D0402766

MAYFLY

JEFF SWEAT

FEIWEL AND FRIENDS
NEW YORK

A FEIWEL AND FRIENDS BOOK
An imprint of Macmillan Publishing Group, LLC
175 Fifth Avenue, New York, NY 10010

Our books may be purchased in bulk for promotional, educational, or business use. Please contact your local bookseller or the Macmillan Corporate and Premium Sales Department at (800) 221-7945 ext. 5442 or by e-mail at MacmillanSpecialMarkets@macmillan.com.

Library of Congress Cataloging-in-Publication Data is available.
ISBN 978-1-250-13920-7 (hardcover) / ISBN 978-1-250-13921-4 (ebook)

Book design by Sophie Erb
Feiwel and Friends logo designed by Filomena Tuosto

First edition, 2018
1 3 5 7 9 10 8 6 4 2
fiercereads.com

TO THE KIDS WHO HOLD THE WORLD TOGETHER,
WHETHER THEY ASKED TO HOLD THE WORLD OR NOT

THERE IS NOTHING TO SAVE, NOW ALL IS LOST, BUT A TINY CORE OF STILLNESS IN THE HEART LIKE THE EYE OF A VIOLET.

—D. H. LAWRENCE

THE PEOPLE OF ELL AYE

THE ANGELENOS

THE DOMINANT PEOPLE OF ELL AYE, THEY ARE A LARGELY PEACEFUL FEMALE-LED SOCIETY WHO LIVE PRIMARILY IN THE HILLS. THEY ARE MADE OF FOUR INTERRELATED PEOPLES:

- **THE HOLY WOOD**

  THE OLDEST ANGELENO SETTLEMENT, ON THE SHORES OF THE LAKE OF THE HOLY WOOD AND THE OLD HOLY WOOD SIGN.

- **THE MALIBU**

  THE FARTHEST WEST OF THE ANGELENOS, WHO LIVE IN THE MOUNTAINS NEXT TO THE OCEAN OF MALIBU.

- **THE DOWNTOWN**

  THE DOWNTOWN GUARD THE FORMER TOWERS OF ELL AYE AS SACRED GROUND AND LIVE IN A GIANT STADIUM IN A RAVINE.

- **THE SAN FERNANDOS**

  THE SAN FERNANDOS LIVE IN THE GREAT VALLEY NORTH OF THE HOLY WOOD AND FREQUENTLY COMPETE WITH THE HOLY WOOD FOR SCARCE RESOURCES.

THE LAST LIFERS

A FERAL BAND OF CHILDREN WHO'VE GONE MAD IN ANTICIPATION OF THEIR EARLY DEATHS; THEY LIVE THROUGHOUT ELL AYE IN VIOLENCE AND CHAOS BECAUSE THEY FEAR NO CONSEQUENCES.

THE PALOS (THE BITERS)

A CANNIBAL SOCIETY FROM THE SMOKING PALOS VERDES PENINSULA, THEY ARE ELL AYE'S MOST FEARED ENEMY. THEY ARE INTELLIGENT, VICIOUS, AND WELL ARMED.

THE ICE CREAM MEN

A WANDERING TRIBE OF TRADERS WHO TRAVEL ON THREE-WHEELED ICE CREAM CARTS, THE ICE CREAM MEN KNOW ALL THE PEOPLES IN ELL AYE.

THE KINGDOM

A MIGHTY CIVILIZATION BUILT BY FORMER GANG MEMBERS, THE KINGDOM OCCUPIES A HUGE CASTLE FORTRESS IN ORANGE COUNTY, THE OC.

CHAPTER ONE
THE HOLY WOOD

All of your years are marked. At thirteen, the changes come, the Olders tell you. At fifteen, you become a Mama. At seventeen, you begin to End.

The words beat through her head as if they've always been there, because they have always been there. Only now she understands what they mean. She's breathing calm on the promontory above the Holy Wood, but the words make her feel as if she's scrambling through the village, legs pumping and lungs burning.

The sunrise breaks over the ridge and lights the roofs below, soft and gold. Jemma can make out all the shapes of her life as the sun blankets them in warmth, one by one: the kitchen, the Smiths' hut, the Gatherers' house. And then the Little Doctors' house, where Zee died, and Jemma is cold again.

There's a cough in the Daycare, and then another. Jemma soaks in the quiet because it's about to shatter. Crying, yelling, fighting, laughing . . . there's nothing noisier than a village full of Children.

The quiet breaks for good, with a baby's wail, and Jemma stirs. She should get out before Trina sees her. Before Lady sees her. Buddha Teevee Jesucristo, before *anyone* sees her.

The sky is bleeding white, and she can see the ruined city just beyond the ridge protecting the Holy Wood. She forgets that there's a city down there, that there's a full world beyond this village. She's relied on the Holy Wood to keep her safe, but Zee reminds her that the world still cuts in. She's not any safer behind the Bear Wall.

Maybe it's time to join the world.

Jemma winds her way down to the village, padding softly instead of running like her body wants her to. There's nothing unusual about a Gatherer getting an early start on her day, even if that Gatherer is fifteen and should have other things on her mind.

She glides through the streets, ignoring the early risers and amazed at how easily they ignore her. All these years, and so few people care if she's coming or going. Until she reaches the house of the Muscle, the guards of the Holy Wood. The Muscle are mostly boys, because boys start to get stronger than the girls in their Tweens, and that strength is useful in a fight.

The house is boxy, mostly greasy glass. It used to be white but looks gray, as if generations of boys have overwhelmed it. Chicken bones and orange peels line the sidewalk. As she creeps by, two Tweens stumble out, hitting each other. She doesn't know what they're arguing about, but it doesn't matter. Tweens—and Muscle—are always hitting each other.

"Oh hey," one of them says, and he disentangles from the other. His name is Jamie, she thinks, but he's only thirteen. "You want to roll with me, chica?"

"You can't handle me," she says. "I'm more Muscle than you."

His swagger only seems to get more swaggy. "C'mon, chica, you look like you need it."

She scoops a rock from the curb and throws it at him. It just misses. "Not from you. I heard about your little pecker." She hasn't, but it's a safe bet.

The Muscle pauses, then punches his friend.

Jemma stops in the Circle, the ring of houses at the heart of the village that beats along with the Holy Wood in work or anger or joy. She fills her water bottles, the Long Gone ones they call litros, clear plastic with red lids. Everything that came from the past they call Long Gone.

She watches for the Olders or the Muscle, and her eyes rest on one of the grand old houses, white walls and orange tiles dripping with creeping fig. But her eyes keep sliding into the sooty pit next to it, charred timbers clawing their way out of the earth. The blackness crawls along the ground into the street, and she can't quite see where it ends.

It was a house that caught the flu, fell so quickly to the disease that the Children couldn't leave. The Little Doctors couldn't save them—they never could—so the Muscle barred the door. When it was finally quiet, they burned the house and everything in it where it stood. Now it sits on the street but doesn't, and the Children pass by it without glances, just tiny shivers and hitches in their step. It's there by not being there.

The embers from Zee's body fire were still glowing last night when Trina, the Oldest, cornered her. "You fifteen tomorrow," she said. As if Jemma had forgotten she was fifteen, as if she didn't have every last year etched in sharp lines. "A good Day to you."

They've forgotten everything else, but they know when your Day is.

"It's time for you to become one of the Mamas," Trina said.

"Just like that?" Jemma had asked Trina.

"Oh, Jemma," Trina said. "Our whole life is just like that."

And suddenly childhood felt so short and the rest of her life even shorter. Even if she survived the baby—fifteen now, a baby by sixteen, and a year feeding it before life is all gone. Two years left, and none of it for her.

Jemma steps away from the water barrel when Lady catches her arm, almost spinning her around. Her hair, curly where most of the Holy Wood's is straight, is wild from her pillow. "Where you going, mija?"

"Gathering," Jemma says, and it's true enough. Gathering is her role in the Holy Wood.

Lady is her best friend. She's named for one of the ancient priestesses who lived in the Teevee, their most important god, but Jemma doesn't see the priestess in her. Lady lives squarely in this world, fierce and open. She studies Jemma's face and says, "By yourself?"

You don't Gather by yourself, not even in times of peace, and Lady knows it. Finally Jemma says, "Just today."

"I miss her, too."

Yes, but you ain't fifteen today. You wasn't walking with Zee when she doubled over in agony, when blood stained her dress. You didn't run screaming to the Little Doctors.

Jemma can't stop thinking about Zee. Zee was the last person you expected to want to have a baby. She led the Gatherers as if it were the most important job in the Holy Wood, and with her you thought it was, as if all it took to keep the village alive was the fruit and shoes and rice in their bags. But no—what really mattered to everyone was in that belly when she got pregnant.

Zee loved it. She did. When she became a Mama, the roundness got rounder, the flush in her cheeks got brighter. A girl in there, she said, a warrior or a Gatherer or a priestess. The other Gatherers were drawn to her, this beacon of life. And then—

She wasn't old enough to End, even. But Zee Ended all the same.

Jemma's not sure she can ever say this about Zee aloud. So instead she simply says to Lady, "You didn't see me today, okay?"

"Okay, this time. But you don't come back by dark I'm gonna kick your ass."

"Deal," Jemma says, just glad to be free before Trina grabs her, too.

A Tween almost clips her with a battered bicycle, and she moves toward the iron gates. They're tall and spiked. They once held off whatever evils kept the Parents awake at night, but now they work just as well against the lions and bears that grow more fearless all the time.

Wagons are rumbling down from the Great Field to pick up the last winter spinach. Their people have claimed every flat space chiseled out by the Parents: their lawns and parks and sacred places turned from grass to vegetables and fruit, their swimming pools holding fish and water for drinking and growing. For all they built, the Parents could never have imagined building a world like this.

The lake below looks like god's hand, blue fingers pushing aside the trees and the dirt, and the Bear Wall a bracelet around its wrist. Maybe the gods did place it there behind the Wall, because in all the hills only the hand holds fish, and water that lasts through the summer when the desert winds slice through the valley. That's why they guard it. That's why it's the Lake of the Holy Wood.

And there is the Holy Wood sign on the mountain, with an aytch as tall as ten Children. You could see it from across the valley, Jemma thinks, see it calling all to the Holy Wood when the priests still walked the hills and the god Teevee talked to Children in their homes.

Today Jemma doesn't want to speak to the gods. She barrels down the hill and doesn't stop until she sees the Bear Wall, a long curved dam that spans the canyon with bears' stone faces guarding the face of it.

Her legs stretch out to cross the Wall, but strong arms grab her from behind. "Not that way, Jemma." The voice is starting to deepen. It will not last, she thinks, and she turns toward Apple. Of course Apple saw her leave. Apple is the best Muscle in the Holy Wood, not because he's the strongest but because he sees everything.

"I need to leave," she says.

"I know," he says. "I saw you at Zee's fire last night." Yes, he sees everything.

"We getting low on fruit."

"Really? I know you your whole life, and you try to tell me you looking for fruit?" He steps close to her, so much taller than she is—even though she's the tallest girl—and still growing at almost seventeen. His chest and shoulders are bare, now that the rains have gone, and she counts the raised scars on his bicep from the lion that mauled him. *Gods*, she asks, *how do we still live?*

"I'm not going back." She feels the fight starting in her stomach, and it has never let her be. Any other Muscle, any other Gatherer, he would have hit her and dragged her back, but this is Apple and Jemma.

"Believe it or not, Jemma," he says as he looks to see who's watching them, "I don't always think like a Muscle. I'll go with you."

Her heart climbs in her chest a little at that, and she pushes it back down.

"I'm sorry," he says.

Jemma thinks Apple of all people knows what she meant when she said she missed Zee. He was as close to her as Jemma was. That's the reason she doesn't have to say it.

They slide down the hill away from the Bear Wall, yellow dust cascading under their feet. They reach an unfamiliar road and push down into the ravine. In just a few turns, Jemma doesn't recognize it and wonders how in all her years as a Gatherer she's never seen this before.

Others have passed this way. The doors are all missing, probably chopped for fires, and the houses start to collapse from the wounds exposing their insides to the world. They don't scavenge those long-stripped houses, just snatch fruit from ancient trees that look as if they're about to stop bearing.

"What you gonna do for oranges when those stop?" Apple says.

" 'You'?"

"We," he corrects himself, but she knows he has stopped always thinking as We.

"Don't you have Muscle-y things to think about?"

"Aren't you supposed to be a Mama today?" She can tell he senses the sting as it leaves his tongue.

The answer is slow to come and then it's gone, because she sees an explosion of red spike before her, and under it a slip of white. A wall.

"A house?" Apple asks.

"Red spike don't always mean houses." The Parents used to plant the spiky vines around their walls, called by a name no one can pronounce. Once Jemma came across a bungalow completely swallowed by red flowers. She imagined a girl like her, a girl from the Parents' time, sleeping ageless in the darkened spiked bedrooms, waiting for the End to end.

Jemma pulls her hatchet out of her belt just as Apple lifts his machete. Both of them hack at the twisting cords supporting the flowers. The red flowers are blinding and beautiful but hide spikes an inch long, so they try to touch them only with their blades.

Apple's breath hisses, two long lines of red welling on his forearm from the spikes. "That'll match your lion scars," Jemma says. "But maybe you should make up a better story about where you got em."

Beneath the spikes are the battered lip of a gate, iron studs pounded into the wood. The iron would trade well. She already knows she'll be back to this place with a larger crew of Gatherers.

"So," he says, and his voice is lower, more intimate, "you don't want to be a Mama."

Jemma swings at the vine harder than she should, and her hatchet digs into the wood beneath it. She grunts, pulls it out. "Why would I?" Talking about a choice that isn't a choice.

She never had the Mama in her. In the Daycare, she was banned from watching the babies like all the other kids did. She'd either ignore them while they wandered into the koi ponds or—worse—goad them into trouble. When she was five, she talked a three-year-old into drinking his own pee.

"We need you to be a Mama," Trina had said earlier today.

"You need me? Or this baby?"

"We need your baby," Trina said.

"If I roll with someone," Jemma said, "it'll be cuz I wanna be with him. Not to give you a goddamn baby." She smiled when Trina flinched.

"Then it's easy," Trina said. "Become a Mama—or leave."

Her life, or her tribe. Jemma feels everything tearing in two.

But as Apple looks at her right now she just says, "Being a Mama's hard. *You* have a baby."

"I tried," Apple says, "but it didn't work."

And he pulls her back. It's so easy with Apple. He lives in her first memories, has always been the shadow over her shoulder, but despite a life together they've almost never been alone. Every boy Apple's age has asked to roll with her, even though she always turns them down. Not Apple. Why?

Now the gate is clear. There's a rusted latch, but a few strikes at the old wood and she can kick it open. Apple lets her. Jemma needs something to strike.

The house still has its door. Jemma lifts her hatchet again, but Apple says, "Wait." He turns the knob, and the door swings open as it must have the day the Parents disappeared.

The air fills the lungs but doesn't feel as if it belongs there. Smells of things Long Gone hit Jemma, and she can't identify anything but decay.

They look for metal and glass in what must have been the kitchen. Everything else has rotted, but in those the Parents' food sometimes lasts. Most of the cans are rusted or bulged. Gatherers know to stay away from those and the death they bring. Three of them hold corn without rust, and she places them in the bag.

Gathering brings riches with it. Gatherers are the ones who find tools and supplies, and sometimes they keep stuff for themselves. Sometimes extra food from the fields can fall into their packs when Farmers need something they have. That's why all the Gatherers are girls—because girls get the good jobs first.

It's getting hard to Gather, though. The Parents' homes near the Holy Wood have been picked over long ago. They have to push deeper and deeper into the Flat Lands, the deserted city blocks at the base of the Holy Wood. In ten years, she thinks, most of it will be gone. Then it's just whatever the Children can grow or make.

"Yes!" Apple whoops. He has disappeared into another room and he emerges, arms filled with tiny rattling bottles. "Look, medsen!"

Medsen will make this trip. It can cure fevers, maybe keep another flu house from burning. Only the Parents could make it, and every year they find less.

She watches Apple celebrate, and sees a dusty fragment of herself in the glass behind him. She can see why Apple never wanted to roll with her. She's not pretty the way the other girls are—hard when she should be soft, gawky when she should be lithe. She doesn't have the kind of body that makes a good Mama, doesn't have the kind of desires. Sex is such a part of the Holy Wood, so important to the survival of the Holy Wood, that the other girls wear it like a fur. But for her it's never fit so well.

She looks down the narrow hallway where they stand. In it are the kinds of pictures that the Parents made, as if they convinced life to stand still. They had that power. She hasn't seen one up close in a long time, and she studies them now: Children frozen in place, one blinking, one crying, but mostly she sees the Parents. Bigger than the Children, faces made of tree bark. Smiling, two of them, in picture after picture.

"Look how light they are," Apple says, pointing at their skin. "I thought only cannibals was white."

It's true. The two of them are the descendants of all the peoples who lived in the Holy Wood, with skin that almost matches the brown of the hills, but this family has pink skin, blue eyes, and unnatural yellow hair. Like the creatures from their nightmares.

"Maybe the Parents was gods to live so long," she hears Apple say.

"Maybe," she answers, feeling all of her fifteen years. "Then why we stop turning into gods?"

CHAPTER TWO

THE STACK

Apple doesn't expect anyone to wind down the choking street—they're the first people to cross the gate since the Parents died, and no one is racing to cross it now. Still, Muscle training doesn't die—he stands with his back to the wall, in the shadow of a barren pomgrant tree, both ends of the road in view. The only motion comes from Jemma.

Apple watches Jemma pull the red spike back, weaving the lighter tendrils across the gap until from a distance he can't see a gate. It only needs to keep till tomorrow when Jemma comes back with a crew, but she's had salvages busted before by another tribe.

He admires her fingers' dance among the thorns. She's a good Gatherer, but not the best. She'd be a good Farmer, if she could stand still. She'd be a good Muscle, if she could handle the blood. He doesn't know if he likes her more for all the things she is, or for all the things she isn't.

Jemma's been marked since they were Middles at age seven. The others are so sure of themselves, of their place in the Holy Wood. Jemma asks and asks. She doubts. It takes a special person not to be sure.

Her questions saved him.

The tribe forbade going to the Holy Wood sign after sunset. The gods return to it at night, and the Priestess says they dance and cry and will kill any Child who comes to the aytch. Jemma said, "Why? Why would they do that? If we got gods on our doorsteps I got a couple of questions for em."

She snuck over the fence and made her way up the hill without a torch, she told Apple later. She sat on the aytch in the moonlight. She didn't find the gods, but on the way back she found Apple getting killed by the lion.

He had been standing sentry over the field, lowly new Muscle duties to keep out the deer and pigs that raided it. And because deer and pigs came, so did the lion. He never heard the lion's cry, just felt the bite at the back of his neck and hot fur bearing him down to the earth. He slipped free somehow, rolled loose long enough to find a rock. The lion pinned him down, ripping his bicep, its tan face and white cheeks snapping at his. He smashed at it, but it only grew angrier.

Jemma had no weapon besides the rock she threw to distract it. Even if she had, she probably wouldn't have attacked. She was too scared. Instead, she drew herself up and screamed, "Look at me, puta! Look at me!" She puffed herself like a bullfrog, made herself taller and wider, and screamed.

Lion Tamer, the Muscle called her later. Even the lions can't stand your voice. She was nine.

It was a stupid taboo, and only the Priestess cared when she broke it, but they sentenced Jemma to the shed for the week. The Muscle were so grateful to Jemma that they let her walk out the very first day.

She walked out with Apple's heart.

"Home?" he says when she steps away from the gate. Jemma shakes her head, and he's glad.

Apple sheathes the machete but takes his bow off his shoulder. All the Muscle carry bows once they pass out of the Holy Wood. They used to send more Muscle with the Gatherers. Then Pablo rebelled with the Muscle, and they don't trust the Muscle anymore. The Muscle get smaller and smaller because the Olders are more scared of their own army than what's out there.

Apple should care more about being mistrusted, about being pushed to the side. But this isn't his time anymore. These aren't his people. The only "people" he has left is holding a hatchet in front of him.

"Can we go down to Ell Aye?" she says. The great city that includes the Flat Lands. He knew that's where she wanted to go.

He nods and gives her a quick grin, showing the dark sockets in the side of his smile that used to be his teeth. Two went missing in his Tweens, and he has never told her the same reason for the loss. Sometimes it's him biting back the lion, sometimes it's a rabbit bone. "How'd you lose your teeth?" she asks, returning to words from older days.

"A cannibal took em," he says, as if he had three more answers after that. "They was the only things sharper than his skinning knife."

"Someday you'll tell me the truth," she says.

"Maybe today," he says, and he touches her shoulder, leaving his hand there until her soft skin gives way under his fingers. He wonders if she knows, if she—

She cocks her head toward him, and he smiles and slowly pulls his hand away.

"Today?"

"Maybe," he says.

They break through trees and the entire lost city stretches out at their feet. The palms soar above the houses, all leaning south toward the sun. From above, Ell Aye looks untouched, unbroken from the Parents' time, but on the street it's as if the city has burst. The houses are falling apart, the streets have overgrown, and the only people who live there are Last Lifers and bears.

The Holy Wood territory ends in the wide wide Flat Lands of Ell Aye, where all territories end. They're too difficult to defend, too open for ambush, too far from water. If you're brave, though, it's still rich. Gathering teams have come back loaded down with tools, food, medsen. The Gathering teams have also come back without people. They left bodies lying in the wide bolvards, carved up with a Long Lifer blade.

The whispers in the Holy Wood talk more about the Palos, because the white skin and the necklaces of teeth make for gossipy shivers. As a Muscle, he knows the Last Lifers, the ones no one talks about, are far more dangerous. They're closer to the Holy Wood, and their minds are gone.

The Last Lifers are kids who turn sixteen or seventeen and lose hope and turn mad, unable to handle what comes next. Nothing matters, so nothing they do matters. They strip down to rags. They paint their eyes black with charcoal and hack at their hair until they look like browning skulls. They slash their skin with scars instead of tattoos. They slip away into the Flat Lands of Ell Aye until they find others like them. They nest in the Long Gone buildings. They eat and sleep and roll whenever. They hunt the Holy Wood for sport.

They should be going down with an army. "You know it's not safe," he says.

"Even more reason to go, huh?" She acts as if she's without fear. He knows it's probably creeping up inside her, and she's fighting to push it down. Jemma does more brave things when she's afraid than someone who's actually brave.

He doesn't respond, because he's looking beyond the city to the lone hill rising up from the sea in the south. The Palos. "Smoke," Apple says. "Always smoke."

"They can't still be eating. They gotta stop to kill people, right?" They laugh, but small. The cannibals put a hush on everything.

"Someday they'll come here," he says.

"They never come this far. Not since our Mamas' Mamas' Mamas' times."

"Then the pull's gonna be that much stronger." Everyone knows the Palos will come. When they do—when they do, Apple knows, they will cook the young and the old in their fires. He's heard the stories, he's seen the camps burned in their wake. But the in-between kids they will steal. They don't make babies of their own, the stories say. They steal you and they turn you into them. And then your tribe will see your own brown eyes in the blue ones killing them.

"Buddha Teevee Jesucristo," Apple says, never sure which god should hear.

Not today, though. And today Jemma wants to go down. She points to the tower she calls the Stack because it's round and stacked like plates in a kitchen, plates stabbed with a sword. "I've been wanting to see it my whole life," she says, and he feels the rest of that sentence. He knows what it is to want for your whole life.

Apple follows her fingers to the spire and shakes his head. He's taken Gatherers there before. "It's picked over, has been before we was born."

"Not to Gather. To see."

To wonder why the Parents built it, he thinks, knowing how she thinks, how they could build such a thing and then vanish.

He shrugs. It's dangerous, but he's a Muscle. And he's not just with her to protect her.

They drop down the hill, speedy on the winding road. Without warning they're at the bottom and the 101 looms above them.

It was the grand road of the ancient people and figures in all the old stories. The Parents would spend days on the 101, they would say, living in the cars that litter the city. Even now, a mass of cars jams the east side of the 101, as if they all stopped and gave up.

Once a flock of birds fell from the sky in the thousands and hit the camp, their dead wings carpeting the streets and everyone scooping them up and roasting them, not caring if they were diseased. He wonders if they simply froze in the air.

Apple has never seen a car move, but these remind him of the birds. Where were they going, and why didn't they get there? He knows but can't bring himself to say it.

"Why is it called the 101? A hundred and one miles long?" Jemma says. This is an old question, but it's clear she's asking it to take her mind off the darkened bulk of the 101 now above their heads. He's feeling it, too. Vines hang down from its belly, leaking decay. Everything the Parents built has started to rot.

"A hundred and one ways to die."

Jemma punches him. "Now you just thinking like a Muscle."

"Maybe," Apple says, trying not to react to the punch or the fact that her hand lingers on his arm after it, "but it's a good place for an ambush."

After the underpass, the Stack climbs before them in a yellowing white pile of plates, hundreds of feet high. The plates that shade the windows are broken in places, as if a giant has chipped them against a doorjamb. A spire juts from the top, like the sundial they built in the village.

The closest door is ajar, and Jemma moves toward it, but Apple stops her. "Not yet," he says, and leads her on a long loop of the building.

"You know peoples who left Ell Aye?"

"I met some traders once. At the Downtown. They go all around our world."

He had escorted the Olders to a meeting with all the tribes of Angelenos, the people who own the hills of Ell Aye. All the tribes were there: the Holy Wood, the Downtown, the San Fernando, even the strange and far off Malibu. During the meeting the Downtown had been visited by traders pedaling bicycle carts, and the giant stadio where the Downtown lived was buzzing with talk about their treasures and the world beyond. He found himself swept up in this strange new world, like Jemma is now.

"What they called?" she says.

"Ice Cream Men."

"They men? Like, old?"

"Nah, they just kids like us, boys and girls both," he says, "that's why I membered their name. It didn't make no sense."

"There are peoples I didn't even know about, and I barely left the Bear Wall," she says. "I wasted so much time."

Apple is thinking the same thing. He's waited too long. He knows he's waited too long. Why hasn't he told her? Maybe because for what he feels, they've lost their words. A boy and a girl, they can't just be.

They enter the Stack after their circuit, and Jemma falters next to him. Nothing about the entry room tells them what the Parents intended; there's no message in its shape. Splinters remain of a wooden table that must have once been bolted to the floor. "Up?" Apple asks, checking her courage. He once dared her to climb down a cliff with him and she did it one-handed. She won't say no.

"Up," she says, and pushes into a staircase. The dim wash of the first room pales to nothing as they climb, even with the door wedged open. The door to the first landing won't budge for them, so they keep climbing. The third door opens, and he breathes in the lightness.

"Nothing is square!" Jemma says, and then laughs. "Of course not." The outer walls are curved. The rest of the room is a jumble of the chairs the Parents seemed to love, with wheels that let you roll anywhere. Jemma steps to the window and pushes. It holds even when the one next to it has shattered.

Apple picks up a phone. They know what they are although no one has ever used one in this life: a way for the Long Gones to talk to you from the dead. Somehow that connection is lost. What would he ask the dead if he could?

He almost imagines he can feel it coming. In the last few months he's found a way of looking at the world, a way of understanding how all the pieces fit, and he thinks: *How cruel, to finally understand it, and then to leave.*

Those are the Children who die first: the curious, the wise, the calm. When the End comes, it comes first for the ones who see the world better, who control their actions, while the beastly and the stupid remain. The Children call them the Touched, as if they're marked for a sooner death. It may be only six months, nine months shorter, but in their lives every month matters.

It feels almost as it did when he was about to leave Daycare to head to the fields before he became a Muscle, that moment when leaving means nothing you do matters. It's not like the Last Lifers, it's not as if he doesn't care, it's just that he floats through the world with a lightness as if nothing he touches will last.

They say you feel better, before the End, so much better that everyone looks surprised when they actually End. They call it the Betterment, for the way that life seems to surge through your skin. Broken bones knit themselves together, scars heal. Your vision clears, your breath arrives quicker. And then you start to bleed through your nose, as if life is draining from the inside of your head. He doesn't feel that way yet. But he knows it's coming.

Jemma shoves a desk out of the way to get to the window; he watches her muscles ripple. He loves that she's a match for his strength. He taught her how to fight last year, and then she started winning. The other Muscle think that their strength is their only advantage against the Olders, the only thing that keeps them from being totally shut out, so they don't trust a girl like Jemma. Seeing that in Jemma just makes Apple think they were born as mirrored selves.

If you asked him where he would want to be on the last day, he would have said here. Unearthing the secrets of the Parents, here. Exploring their own lives, here. The important thing is that the *here* is Jemma.

Now they're looking at the towers the Downtown people worship almost as gods but never visit. She reaches out, touches Apple on the shoulder. She would never have done that before this day.

"We should leave the Holy Wood," she whispers, and he's not sure if he's meant to hear, the way the sounds seem to melt right into his skin.

Apple doesn't answer because his eye catches more pictures, this time on a table next to a kind of glass rectangle. Two Parents, two Parents with two Children. On the next desk, two more Parents, smiling.

"Something else in those pictures, Jemma," he says. "They was always together." He hasn't been able to explain what he felt, but the pictures show it.

"So?"

"They didn't just live forever. They was together. That's what made the Parents the Parents."

"I would take either," she says.

"I don't think it works that way," Apple says. "Together takes time." Enough time. *Now now now,* he says, only to himself. *Now.* He leans toward her, and her lips are just open so that they fit right between his.

He's waited too long.

CHAPTER THREE
THE BOWL

Jemma hadn't imagined his look from before, the one that left her open and naked in the center of the room, because he's looking at her that way again and then he's kissing her, brushing her lips softly while she holds completely still.

She pulls back. "You never asked me to roll," Jemma says.

"I never asked no one to roll," he says, and she realizes she's never seen him with anyone else.

"But why?"

"Cuz I feel something different for you." Before she can show the way that cuts, he says, "Something good. Something like the Parents. And no one told me how to show it."

"Oh," she says, spinning that thought in her mind but still, this time, kissing him back. This time, allowing herself to feel it: the cracked skin of his lips growing softer, wetter, as they explore hers. She's kissed lots of boys—all the girls have—but all that is gone with those lips. The two of them are kissing as if they're trying to uncover the truth of each other under that skin.

The sun interrupts them, its rays pushing under the window coverings as it swells onto the horizon. "It's time," Apple says, and they reluctantly pull apart.

"A little more. We could see so much more higher," she says, a pleading note. She knows they will never be back, and maybe Apple sees that, too, because he doesn't argue, just climbs. Is that why he left with her today, because they are running out of time?

The other floors are more of the same, and when the sun finally sets, she's ready to go at the next flight of stairs.

They reach what must be the top of the tower and crack the door. Unlike the other floors, it's dark inside. Apple chokes and backs into Jemma. "You smell that?" he whispers.

Yes, oh gods, she does. "It smells like shit!" she hisses. Shit and something else, blood and death and something wrong. And as the darkness through the door resolves, she sees dim shapes moving, clothes rustling. Something waking up. Something they woke.

Jemma is bounding down the steps before she knows it, trusting the railing that slides under her hand in the blackness. She barely hears Apple behind her, both of them knowing the only thing that matters is speed.

Death whispers past them—really there or not? It doesn't matter. At any moment a knife will pierce her back; she can feel it between her shoulder blades. But then she hears the shouts, hears the voice of the Last Lifers, and knows a quick knife is more than she could hope for.

They burst through the greasy white room and into the street.

"Home?" Jemma says, attempting to sound casual.

"It's probably dinnertime," Apple says as calmly as he can for someone running for his life.

When they reach the underpass, though, Apple steers her away from it, even though the voices pour out of the Stack into the streets.

"That way's home!" she says.

"Look in the shadows," Apple says. And then Jemma looks at the underpass the way Apple does and sees an elbow and then an arm and then an ax.

Then she sees something more, a sharp flash from the overpass of the 101, a long tube of something, and Jemma screams. "Gun!" A gun? How did the Last Lifers get a gun? And they dive behind a low wall before something loud bites into the bricks, like an unseen chisel.

The Last Lifers are coming at them from the south and the east. They're blocking the way home. That means that, for now, home is to the north and west.

"With me," she says, and she pulls Apple to the north side of the street, the uphill side, as they push west. She looks over her shoulder at one of the Last Lifers and she knows the scowl under the blood and the grime, knows it from her own village.

"Andy!" she pants to Apple. "That's Andy!"

"That *was* Andy, then." And that's why the Last Lifers are so terrible. They're not demons like the Palos, they're brothers and sisters. Andy once gave her blackberries that he found bursting through a car overwhelmed by bramble. Now he has a spear raised toward her, and if Jemma stopped to greet him, he would bury it in her guts and twist. That and worse before she dies.

There are more behind Andy, still visible in the thickening dark. Seven Last Lifers at least, more than you'd ever find together at once. They don't usually get that big because they kill one another off. They run in packs like coyotes, but coyotes don't tear one another's hearts out. These animals do. They'll idly attack one another if they don't have other prey.

Jemma knows where to go now, remembering a Gather with Lady and a Muscle long gone, looking for a Long Gone store of medsen. They stumbled upon another way home, and—and here it is, so fast that they almost run past it. She tacks hard to the right, almost losing Apple and maybe losing the Last Lifers, through a long narrow alley and then up a flight of stairs.

At the top, the stairs are flanked by walls, and they crouch behind one. Apple pulls back his bow and looks down the steps. She can't see over the wall as she ducks, only watches him unleash an arrow and hears a scream below. Six. Apple notches a new arrow, but he must have missed because he quickly fires another before there's a gurgle, closer than before. There's a quiet as the Last Lifers regroup.

"I never seen you work before," she says. "It's nice to look at."

"It's nice to be looked at," he says, with a little smile. "But you a better kisser than the other Muscle."

"Now what?"

"The rest gonna charge at once," Apple says.

"How you know?" she asks.

"They used up all their strategy down on the street," he says. "Now all they got left is crazy."

Ahead of them in the dark, away from the staircase, is a tangle of streets, narrow and twisting even in the Parents' time but now choked by brush. If she barely knows her way, she has to hope the Last Lifers, maddened as they are by the End, will know even less. She twists left and right, hoping that the circles they're running will take them north to the next underpass through the 101.

Behind them they hear the screams of the Last Lifers, closer than they should be.

The street drops them back down the hill, and they pull up at the bottom, lungs burning, the underpass not where it should be. They're in a sort of glade, a place where the Parents used to park their cars, and there are still a few of them, overgrown until they're just ivy-covered mounds. But there is no 101. "That's not right," Jemma says. Beyond the glade is a street, and they race to it, hoping to get their bearings.

Jemma spies the letters then as she sees all of it at once—the first of the Last Lifers pouring off the hill, the 101 farther than she thought, too far to reach now, and the forbidden gate in front of them. They're at the Bowl, one of the Gathering places of the Parents. It's the place all the stories warn about, and they're going to have to enter it if they want to live. She can only hope that whatever force has guided the Last Lifers, maybe the evil in the Bowl will be enough to throw it back.

She can't move, even though she knows she must. Apple pulls her shoulders toward him, looks at her with clear eyes. "Time to meet our ghosts," he says. Somehow his gentleness makes her feet budge where the Last Lifers couldn't, and they're past the gate and into the terror that seems to close in on them.

None of the Holy Wood have ever entered the Bowl, even though they can see it from their ridge. It's not that they don't dare, although they certainly do not. It's that every taboo, every confusing, conflicting legend, agrees on this: Stay out of the Bowl.

It should smell, she thinks. She thought it would smell, of death and worse. But even as she wonders how long the smell lasts, she does sniff something, the scent of the pines that line their path. Then she thinks it's far more beautiful than she could have imagined, with ponderosas thick and green, and pine needles up to her ankles—

But then a final turn and it opens up before her and it's worse. It is a bowl. She sees immediately how it gets its name, like a giant scoop from the hillside. Seats climb the walls of the Bowl; at the bottom is a platform and a kind of shelter like a clamshell. She couldn't have even thought of how the Parents used it—religion, games?—except the old stories said they used to sing here. The Holy Wood Bowl, they called it.

It doesn't matter, though, because now the Parents use it in another way. Everywhere she looks are bodies: draped over chairs, tossed roughly into walkways, piled seven deep, tangled arm over leg over head, the Bowl filled with them. The bodies are bigger than they are. There's no flesh on them anymore. Jemma feels horror rising in her throat, but also a sort of awe. This is the place where the future came to its End.

"We found the Parents," Apple says.

There is nowhere to hide among the bones and smiling skulls. They climb midway up the Bowl before they hear the shrieks of the Last Lifers. Jemma looks around, panicked, for some kind of hole. "Help me," she whispers, to whatever god will hear.

Crunches of bones at the bottom, the crackling cries growing louder. "Help us," she says, the fear rising. "Show us where to hide."

And—and something does. There's a buzz in her ears, like the beginning of a headache. It's like her head can't quite grab on to the sound, and the disconnect hurts her head. The sound recedes. In the silence, a blue haze floats down over the Bowl, like scattered ash at first, then brighter and brighter like stars.

She worries that the Last Lifers will see it, but even Apple doesn't seem to notice it. The haze swirls in clouds around her, until it takes the form of Children.

It's showing me the Last Lifers about to attack, she realizes. Not in perfect images—the edges of the Last Lifers are blurry, as if the haze doesn't know how to draw bodies. The features are sketched out in dots. She saw a painting once, in a grand Long Gone house under a giant banyan tree. It was of a girl, a dancer made of little dabs of paint. When Jemma looked at it up close, she saw only the dots and an impression of the shape. When she stepped back, she saw the girl.

The haze looks like that kind of painting—vague and blurry if she looks right at it, but falling into shape if she looks at it out of the corner of her eye.

The Last Lifer shapes in the haze come toward her. When she looks back up the hill, this time, she sees a passageway under the bones. One of the benches has been dug out by a coyote—a burrow in the bones. It's invisible to her real eyes, but the haze shows her a way in. In the haze, the Last Lifer figures seem to walk right past it without noticing.

Jemma hesitates. *Is it safe?* Then she thinks, *You asked for help from the gods. It'd be rude not to take it.* She leads Apple straight to where the burrow should be. She moves two skulls, and it's there. Under a long bench, under the bodies, there is a pocket big enough to hold them both. Jemma crawls under, followed by Apple.

"Did you see that?" she says, but Apple looks at her blankly. She shakes her head, but a loud bone crack below stops her next sentence. Apple slides up behind her as she lies down on her side, staring out into the bones. The smell of ancient death settles upon them.

She whispers quietly to ward off the panic that threatens to smother her under the bones. "This ain't what I planned today," she says.

The Parents used to bury their dead, but when the End came, they died so quickly that there was no one left to bury them. All the Children could do was drag their Parents into the Bowl and leave them there to rot. Now they burn their dead the day they die.

Now, she thinks, *we're all orphans.*

The Last Lifers are supposed to be afraid of the dark, because the gap between worlds is narrow then. They're supposed to be afraid of deaths and ghosts and anything that can steal their souls quicker. But these Last Lifers move as if ghosts aren't real, smashing through the Bowl, angry and sure.

She can hear their calls as they divide and scale the sides of the Bowl. They sound wild, like lions or bears, but neither. A bear never talked or thought or loved like they did, so in those cries are everything lost and abandoned. Jemma finds something strange pushing aside the fear: sadness for Andy, the ten-year-old who loved the Long Gone cars, the thirteen-year-old who dove off the Bear Wall first.

She breathes hard and sharp, and Apple mistakes it for panic. He wraps his arm around her waist, threads his leg between hers, until their hips and shoulders and breath match and her head nestles under his chin. For the first time since they ran down the Stack, she feels a flash of calm. When she was seven she hid from the Olders and the others looked for her. Apple found her under a table, crying. Instead of pulling her out, he put his finger to his lips and climbed under.

Jemma is aware of every place where Apple's skin touches hers. Her skin seems to heat on contact and spread until all those places are linked and on fire, as if he's touching her everywhere. He feels it, too, because he rubs against her, presses his fingers wide across her belly. *We can't be feeling this here, among all this death, with people hunting us,* she thinks. And yet, why not? Isn't it all part of surviving?

She can see windows of the sky through the lattice of bones before her, but can't see down any deeper into the Bowl. Someone is two rows down, stomping the skeletons as if they're dry wood. The cracks shoot through the still air.

Footsteps fall in their row, and she can't help shaking until Apple's stillness draws the shivers out of her. Three people, just like in the haze.

The feet crunch closer, closer, closer, in front of her eyes, and then they're past. She doesn't breathe.

Then they fade away.

The buzz comes back, and then the haze does, suddenly, as if it's just popping in for something it forgot to tell her. In the dots of the haze she can see Andy's face, those empty eyes. The haze can't quite draw his features, but she recognizes the pain in him. Is it real? Is Andy coming back for them?

"I think they're gone," Apple says, starting to move.

"Wait," she says.

They wait long moments, listening for the sounds. Maybe Apple was right. But a smaller set of footsteps start again. Toward them.

She feels Apple tense to reach for his machete, but he can't swing it properly while he's wrapped around Jemma. Her fingers reach for her hatchet but they're not quite there and she doesn't know if she could bear to swing it, and then a foot smashes away the bones in her face and it's Andy's face but not, Andy lost in eyes rimmed with coal, reaching in to tear them apart.

"Andy," Apple says calmly, probably seeing that Andy doesn't have room to swing his spear under the bench. "It's us. Your friends."

Andy hesitates for a moment, life flashing across his eyes before flickering out, and Jemma swings the hatchet, buries it deep into his skull. He collapses without a whimper, with a face as clear and confused as a baby.

Jemma pulls out the hatchet, wipes it off. Carefully. But her hands shake so much that she's worried she'll cut herself. *Andy. Andy. Andy.*

They huddle close together in silence, hoping that no one heard Andy fall. Jemma shivers so hard she's afraid the bones will rattle signals to the Last Lifers, and Apple pulls her closer to calm her. "We ain't meant for this," he whispers.

"You almost seventeen," she says. "How you keep living?"

"You gotta remember what it's like to be alive."

They listen for the crashes as the Last Lifers move to the top of the

Bowl. If they knew Andy, if they remembered him, the Last Lifers don't look for him. Just when she's shaking with cold and exhaustion, Apple pushes with his thigh. Out.

They make their way down through the Bowl, the only Children to visit the Parents.

CHAPTER FOUR
THE OLDERS

On top of everything else, there are goats in the koi ponds.

Trina is almost seventeen, but she doesn't have to worry about floating off the earth anytime soon. As the Oldest, the leader of the Holy Wood, she's tethered to this life through an endless string of annoyances.

The Little Doctors started throwing scissors at one another in the middle of trying to patch up the leg of a Farmer. They fight all the time. The Farmer lost the leg and now, if he lives, he can only work in the Daycare. Jemma threw a fit last night, and now Trina has to fix it. The goats are eating all the plants in the koi ponds.

And then Zee—she was wrong, it's not the goats on top of everything else.

Trina doesn't believe in grief, but she's setting some of it aside for Zee. She talked Zee into becoming a Mama. She was the only person who thought Zee would be a good one.

Before she became an Older, Trina was the head Farmer while Zee was head Gatherer. They were the rare Children who did their jobs thoroughly because they liked doing things right.

They used to wonder if they came from the same Dad, but no one kept track of the Dads. Then they would hear the identical tones in each other's voices when they yelled at a Middle and thought that they were right.

After she heard about Zee, after she lit the fires to burn her body, she pulled out a bottle of whiskey, a gift from Zee, and drank it until her forehead was numb.

Now she's walking down the main street, taking the pulse of the village around her. Nothing feels different from yesterday, before Zee. Grief doesn't live in the village; that's the good news. It just lives in the few people too slow to run away from it.

The life in the street, though, it has a way of rubbing off. Everyone seems to be running, to be shrieking. Two five-year-olds kiss on the ground. A line of kids leave the Daycare, from shortest to tallest, and every one of them is singing. A different song. As much as she hates it sometimes . . . for Trina, this is the center of the world.

She sees every age group out there. The Angelenos have all the kids marked off in neat bunches by age, each with their own roles. The babies go to a year and do nothing. The Toddlers go to four and terrorize the Holy Wood. Nino goes to six, and that's when kids start to learn how to work in the kitchens and fields. The Middles go to nine; they start watching the Toddlers in Daycare and teaching them the stories. By Tweens, they have found a trade. The Teens start at thirteen and get ready to become Mamas and Dads. At fifteen, they stop naming you. You make a baby or you don't, and you End.

Never leave the Holy Wood empty, they say.

The memory of her talk with Jemma is rawer than it should be. "You fifteen now," Trina had said.

"You talking to me about that *now?*" *Ah, that bitch.* Did she think she wanted to be here talking about Mamas when she's talked her friend to that death? "You ain't had to do this. The Oldest don't got to make no baby," Jemma said.

"I couldn't," Trina said, remembering the clumsy hands on her from all the boys they sent her way, the pain in her stomach when what would have been a little girl died and all her hope did, too.

"If I roll with someone," Jemma said, "it'll be cuz I wanna be with him." And Trina flinched and remembered the boy she liked, who died before she even tried to become a Mama.

Trina almost likes Jemma. But right now she needs her to just say yes. She has enough pendejas to deal with today.

The rest of the Olders are already at the Older House when she gets there.

When Trina enters the front room, Mira is draped across the big chair the Olders use for ceremonies. "Jesucristo, Mira, get off the throne," she says, and Mira lazily swings her feet to the ground. The rest of her doesn't move.

The Olders aren't really the oldest in the village. Just five hags who can't have babies and like to mess with people, she thinks. This is who leads the Holy Wood. It's supposed be an honor to be an Older, but everyone looks down on them a bit because they couldn't make babies. Olders might have power, but the Mamas get all the honor.

Trina's in charge of all the Olders as the Oldest, but "in charge" just means someone willing to do all the work. Mira is the actual oldest girl in the Holy Wood, grown unmoored in the way all the seventeen-year-olds tend to be. Trina almost wants her to go. In-sook milks her spot as an Older for everything—the first meat, the best Gathers, sparkly rings. Lupe is still young and wants to fix things like the Carpenter she used to be.

The only one who's dangerous is Heather, who leans against the wall and watches her. Heather is smart, and all that smart pours into an acid tongue. She talks like a true believer in the gods, but mostly she talks of the weakness of boys. Every mistake the boys make is a reason to take something away. Heather got the Olders to create a rule that made boys get a girl to speak for them before the boys are allowed to become anything that isn't a Muscle or a worker.

The boys get only the strong jobs, not the smart ones, which means most of the Muscle are boys. Any girl can be a Muscle, but with so many other things girls are allowed to do, most don't bother.

A group of girls, mostly Tweens, have started following Heather around: the Hermanas. They carry big sticks. When a boy breaks a rule, increasingly it's the Hermanas, not the Muscle or even the Olders, who punish him. There never used to be beatings. Now the boys find themselves under the sticks all the time. Trina tried to make a rule against the Hermanas, seeing how much power that gave Heather, but that time she got outvoted by the council. "Girls need girls to protect emselves," In-sook said.

None of this would have happened without Pablo's Rebellion. Pablo was the head Muscle of the Holy Wood, one of the best they'd ever had until he decided that the strongest should rule, not the Olders. Trina was thirteen when Pablo rose, when he peeled away a dozen other Muscle. He was tall, cunning, full of fire.

He claimed the gods spoke to him. Their voices rang in his ears. He saw visions tinged in blue. He said that boys were not meant to serve.

"We ain't Muscle!" she remembered him rage in the Circle the night he declared war. "*We* the rightful Oldest. You oughta be following us." He claimed that boys once owned the earth, a lie that shook the entire Circle, it was so bold. None of the girls believed him, but it was the lie that some of the boys needed. The Olders didn't see the hunger the boys had to be equal. When the Oldest exiled him, most of the Muscle followed, with scores of Tweens.

The weeks that followed froze the Holy Wood. Pablo burned wagons full of corn, killed Gatherers in lonely houses. Some of the Muscle rallied in defense, but most of the strength was with Pablo.

When the sentries saw him coming in force with burning arrows, the village retreated to the Zervatory, the holiest Holy Wood place in the hills above them. If the gods had brought Pablo to that place, they abandoned him there. He broke on the Zervatory walls.

The Zervatory was big enough to fit the entire village behind its barred windows, which Trina knows from a long week hiding in the lower chambers with barrels of water and rations while Pablo's Rebellion went on above.

She heard the shot that ended the rebellion. The rebels rushed the gates, most of the first wave falling to the archers. Pablo stepped out from behind the Star Watchers Pillar, a monument in the center of the Zervatory's great lawn.

"The gods do not speak to girls," he said, his speech flowery and unnatural. "They've shown me what used to be in the Parents' day, and what is yet to come." She remembers thinking: *Even the priestesses don't claim to speak for the gods. Why is he different?*

The Zervatory was silent. Between his pauses, Trina could hear a drop of water escaping a cask.

"The Holy Wood will fall," Pablo said. Trina can almost remember seeing his face, but of course she couldn't. "There are weapons that will destroy—"

The Oldest shot him with the One Gun, resting the rifle on the Zervatory wall to steady her aim. The bullet tore through his throat and burrowed into the feet of the bearded Star Watcher behind him. The rebellion was over. No amount of boys could fight the One Gun.

That's the biggest secret the girls keep from the boys. The boys think all guns died with the Parents, although some wonder. There is more than one gun still out there—but for the Olders to stay in power, there can only be One Gun. When the Gatherers find guns, the Gatherers who are always girls, they bring them to the Olders, who destroy them. If the Muscle ever believed they could have their own guns, if they didn't walk in fear of the Olders' gun, the balance of power might shift to them.

The lie bothers Trina, just a little, but it's one that has gone from Oldest to Oldest to Oldest since the Holy Wood began. And it has kept them safe.

The Holy Wood beat Pablo, but it never recovered from the terror. The Olders set curfews for boys. No one balked. They gutted the Muscle, left their defenses weak. No one protested. By the time Trina became the Oldest, the boys found themselves hemmed in, weakened.

The Hermanas, the girls who follow Heather, are supposed to keep the girls safe as well, but they terrify the shit out of Trina. They hang out near the kitchens and demand that smaller kids bring them their food. The Hermanas cut marks in their wrists to show that they can hurt themselves worse than a boy ever could. They wear matching pink lipstick, freed from some Gatherer's stash. Only the Mamas were supposed to wear lipstick, the red lips of their Waking. Trina tried to ban the pink, too obvious a sign of defiance and violence, but it keeps coming back.

Trina has no love for boys, for all the chaos and violence that comes with them. But if she had to choose between them and anything Heather wanted, she'd bring in a whole army of boys.

Heather doesn't waste any time. "The Muscle been leaving the gates without asking," she says.

"Everyone leaves the gates without asking," Trina says.

"Yeah, but the Muscle are a lot more dangerous," Heather says.

"That's what makes em good at their *job,*" Trina says.

"We should make em ask before they leave," In-sook says, and just like that Trina loses the vote: Heather, Mira, In-sook. They usually don't have to vote on things, really—Trina could look around and see which way the group's decision will go.

"I been thinking," Heather says. "Don't you think we got too many Muscle? I talked to Hyun. He says it's hard to train em all."

"So he just wants to . . . not train em?" It should surprise Trina, but it doesn't. Hyun is the head of the Muscle and has tried his hardest to run them into the ground. Ever since Pablo, the Olders have been scared of anyone too strong or smart heading the Muscle, afraid he'll take their power. They picked the exact opposite of that with Hyun. They should have picked Apple, who's as smart and calm as a girl.

"What would you do with em?" Lupe says.

"Keep some as Carpenters or Farmers—or Exile em," Heather says. Trina just stares at her. Some boys go through the rage when they became Teens; some get it so bad that the Olders make them leave. But they've never Exiled them just for being boys.

"Aww, don't get rid of the Muscle," Mira says, squirming a little on the throne. "They're my *favorite.*"

The past few months, Mira has been rolling with any boy she can find. It's her version of the Last Life. Instead of not caring how she dies, she doesn't care how she lives.

"We ain't cutting down the Muscle," Trina says. "We need the protection. And if we wanna make babies, we gonna need *someone* for the girls to roll with."

"We ain't had a vote," Heather says.

"You don't got the votes. I can tell you that right now."

"We gonna." They don't vote on it now, but Heather will push and push it until one of the Olders goes her way.

On the way out, she watches two kids go, in moments, from hoisting well water to shouting to punching. She grabs the bigger kid's shoulder.

"What you doing?"

"He said I ain't doing it right!"

"Are you?"

"He can't tell me what to do!"

Trina looks at the two boys, both trembling with anger, and the water sloshed all over the dirt. She's about to answer, then just shakes her head and walks away.

There are shouts at the gate, and Trina looks up in time to see them clanging shut. They're never shut in the daytime, except for in times of danger. She sprints toward them. If Hyun is manning them, he might end up killing someone. It won't be the right someone, because he's too stupid to know the difference.

Trina shoves through the crowd that's sprouted in front of the gate. Behind the fence, behind a wall of machetes, are three dusty boys. "Exiles," Hyun says, suddenly at her side. But she didn't have to be told. Exiles—Malibus, based on the shorts they wear.

The Malibus live along the ocean and eat fish. It's too far for the other Angelenos to fish themselves. When whales beach, though, the Malibus tell the other Angelenos so that they can all feast on the whale. Trina has made the trek to the water to harvest the whales, one of the only Holy Wood to see the ocean. She'll never forget when she stood on a cliff and saw the blue open up beyond the fringe of pounding white. She felt as if she were about to fall off the edge of the world.

Every few months boys wander in from the other Angeleno peoples:

the Downtowns, the San Fernandos, and the Malibus. The Angelenos are a united people. They keep the peace, although squabbles over land are common, and they trade. Sometimes, they trade boys.

The Exiles are cast out from the Angeleno tribes because they were too violent or too strange for their people. So they roam in packs, sometimes looking for a home that fits them better, or they die. But sometimes those Exiles are what other tribes need—a boy who steals from the Downtowns might fit into the San Fernandos because he's a good hunter. All of the Angelenos do this. It keeps their boys calm, their babies healthy.

The first Exile at the gate is a giant compared to the other Children. He must have been a threat to the Malibu Olders, who are stricter than other Olders and don't tolerate even a little rebellion. With his size he will be in demand as a Dad. Trina knows the tribe will vote to accept him, even if it means they kick him out in weeks for the rage he shows simply standing there. That's the line with the boys: You want someone strong enough who will create strong babies, but not so strong that you can't control him.

The second Exile looks strong like him but smaller. The third, though, doesn't look like an Exile. He's too young, too small, as if an earthquake would topple him. If they expelled him he must have caused harm of a different kind. He's the one Trina watches.

And he is the one who speaks. "We traveled through the lost city and hidden hills to the Holy Wood," he says in the stiff official speech that only gets used when you talk to other Angelenos. "Under the ways of our peoples, we Exiles ask you to accept us."

"Bad timing—we was just talking about how we got too many boys," Trina says. She doesn't even try to echo his tone.

"We got strength and skill to share," the little one says. A standard Exile line.

"We all full up. Try the Downtowns." She doesn't like the look of the first two, and if the little guy was too much trouble for the Malibus . . . Less than half of the Exiles find a new home. These will be ones who don't.

Trina turns to Hyun. "Keep the gate barred. If they reach through, chop off their arms."

She's stopped by that small, calm voice. "Please," the little one says. "We got news of the Malibu."

"I hear more than I want," she says.

"You ain't heard this," he says. "The Malibus got someone who lived."

Trina doesn't breathe. Someone who didn't End? A way to dry the trickle of life that seeps out of this village every year. Maybe the kid's lying. But what if he's not? She has to hear more.

She tries to keep her expression neutral as she says, "Open the gate."

CHAPTER FIVE
THE CIRCLE

Gonna kill that girl. If she's alive. Lady stays at the gate long after the Exiles have passed through, long after the coyotes have started howling, long after the gates shut in her face.

She should have known. No, she knew. She's been best friends with Jemma her whole life. She saw that set in the jaw last night at Zee's fire and read it again this morning for what it was: Jemma was already halfway to stupid. She has a little bit of Last Lifer in her, Lady thinks; ready to shank the world the second it pushes too hard. Lady has a short temper, but Jemma has something different, sometimes worse.

Apple is with her; that's what the sentries told her. That's the only thing that doesn't send Lady out into the night after her.

Lady hears the rising sounds of the Children in the Circle, the night promising a jolt. Whenever Exiles come, the Holy Wood changes, its pattern weaving in new threads from the Exiles, and becomes new cloth.

She saw the big Exile, the beautiful one, looking like the old pictures of the holy ones on the billboards in the Flat Lands. When he came through the gates she rushed toward him to be seen. That has less to do with him than the ball of excitement she feels all the time lately rising in her chest, threatening to burst out whenever someone touches her skin or casts her a lingering look. His eyes slide right past her.

The sentries see Apple and Jemma before Lady does, stumbling out of the night. No, not stumbling. There's nothing wrong with them, but something drags their bodies down, slows their step. Something happened to them in the night.

Anger fights with relief, and for a moment anger wins. Luckily for Jemma and Apple, it's directed first at the sentries who are blocking the gate with drawn machetes.

"Open the gate," she hears Jemma say, her voice sounding old.

"Hyun says don't open the gate. Why you out?"

"We was jumped by Last Lifers," Apple says. "Let us in."

"But you was outside the wall."

The other sentry says, "Hyun says we gotta ask him first."

"Jesucristo, you idiots, let em in," Lady says, pinching one of them hard on the neck and dragging him away from the fence. He's a little bigger than her, but she's madder. She glares at the other one until he sheathes his machete and draws back the bar.

"Thanks, Lady," Jemma says, walking through the gate and leaning forward to hug her. "It's been—"

"You shut up," Lady says, grabbing Jemma in a headlock that Jemma barely resists. "I been waiting for two hours. Last Lifers? What the hell you doin anywhere near em? What the hell you—" But then she sees streaks of tears on Jemma's cheeks under the headlock, Jemma who she's only seen cry when she fell off a house and knocked her wind out. And the always-calm Apple, jaw now tense and tight.

Lady releases Jemma but keeps her hand on Jemma's arm. "Last Lifers? You—you okay?"

"It's . . . it's tranquilo now," Jemma slowly says.

Tranquilo. All good. But Lady knows from that voice that it isn't all good—and whatever happened out there, Jemma won't tell it right away.

Then she remembers why she came to the gates in the first place, the news that couldn't wait until they were back in their house.

"Exiles," she says. That should be all she needs to get Jemma's attention. But Lady has more. "The Malibus," she says. "They got someone who lived."

"I don't understand," Jemma says, seeming to stumble over the idea.

"Someone's—old. Actually old."

Jemma squeezes Apple's hand at that, and he squeezes back. Lady catches the movement but looks away. The two let go, but as they walk toward the Circle, she sees the way they lean toward each other, providing invisible support. They went out two. They came back one. *What else happened out there?* Only the waiting Circle keeps her from asking.

There's a difference in the Circle: part party, part war council. The bonfire is lit, the Tweens dancing around it, and the Olders sit back in a tight knot.

Across the flames she sees Trina, remembers her arguing with Jemma last night. Trina starts speaking. The Tweens stop dancing and are pulsing around the Circle.

This is the Story. Every night starts with the Story.

"Once we was a family, Children and Parents," Trina says. She's flinty. You have to be like that to be the Oldest, the keeper of the One Gun. "They stayed with us forever, and we grew old and grew Children of our own. Then came the End. The End of the Parents, the End of our lives. We wasn't warned, and the Parents died in minutes. They didn't know what killed them, but still they died. In oceans and the hills, still they died."

"Still they died," the crowd repeats in unison.

Trina glances around the fire, watching the red glow flicker on the faces. The Children are still rapt after hearing it every day, because, really: It is the only Story. "The Parents died. The weak Children died, them who lived in high places. The strong and humble lived. We was all colors, Whiteys, Tinos, Korenos, and now we one. We grew our food, we Gathered. But even that wasn't enough, cuz we lived but we didn't make new life. We died before we could become Mamas and Dads. But we learned how the body dies fast, and we lived our lives faster. Of all the people of the world, the Angelenos last, cuz we remember this: 'Never leave the Holy Wood empty.' "

"Never leave the Holy Wood empty," they repeat.

"To keep the Holy Wood full, we bring in Exiles," Trina says. "Do we accept them?"

The biggest Exile, named Li, goes first. At least half the thirteen-year-olds raise their hands to accept him. Lady's hand shoots up first. They accept the second Exile, Tomas, although with fewer votes. Lady doesn't raise her hand.

The third Exile is so small. So small. Lady didn't notice him before when he came in the gates, but now she can't quite look away. Such a strange kid, the way he watches them, as if he's the one who decides who stays or not. Lady can't tell his age. She guesses fourteen, but he's twelve in size and seventeen in his eyes.

"Do we accept him?" Trina says, and no one shouts "Yes." He's too young for a Dad, too weak for a Muscle. None of the Holy Wood see him in the future. The ring is silent.

"He's gonna die out there," Jemma whispers. Lady knows it's true. He won't have an Exile gang to protect him in the wild.

"He will," Apple says. Lady can see his jaws working. He's seen the bodies of those who've been forced to wander alone. Only the girls can accept an Exile, though, so he can't say anything.

Lady sees Jemma's mouth start to open, her shoulders tighten. She's not sure why Jemma cares—they've rejected lots of Exiles in the past, and it hasn't bothered her. Lady elbows her. "You can't. You just gonna get more trouble." Trina's already mad at her for staying out, Lady heard. Heather shot her dirty looks after she walked in with Apple. Why make it worse?

"Do we accept him?" Trina says. Jemma's mouth almost opens again.

"Do we accept him?" Trina says. It's the third question, the last question, then the boy will die unwanted as he should be. The Angelenos have stayed strong by only taking the strong.

There's no fear in the boy's eyes, though, and Lady wonders if they've read him wrong. His eyes are filled with an almost lazy curiosity, and they alight on everyone in the Circle, touching faces and moving on.

Whatever happened out there today, Jemma doesn't seem to care anymore. So when Trina says, "Exile from the Malibus, the Holy Wood people don't accept—"

"I do. I accept you," Jemma says. The rest is a clanging of Lady seconding the acceptance, of Trina shouting, of Apple squeezing Jemma's waist—squeezing Jemma's waist?—and through it all, the little Exile staring at Jemma without emotion.

Jemma, stepping on the world's neck again. Lady is proud of her, even though she doesn't know what it will cost them. "I hope you like trouble, puta," Lady says, watching the Olders watching Jemma. "Cuz you just bought it."

Jemma's ribs move under his hand. Apple's aware that she is speaking but feels it as a vibration under his fingertips and not a voice in his ears. Claiming the Exile. Saving a life. He smiles wide at that, at the good under the tough.

Until he sees Hyun tramping toward them through the Circle, Apple in his sights. Hyun's cheeks puff out, building himself up for a fit. The leader of the Muscle. The Head. That's the perfect name for Hyun, who has the biggest head in the Holy Wood, sitting on his shoulders like a sweaty egg. If there ever was a visible neck, Apple doesn't remember it.

Hyun motions him away from the fire into the shadows, and Apple steps toward him at the closest speed to disrespect. He doesn't want to leave Jemma. He catches her eye, though, and walks into the dark.

"You went past the Bear Wall," Hyun says.

"I pass it every day," Apple says.

"Nobody asked me."

"Gatherer needs protecting, I protect her."

"You heard Heather. One Muscle to five Gatherers. She wants to go off, you let her."

"That ain't safe."

"You heard Heather."

"Why you letting Heather tell the Muscle how much Muscle we use?" Apple says. "You the Head."

Apple should have been the Head, until Pablo terrified the Olders with his rebellion. Anyone smart enough to do the job was ruled out after that because they were too big of a threat to the Olders, and Hyun was the most qualified idiot left.

"Yeah, I'm the Head. And I tell you this Muscle stays home if Heather says." Hyun grabs Apple's arm, and Apple remembers his one qualification. Hyun is strong, maybe stronger than Apple, even with a coat of fat and a chest like a girl's. That he's fat in a village where no one's fat shows how good being the Head has been to him.

Apple brushes off the hand as if he weren't really being held. "We got bigger problems than your boner for Heather," he says. "The Last Lifers."

"Stupid jwi," Hyun says. It's an old Koreno word for rat but means something else now. "They ain't getting over the fence."

"They changed. They got smart. They got a gun." Apple remembers the way the Last Lifers ran in formation, the way they plotted to head him off—most important, the gun. None of that is like any Last Lifer pack he's ever seen—usually they're just a pile of crazy. But Last Lifers who can plan? That's a danger.

"I ain't believing that if I ain't seen it."

"Then you gotta see it."

"Nah, I don't," Hyun says. "Heather says no."

This time it's Apple grabbing an arm and Hyun brushing it off. "This matters, pendeja," Apple says.

He shouldn't have called him that, because Hyun puffs up even bigger. "Oh, pendeja? Don't you got some sentry work to do?"

"That's for juniors," Apple says.

"You a junior now," Hyun says. "Ya lo cagaste." *You screwed it up, Apple.*

Apple never cared about being passed over as Head of the Muscle until now, until he sees how vulnerable the Holy Wood is, from inside and out. He shouldn't care. His time is Ending, right? No, that's not right. Apple looks back over his shoulder and sees Jemma with Trina and Lady and the Exile.

The End is gonna have to wait.

The Exile seems untouched by the uproar he's caused. The tribe flows around him like he's a boulder in a flood.

As the only one who spoke, Jemma will have to introduce him to the Holy Wood. For the next thirty days, he will be her shadow. She's not sure what she expected from him—gratitude, fear?—but she doesn't get any of it as she approaches. He just watches her, and she doesn't say anything for several long seconds. "You little for an Exile," she finally says.

"Yeah, but my mouth is big," he says.

"I believe that," Lady says. "You got a name?"

"Pico."

"From the Malibus, right?" Jemma asks. He nods, and she whispers the next question without intending to: "It true that someone lived?"

"Ah," Pico says. "Only question worth asking. Yeah, it's true. And I think I know why."

Jemma feels the shock run through her chest, little tremors pushing into her lungs and stealing the breath. "We could live longer?" The picture Apple was holding settles in her head, and in it the two of them are now the Parents.

"Maybe. But not sure you'd want to."

She's shaking her head at that, at the stupidity of that, when Trina blows in like a dark cloud, trailing angry daggers of rain. "You!" Trina says, digging her fingers into Jemma's arm. "You . . . !" she sputters again, but she runs out of words.

"What, Trina, what?" Jemma says, matching Trina's anger.

"Accepting this Exile when you never cared about Exiles before. You messing with me?" Trina says.

"This ain't got nothing to do with you!"

"Then what?"

"Ain't gonna kill someone else today," Jemma says. Softer than she meant.

"What?"

"I saw Andy today, me and Apple did," she says, hearing her voice crack but unable to stop it. She meant to sound like a Muscle, a warrior. She doesn't. Instead, she sounds like someone who had to kill a friend she loved, and that opens her insides to the world, raw and sad. "Me and Apple got chased into the Bowl by the Last Lifers. And one of em was Andy, and he tried to kill us, and I split his head."

"Oh," Trina says, and their argument is forgotten. She's the Oldest again. She pulls Jemma to her chest and holds her there until Jemma finally feels herself stop sobbing.

Trina releases Jemma, gently pushes her toward Lady and the Exile. "Go to bed," Trina says, but catches Jemma's wrist. "We gotta talk, though. About the Mamas."

Jemma sees Apple standing there watching them. She doesn't know how long he's been watching. She feels herself floating toward him, away from Trina and the others. "About the Mamas, sure," she says. "It's all about living, right?"

"About making babies, about keeping us alive as a people," Trina says.

"I think it's about live like you're alive," Jemma says.

Apple takes three steps, Jemma takes five, and she folds herself into him. His arms form a protective shell around her and she's kissing him, kissing him hard, with everyone watching, and she doesn't care.

In the Holy Wood, they want you to kiss, they want you to roll. Your whole life is meant for you to be a Mama, because making a baby will save the tribe. You don't have to like someone to make a baby. But touching lips and brushing thighs, that's one thing. This feels different. This feels as if they're a whole.

Apple holds her face in his hands. "Jemma," he says wonderingly.

"Why does it feel like this?" Jemma asks.

"It's deep, it runs deep." Apple points to the gaps in his teeth. "I earned these when I was a Tween, the day I learned it. Two Muscle was talking about you, and I told em I didn't like it, and so . . ." He smiles.

She touches his lips, says, "It's always been you, ain't it?"

"It's what the Parents—what the Parents called love," Apple says. "But we don't got time for love."

Love. If that's what it meant, then yes. If it meant being two halves of a circle, meant breathing the same breath, meant melting into each other's hips. Maybe she could be a Mama and more than that. She would love like the Parents did.

"Jemma," Apple says again. She sees smiles in the firelight, then the glare from Heather, the Older. Heather has never liked seeing Jemma with Apple. And even as Jemma pulls Apple tighter, she realizes: It's not just that we don't got time. We're not brave enough. The most dangerous thing in this world is to love.

CHAPTER SIX

THE LONG WALL

Lady pushed Jemma hard—really pushed her, with her hands—after Apple left the Circle last night. "What's your problem, Jemma?" she said. "You can't tell me?"

"Which piece?" Jemma said. "Almost getting killed? Or kissing a boy?"

"Hell yeah, the boy," Lady said. But she really means almost getting killed. Lady should have seen it, should have asked more. Jemma should have collapsed into Lady's arms the second she walked through the gate. But she didn't tell. Instead, she leaned on Apple.

On Apple. Who was at the edge all their lives, and now was in the middle.

Ah.

It's no surprise to Lady that Apple likes Jemma. They're good with each other, even though she's pissed that Jemma didn't tell her. The real surprise is that Jemma likes him back. She's never admitted to Lady to liking a boy, nothing real, nothing more than weak Tweeny talk of rolling.

But yesterday Jemma moved as if the End were chasing her. Zee was dead. Andy was dead. It was time to become a Mama. Jemma whispered something as they argued last night, her chin tucked in to her chest. Lady couldn't hear.

"Repeat it," Lady said.

Jemma lifted her head. "We gotta live now, Lady. We all gone tomorrow."

We all gone tomorrow. Life is always running out. That's how Jemma sees it. As Lady combs the Holy Wood for Jemma this morning, she can see it, too. A pair of sixteen-year-olds walk through the village before her, but they don't talk to the younger kids. The old kids don't mix the way they did before. They cluster in groups of two and three, drawing back as if afraid to touch the life around them.

Some of them will slip away altogether, like Andy did. He was dancing in the Circle one night, and then he was gone, off to the Last Lifers. She's found Last Lifers collapsed on the streets of Ell Aye, no one to light their body fires.

Lady shakes her curly hair, clearing the thoughts as if they're hovering gnats. They don't have a place in her head, because no one loves the Holy Wood, no one loves life, the way she does. Chasing through the streets, Gathering in the Parents' houses, lazily kissing a boy in lemon-scented shade—it's as if they created this life for her.

A Carpenter named Ricky steps away from the food sheds, carrying a potato roasted in coals. He won't wait until it cools to eat it, so he bobbles it between his fingers while he licks his burning skin.

"You seen Jemma?" she says. He yelps and drops the potato.

"Tall one? Nah." He leans over to pick up the potato, and she stops him.

"Use your head," she says. She stabs it with a stick and hands it to him.

He just shrugs. "You wanna roll?"

"Help me find Jemma and maybe."

She's not really interested. He's only thirteen, with a skinny body. Okay, maybe she's interested. Maybe she's always interested.

Lately she feels as if her skin is always tingling, as if her eyes are always wide, as if her breaths are always shallow. It's all about the boys. It's all about becoming a Mama.

Life running short? She feels as if she has enough life for the entire Holy Wood flowing through her fingertips.

Ricky doesn't help her find Jemma, being the age where a hot potato still matters more to a boy than a kiss. So she leaves him behind and enters the Casa de las Casas.

The Casa de las Casas was the first house, the one where the First Mamas fled the End and the madness in Ell Aye below. It was the house where the Three Peoples—the Tinos, the Korenos, and the Whiteys—became the Holy Wood.

It echoes silent today, just her footsteps and the whisper of her fingers along the Long Wall. On the Long Wall are stories in pictures, drawn by each new batch of Children. Traveling its length takes her back in time to the First Mamas.

On her right, Lady sees the memories that are still fresh: the raw red lines of the Winter Fire that licked the hills right to the edge of the Holy Wood and burned down seven houses, the brown of the cabbage blight, black arrows of Pablo's Rebellion.

The people change as she moves. The drawings are crude at first. With each step, the lines become clearer, the shapes more graceful as the pintadores get closer to the Parents' time. The Long Gone pintadores could make pictures that practically breathed, but the Children lose the feel of the brushes with every new batch of kids.

The skin colors shift along with the shapes, from the dusty brown they all share now to shades of the Tinos, Korenos, and Whiteys, who used to hate one another but when the world was in trouble became one. She traces over the details of the first drawings with her fingers. A fold of skin over the corner of an eye, white skin with freckles, broad cheekbones, all gone now. Well, not gone—peeking out here and there among the Children of the Holy Wood. All one now.

The wall farthest away from the entrance is different, because there they used letters. She sees letters everywhere on her Gathers, but now they mean nothing. Whatever magic the Parents found in them, it's gone. The only letter that matters is the aytch, the one that stands at the beginning of the Holy Wood sign and tells the people of the Holy Wood where they belong.

"Buddha Teevee Jesucristo," she says, and whispers the other ones: "Mama. Dad." They all add that whisper laced with longing, because what is a god next to a Parent?

Padres. Mamas. Parents. Fathers. Bumonim. So many words lost and still they have words for Parents.

Even in the Daycare they whispered about the real Mamas, the real Dads. Not the ones who made them, but the ones who could save them from the End. "Be good and the real Mama comes back," they'd say. "Drop that stick or they'll never come for you." The priestesses who talk to the gods don't talk like that, but they don't have to. Some longings run deeper than churching.

"Catching up on your stories?" Trina emerges from what would have been the kitchen back in the Long Gone. Lady's a little scared of Trina, and Lady's not scared of anyone.

"Looking at the First Mamas," Lady says.

"We wouldn't be here right now, none of this would be here now—not if they hadn't been brave," Trina says. "They knew the need."

Lady knows. That back then they used to wait to become Parents to roll, to make babies, and the First Mamas were the first to realize they'd have to roll younger in order for the Holy Wood to survive. But Trina seems to need to say it. So Lady just nods, and remembers why she came to the Casa de las Casas.

"Looking for Jemma," she says.

"Walk with me," Trina says. "This matters more."

Instead of turning left to the lake when they leave the gates, they walk to the right until they reach one of the streets that snakes along between the Holy Wood sign and the Circle. It's part of the Holy Wood, but no one lives there. It's too far from the Circle. Lady and Jemma used to sit in a glass house, an old mocycle parked inside the house in front of the window, and pretend they were the old starlet priestesses they found in tattered magzines.

"People used to live up on this street," Trina says. "My nanny in the Daycare used to."

"Why'd they leave, then?"

"They didn't need to live here no more. There's enough space down by the Circle now."

Lady doesn't know what to say. She doesn't know why Trina is saying what she's saying.

"They didn't need to live there cuz the Holy Wood has less and less people every year," Trina says.

"We always been small," Lady says. "Right?"

"We used to fill the houses of the Holy Wood. All the Holy Wood, not just the streets by the Circle," Trina says. "You think that was all Parents down there?"

"I—"

"We getting smaller. There was nine hundred Children in the Holy Wood when my Mama was alive; now there are eight hundred. The numbers don't work," Trina says. "It takes two to make one. Sometimes a Mama has twins, sometimes she gets two babies in before she dies. But mostly they don't."

"Oh." Lady sees it now. "What if we started Mamas younger than fifteen?"

"The Olders tried that once. You think we lose a lot of Mamas now? We lost a lot more then. Ain't enough bodies ready to have babies."

"Mine is," she says, and she can feel it. She's not even two months away from fifteen, and she's ready. The way her stomach tightens when she's with a boy, the feel of a baby in her arms. She's ready.

"It is," Trina says, looking at Lady's body like the Farmer she used to be, looking at a goat. Lady feels no shame. "Those hips, you ain't gonna lose no babies."

Lady smiles. It's true. Everyone knows the wide Mamas make the best Mamas, because they don't get hurt as bad when the baby's born. And Lady's wide. Maybe that's why Jemma doesn't want to be a Mama. She's not built for it.

"Being a Mama is all I ever wanted," Lady says.

"Good," Trina says. "Join the next Waking." And that's it.

The Waking is the ceremony that every girl goes through before she becomes a Mama, and the rolling that comes after. It's the first full moon after she turns fifteen. They will go to the Zervatory, the holiest of places in the Holy Wood, and they will pick a boy to be the Dad of their baby.

"More babies'll help, right?" Lady says.

Trina doesn't respond at first, lost as her eyes wander through the empty streets. Then: "It's gonna take a lot more than you."

"What else we gonna do?"

Trina almost snorts. "Live longer, I guess. Grow faster."

"That ain't possible."

"I know," Trina says. She points to the house where her nanny used to live. "If we can't, that ain't just an empty street. That's the real end of the world."

CHAPTER SEVEN
THE MAYFLIES

The night after the Circle Jemma dreams, not of Apple, but of the Exile. It doesn't feel like a regular dream. The Exile's still still eyes peep out of a blue haze that seems familiar. He limps. He pulls a silver case out of a hole in the floor. He's followed by a buzz in her ear. *The haze showed me something new*, she thinks. *But why does it care about the Exile?*

The next morning when he's sitting in front of her door, only the quiet eyes are there. She almost wonders where the case is.

She lives in El Tercero, the third house claimed by the First Mamas. Only the oldest Gatherers live there, so Lady has not yet made it to El Tercero. It's the first time they've ever been separated.

El Tercero is on a winding, quiet street away from the Circle, so he's the only person outside it. He sits as he did before, taking in the street as if he's not even on it.

Jemma looks at him, trying to puzzle it out from his face. All her memories from last night are crowded out by Apple. Finally she gives up. "What's your name?"

The Exile doesn't look offended, and she suspects he never is. "Pico," he says. "What, you forgot that you saved me?"

"I save a lot of people. It's easy to lose track," she says. She looks around the deserted street. "No one would show you around?"

"They hope I'll just go away."

"I understand that," she says. "You need a guide? Fine." Lady's probably still mad at her. Trina, too. Apple got sent off on night watch as punishment for taking her to the Stack, so he's sleeping all morning. Showing the kid around will keep her out of everyone's way.

The Holy Wood and the Malibu are supposed to be the same people, but nothing Jemma shows Pico seems to be the same as what he knew in the Malibus. He looks like the type who would mock her little tour. Instead, he listens like he's stowing it all in a box for safekeeping.

The Bicycle Kids are a team of Middle Children, seven and eight years old, who learn to repair the prized fleet of bicycles—patching tires with ancient glue and raiding the Parents' bikes for parts. "There's always three?" Pico asks.

"At least three of almost anything, of all ages," Jemma replies. "That's new. Two of our Animal Doctors died a few weeks apart, and no one could deliver a goat."

The Daycare is in a sprawling single-level house. Babies and Toddlers live there, but their caretakers are not much older: Ninos, five and six, with some Tweens watching everything. "Daycare?" Pico asks. "Even though they stay all night?"

"That's what the Parents called it," Jemma says.

On the way to the Great Field, Jemma shows Pico the kimchee pit, where they bury cabbage and peppers in pottery and let them ferment for weeks. This is one of the foods the Children remembered from the Parents, from the Korenos. They can smell the kimchee long after they pass it.

Most of the Middles work in the fields, and Pico can't stop staring at the plants. In the Malibus they eat so much fish that farming is only some potatoes and squash. But the Great Field is full of peas and favas, which heal the ground for the other vegetables. The Middles are harvesting the last of those to get ready for the summer crop of tomatoes, melons, and peppers. Behind them, an ancient sign shows a dog squatting. "We think they used to raise their dogs here," Jemma says. "Maybe they ate em, too?"

The Great Field Pump is a miracle from the past, fueled by donkeys that move in a slow circle to pull water from the lake. "But that's two hundred feet below," Pico says.

Jemma doesn't answer. She's never thought of it before.

"Did the Parents make it?" Pico presses.

"No, the first Children did."

"Children made that?"

"That's what the stories say."

Pico falls silent, the first time all day. It's not until they're on the lake in the canoe, trying to net one of the koi that live there, that he speaks up again.

"If Children could make the pump, they could make something like it again," he says.

"If you say so."

"We keep talking about the Parents—but we used to be almost as smart."

Jemma digs in her paddle and pulls them into one of the lake's fingers. There the koi are bigger—some as long as her arm. The fish avoid the surface, but she can see distant glints of red and orange below. In the afternoon sun, none swarm after the bait.

"Those fish aren't meant to live here," Pico says almost absently. "They're too bright."

They paddle into a cloud of flies, not dragonflies but something daintier. One of them lands on her knuckle. It looks as if it's trailing threads behind it—twin tails that stretch almost the length of its body. Wings like bows—in fact, the whole body curves like a bow already fired. Jemma twitches her finger to let it go, and, sputtering, it dives into the lake.

"Mayfly," Pico says.

"What?"

"They got em in the creeks in Malibu. The eggs last a long time, like a year. Then the flies all climb out, they look around, they roll with each other, they lay eggs. They're dead a day later. Before the eggs even hatch."

"They don't even got time to be Parents."

Together they watch the lacy swarm, the water giving way to the tiny pressure of the flies' feet. They think of it at the same time, but only Pico voices it. "We the mayflies," Pico says.

"No," Jemma says. "I ain't a mayfly."

"You sure?"

She isn't. But with Apple she'll make it sure. And then Jemma remembers one of the first things Pico said to her.

"You said something last night," she says slowly. She doesn't know why she looks over her shoulder at the shore, but she does. There's no one there.

"I thought you might not remember, with everything else."

"It's the only question that matters, right?"

Pico begins slowly. "I wanted to be a Little Doctor, in the Malibus. They wouldn't let me."

"Shaky hands?"

"No. Cuz I'm a boy."

"Oh." There aren't many boy doctors in the Holy Wood, but they happen. "You smart enough."

"Too smart for a boy," Pico says.

Yes, she thinks, too smart for a boy. Probably too smart for an Angeleno. And if he didn't do a better job hiding it than he's doing now, the Malibus would have shied away from him because they thought he was Touched, someone who was marked for death because they were too smart or too Grown-Up for their age. The smart ones, the mature ones—the End always comes to them first.

"They had me haul the trash," Pico says. "So I hauled it for the Little Doctors, watched as much as I could without em noticing."

"You know how to do the doctoring?"

"Not all. But some I know better than em." There's a wisp of anger in his voice, the sound of a boy who's smart where boys aren't allowed to be smart. "There was a Tween in the Malibus, Leong. He was almost thirteen, and he fell off some rocks and hit his head."

"But he didn't die," Jemma says.

"Not then. And not now," Pico says. "That was six years ago."

"Then . . ." And she remembers how it hit her the first time Pico told her, and she struggles to find her breath again.

"No one's ever lived that long. Not since the Parents."

Even Old Steve, who died when Jemma was six, didn't make it past seventeen. "How?" she says.

"When Leong woke up, he wasn't a Tween anymore," Pico says. "He was more like a Middle. And he don't change. He don't grow . . . up."

"But he don't die."

"I think—I think we die cuz we grow up. Something changes, and that's the End. That's why the Touched die first." Like himself, she can see. He expects to die young.

"What they doing with Leong?"

"The Priestess says that Leong is defying the gods. She wants him put to death."

"Like the fools," Jemma says.

"Like the fools."

Sometimes babies are born, and something is wrong with their minds. When they're Toddlers and the differences show, the tribe pushes the child into the Flat Lands of Ell Aye. Jemma has seen mama coyotes fight bears to protect their pups. But in the Angelenos, there are no Mamas left to protect their kids—they're dead by the time the kids become Toddlers.

"But ain't no one gonna let the Priestess kill him," Pico says. "And some said it might mean we don't all have to die."

Jemma sees everything that he doesn't say washing over his face. "Some, eh? I think I figured why you had to leave." Some of the superstitious shun the Touched, because they trail death after them. In a world where death comes quickly, you don't want to be next to a smart kid who's going to find death even quicker. That's why so many kids pretend not to be smart, and, the whispers say, why the Children stopped reading the letters. The ones who could read them didn't want to admit it.

Malibus are supposed to be churchy freaks, and the churchy freaks like smart even less than the other Angelenos. If he gave the Olders even the slightest excuse, they would send him off.

Thoughts spiral through Jemma's head, too fast to grab for long, but one keeps circling back. "Would that work for others, too?"

"Getting hit on the head?"

"Yeah."

"Getting stuck in the Middles forever?"

Jemma thinks of herself at seven, dancing with Lady, feeling that the Middle wasn't really the middle of her life, watching Apple in the corner of the room watching her. "It would be worth it," she says.

Lady sees Jemma and the Exile coming up from the lake and descends upon them, angry, giddy, and protective all at once. "Where the hell you been?" she says, half hitting, half hugging. "You shouldn't be wandering around without me."

"Like every day since I was born?" Jemma says.

"Since yesterday."

"She can take care of herself," Pico says.

"Shut up, Exile," Lady says. He's got a lot of sass, speaking up like that.

"You remember the Exile," Jemma says. "Apparently I saved him last night."

"Among other things," Lady says.

Lady puts her arm around Jemma's shoulder like she's shutting a door on Pico and shifts her focus to Jemma. It's a mark of her concern that she can hold that focus for more than a few seconds, with everything else happening. "How are you feeling? After all you been through last night?"

"Okay. I didn't get hurt."

"And . . . Apple?" Putting a lot into that word.

Jemma smiles like her face might freeze that way, shakes her head. "Apple," she says.

Lady smiles back at that, but she's mad again, and Jemma notices. "I shoulda told you," Jemma says. "About everything."

"You shoulda," Lady says.

As if that gives Lady permission to move on, she does. "I got news," she says.

"Yeah?"

"Trina says I can join the Mamas early—even though I'm not old enough! Cuz my bod's ready." Lady gestures down at her curves. "This Mama's ready to roll."

Jemma hugs her.

"Salud," Pico says, giving the traditional blessing. They'd forgotten he was there. He's watched the whole thing without blushing, unusual even for an Angeleno boy.

"Shut up, Exile," Lady says.

"You still wanna run away from here?" Apple says, then punches her in the stomach.

"I never said run away," Jemma says. "I said *leave*." And she swings for his head. He ducks.

"What's the difference?"

"Speed." She fires two tapping blows at him, and they both connect, on each cheek. He looks flustered and confused for a moment, then smiles.

"Show-off."

Apple believes anyone could be a Muscle, even a girl, and has been fighting with Jemma since she was seven. From the beginning she couldn't shoot, couldn't hold her quivering muscles still long enough to aim properly. But with fists or a machete or an ax, she was nearly the match of him.

Still, this comes second nature to Apple, not to her, and he still teaches her. "Where's your guard?" he says when his fist makes it to her chin.

She takes another punch to the gut.

"Why you giving me such a big target for such a skinny girl?"

She connects with his chin, but not with force.

"Don't swing for my face. Swing through the back of my head," Apple says.

She grabs his head with both hands, holds his face a finger away from hers. "You talk too much," she says, and kisses him hard. He seems to pull away, and she pulls him back.

"Yield," she says.

"Too late," he says, and pushes her away. She feints at him and he catches her arm somehow, rolling her over his shoulder and throwing her hard to the ground. Her wind gets knocked out, and she breathes in raggedly before she can exhale. And then he's on the ground with her, wrestling at first, and then not. She holds her lips to his until they have to break to breathe.

"When I said we should run, things was bad," Jemma says.

"Now?"

"Things got better."

"Same for me," Apple says. "A lot better."

They fight even more since they became boy and girl together. It gives her a reason to be close to him, to touch his skin. And somehow, by fighting, they're protecting the space between them, a space that feels as fragile as a bubble and just as hard to hold in her hands.

"Maybe we should stay here. The Holy Wood is safe," she says.

"Yeah," he says, "only . . ." Only no one's safe from the End, so no place is really safe. She knows that never leaves his mind, the End looming over him. It pulls him away, from time to time, and she has to pull him back.

"But still," Apple says, "I seen the maps and heard the traders talk, Jemma. There's places and places beyond the mountains, more than we can ever think on: trees as thick as a house, trains that go in upside-downy loops, boats big enough for three Holy Woods. Places where the earth breathes fire and the deserts are painted red. We could walk the world and never reach the end of it in my life, in yours. You don't think one of those places has figured out how to grow old?"

There it is. Asking her to run. There is a buzzing in her ear, and she can see the haze of blue that she's started to believe is showing her things, true things, and it shows her a forest made for giants. As if to say, *Yes, it's there.*

She gets herself ready to say yes, but fear grabs at her guts and this is what comes out: "But we ain't never gonna get to one of those places."

Apple collapses a bit. "If they leave us alone, if they let us be together, then maybe we could stay," he says.

"Won't they?"

"You got the Waking coming up. The Waking of the Mamas."

"Well, I'm ready to roll now." Only she's still not, even with Apple sitting in front of her.

"What if they don't let you pick me? I ain't even sposed to be one of the Dads this time." They pick enough Dads at each Waking for each of the Mamas—the boys who've never been a Dad before, but also a few who have. It's the strong ones they want. If a Dad has helped make a baby or two, they want him at the Waking again and again. Apple has been picked for the Waking before, but he's never made a baby. He might not get asked again before he Ends.

Jemma hadn't thought of that. Once she kissed Apple, she's only thought of him. If she was gonna roll, it would be with him. But what if they didn't let him be in the Waking, or let her choose him? "I'll ask Trina," she says.

"Cuz she likes you so much right now. Like Hyun and Heather like me."

She's distracted, though, by what he said to her in the Stack, right after he kissed her. "Apple . . . you never asked anyone to roll with you."

"No. I didn't."

"But you rolled with someone in the Waking?" She knows she's seen him there in the Zervatory, gleaming in the torchlight, waiting for a Mama to pick him. But she's never thought about it.

"I did. Cuz we sposed to. I—I didn't want to, but I did. Twice. The third . . . both me and the Mama didn't want it, so we told everyone we did."

She knew that he must have rolled with others, but she's never let herself think it. The Holy Wood doesn't really trade in jealousy. No one owns anyone, the way the Parents seemed to do. If the boy you want is with someone else, another will roll along. But Jemma feels it grab her, refuse to let go. He had to do it, or he would have been Exiled. It's the rules. Still: Her Apple. Her boy.

He doesn't say he's sorry. He shouldn't be. But she thinks he is sorry all the same, as she is. "It'd be different," he says. "To want it. To want you."

"That kid who lived, the one the Exile talks about," Jemma says. "Would you do what he did if you could? To live longer?"

"To live longer?"

"Yeah."

"Would I know you?" he says.

"Maybe not."

"Then . . . no."

Jemma pulls him close to her, twining their legs together. She pushes her pelvis into his. "You ready to roll, aren't you?" she says.

"Yeah. You?"

She looks into his eyes, finds the calmness there and holds on to it. When she shakes her head, it's with a promise. *Not yet. Soon.*

CHAPTER EIGHT
THE EXILE

It's a strange thing to be accepted for the first time in your life, and the little Exile doesn't know quite what to do with it. Pico looks down at the village from the remnants of the Holy Wood sign and wonders if he really has a place in it.

The second night he's there, the girls sit with him by the fire in the Circle. There's no dancing that night. All is quiet. He can already tell that Lady doesn't like quiet.

"Who's got a story?" Lady says.

"Of the first Children?" Jemma says.

"Sure."

"You better at it. You worked in the Daycare longer."

"The First Mama, our Oldest Oldest, was Angela," Lady says. "She lived before our Mamas' Mamas' Mamas' Mama."

"Ours was Carmen," Pico says.

"Angela lived in the Holy Wood, not in the hills, but down on the Flat Lands with her Parents and her brother, Long Gone years ago," Lady says. "She was a worshiper of the Teevee, and a follower of the great priestess Lady." And Lady points at herself, smiling.

"One day the Parents didn't come home, and it was just her and her little brother. They waited and waited. Parents fell in the street, and when Angela ran out to help them they was already gone. She thought the gods was coming to punish them, but the bodies lay still and she hid and hid. And on the third day they looked out the window and only saw Children's faces staring back at them, and she knew they was alone. And if they was alone . . . they had to take care of themselves."

"And her brother, Miguelito, was the first Exile," Jemma says. "But that's another story."

"Do you know your Mama?" Lady asks.

"I do," Pico says. "Her name was Mary. She was the head Fisher, and when she got pregnant she wouldn't stop fishing. She had me, and then she went to sea and never came back—I guess so she could leave the way she wanted to. They say she didn't End. She drowned."

"Mine was a cook," Lady says. "She made really good beans. She loved to hold me. Sometimes I think I remember that."

"That can't be true," Pico says.

"I remember her face, looking up at her," Lady says.

"That coulda been anyone," Pico says. "Just cuz you remember—"

Lady jumps on him, pins him back against the ground.

"I remember her face! It was soft. Her voice was soft," she says, and the wistfulness of her voice doesn't match the arm pressed against Pico's throat.

"Okay," he says, and he lifts himself up on his elbows when Lady releases his neck. Apparently Lady hits a lot. "What about you, Jemma?"

"No one remembers her Mama," Lady says.

"Just one thing," Jemma says. "She was tall."

For Lady, he's someone to tease. He sees she teases people she likes, so he just smiles. Jemma, though, looks at him as if she's trying to unlock his head. Her gaze is one of the few that makes him want to shift his eyes. But he never does.

No one quite knows what to do with him, though. He's seen it with Exiles in his own tribe. The people of the Holy Wood give Pico an odd job here or there, but mostly he's allowed to explore alone in ever-widening circles in the hills.

Today is his farthest arc, all the way to the ridge above the Lake of the Holy Wood. The trails along the ridge are so worn with so many feet that they sink deep into the sandstone, years and years after the

Parents abandoned them. He walks through a passage slotted so deep that he can reach out with both hands at his waist and touch the banks on both sides. *How many Parents was there?* He's tried to count before but gave up each time.

In the Malibus, he wasn't given the gift of neglect. He was Touched, a bearer of the End. Unlike Leong, nobody loved Pico enough to keep him from being sent away.

He didn't love them either, just his nanny and Roberto and the idea of his Mama. He wanted to, but they would fall quiet when he walked into a room. The Malibus, like the other Angelenos, never asked questions, so they couldn't stomach a kid who *only* asked them. It didn't bother him, but in failing to win their love he felt like he failed to rack up one of the only things he could earn in this life.

Still, he loved it enough, loved the mountains and the waves, that it hurt when they cast him out. He had found a Long Gone house on the cliffs above the ocean, stripped by the Gatherers long ago of everything useful but the things that he needed, his precious objects. Pico spent hours there each day until one of the Muscle reported him to the Olders. They crashed through the door, saw the book in his hand, and shrieked.

"Brujo," the Oldest said, her finger outstretched and trembling. Witch, she meant.

The Priestess would have killed him, but the Olders took mercy, and before sundown he was walking away from the cliffs with three other Exiles.

Pico pauses on his path, a knife ridge that leads away from the Holy Wood sign to the west. To his north is a cliff; to the south is a slope that might as well be a cliff. A fire has eaten all the brush on the south slope, leaving the earth bare and dark as a bruise.

There's a sound back along the trail, a whisper of cloth against grass. It's someone who knows how to move through the wild. He wouldn't have heard it if he hadn't been watching and listening his whole life. So the Holy Wood sent someone to follow him. *Ah well. No sense spoiling the view.* Pico walks on.

He didn't know the other Exiles from the Malibus when they sent him away and didn't trust what he did know. Cole was sharp and sneaky, exiled for trading weed he found growing in the creek bed. Tomas was kind enough but stupid and quick to fight.

Li was different. He came to the Malibus from the San Fernandos and was only there a month before they decided Malibu was too small to contain him. When he spoke, Pico felt tremors of malice running under the surface, like the quakes that burst out of nowhere to terrorize the Angelenos.

It only took one night for someone to die.

They caught a raccoon the first night. Cole turned out to be a good mark with a spear, and they had a raccoon roasting by dark. Li took the raccoon off the spit, letting one end drop in the fire. He tore off a leg.

"Oy! That's mine!" Cole said.

Li lifted an eyebrow.

"I catch it, I got first bite. Don't you dirty San Fernandos know nothing?"

Li didn't say anything. Pico had hardly ever heard him speak, angry or not. Cole opened his mouth—and Li swung the burning spit through the air and caught him in the cheek.

Cole howled but somehow kept his feet. Li stabbed him again through the left shoulder. Pico almost heard a sizzle. This time Cole dropped.

The fire was quiet, they were quiet. Even Cole refused to scream. That ended when Li drove his heel down on Cole's knee, shattering the joint, then twisted until the leg jutted wrong. Pico knew Cole would never leave that spot—not in the wilderness.

"I'm gonna eat," Li said. "Help him if you want." They didn't help him, not with the menace in Li's voice, and Pico pretended the deadening whimpers were the sounds of the fading waves. In the morning Cole's chest was moving but his eyes were glass. They left him by the fire. Pico knew if he touched him, they were both dead.

Without the Olders to contain him, Li's thin layer of control melted. The other two boys stayed always at the edge of his sight, all calm voices and cocked legs. Even so, the only thing that kept Tomas alive was that he could almost win in a fair fight. The only thing that kept Pico alive was that he knew where to go.

"You never get lost," Li said, almost admiringly, as Pico led them through hills of fallen mansions. And Pico never let him see what was in his bag.

Pico pulls it out now—a map, folded in eight pieces, gilded in yellowing plastic so it's almost as fresh as the day the Parents made it. On the map the Holy Wood is an oasis, an island, the only patch of green in a sea of gray. That's why he led the Exiles to the Holy Wood. Because he saw the green mountains thrusting up from Ell Aye and thought, *This is the only place that looks safe.*

Despite the rustles in the grass behind him, Pico thinks he was right.

At the end of the trail is a clearing, and at the end of the clearing is a tangled tree, stark against the western sun. It's a tree that probably isn't old but feels like it is, the way the branches twist toward the sky, the way the roots seem to have fought for every inch of earth, the way the needles reach for the sun.

The peak is the last hill before the mountains drop down to the 101 in the pass below. Pico wonders if it held some churchy place for the Parents, because below are hundreds of flat rocks, stacked in sand-hued towers like altars. The towers almost mimic the Downtown, clustered together like a neighborhood. Each tower is roughly two feet high, with plate-size rocks at the bottom and skipping stones at the top.

Were they built by the Parents, or the Children? If the Parents, how could they have survived the quakes and the winds and the wild animals? Some are clearly made by the Children, splashed with crude red pigment from the ridge trail. But some—

Pico spies slips of battered paper peeking out between the stacked rock. Children wouldn't have written them. The first one he ferrets out crumbles in the wind. With the second, he takes more care, moving the rocks above before teasing out the slip.

It's a message from the Parents, to their friends and their Children.

Pico recognizes more of the letters than he would ever admit. "Jory Weinstein, if you get this, we're leaving town. Meet us in Ventura at the 101," it says. He doesn't understand what they mean.

The next: "Have you seen my dog? It's a husky and he goes by Scott."

Just messages, gifts to those who are still living. But then this one:

"The End can be ended."

There's a scuff on the trail, rock against rock, and the paper flutters away from his fingertips. "I ain't *that* interesting," Pico says.

"No, but you weird." The figure steps out of a low overhanging tunnel of oak. It's the boy Apple, who was there the first night but who Pico has somehow never seen next to Jemma since. Odd, since even Pico can tell they must be rolling.

"What's with the rocks?" Pico says.

"Dunno," Apple says. "Always been there. We build new towers sometime, but mostly people stay away. They get the creeps."

"The Parents' work?"

"That's the Tree of Wisdom," Apple says. "The gods put it here."

"They carve up its trunk, too?" It's covered with ungodly scratches. Pico sees a penis. Apple shrugs.

"So what makes it the Tree of Wisdom?"

"Priestess says Eva and Aidan used to live here."

"It ain't that old," Pico says.

"That's what I told her."

Pico remembers other barely heard footsteps, shadows where they shouldn't be. "You been following me the last two days?"

"Three," Apple says. "I ain't normally sposed to track Exiles, but the Olders are pissed at me."

"Hope I'm worth it," Pico says.

"Nah. Keep hoping you'll stab someone."

"They don't trust us," Pico says.

Apple hunkers in the midst of the stacks, so Pico just sees his eyes. "No. No, they don't." And Pico knows he's not talking about just the Exiles. He's talking about every boy in the Angelenos, who is used for strength of muscle and bone, who only lives to carry out what the girls think. And Pico realizes that the little Exile and the tall Muscle probably have more to talk about.

Pico says, "You wanna hike down with me, or you gotta follow fifty steps behind?"

They take a different trail down, Apple leading this time along a nearly invisible trace that must have been used only by deer. On a lower ridge, facing them, Pico sees the regular outline of crops covering the hill. Middles pull weeds away from vines lashed to rusty fences.

"Grapes?" he says.

"Yeah."

"You plant em?"

"Parents did. Weird thing for a city."

The lake, the fields, crops already in place—the First Mamas were lucky or smart. "You got a great spot," Pico says.

"That's what we fight for," Apple says. *Yes, that and Jemma*, Pico thinks.

Apple's next question surprises Pico. "You got Last Lifers in the Malibu?" he says.

"There's Last Lifers anywhere there's the End, ain't there?" Pico says.

Pico remembers his nanny, who still kept watch after him when he left the Nursery at seven. Ceci would set aside food for him because the older kids would take his away, and he was too small to miss many meals. Until the day he met her behind the kitchens as they always did, and she was on all fours over a bowl of black beans.

"What causes the Last Lifers to lose it?" Apple says.

"Dunno. People get sick of holding on."

Something in Ceci's posture that day, in the desperation that seemed to radiate out from her, made Pico stop. That was lucky, because he was still far enough away from her when she looked up like a coyote guarding her kill. She had a snarl set in her teeth and didn't seem to know him. She was a Last Lifer now.

"Ceci?" he had said, and without a word she leapt to her feet and sprang at him. The distance was just enough for him to make the edge of the kitchen and into the middle of a pack of Muscle before she caught him. They stomped Ceci until she stopped moving.

Everyone forgot Ceci in weeks and forgot Pico, too. The Angelenos are always moving forward.

"Jemma told me about the kid. The one who lived," Apple says. "He lived cuz he got stupid, right?"

"Kinda. He hit his head, and he's stuck that way."

"Shouldn't Last Lifers live longer if all of a sudden they get stupid?"

"It ain't the same thing. Last Lifers ain't stupid, they just gave up on life and went crazy," Pico says. "They just stop thinking cuz that's the easiest thing to do when life gets so hard. What's the point of planning and thinking when you know none of it matters anyway?"

"Okay." Apple stops in the middle of the trail and looks back at him. "So . . . what'd make Last Lifers start acting smart again?"

"That a real question?" Pico says, but the look on Apple's face says it is.

"When we were out there," Apple says, "I saw the Last Lifers acting like they never done before. They had a gun, which meant they found it and knew how to find and load the right bullets. They used strategy. They stuck together and hunted us in a group instead of just going berserk. Something changed."

"The only thing that could bring the Last Lifers back is if they thought there was more to life than just Ending," Pico says.

"So something's changed them."

"Someone gave em something," Pico says. "A reason to want to keep on living."

They walk in silence until they crest the hill above the sign. From there Pico takes in the valley of the San Fernandos, the towers of Downtown before him. "You all too close together," he says. "San Fernandos, Downtown, Holy Wood . . . you all fighting over the same patches of green."

"Someone showed you where the lines was?"

Pico shakes his head. No one did. He figured it out from the map. It's probably dangerous to reveal that to Apple, but he trusts him.

Apple seems to make the decision to trust him, too, because a look breaks across his face as if he wants to tell a secret. "Pico," he says, using his name for the first time, "if the Last Lifers are getting organized, if they've got guns, then it's really bad for the Holy Wood. I need to stop them, and I need your help."

Trina doesn't leave Jemma alone; none of the Olders do, they just let her breathe for a few days. That's the most you get for mourning.

When Trina sits next to her outside the Mamas' house, though, it's as if the other Trina has disappeared after Andy and Zee died. No more arguing. No more forcing. They sit in the lush grass together, the blades brushing their chins, and she talks as if she's trying to coax a fawn. "You know why we need you as a Mama," she says. "I just don't know why you think you can't."

All the reasons are there in Jemma's mind—the End speeding toward her, the motherless babies, the love the Parents had—and she doesn't know which to pull out to show to Trina. Finally she says, "It's all wrong. It just seems wrong."

Trina seems to hear it the wrong way, as if it's just about the Mamas. But her words are gentle. "It feels impossible. But we ain't gonna survive if we don't ask it."

"It's all about survival," Jemma says, shaking her head. And none of them ask why they can't have more than survival, when the Parents had so much.

"But you got Apple now. Don't you want him?"

Jemma grits her teeth, shaking that thought away. That's all people have said the past days. *You got Apple. Ain't you excited to be a Mama now?* "Sure. I mean, I want him," Jemma says, telling Trina what she hasn't been able to tell Apple, although he probably knows. "That don't mean I ain't scared. That don't mean I'm ready."

"We all get nervous. But we still gotta do it."

"How many people died making a baby, even before Zee? I count three since Chris Mass," Jemma says. "If the gods want us to do it, maybe they make some kids with smaller heads."

"I didn't want to do it, either, my boy Ended early." Trina looks down at her hands. "And then I couldn't, and they kept putting me with new boys who might have stronger seed, and some of em was kind, and some of em was not. And then I was pregnant for just a little while, and the Doctors just—" Trina looks angry when others might look sad. But anger is just a swifter form of sadness.

"That's awful," says Jemma, seeing Trina as something other than the Oldest.

Trina moves to stand but only makes it to one knee. "I ain't the best person to tell you this is a good thing," she says, shaking her head. "Just this: I ain't leaving nothing behind me when I go. What stays is the Holy Wood. And I want to leave it full."

There are Last Lifers down in the streets, too desperate about the End to let someone else live, and Trina is just trying to bring life into the world. Jemma feels her cheeks redden as she tries to meet Trina's gaze.

"If I do the Waking—could I be with Apple? I only want to be a Mama to him."

Trina seems to think for too long. The Mamas aren't supposed to choose in advance. The Olders decide who picks first, and then each Mama chooses a Dad one by one, like picking sides in a game. Jemma isn't anyone's favorite to pick first.

"Yeah, I can make it happen," Trina says. "I'll get the other Olders to let it go down. But none of that craziness like you and Apple pulled the day the Exiles came. You gotta stay inside the walls unless we say you can leave. Girls who play nice get the boys. Got it?"

"Got it," Jemma says.

"And you gonna want to watch your mouth with me," Trina says. "Not cuz I'm the Oldest but cuz you need more friends."

Trina stands all the way up, and she's back to being the Oldest. She can't be friends with Jemma anymore, she can't seem to take her side, because she needs to be seen as the person in charge. Jemma knows they'll never have a talk like this again.

CHAPTER NINE
THE LANDS BEYOND

In her dream, Apple is driving. Jemma doesn't know why she knows the word "driving," but he is: driving down the 101 to Downtown, on the empty side, flying past all the Parents' cars stranded on their left. "So sad," Apple says. "They took the wrong way."

Jemma sees them in their cars, still living, waiting for something. They're not screaming in fear as she would expect at the End. Some are tapping the wheel in front of them, some are singing, others glance at the pieces of jewelry on their wrists.

For the first time she sees that she and Apple are in a car—of course, a car! It's a type of car she's never seen. There is no roof. The car is made of gleaming blue that ends in dolphin fins. Apple's left arm rests on the door, and only his right arm drives. Their hair whips in the wind as they race through the air. She has never moved this fast before, and she feels words pulled from her lungs before they even leave her mouth. For the first time, Jemma realizes they're living inside a picture frame, like the ones the Parents hung on their walls.

"I wish we had longer," Apple says.

"I know. You not even fifteen," Jemma says.

"Wish we had longer," he says. He smiles at her with a mouth full of perfect teeth, and she can't say why that's wrong.

The frame of the picture they're in starts to blur, a haze of blue that she remembers from somewhere. A buzz overpowers Apple's voice, and she fights to hear him. This is a dream. Maybe it's a vision. Apple isn't really driving. She holds on to him harder.

Apple stretches his hand toward the window in front of them. She can see a band of clouds near Downtown, so gray they're black, smothering the 101 where the road punches through the horizon. "Starting to get dark," he says. Then the clouds tighten around her, squeezing out the light.

Jemma hasn't moved, hasn't spoken in the past thirty minutes as they grab shelter from the sun.

At first Lady thought she was wiped out from helping in the fields. All the Gatherers have been called in for Farmer duty. They don't normally help, but the ground needs to be prepped for the summer crops and the favas need to be picked. With Heather reducing the Muscle for the Gatherers' guard and with Zee—well, with Zee dead—it's not safe to Gather, anyway.

"Stupid greenskins," Lady says. "I don't wanna see another bean." If there's anything they agree upon, it's that Farmers' jobs are beneath Gatherers.

"We gotta get outta here," Jemma says.

"What?" Lady says. "Like, from the fields?"

"Huh?" Jemma is somewhere else.

Lady watches Li, carrying a bundle of stalks on his shoulders. The boy has a bad attitude, but he works hard when they point him the right direction. He's sweaty. Lady doesn't know when the sight of a sweaty boy started to do it for her, but it's doing it now.

"Have you seen his arms? They're as big as my legs," she says. She can't stop thinking about the Waking, about which Dad she'll choose, about how quickly she'll have a baby. Lady has kissed most of the boys her age in the village. Maybe that's why she only thinks about the giant Exile.

He passes in front of her, scowling. She likes a boy who scowls. Li always scowls. *Jesucristo, Lady,* she thinks. *He got you, or what?*

"Hey, Li," she says. He doesn't look her way. It's okay, because the boys don't do the picking in the Waking. He just has to be there to be picked.

Mira, the Older in charge of the Waking of the Mamas, told her Li would be there in the Waking. It's supposed to be the Priestess's decision, but when an Exile is this old and this pretty, he's a sure pick for the Waking.

There is Mira herself, ahead of Li in the road. *She* makes sure Li sees her, almost blocking him. Mira has a reputation for taking the best Dads before the Waking. "Just making sure they know what they're doing, mija," Lady heard her say, all fake smile. Lady feels the jealousy Jemma described about Apple stabbing her, too.

"We gotta get outta here," Jemma says again, and Lady looks at her closer. She's gone, her eyes vacant. Lady watches the way her fingers tremble, as if they're tapping out some Long Gone code. Jemma blinks once, twice, and she's back.

"Where'd you go?" Lady says.

Jemma doesn't answer, but she looks as if she's holding back panic. "Would you ever leave here?"

"Why?"

"If someplace was better."

"Ain't no place better than the Holy Wood," Lady says. She doesn't understand what Jemma is saying.

"If someplace was, though."

"I got the Waking coming up. One of us could be Head Gatherer to replace Zee."

"Yeah, I know."

What else was there out there? Their enemies wanted to kill them. "Out there you got Last Lifers and Palos, Jemma," Lady says. "This is the safest place in the world."

"But not for long, Lady. Apple's almost seventeen. We got no time left."

Ah. Apple again. Lady doesn't understand that feeling Jemma tried to tell her about, that wanting one person forever. She likes Apple, but people die all the time.

"Look, mija. Nothing out there gonna give you guys time. You get what you get," she says. She gestures at the blue sky, the brown hills, the green fields. "At least you can spend it here."

She can tell from Jemma's face that it isn't enough.

Apple comes to Jemma after the final Sacred before the Waking, when she and the other Mamas wore the red lipstick on the lips and the black on the eyes for the first time. Any time you do a ceremony that's mostly for the gods, it's called a Sacred. The Priestess took them to a room in the Mamas' house, lit with candles on altars made from old coffee tables.

The new Mamas knelt in front of flickering images of priestesses torn from Long Gone magzines. Jemma knows they're sacred, that beauty is sacred—that's why the pictures of the priests and priestesses are plastered everywhere on the buildings of Ell Aye. How do the red and the black help her to Gather, though, to fight? How does it help her be anything but a Mama?

Apple finds her on a rusting swing set next to a koi pond, trying to see herself underneath the black around her eyes. The moon is almost full because the Waking is soon, and she can almost make out her face in the water. He barely notices the black and the red. He only sees Jemma.

Apple is leaving to hunt the Last Lifers in the morning. He'll be joined by five Muscle—and the little Exile. Jemma can't talk Apple out of going, of sneaking out without Hyun knowing.

"Can't you get Hyun to send someone else?" she says.

"Hyun'd Exile me for it. He can't look past his pecker, and Heather got that. So it's got to be—"

"I know. It's got to be secret. We'll cover for you."

They'll leave before the Squawk, the monthly meeting where the

Olders and Heads talk about the crops, safety, babies, everything. And since everyone wants to talk and no one listens, the Squawk lasts forever. They'd be gone for most of the day before anyone notices they've left. Jemma hopes.

"Pendejo. Why you gotta go after the Last Lifers?"

"Something's wrong with em. You saw it. I gotta keep you safe."

She pulls him down toward her, trying to kiss him into staying when words won't work. "I'd rather keep *you* safe. It's dangerous in the Flat Lands."

"Oh, now you think it's dangerous?" Apple says, smiling. "The nice thing about Ending soon is I get to do all sorts of crazy."

The goodness, the bravery, the protectiveness—all her feelings for Apple come to a point like a spear. Jemma pulls him down in earnest, makes him sit on the swing next to her, and straddles him. "I want you," she says.

"Here?"

"I'll let you go back to my room," she says. "I'll even give you a running start."

She kisses him on the swing, though, wrapping her legs around his waist. He breathes deep and she feels the muscles of his back under her hands. Her tongue reaches his and it's hard to remember to breathe and it's hard to remember where she's felt something before like the sensation she's feeling in her mouth.

I'm thirsty, she thinks. *That's what it is. I'm thirsty and the only thing I can drink is him.*

Apple whispers, and she hears it through her cheekbones before she hears it in her ear. "We should wait."

"What?" That can't be what he said. She can feel that he's ready.

"I'm gonna go to the Flat Lands tomorrow. I gotta be sharp."

"Oh, do you?"

"I gotta keep my Muscle alive tomorrow, and that means sleep. And the Waking is in two days. We gonna be together then."

"I don't want that to be our first time to roll," she says. "I don't want the gods anywhere between you and me."

"I'm gonna be back tomorrow," he says.

"You better," she says. Tomorrow night.

Apple disappears to the Muscle's house. He'll be gone by dawn, and she already wants him back. Jemma slips down a back path to her house, trying to avoid torchlight and moonlight both. She almost stumbles over something in the path. She looks closer. It's Pico, huddled in blankets, definitely not in his bunk.

"Oh, you," she says. "What?"

"My bunkmates decided they'd sleep better if, uh, I slept here."

"The Farmers?" That was the only opening for him when he arrived.

"Yeah. I showed em a better way to pick corn."

"Teevee Buddha, Pico," she says. "Trying to get Exiled here, too?" But she helps him up and shoulders his pack. She leads him to her house and shows him the patio. It will be warmer there. "Farmers don't like nothing too smart to pull a plow," she says.

Pico stifles a laugh. "Thanks," he says.

Jemma looks at him while he settles into his blankets. She can just find the outline of his face in the filtered moonlight. "Apple taking you tomorrow?"

"Don't worry, Jemma," he says, so serious. "I'll keep him safe."

The image of tiny Pico keeping Apple safe is so funny that she laughs, too. A big one. "Right," she says. "Right."

"I got a lot of sperience wandering in the wild."

"I spose you do," she says, thoughtful. "Let me ask you this: Would you ever leave a place like this?"

"This's a good place," he says, and is silent so long she thinks that's the end of it. "But you can always find a better one."

"Well, what if there was a place where there ain't no End?" She feels stupid saying it, and stumbles over her words trying to take it back. "I mean, there ain't a place like that. We can't run from it. That'd be—"

"The End can be ended," he says.

"Say that again?"

"The End can be ended."

"Like that Leong kid. Right. Only that don't seem like living."

"You think we the first people to ask, Jemma?" He speaks so intensely that Jemma thinks this is the first time she's gotten a good look at him. The rest has been the reflection he wanted her to see.

"You think someone got it figured out?"

"Dunno. But if there's one way to beat the End out there, there's gotta be another one."

Jemma feels something, looking at Pico. It feels like hope.

CHAPTER TEN
THE HOLY MOTEL

Apple bursts through the door on the top floor of the Stack, bow drawn and machete close to his side, ready for a fight. The other Muscle scream in behind him: With him are Blue, Hector, Jamie, Pico, then Shiloh the Archer and Ko the Asshole. The last two are difficult but the ones you want in a fight.

The smell hits him almost as strong, of violence and shit, but it's the only thing left in a dead room.

The Last Lifers aren't in the Stack.

The old Last Lifers would still be there after they chased out Jemma and Apple, eating and rolling and stabbing one another. They would stay in a den until they burned through all the food nearby.

"They been gone for a while," Hector says. The tracker. "Maybe three days."

It's because of us, he realizes. *They knew we'd be back, with more swords and bows. Which any normal person would*—but Last Lifers aren't normal.

"Check it," Jamie says, the littlest Muscle, only a little bigger than Pico. He points out eight, possibly nine bare patches on the floor where they would have slept. The group was even bigger than the ones who attacked Apple and Jemma.

Pico squats near the ashes of the fire and pokes them with a charred stick. They put the fire near the window on a once-white marble surface, in the hopes that the smoke would be drawn out the window and nothing would catch flame.

"Apple," Pico says, "Last Lifers don't cook stuff."

"No," Apple says. Everyone knows they eat meat raw.

"These ones do." Pico taps some ashy bones with his stick. But not just that—there's the remnant of a pot of beans.

"They get along, they cook," Hector says. "Starting to act like people."

"They got my boy from back when," Blue says. "He ain't turning back into a people." She's the only girl Muscle. Any girl can be a Muscle, but with so many other things girls are allowed to do, most don't bother. Blue is faster than anyone else in the Holy Wood, so fast that when she fights she doesn't always need a machete.

Blue is supposed to be a Mama, just like the other girls. But she keeps on not having babies. Word is she gets the boys drunk during the Waking and sneaks out before the rolling begins.

The seven of them wind down the stairs. Apple remembers when he and Jemma ran down them, death at their backs.

"How they got guns? I thought there's just the One Gun," Jamie says.

"You telling me there's just one gun in all of Ell Aye?" Pico says.

Apple has wondered this, too. He's never gotten an answer, but it has to do with rebellions like Pablo's and how easily the gun helped put it down. If Pablo had his own guns . . .

"Maybe that's the only one that survived?" Blue says.

"But it's not," Apple says. "I had one shooting at me."

They pause at the Holy Wood Road, usually considered the southern reaches of the Holy Wood. Anything beyond that is pure wild. The Road may have been grand once, but it's Long Gone, torn apart by giant fig trees that buckle sidewalk and street alike and break through second-floor windows. One tree has taken over the entry of a building and wrapped it in roots until it looks as if it's more tree cave than door. A sign with a naked woman is all that juts out from the strangling branches and marks the building for what it was. Apple catches Jamie smirking.

It's what's left of the sidewalk that fascinates Apple, just as it always has. It's made of a kind of cement that's polished like marble. Set in the middle of each square is a pink star, each stamped with a different set of gold letters. They're names, he thinks. What were they? Priests? Priestesses? Minor gods? Was this some kind of holy road?

Pico scrapes away the leaves and dirt from one of the stars. Apple marks Pico's eyes, moving back and forth quickly, and his lips, silently sounding out something. *I was right about you,* Apple thinks. *Better be careful, Exile.*

"Where we going?" Hector says, but he's probably already guessed.

"Where else?" Apple says. "The Holy Motel."

"I hate that dude," Ko the Asshole says.

"You hate everyone," Apple says.

"I like your girl," Ko says.

Apple brushes off the taunt. "We can wander around waiting for the Last Lifers to jump us, or we can talk to someone who maybe seen em," Apple says.

"Who's the Holy Motel?" Pico says, looking confused.

"It's a what and then a who," Apple says.

The what is a shambly structure on the Sunset Road a few blocks away, climbing with ivy so that you almost don't notice the tight iron gate set in the green like a belly button. The who doesn't open the gate unless you know exactly what to call him, and that changes all the time. "Watcher!" Apple calls up to the windows above the gate. The others watch the street. "Half Holy! Watcher!"

Nothing. What was the name he gave Apple last time? Right. "Tim!"

There's a long silence, but one that carries the expectancy of motion. Soon he can hear keys jangling on the other side of the gate. A hole the width of a thumb is blocked by an eye. Apple can see it blink. "Tim?" the voice says.

"That's the name, right?"

"Timmy."

"Right. Timmy."

"Tim—okay, fine."

The gate swings open.

Apple is curious what Pico makes of the Half Holy. Even the other

Muscle stare as if this is the first time they've seen him. The Half Holy is dressed like the priests on the posters of Ell Aye, in a battered black suit with a raggedy black cloth tied around his neck in a bow. His hair is cut shorter than an Angeleno's, parted neatly and held in place with some kind of grease. On his lip is a mustache, thinner than eyebrows with a blank space in the center. Apple knows it's painted on somehow, but he's never seen him without it.

The Half Holy never fit in the Holy Wood, just like his Mama. She arrived in the Holy Wood in the middle of the night from the Downtown or San Fernando or somewhere, heavy with baby. The Olders took her in because they always wanted babies, but something was different with this one. Apple thinks it's because she came to the Holy Wood under the cloud of rape—whoever put the baby in her had forced her. All babies are the will of god, so a girl who says otherwise is dangerous.

They took her baby, but they shunned her. The baby didn't escape his mother's sin. He had a name once, but he was only ever called the Half Holy, because he only half belonged in the Holy Wood. At nine, he just disappeared.

Apple knew him and liked him, a Gatherer who spent all his time scouring the shops along the Holy Wood Road. When he disappeared, Apple thought he'd died like any other single Exile would. But the Half Holy showed up a year later, dressed in his suit, living in the Holy Motel.

Pico barely looks at the Half Holy, though. His eyes focus on the Motel itself. The gate takes them under a second floor, and once inside they find themselves completely enclosed by the rooms of the Motel. A narrow balcony circles the courtyard of the Motel, fringed with dozens of doors, most of them in disrepair. On the balcony are at least three goats, watching the visitors in placid silence.

In the center of the courtyard, there's a patch of ground that once was asphalt but has given way to dirt. Winter vegetables, cabbage and peas, stand ready to be picked. A swimming pool is filled with enough water to last the Motel through the dry season.

"Incredible," Pico says, and it is. That it was built by one kid.

"News from the Holy Wood?" the Half Holy says. That's the payment for visiting him here—that and the parcel of dried meat, wrapped in an old shirt, that Blue has carried from the village. She tosses it to the Half Holy while Apple talks.

"You got what you need?" Apple says.

"Nuff," the Half Holy says. Away from company, the Half Holy seems to be forgetting how to speak. Apple wonders how he survives here by himself, because no one ever has. He suspects the Downtown leave him gifts. They have a weakness for storefront prophets.

The Half Holy motions halfheartedly for them to follow him, and he leads them into what once must have been the Motel's lobby. A long line of golden statues, of men with bare chests, covers a desk. Every vertical surface, including the glass, is covered with priests and priestesses in black and white. At some point the boy must have found posters in the Holy Wood Road stores and plastered them on the walls with glue. Light shines through the windows in muted shades of gray.

For the first time in his many visits there, Apple looks closely at the glowing pictures. These Parents somehow seem more graceful, more set in the Long Gone, than the other pictures he's seen. No wonder the Half Holy modeled himself after them when his own people failed him.

"Whaddya want?" the Half Holy says, nowhere as graceful as his pictures.

"The Last Lifers," Apple says.

"Whatabout?"

"You seen any? You seen any acting weird?"

"Like, smart?" Blue says.

The Half Holy falls silent. He has a sort of nest on his roof where he can defend the Motel from anyone smart enough to find their way in, and he can watch most of the streets without being seen. He seems to talk to anyone who passes through Ell Aye, when he wants to be seen. So if there is anything to be seen, he would have seen it.

"Gonna need more'n meat for that," he says.

"Uh-uh," Blue says.

"What happens if they getting smart, Watcher?" Apple says. "You don't think they ain't gonna see your nice little gate, wonder why there's goat sounds in an old motel?"

"Got plenty a weapons," the Half Holy says.

"You only got two hands, though," Pico says.

Blue blasts out a laugh. Ko the Asshole joins her. "One of em for jerkin," she says. Blue's got a wicked knife, a wicked mouth. The Asshole sits a little too close to her, and she doesn't seem to notice. Doesn't seem to care. Apple thinks, not for the first time, that Ko has a thing for her.

The Half Holy ignores her and eyes Pico, his shorts. "You ain't Muscle. Ain't Holy Wood."

"We got that in common, then," Pico says.

"Need a drink," the Half Holy says stubbornly. He's heard the clink of the three vodka bottles in Apple's pack. Drinking is usually forbidden in the Holy Wood, although the Gatherers find the Parents' stashes and even trade illicit bottles for extra food or supplies. Or in this case, information.

"Not until we decide it's worth something," Apple says. "What you seen?"

"The Last Lifers, they formin up. Lots and lots."

"We seen that," Apple says.

"They moving like Muscle, all orgnized," the Half Holy says. "They got guns."

"Guns? More than one?" Apple knew they had at least one.

The Half Holy holds up one hand, all fingers out. Five guns that he's seen, Apple thinks. And the Holy Wood just has the one.

"Where they getting em?" Sure, there have to be guns hidden in Ell Aye, but it would take the Last Lifers some serious brains to get them working again.

The boy in the black suit hesitates, almost checks the shadows behind him for listeners. "Ain't seen it, but heared it," he says. "They say Palos. Palos stirring em all up."

Apple goes still, just like everyone else in the room. He hadn't expected that. Maybe somewhere deep, he feared it. They lived in fear of the Palos, saw the smoking mountain every day from their borders, but the Palos almost never ventured into the Flat Lands near Angeleno territory. If the Half Holy is right, they're at the door to the Holy Wood. Worse, they're helping the Holy Wood's closest enemy.

"Where they at?" Apple says.

"All goin south. I heard em say tarpits."

Apple's heard of the tarpits. Some of the Gatherers have gone there, but not with him. "You know where they are?"

The Half Holy shrugs. He's probably never been more than a few blocks from the Holy Motel since he left the Holy Wood. Apple looks at Pico, who pauses for just a few moments before answering. "I know," Pico says.

"What do they want? They gonna attack us?"

"Maybe. Probly."

"We gotta—"

"Ain't all. I heared them. They talkin—they talkin about endin the End."

Pico's head jerks sharply toward the Half Holy. All of them are listening to his words, but Pico is hanging on them. That's the reason to live that Pico was talking about. It's not just the guns that make them different. It's hope. Apple feels the hope, too, before he pushes it away. That's too much for him to think on right now.

"No one knows how to do that," Pico says.

"No?" The Half Holy smiles, smug at the reaction he got. "Talk to other wanderers fer a bit. Get outta Ell Aye. End ain't no big secret. Parents knew it, they jest couldn't fix it."

"You think the answer to the End is out there?"

"Jest told you that," the Half Holy says.

"Sorta," Pico says. "You kinda mumble."

"Fine. Gonna show you," the Half Holy says. He rummages through a pile of books and grooved discs made out of shiny black plastic.

Finally he pulls out a heavy book with a priestess on the cover, wearing the red and black makeup but almost nothing else.

"Someone brought me this," he says. "Knew I liked pics of the priestesses. But something different bout this. It gots stuff bout the End. Stuff the Parents knew."

He shows the book to Pico. Pico flips through until he reaches pages that were added. The paper is rougher, less shiny. Pico looks at them more slowly. His eyes go from side to side of the page. Apple watches his face bloom with carefully masked surprise.

Pico's head lifts up. "I think we can part with that bottle of vodka," he says.

CHAPTER ELEVEN

THE TARPITS

Pico studies the tar while they wait for Jamie to come back from the Last Lifers. They found the only place the Last Lifers could be hiding near the tarpits, in a pyramid-shaped hill surrounded by dense, dry brush in the middle of an old park. Something had seemed strange about the hill, so they headed right for it until Jamie pointed, quietly, at something they all missed if it was there earlier: a single column of smoke rising from the center of the hill, so faint you would miss it unless you were standing still yourself.

The hill is only about thirty feet tall, capped by a white wall maybe eight feet high and a crown of trees behind it. Just below the crest is a door cut into the hill—and someone standing in front of it with a spear. The Muscle had almost stumbled across the sentry but dropped back to wait in the thick brush around the pond at the south edge of the park while Jamie slipped away to see how many Last Lifers waited for them.

The sentry scares them, because it's such a departure from Last Lifer ways. Taught by the Palos? Some of the Muscle sharpen their knives nervously. Pico looks at the pond.

He knew about the tarpits because the Angelenos sometimes scavenged the remains of animals there. He had expected them to look something like a parking lot, bubbling with blackness. Tar washes onto the beaches of the Malibus, and they patch boats and roofs with it. Sometimes they burn it in the winter for heat. It smokes and smells, but burns longer than wood.

Instead, it's a pond with a greasy rainbow sheen. At the southwest corner of the pond, the water has evaporated—or the tar has pushed up—so there's a thick, sticky glob of pitch on the sand. Animals would avoid that. But the water elsewhere looks like water, with a denser black under the surface. That's the trap, he thinks. It don't look like tar until you're in it.

In the pond there's a statue that startles them all: a giant creature that Pico has seen only in books, that he assumed wasn't real: an elfant, with huge teeth horns and a hose that must be its nose. The elfant is up to its knees, and next to it a baby elfant sinks in to its waist. They seem panicked. Pico follows their eyes to another elfant in the middle of the pond, sinking to its eyes in the muck. Only the nose stays above water.

He's heard about this place—tarpits that trapped the animals. The elfant statues are all swallowed up in the tar. A small tree half buried in tar. Pico can see where the branches have turned a deep brown-black from soaking up the tar for years. They're probably more tar than wood.

Pico understands this place now, the pictures of bones on the signs, the giant statues of fantastical animals he could glimpse through the trees. The whole park is some sort of museem to animals that have died here, animals who died long before the humans came. Humans may be dying out, he thinks, but we're only the latest. Life keeps looking for ways to kill us.

He hasn't stopped thinking about what the Half Holy said. Did the Parents know what caused the End? Had they discovered a way to fix it, but it came too late? The answer could be in his backpack, but he doesn't want to study it with the Muscle around.

When the Parents died, they left a million puzzles—a world that makes no sense, machines that can't be started, a death that can't be fixed. Pico wants nothing more than to unlock them all.

"La Brea," Hector says, at his side.

"Huh?"

"Holy Wood for tar," Hector says.

"In the Malibus, we just say tar."

Just to the right of the glob of tar, bubbles of air push up through the black water like blisters the size of his hand. He waits for them to pop. They quiver but don't quite break, surfaces shiny like a blackened rainbow. Impatient, Pico pokes one with a stick and startles when it pops—not because of the sound, since it's noiseless, but because of the fumes. The bubble smells like gas from a Long Gone car. Maybe gas is made from the tar, or something like it.

Back along what used to be the street, past the flattened remains of a museem building, Pico sees a forest of lamp posts. Real trees are elbowing them aside, but Pico can imagine children lost among the glowing trunks. Pico wishes Jemma could see it—more than anyone, she seems to love the things the Parents left behind. He doesn't have an eye for that kind of beauty, but still . . .

"That's a lot of lights," he says, and the others nod. Although the Muscle have seen many new sights today, this is the one that makes no sense.

Jamie is suddenly in their midst, returned without a sound. Pico thinks, *I need to learn to move like that.*

"It's a whole Last Lifer village in there," Jamie says. The Muscle tries to explain the hill, but it makes no sense to anyone, not even Pico, so he draws a map. It's a building built under a hill. The center of the hill is actually an open courtyard where a much-tamer garden must have grown under huge panes of glass. The wall Pico thought he saw at the top of the hill actually acted like a cap for the garden, holding the glass in place, but the trees have burst through the glass now.

"They living inside a hill," Blue says. "How we sposed to fight that?"

"Maybe we go back, get help?" Pico says. Just so someone says it.

"From Hyun? What he gonna do?" Ko says.

"Hyun'd just make sure we never gonna leave the Holy Wood again," Apple says, "and someday these Last Lifers gonna march up to the Holy Wood with guns and numbers and smarts. We can't say told you so then cuz we'd be dead."

Jamie was able to get close enough to look down into the courtyard.

Some of the Last Lifers seemed to be in there, others in the rooms of the museem located next to the courtyard, buried in the edges of the hill. Even if they could fire into the courtyard from above, all the Last Lifers would have to do is retreat into the rooms of the museem, out of sight and out of range. The fact that there's only one door, and walls protected by earth, means they can't storm the museem from the front entrance without heavy losses.

"How many you guess?" Apple says.

"I saw five inside, the two outside. Heard more. Could be a dozen."

"Huh," Apple says. The Last Lifers are ferocious and unpredictable, but most weren't Muscle before they turned—they were Farmers, Cooks, Gatherers, Doctors. Six trained Muscle could possibly take them.

"And I saw at least three guns," Jamie says. "There's probly more."

The Muscle deflate at this. Apple is silent. Pico watches his face work, calculating the odds. Finally he says, "We gotta go back."

"We got this," Ko the Asshole says. Pico has begun to realize that Ko needs almost no reason to fight, and the other Muscle know it, too, because they ignore him.

"We don't got it," Apple says. He doesn't have to spell it out. There are twice as many Last Lifers, holed up in a fortress with only one door. The Muscle have bows and machetes. The Last Lifers have guns.

"We don't got the weapons," Hector says.

Pico smells the whiff of gas and tar. He looks around at the underbrush between them and the hill, at the sticky pitch and dark dark water. He remembers the clink of bottles in Apple's pack. "No," he says, wondering whether he should be saying it, "we got the weapons."

Hyun shows up while Lady's still helping in the fields, more puffy-red than usual. Apple's got him real mad.

"Where's Apple?" he says. As if there were any other question he'd ask.

Lady knows, but she's supposed to lie. She can lie better than Jemma, who told her about Apple's mission this morning, after they'd already left. "Why didn't you tell me before?" Lady had said.

"Apple told me yesterday. And if I told you, you woulda tried to go with em."

"No, I *woulda* gone with em." Sometimes she wishes she'd become a Muscle like Blue. She would like fighting, anything that fills her body with life.

"How much harder would it be to cover for em if we ain't here?" Jemma said. So now here Lady is covering for Apple with Hyun.

"I saw him, middle of the morning," she says to Hyun. "Hanging out near the stables." The Animal Doctors have been gone all morning, so they can't tell Hyun she's wrong.

"Why'd he go there?" Hyun says.

"Maybe he likes goats," she says. She pauses. "I hear you like goats."

He's so easy to make mad, it shouldn't be fun to make him madder—but it is. He can't even hit her. He may be a Head, but she's a girl.

Hyun is back an hour later. "He's not at the stables."

"He wouldn't still be there. You check the back?"

"The back of what?"

"The back of your butt."

Hyun stomps away.

When Trina shows, an hour after that, Lady has to be more careful. "You seen Apple?"

"I—"

"Before you say it, he's not at the stables. And wasn't."

"Oh."

"He's not helping fix the pump. Or with the Little Doctors. Or sleeping."

"I seen him around since this morning. I just can't remember where exactly."

"Exactly, no. Or Hector, Jamie, or Blue."

"No."

"Or that Exile kid."

"Defintly not the Exile." Lady's mad at Apple for taking Pico with him. She doesn't know why.

"Look, Lady. You making my job hard."

"I wish I knew where—"

"I don't care where they are," Trina says, her voice crackling with anger. "Apple's smart. He'll be fine. But Heather wants to rip the shit out of the Muscle, and Hyun is gonna help, and all your pendejo friends are out there handing her the only reason she needs. I don't care about em, but I bet the Holy Wood is a helluva lot safer with an army. Got it, mija?"

That rattles Lady, and she searches for Jemma. When Lady finds her, with the sun low in the sky, Jemma's standing in the closest backyard to the lake. From there she can see the Bear Wall and all its approaches. If Apple—or anyone else—returns, she'll see them first.

If Apple returns. Lady can see that's what Jemma's been thinking, over and over.

If Apple returns.

"He said he'd be back by now," Jemma says, sounding small.

Lady doesn't feel like answering, because any answer would be meaningless.

"I hate this," Jemma says. "We girls. We meant for sploring and Gathering and fighting and—and whatever the hell we want. Waiting's for pendejos."

That's how Lady feels. That's why she wouldn't want what Jemma has, what Jemma is feeling. Only that's not true. She'd like to know what Jemma's feeling first, then decide for herself.

Heather finds them there, watching for the Muscle and not particularly trying to hide it. It's almost dark now. If Apple and his Muscle hadn't slipped back in before, they certainly can't with the gates shut.

If Lady thought Trina was scary, it's because she's never really talked to Heather and her staff-wielding Hermanas. Three of them, the biggest, follow her here. They lean against the wall of the house while Heather strides across the lawn.

"Where the hell is Apple, puta?" she says to Jemma.

Lady knows Jemma is scared, but she doesn't flinch. "He ain't with you?" Jemma says.

Heather doesn't smile. "No, he ain't with me."

"Oh," Jemma says. "Thought he was with you."

"You tough, ain'tcha?" Heather says. She bellies up to Jemma, and although she's inches shorter, the three Hermanas at her back make up for it. "I hope you got your rolling in with Apple. Cuz tomorrow, at the Waking, you gonna be on your back with someone else."

She starts to walk away, the Hermanas folding around her like a coat.

"Hey, mija," Lady says. She doesn't dare say "puta," although that's what she means. Even "mija" is too familiar for an Older. "Why you hate boys so much?"

"Not all boys," Heather says. "Not all."

CHAPTER TWELVE
THE LAST LIFERS

Even with Pico's help, Apple doesn't like this. They should be coming in here with an army, stamping out the Last Lifers like they would a hornets' nest. But going in as light as they are—these hornets will sting.

The Muscle have never fought a war. They've defended Gatherers from bears and wild dogs, they've clashed briefly with San Fernandos and Last Lifers. But they haven't experienced anything like this.

"We gotta attack at night," he said as they prepared for the fight, realizing they need every edge they can get. Night will throw the Last Lifers off balance.

"So much for that," Shiloh the Archer said. They were all thinking the same thing: No sneaking back into camp now. The absence of six Muscle when Hyun is supposed to have them locked down will be impossible to miss.

"I'm gonna be cool, I'm too old," Apple says. "What they gonna do—Exile me? The rest of you ain't gonna be so lucky. You should go back."

"Screw you, pendeja," Hector says.

Apple waits at the pond with Pico, kneeling by the edge. Three of the Muscle slip through the bush toward the north side of the hill, loaded with Pico's tricks. Blue and Ko the Asshole stake out spots on each side of the big southern sidewalk leading up to the museem.

Apple knows that without the Exile, they would be home by now, beaten by this search. Part of him wishes they could be home. He's not too far gone to be past fear, and he wants his Muscle to outlive him. Mostly, though, Jemma told him to come back.

The sunset is their cue, and now it's his and Pico's turn. Apple fingers his knife and worn flint. The Parents seemed to be able to wish fire down from the sky, but like everything else they do, the Children have to work harder for it. He scrapes the flint down the back of his knife as he has hundreds of times before, and a thick cloud of sparks showers into the nest of bark shavings at his feet.

They catch. He blows, feeding the fire with kindling the size of his finger. He shields the blaze with his body, not just from the wind, but from the Last Lifers. They can't see the flames until it's too late to do anything about it.

Pico holds out a sturdy branch, wrapped in cloth and coated in tar. They tried just dipping the stick in tar, but it didn't stay on the wood. The cloth smolders for a few seconds over the fire, then lights. Pico swishes the branch with a few experimental strokes—*whoosh, whoosh*—and the flame stays lit.

The surface of the water gleams ominously in the flame. Pico raises his eyebrows, and Apple nods. Pico thrusts the torch into the thick tar at the edge of the pond. Apple holds his breath.

Nothing happens. The tar refuses to light. The torch threatens to flicker out.

"Don't it burn?" Apple whispers.

"It should," Pico says, and holds the torch near the clumps of tar. Still nothing.

Small as it is, the torch seems to glow huge to Apple. How long before the Last Lifers see them?

"It needs to be hotter to catch fire," Pico says decisively.

"Ain't that what the fire is for?" Apple says. It's all so backward. Does he hear movement? Shouts?

Pico moves the torch two feet to the right, where bubbles break through the pitch. He holds the torch above them until a bubble bursts. And a jet of flame shoots into the air.

"The gas," Pico says. "It burns quicker."

Apple grabs two other torches, all ready to burn. He lights them and reaches for the bubbles. Instead of waiting for one to burst, he pops it. More flame. He pops another. This time, the tar next to it starts to catch, a low orange flame. He blows on it as best as he can from the shore, and it picks up.

The sky lights up next to him. Pico has lit the dead tree in the pond on fire. Stuck as it was in the tar, it must have soaked up the oil until it was flammable. "Like a big candle," Pico says.

The tree burns bright and hot, and with Apple's attempts to light the tar, they now have what Pico wanted: a burning lake. A burning, smoky lake.

The heat starts to push them from the edge of the shore. "Now they're gonna notice," Pico says. That's what they hope, at least. Apple shoulders his pack, makes sure Pico is right behind him, and charges off into the brush around the western edge of the pond toward the north slope of the hill.

The sky turns orange at their backs. They've only made it fifty feet before Apple hears a stifled scream. That'd be the sentry, meeting Blue for the first time. She probably used a knife—less chancy than a bow.

They scramble up the slope, hearing noises from inside the hill. No screams, just the strange laughs and shrieks only the Last Lifers seem to make. That's good. Right now he doesn't need them frightened. He needs them to stay.

Apple glimpses the white wall above the courtyard, already illuminated by the hell glow of the burning lake. The corner to his right, at the northeast corner of the courtyard, has collapsed, twisting the wall until it appears ready to fall into the courtyard. He marks where his Muscle are—on the west and east walls, next to carvings of strange long-toothed lions.

The night is split by a flaming arc from the east. That'd be Shiloh the Archer. The center of the courtyard catches fire. Shiloh was looking for dry brush, and he found it. Another burning arrow, this one streaking from Jaime in the west into the room under Shiloh's feet. It catches something wood, but the fire starts slower there. If it fills the room, though, it will push the Last Lifers outside and toward the street.

Now the screams begin.

The arrows are coated in tar. Pico's idea. So are these. Apple pulls the vodka bottles out of his pack. They're partially filled with tar—so they'll stick to their targets, Pico says—and stuffed with a wick made from a shirt. Jamie has another torch wrapped in tar jammed into the ground, already lit so that they only have to light a fire once. Apple lights the first wick, waits for it to catch, and throws.

The bottle drops into the only bare patch in the courtyard, at its dead center. Pico has told him how it might work, but none of them are prepared for how well it does. The bottle erupts in a flash and a boom, and the floor of the courtyard is covered with a carpet of flame.

More arrows fly. Pico throws a litro, cut in half and filled with tar, into the flames below. They flare again, so bright that their imprint lingers in Apple's eyes. He hears more shouts, more screams, no more laughs. If the Last Lifers can move, if they still have the instinct to save themselves, they're running toward the exit.

Apple spots a eucalyptus tree. They're filled with oil. Apple saw a row of them explode, one after the other, in a swamp fire. The second bottle goes there.

It doesn't blow right away, but flames spread from the bottle before he can blink. The entire tree is coated in fire, and it's brushing the other trees with its touch. A bang from below sends a wall of heat their way. Any longer, and they won't be able to stand near the wall. But there's not much of a need.

"To the front!" he says, and he sees Shiloh the Archer running toward the top of the south slope. Pico and Jamie are with him, and they catch Hector as they run along the western wall.

The Last Lifers are streaming out of the hill, as Pico predicted, as Apple looks down from the top of the hill to the entrance. Five, six of them—the rest must be dead or trapped inside—belt noisily out of the doorway, where Ko and Blue wait for them. The first Last Lifers go down, from silent arrows. They look the same as the Holy Wood, just fewer clothes and more black around the eye. And more dead.

The runners behind them see what's happening, though, and they're the ones with the guns. There's a statue of two fanged lions, and one of the Last Lifers drops to her knees behind it. She rests her rifle on the pedestal of the statue. Apple hears a crack, quieter than he would have thought, then another and another, and this time he hears a cry. Ko. Blue. It has to be one of them.

The guns fire so fast. This has happened in the seconds since Apple arrived at the front of the building, in the time before Apple can pull an arrow out of his quiver and draw a bow. The gunner waves to the other Last Lifers to move forward, and Apple puts an arrow in her neck.

The other Last Lifers aren't as deliberate as the gunner, especially when arrows start raining down from the top of the hill. They fire their guns, but it's clear they can't really focus on the source of the arrows or decide which is the most important. Apple hears a bullet slam into the wall behind him and turns to see one of the lions with a hole in its chest.

Shiloh the Archer gets to work on them. In moments three are down, and the only Last Lifer left is a boy, jumping over a low wall and leaping into the brush. The fire by the lake is roaring now, pushing into the park. He'll have to swing north if he wants to escape it.

"Get the guns!" Apple motions to Shiloh and Jamie. "Check our wounded!" Without being told, Hector and Pico follow Apple down the west slope into the park.

Ashes and smoke fill the air. They wanted confusion, and they succeeded. Apple pauses for a moment to get his bearings amid the press of the branches and the burning air, but Hector pushes past to track.

They barely need to track. The boy ahead is crashing through the brush so loudly that they can hear him from fifty yards away. Hector lopes after him silently and smoothly, his feet finding a trail where Apple can't see any. Forty yards, thirty yards. If they can catch the boy before he reaches the street—

Then there is no sound in front of them and still they run and Hector is on his toes, windmilling to keep from falling into something that Apple can't see, and they're all skidding at the edge of a pit that yawns deep into the earth, a foot away from their deaths.

"The boy?" Apple says after he's sure they've all stopped.

Hector points down.

The pit looks a hundred feet deep at first, but as Apple looks closer he realizes it's just the tar, sucking down all the light. The red glow of the sky brushes the edge of the pit. It's perfectly square and lined with rotting timbers.

"The Parents dug this. For tar or for bones," Pico says. Bones. How strange the Parents were.

There's a thick splash in the southwest corner of the pit, out of the fire's light. Apple kneels near the edge and waits for his eyes to adjust to the light. There. A head, barely jutting out of the water, whites around the eyes the only things letting you know it's alive. Arms reach out of the muck, try to find a grip on the timbered walls, strain, and then release without a sound. It looks as if there's water on top, just like in the pond, but Apple bets the boy's legs are trapped in tar.

"Stuck, huh?" Apple says, not unkindly. The head doesn't answer.

"We can help you out," Apple says. "I just need you to talk. You want that?"

The head nods, slightly. Hector fishes a rope out of his pack, ties a loop, and lowers it to the shape. The arms go through the loop, cinch it tight, and they begin to pull. It's harder than he thinks, as if invisible hands are pulling on the other end. There's an elastic feel to each pull, a sense of almost releasing, then snapping back. One more, and then the shape is free from the muck.

Once the boy is free and almost to the top of the pit, a drastic change takes place; he comes to life. Instead of dead weight on the rope, they have a thrashing, fighting bundle striking at everything, bouncing off the wooden walls. A caterwaul like a lion's splits the night.

"Drop him," Apple says, and they let the rope slide back through their fingers until the boy splashes back into the tar. For a moment they're not sure if the boy is still alive, but they hear a panicked sob of a breath below.

"Wanna try it again?" Apple says. "We can get you out. If we don't, you never leaving. You starve, you drown. Or worse, your friends come looking for you." If the Last Lifers come back, find this boy, they would tear him to bits. There's something about Last Lifers that sniffs out weakness and attacks it. It's like a chicken coop—you're fine unless you get a bare patch in your feathers. Then everyone pecks.

The boy knows it, too. Apple thinks he sees him nod, then hears what he thought he'd never hear: the voice of a Last Lifer. "Help me," it says.

It's not a boy, he realizes once they've hauled up the Last Lifer, tied her to a tree, and cleaned enough of her face that they can see her lips move. It's a young girl of twelve or thirteen. Too young, normally, to join the Last Lifers.

"Where you from?" he says. He doesn't want to ask her name.

"San Fernando," she says, and her voice sounds strangled, as if the throat has been closed for months.

"That's a long way," he says. Over the mountain to join up with other Last Lifers? Usually they just stay where they turn.

She shrugs. "Everyone comes when the Palos call," she says.

"Why you gathering? Why you trying to fight?"

"For . . . our place in the world."

"But you left your peoples."

"You left us," she says. *Is that how all the Last Lifers see it?* Apple wonders. Rather than them leaving their tribe behind when they go crazy, they feel as if their tribe left them?

"Where'd you get your guns?"

"Found some broken ones. Gave em to the Palos. They . . . traded?"—as if she's not sure of the word—"They traded us for fixed ones."

"What do the Palos want with you?" he says.

"To . . . give us our place."

"What do they really want?"

The girl looks blank. Maybe the Last Lifers believe the Palos.

"Did they offer you anything? Besides guns?"

"Yeah. Little Man says we gon live forever. He showed us someone who got old." Dreamily.

Little Man. He's never heard the name, not even in whispers from the traders. "Who's Little Man?"

"The one who says we gon live forever." Then she falls silent.

Apple decides to let her rest, and walks away from her toward the pit. The sky still glows. He thinks the fire will be burning a long, long time. He has to decide what to do with the girl. He wants to keep his word. She's just a Tween. But if the Last Lifers are gathering an army, then he's helping add to it. She's young still. Maybe he can take her to the Holy Wood, and they can bring her back from the Last Life.

He turns back to the tree. The Last Lifer girl has an arrow in her throat.

Near the edge of the pit, three of his Muscle have returned. Shiloh carries two guns. Jamie carries another. And Ko the Asshole holds a bow upright, the string still thrumming.

"What did you do?" Apple says. "We needed her. She was a *Tween*."

"They killed Blue," Ko says, his jaw so tight he can barely speak. He realizes that he almost never saw Ko without Blue somewhere next to him, that Ko's eyes always followed her. Turns out Ko did care for someone, after all.

CHAPTER THIRTEEN
THE HARSH

The Hermanas have the crowd at the gate whipped up and ugly long before Apple returns. Any hope Trina had of bringing the rogue Muscle in quietly is gone.

Somehow Heather knew the Muscle had slipped out, even before the Squawk ended. And she's been building a case against them. "They searching for weapons to fight the Olders, just like Pablo," she shouts as Trina moves into the crowd.

"Apple is nothing like Pablo," Trina says, trying to keep her voice calm.

"He's acting like Pablo," Heather says. When Trina looks around the gates, she realizes she's lost the crowd. The Hermanas must have spent the rest of the day whispering to the village of rebellion.

How did Trina not see this happening, not see what Heather is trying to do? She was so focused on getting her way on the council that she didn't notice that Heather was building her power outside the Olders. She doesn't need the votes. She has the Hermanas.

She has the other girls, too. Most of the oldest Mamas have slipped quietly away, but the Middles and Tweens are chanting along with the Hermanas. A hundred, maybe more.

"Down with Muscle!"

"Girl home, girl rule!"

"Chicas por las chicas!"

Even the Middles have to realize that they need the boys for more than just the babies. They need their strength, need what smarts they have, even need whatever it is that makes them annoying. But by the time the Hermanas' spell is broken, the Muscle could be gone.

"Get em out of here," Trina says to Hyun.

"You ain't my boss," Hyun says.

"I *am* your boss. That's why they call me the Oldest."

Hyun acts as if he can't hear. He's riding with Heather as far as he can go. "What happens if Heather decides to get rid of the Muscle? Who's got your back then?"

"Heather does," he says, muttering.

"You fool," she says. "If Heather's got your back, she's gonna stick something in it."

He turns his back. Then she realizes: Hyun sent the Muscle away from the gate. None of them are here to help Apple. *Stay away, Apple,* she thinks. *Just stay away, if you don't want to get hurt by this crowd.*

"Everyone!" she says, and she's still the Oldest, so they have to listen. "Everyone go back to your casas! This is Older biz."

"The Muscle do what they want, when they want. They ain't safe," Heather says. "This is everyone's biz."

The Hermanas start to chant again. "Chicas por las chicas!" Their voices are so loud, so rhythmic, that it hurts Trina's chest. Everyone's lit by the flame of the Circle, sweating, jumping, pinging off one another like rocks in a landslide. *This is what crazy looks like,* she thinks. Not the Last Lifers. This.

A Middle boy is stupid enough to walk through the crowd, and a girl bumps him. He cocks his arm as if to punch her, and the Hermanas are there, two of them beating him with their sticks. She sees him under the staffs, screaming, and then the other girls are pulling at the kid. Trina pushes through the crowd to stop them, with no real hope. All she hears are the shouts.

It's to this that Apple comes home.

Half of the crowd goes quiet, and Trina sees Apple, still, trying to make sense of what he's seeing when he looks at the Holy Wood. Behind him are four of the missing Muscle—just four—and the Exile. They look tired, determined, smeared with tar. Changed. Then they see the Hermanas beating the boy, and they spring to life.

"Get away from him!" Apple bellows, and Trina realizes what else has changed with them. They have guns. *Jesucristo, Apple*, she thinks. Guns. Apple shoulders his, and so do the two Muscle who carry weapons. Two of the guns aim into the crowd, and still the shrieks continue, and then Apple fires into the air. The sound is so unfamiliar that a few of the wildest rioters continue, but the rest of the crowd falls still and then even the wild ones do. When Apple speaks, he has almost total silence.

"Get away from the boy," Apple says, quieter. People don't really hear his words. They only see the gun. A *boy*, holding a gun. Only girls are allowed to touch the guns. All their fears of a Muscle rebellion are going to be fanned by that sight.

The crowd parts, the Hermanas part, and the Middle boy is exposed on the pavement. Even from here, Trina can see he's breathing. Behind him, Jemma and Lady push through the girls. Trina sees Jemma's panicked face but warns Jemma with her eyes not to rush in. *It's only gonna get worse for you from here, mija.*

Trina steps toward Apple and holds out her hands, palms up. "Give me the guns, Apple," she says. He doesn't resist. He holds out his gun and nods at the others to give her theirs. Trina reaches out, then stops.

There's another body on the ground, sprawled on a makeshift stretcher. Blue. Somehow Apple has killed the only girl Muscle.

"Oh, Apple," she says, taking his gun from his hand and speaking so softly no one else can hear, "there ain't much I can do for you. Ya lo cagaste, mijo."

"That's what people keep telling me," he says. Grim.

He's done so many things wrong: Picked up a gun. Killed that girl Blue, maybe. All unforgivable. He's gonna be Exiled the second Heather gets a chance.

If Trina can pull Apple back to the Olders' house and let the crowd die down, she has a chance of quietly saving him. But Heather knows that. She won't let it happen. She wants a Questioning now, in public. Trina settles for moving them to the Casa de las Casas, because it's smaller. Fewer people to tear Apple apart.

Heather's case is what she's been telling everyone all day. Apple left to find weapons to overthrow the Olders, to take over the Muscle, to rebel against the girls. He disobeyed his own Head's orders.

Actually returning with guns and a dead Blue—those are gifts that even Heather couldn't have hoped for. By the time she finishes talking, the crowd is just as ugly as it was outside.

This time, though, the crowd includes boys: Muscle without weapons, burly Farmers, Gatherers and Carpenters and Smiths. Apple is respected by almost all the boys—and girls once, too, she has to remind herself—and they're here to make sure things are fair. Well, even with the Hermanas breathing down her neck, she better make it fair.

"Tell us what happened, Apple," she says, and he launches into his best weapon: his side of the story. He's the kind of kid everyone trusted. He needs to remind them of that.

The story unreels without drama, just a quiet retelling. Apple's suspicions about the Last Lifers, his orders from Hyun to do nothing, his visit with the Half Holy and the attack on the museem, the tar arrows and the vodka bombs and the questioning of the Last Lifer. He seems to claim all the actions for himself, as if he did it all, ordered it all. That way no one else gets blamed. This Questioning is about Apple, now. They might escape, even if he won't.

When Trina hears about the Last Lifers, about their guns, their numbers, their alliance with the Palos, she can't hide her expression. *The Last Lifers and the Palos could have come to destroy us, and we never would have seen it coming. You should be Head of the Muscle,* she thinks, not for the first time. *No. You should be an Older.*

The crowd feels it, too. If Apple's telling the truth, then he saved them from terrible deaths, something worse than Pablo's rebellion. People start to murmur in approval. Some of them slip away. Heather can feel it slipping away, too. Trina can tell by the pukey look on her face, then permits herself a moment of snark: Heather always looks pukey.

"We owe you, Apple," Trina says. She sees Hyun melting back into the crowd. "Hyun, we should talk."

"Nah. That ain't right." It's the voice of the Muscle they call Ko. Ko the Asshole. Trina doesn't like him much, but with that name she didn't expect to. Ko's the one who kept trying to roll with Blue. Blue wanted nothing to do with him.

"What he sayin ain't right," Ko says. "He told us it was Hyun's orders. Older orders. That we was just gonna scout for Last Lifers and report back. But he wanted to meet up with the Lifers and trade em vodka for guns."

"That don't sound like Apple," Trina says.

Ko's face is set hard. He's not looking anyone in the eye. "He said he was gonna make the Muscle great. The Last Lifers was gonna help him get rid of the Olders."

The room is still again. "Blue, she didn't want us to be out there. She said he was wrong—said that wasn't our orders. And so he shot her." The room erupts. Jemma looks as if she's the one who's been shot.

"Bullshit!" Jamie shouts. "That's bullshit, Ko! You just mad because they killed Blue! You blaming it on Apple. Apple didn't kill her!" But the little Muscle is lost in the madness of the room.

It takes almost a minute for Trina to calm the room down. She takes stock of it, even while she's shouting for quiet. She sees Jemma's face stretched tight over her jaw, which is grinding back and forth. She's being careful not to show any expression, but all Trina reads is anger. Lady is just as still, and so is that Exile who tags behind Apple.

They're smart not to say anything—it will only make things worse for Apple. *Those three are dangerous*, she thinks. She wouldn't mind sic-cing them on Heather.

"The other Muscle got stories to tell?" she says when the room dies down, hoping that Hector or Shiloh will contradict Ko. But Heather cuts her off.

"We got enough! It's time for the Harsh," Heather says—time for the sentencing. Of course she has the room on her side, but now Trina can see she has the Olders, too. Mira, who'll do whatever Heather says. In-sook looks smug and satisfied, a glittering chain of diamonds around her neck. Heather got to her in the terms she understands. Only Lupe, the former Carpenter, looks unsure.

"Exile me," Apple says. "This ain't my Holy Wood no more."

You trying to piss off everyone? she wonders.

"Exile me," he says. He *is* trying to piss them off. So they punish only him. But he's wrong about this.

"We Exile him," Heather says, pointedly refusing to talk to Apple directly, "he'll come back here like Pablo did. He'll attack the gates with his Last Lifer army and more guns, he'll get the Muscle to rebel."

"Last Lifer army." Jesucristo, Heather. It's true that the Olders had talked about harsher punishment for rebellion. Trina agreed to it. It just seemed safe. She never thought it would be applied to someone like Apple.

"Exile is too dangerous. It's too good for him," Heather says. "We want another Muscle rebellion?"

Shouts puncture the crowd. She's speaking in the language they fear. Even someone as kind and brave as Apple can be swept up by that unthinking fear, as he's about to be now.

"The Harsh for rebellion is death," Heather says. Trina hoped that would sober everyone. If anything, the crowd grows more raucous, more bloodthirsty. Apple and his friends are resolute, deathly still.

Trina catches the eyes of the other Olders. They're supposed to agree; the Oldest is supposed to say the sentence. Every face says to kill him: In-sook, Mira, Heather. Even Lupe's face says it now, swayed by the lies and the shouting of the mob.

She feels so alone. She grew up with Apple in the Daycare. They were the same batch, Trina and Apple and Zee. Always she relied on Apple for kindness, common sense, strength—and she can't give him any of that now.

If the crowd doesn't hear the Harsh it wants to hear, she loses the room. And if she's not the one to give the Harsh, she loses the Holy Wood.

"The Olders agree," she says, and she sees hope draining out of Jemma's face. Apple's face stopped hoping the moment he walked through the gates. "For rebelling against the Olders, for threatening the Holy Wood, for working with the Last Lifers . . . for all these things, Apple is sentenced to be Ended at the barrel of the One Gun."

No one has ever died like this in the Holy Wood, and Trina can't stop it, not with the crowd watching, with the Hermanas ready to strike, the Muscle missing, and no fighters of her own. But maybe she can delay it, and give Apple a chance. Maybe give people a chance to come to their senses, or—or maybe give them time to come help Apple. "The Waking is tomorrow, and we can't start a Waking with death. He will End at dawn after the Waking."

Jemma's eyes were focused on the floor, and she lifts them now to Trina, who nods. Jemma gives the faintest of smiles, just a shadow across the cheeks. Trina finds herself liking Jemma just a little bit despite—well, not liking her. *That's right, chica,* she thinks. *I just opened you a window.*

CHAPTER FOURTEEN
THE WINDOW

Jemma had one moment with Apple after he entered the gates. When the crowd saw Blue dead, they pushed Apple toward the Casa de las Casas, only his long legs keeping him from getting trampled. Jemma stood in front of him like any other kid too stupid to get out of the way, and the mob didn't know the difference. She planted her feet. He hit her, chest to chest, so hard that it almost threw her back. She didn't wrap her arms around him the way she wanted to, just pushed back against him as the mob streamed around him and tried to wash them both away. She dug her feet in more and held him there. The look on her face wasn't fear, it was fire and steel.

"Hope," he said, and the mob closed in. She pivoted sideways and the mob carried him away.

Apple managed to turn his head once as she followed him to the Questioning. "Pico!" he said.

"What?" Not the name she expected him to call out.

"The Exile," he said, adding something else that disappeared into the crowd.

Then the crowd cleared and the Exile was there, standing quietly at her side. He was bloodied and smudged and he placed his hand on her arm. She jerked away from him and took three hard steps out of the Circle.

"Where you going?" Pico said.

"To get my hatchet," she said.

"Wait," he said. "I can help, but we ain't gonna out-talk or out-fight that crowd. Wait and see what happens in there."

"But Apple—"

"Wait," Pico said.

They did. Because Apple trusted this kid somehow, Jemma and Lady waited. Through the Questioning, when all she wanted to do was split Heather's head, they waited.

Now she won't wait anymore. The three of them walk quietly away from the Casa de las Casas. Half the village is celebrating Apple's death. The rest are in shock, almost like they are.

"Heather was right," Lady says. "You gonna have to go through the Waking without Apple." She sounds as if she doesn't believe it could happen. She sounds sympathetic. At first all Jemma can think is: *That's what you take from this?* And, then, absurdly, meaning all of it: *I wished I'd rolled with him when I had the chance.*

"Got to go through everything without Apple," she says sullenly.

"I know. I didn't mean it like—" Lady says, but Jemma's already made up her mind.

"I . . . gotta talk to Pico. Alone," she says.

"I wanna stay with you," Lady says.

"Apple asked me to talk to him. About the Last Lifer raid," Jemma says.

"I wanna—"

"It's okay," Jemma says. "I'll see you in a little." Lady looks hurt. But she can't hear what comes next.

When Lady walks away, though, and it's just her and Pico, Jemma doesn't know what to say. She doesn't know where to begin. The two of them walk. Everyone they pass acts as if they don't see them. Because they're friends with Apple. It's as if they've got a flu that no one else wants to catch.

Finally she speaks. "Apple . . . thought I should talk to you."

"He say why?"

"He was getting dragged off at the time."

"Ah."

"You know why?"

They head away from the gates, to the part of the Holy Wood closest to Ell Aye. There's a dirt trail that leads through the brush. If they take it far enough, it will dead-end at the fence that holds in the Holy Wood. No one will be there to overhear.

"You want me to break him out," he says.

"No," she says. "I want you to tell me there's a better world than this."

"I only been to the Malibus," he says.

"I know you know," she says. "I don't know how, but you know about the world. You know about the Parents. And I . . . and I—" *And I need to believe what's out there is better than what we got.* That peoples don't kill their bravest and truest for being brave and true. That not everything is driven by the wants and fears of a sixteen-year-old girl. That if she rescues Apple, they have the slightest chance at a life together.

Pico doesn't answer, not right away.

"You told me there could be a place that got the End beat," she says.

"There *could* be," he says. "I don't know it. There just could be a chance."

"There's no chance at all here."

Pico, silent again, places his pack on the ground and opens it. He hasn't had a chance to take it off since they got back. He pulls out a heavy book with a once-glossy hard cover and opens it. The pages creak with age.

"Old," she says.

"Not as old as it should be," he says. "This was made after the Parents died."

"How do you know?"

"I spend a lot of time looking at books," he says.

He turns the pages. The moon is so bright that she can see almost every detail. At first she sees old pictures, of the priests and priestesses. It's the way they're supposed to look for the Waking, but these pictures are in black and white. Then she sees pictures of bodies stacked up carelessly, and she's back in the Bowl. It's the look of death that happened too quick to bury.

"Why would it be in there? With the others?"

"Someone wanted someone to find it. They wanted someone to do something about it."

The next page is more pictures, of ambylances and bodies shrouded in white. Below them are huge blocks of black letters. Jemma can't read, but the pictures tell the story.

"I don't know if there's a way to fix the End," Pico says. "But I think some of the Parents knew what caused it. If they did, maybe they put the answers somewhere we could find em."

How would they recognize the answers even if they found them? But then she understands.

"What does that say?" she says, pointing at the page.

"Children Immune from Mystery Plague—" Pico looks up as he realizes what he's said. If they were in the daylight, she bets she could have seen his skin turn pale. His eyes are panicked. She thought she would never see that in him.

"You can—you can read it?" Jemma's not sure what else to say. She's never known anyone who could read.

"You can't tell anyone, Jemma," Pico says.

"How long you known?" she asks.

"What really matters is how long my tribe knew."

That's why they kicked him out. They knew the Parents used letters, but that was lost long ago. And at some point someone decided that all the Parents' learning must have caused the End, and they started to think that reading meant you were a witch. A bruja. It meant you were dangerous.

"Your priestess could have—"

"She coulda killed me," he finishes for her. "I was already Touched. But they Exiled me. The youngest Exile in—well, my whole life."

"But what is it like to read?"

Pico is silent so long that he seems to have forgotten to answer. And then, quietly: "What if you was surrounded by pictures that the Children drew after hunts, after worshiping, and your eyes was closed? What if you never saw em? And then one day you opened your eyes and the walls all meant something?"

Jemma imagines the hallways of their homes, the way they're covered with exploits in chalk and paint. The capture of the deer. Trading with the San Fernandos. A lion attack.

"When you walk through the city down there," he says, "you walking through letters and signs and books, and they all tell you where to go and what to do, but you don't know what they mean. But when you do—you unlock the world."

Unlocking the world. There's a thrill buzzing through her now. Unlocking the world is all she's ever wanted.

"I want to read," she says.

"I'll teach you."

"But first—"

"But first you want me to break Apple out."

"Yeah, I do." She pauses. "Why do I feel this way about him? Why I gotta have him so bad? This . . . love . . . was that normal?"

"I don't know love," he says. "I barely got friends."

"The Parents, they write about it?"

"That's all they wrote about," Pico says. "Love. Love and death."

"Now all we got is death."

Pico nods, then says, "Why not Lady? She'd do anything for you."

Jemma's fought with herself. "Lady *would* do anything for me. But she deserves to be a Mama. I ain't gonna take that from her."

Even though she doesn't say everything, he seems to understand. "Okay."

"We need some tar, some brea? Some booze bombs?"

"Nah," he says. "Think this one's gonna be a whole lot simpler."

The shed is windowless. The door is steel. The walls reek of pool chemicals that seeped in for a hundred years. Apple is staying in the only building in the Holy Wood capable of holding him: a concrete-block shed next to a swimming pool.

The Hermanas haven't bothered with a bed for him, just a single blanket on the ground. It's covered with yellow bears in red shirts. Whoever drew them has never met a real bear.

He feels better somehow that only the Hermanas are guarding him. Hyun tried to put some Muscle on guard, and they walked away. They wouldn't guard their friend. But they're still too scared of defying the Olders to break him out. No one wants to be another Pablo.

Apple should have seen the Hermanas coming. Maybe he believed Heather was still the fifteen-year-old he used to know. Or maybe he got too removed from everything toward the End.

It's pointless, he knows. His death doesn't change anything for anyone except Heather and her stupid power grab. What does he lose? Eight weeks? Six months? It's nothing.

Only it's not.

Six months would be everything. Another week would be everything. What if that was the last time he touched Jemma, at the edge of the Circle with all the Holy Wood pouring around them? He feels tears welling.

"Stop it," Jemma used to say when they were only Middles and she found him crying. "You never see me crying."

"Just means my heart is bigger than yours," he said back then. And that look of impatience and kindness on her face may have been the reason he fell in love.

The door opens, and before he can blink away the sunset, two of the Hermanas leap through it with their staffs raised. The first blow catches him by surprise, catches him across the ribs. He rolls to avoid the second and the butt of the staff hits him by the spine. Another connects with his legs. The Hermanas have pounded nails into the sticks so that the nail heads make the staff hurt even more. All he can think of is the studded tip, hammering a mark into his back.

He wasn't planning on fighting, although he probably could. The Hermanas have started wearing machetes, too, and if one decides to pull hers out while they're whaling on him, he could lose a hand. After the third blow he starts to change his mind, but now it's too late. Now his breath is ragged and the best he can manage is not getting more hurt. A fourth blow glances off the side of his head and his vision blanks for a moment.

"Jesucristo, don't kill him," a voice says, cool and amused. The sticks halt, and another shadow crosses the door. "It ain't smart to have the best Muscle in the Holy Wood guarded by a couple a girls who don't got their boobs yet," Heather says. "I figured this'd make it even."

Apple touches the side of his head. It's bleeding. Imagine if the Hermanas were *less* good at their jobs. The door remains open for the light, but he counts at least four Hermanas outside besides the two in here. Taking no chances that he will run or fight. Heather crouches down to get close to his face.

"You thinking that I'm picking on you," Heather says.

"Nope."

"Not a little?"

"I think I tried to do something about the Last Lifers that you woulda never let happen, and that's the one thing you can't afford. You want to replace the Muscle with something you can control."

"That's part true. Don't want anyone to think the Muscle can be trusted after all this," she says. "But Apple, it's also true I *am* picking on you. You deserve this."

"I didn't do anything to you."

"It's what you didn't do to me."

"You asked me not to." That's not accurate. She begged him not to. Heather was a frightened fifteen-year-old, small for her age. She picked him at the Waking, he suspects, because she knew he didn't want to roll, either. He kissed her once, but she was shaking so hard that he stopped even before she asked. They wouldn't do anything. They would keep it secret. She slept with her head on his chest, and in the morning he walked her back to the house of the Mamas, where she didn't have a baby.

"You was wrong, though. You should've rolled with me. You should've made me a Mama." As if he were the only one who hadn't wanted to.

"You mad with me . . . cuz I didn't put a baby in you?"

"They made me keep trying, with worse and worse people each time. Fat and small and sickly. Then I got pregnant and . . . you know."

The whole village knew. The baby was stillborn. That happened often enough, but people remembered hers because Heather acted like she didn't mind.

That has nothing to do with him, though. He says so, and she shakes her head. "If it was your baby—he would have lived. I would've been a Mama," she says.

"You wanted to be a Mama?" He's never seen Heather hold a baby. She speaks of the Mamas with disdain.

"I didn't want to have a baby," she says. "But I wanted to be a Mama."

"I don't get it."

"You don't. Cuz you a boy," she says. "Now I'm an Older. I got an army of Tweens. I'm about to become the most powerful girl in the Holy Wood. And none of it counts half as much as being a Mama."

It's true, he realizes. The Olders are tolerated as barren failures. "So you want to End me and the Muscle for that?"

"I want to End all of this. Where the girls only get to be Mamas and the boys get to go out and fight."

"Cuz you only *let* us fight."

She ignores him. "I'm tired of people telling me I'm only as good as what my body can do."

"Funny," he says. He understands Heather better than he ever has, better than probably anyone does in the Holy Wood. "I feel the exact same way."

Heather nods at the bigger Hermana, who hammers his collarbone. This time something snaps.

CHAPTER FIFTEEN
THE WAKING

The new Mamas are blessed by the Priestess every month when the moon is full. Like everything meant for the gods to watch, the Waking of the Mamas will happen where the Parents used to watch the gods: the Zervatory, the giant domed building that overlooks the city.

The Zervatory is too far from the lake to be part of the village's daily life, but it's its heart all the same. Every week they trek along the ochre pathways through the hills and hear the Priestess tell equally dusty tales of life before the End. When Jesucristo and Buddha talked to the Parents and the Children through the most powerful of gods, Teevee, the faceless one.

For the Mamas, they unhitch the donkeys from the pump so they can ride them to and from the Zervatory. They joke that the Mamas won't be able to ride a donkey for days after, so they should take their chance now. It's probably true, but Jemma is tired of hearing it.

Jemma barely recognizes Lady next to her and knows she is just as unfamiliar. They are made up like the priestesses on the billboards, smoky eyes and red lips. They wear gowns rescued from the moths, draping down the donkeys' flanks and almost touching the ground. Once the Parents wore them to meet with the gods, on red carpets as long as entire streets.

The Zervatory takes her breath as it does every time she sees it. The Parents built other buildings, but few so filled with such grandeur and purpose. It has three copper-green domes, two of them flanking the big one like a Mama with twins. The small domes house the scopes the

Parents used to watch the stars, and even that sentence thrills Jemma: The Parents built a building just to watch the stars!

It's even more dominating from below, with a sheer white wall that could repel attackers. And it has. The Zervatory isn't just for Sacreds like the Waking. Halfway up there is a circular pathway, guarded by buttresses, that lets their archers rain arrows below. More archers can guard approaches from the roof. It's the Zervatory that helped end Pablo's Rebellion.

As Jemma rides up to the Zervatory, she sees the wounds that the rebellion left. Bricks fill the windows once left open in peaceful times. Axes scarred the massive iron doors, and flame blackened the ancient white.

The Star Watchers Pillar still bears the bullet hole that killed Pablo. It's a Mamas' story already, the one bullet that killed a rebellion. The One Gun keeps the village protected and in balance. If you touch it without permission, you are Exiled. And this hole is why.

That's why Apple was doomed when he walked in the gate with more guns. If she'd told the secret of the One Gun to Apple, how the Olders conspired to have only one at a time, he might be safe now. But she never thought he'd find a gun on his own.

There is time for rest after they dismount, before the Waking. She catches Pico in her sights while he studies the Zervatory. The Exiles, now that they are part of the Holy Wood, can join the Waking.

Jemma slips toward the stairs on the west side of the Zervatory, trusting Pico to follow. During times of war the stairs are blocked with sandbags, boards, and spikes, but now she can climb right to the roof on the outside of the building, the stairs tracing a circular path. They open onto a deck that spans the entire building, broken up only by the green of the three domes.

From where she stands, the broken towers of Downtown almost float between the domes, separate from the world. As she steps closer to the edge, though, the city widens and fills the horizon.

"The Parents liked a good view," Pico says next to her. He's slipped up almost to her side without her hearing, something he does a lot. He prefers the ancient shoes with the rubber soles and can move almost without a sound.

"Welcome to the Zervatory," Jemma says.

"Ob-servatory," he says automatically.

"What?"

"Observatory. It's on the sign."

"It's gonna take a while to get used to that," she says.

Jemma looks out to the towers of Downtown, their remaining windows glinting gold in the late-afternoon sun. "You just got here. You sure you want to leave again?"

"There's no here," he says. "You and Apple saved me, not them. I'm just someone eating their food."

They wouldn't let her see Apple like she knew they wouldn't, although she had to try so that it wouldn't look strange. The Hermanas have been at the jail all day. Sometimes as many as six of them, never fewer than two. "Are the answers down there?" Jemma says, pointing Downtown.

Pico says, "There's a building called a library, where all the books are. That's where the Parents kept their knowledge. If they wrote down what caused this, it'll be there."

"How do you know this?"

"Reading," he says, and then triumphantly pulls a folded piece of paper out of his pocket. It's a map, encased in plastic. When Pico lays it on the wall and twists it, she can see that it matches exactly what she sees before her. She can almost see the lines of the streets click into place.

This map has pictures of some of the buildings printed on the map. Pico points at one of them, the Zervatory—Observatory, she corrects herself—and taps the map with his finger.

"This is it, this is where we standing," he says. His finger slides left along the map to a tight cluster of pictures. Even Jemma can tell he's pointing at Downtown. "This is the Library Tower. We look there."

"Let's look now," Jemma says. She steps to one of the little scopes lined up against the wall, a weathered silver shell with fingerprints carved into it. The scopes require a coin to work, but the Children don't require a coin for anything. So they just pry open the bottom of the scope, and the coins cascade out onto the roof. She holds her eyes to the holes, places a coin in the slot. The city whirs into place and the disc clatters to the deck.

The scope is stuck in the streets directly below the Observatory. A church tower, an open belfry with four tiny spires flanking it, is so crowded with crows that she wonders if someone climbed into the belfry and died. But then Downtown and the Library Tower.

The tower isn't a perfect cylinder, Jemma can see right away—it's wrinkled with folds like the barrel of a cactus. The top is crowned with glinting pieces of glass.

"It's as tall as this mountain! So . . . all of that is books?"

He answers with a question of his own. "It ain't that far away. How come you guys never went?"

"It ain't safe to travel the Flat Lands," she says, although he knows that. "But mostly it's cuz the Downtowns would kill you if you tried. All them towers is sacred to em."

"It ain't that far," he says again, but softer.

They are quiet for a moment, and they can hear the bell that means the Waking is to begin. "You know what you gotta do tonight," Jemma says. "I'll be busy for a bit."

And then they go down.

The Waking is in the chapel, under the great dome at the center of the Zervatory. The ceiling is blue, like a miniature sky. Only a little daylight reaches it, so torches line the walls and soot flares up into the dome. All the chairs, shabbily padded and able to point almost to the ceiling, face a central altar that looks like a keyhole. Inside the altar is the Ball: a bronze sphere with dozens of eyes, looking like pictures she's seen of the moon.

The Priestess is at the altar already, dressed in a white gown with sleeves that billow like wings. She is not made up like the Mamas, because she will never be a Mama herself, so her face is unadorned and stern. Her name is Pilar, but no one is allowed to call her that now. Jemma doesn't know her. None of them do. She was chosen for her sight when she was seven, and she's lived here, alone, cut away from the village for almost half her life. Her only company now is her novice, who lives here, and the sentries, who don't.

Lady seems to glow. She's been kind to Jemma all day, but grief and sympathy don't sit long on her. Jemma doesn't force the pity from her. This will all be over soon. The least Jemma can do is not ruin Lady's Waking.

Jemma looks at her oldest friend and wishes again that she were coming with her. It would never work, though. Because Lady's mind is on becoming a Mama, yes. But also because Lady has room in her life only for this life.

A trip Downtown for Lady would be like a trip to the stars.

The sermon starts as it always does, with the First Mamas, and Jemma chants at the moments they chant without really listening. The words throb like a heartbeat.

The Priestess says that Jesuscristo will come back, the Parents at his right hand. The cars will start again, the skyplanes will fly, the medsen will flow. The Children will have the shelter they've always wanted, the arms of a Parent, and the End will be beaten at last. *Come, Jesucristo,* she thinks. *But only if you bring the Parents with you.*

Then Pilar's voice changes, somehow flatter and faster, and Jemma looks up at the altar for the first time in minutes. "The Children are waking," she says, each word clipped. "I see the Palos moving, the Last Lifers joining them. They're growing, getting stronger. The Little Man binds them together."

Jemma slides her eyes to the side and sees that no one else is tracking Pilar. How are they not hearing this? Every word Pilar says, every time her mouth moves, Jemma hears it as if it's coming from inside her own head. Jemma feels the buzz in her head, the way she did in the Bowl, although the buzz has started to dim now that she knows to look for it. Pilar is having a vision from the haze, and the haze wants Jemma to know it.

Jemma closes her eyes and there's a hazy burst of images in front of her, wrapped in the blue dust that she thinks means a vision. Maybe that's why no one else can see it. All she can focus on is a bear, charging through—a forest? A building? She can't tell.

"The Mamas are fertile," Pilar says in her regular voice, and her strange words exit Jemma's head. So do the pictures.

"The Mamas are fertile," the village says.

"The Mamas are ready," Pilar says.

"The Mamas are ready," the village says.

And so the gods are ready to make her a Mama.

The five Mamas stand up—*I'm a Mama, too,* she has to tell herself, even if it doesn't feel like it—and climb onto the narrow end of the keyhole altar. Jemma sees that the altar is covered with thin sheets of bronze. She's never noticed before, but she has always tried to sit as far away from the altar as she can.

The Mamas choose their Dads now. The Olders pick their favorite Mamas, who pick their favorite Dads. Jemma already knows she'll be picking last, and who will be left.

Ming, the oldest Gatherer, picks a Farmer named Jax. He's built like a Muscle, but too gentle to ever swing a machete against anything but thorns. She's seen the two kissing in the Circle before. Consuela, one of the Little Doctors, picks the new Muscle, the one who's smaller than Li.

The Priestess calls out Lady, and Jemma holds her breath, wishing her a good choice. Carlos is slight but a smart Mechanic and kind, and he likes Lady. But Lady can see only the giant Exile, and when she says "Li!" Jemma feels something come ajar inside her. It only gets worse when Li lifts Lady off the altar without really looking at her.

There are always more Dads than Mamas during the Waking, so there are four boys left over by the time they call Jemma's name, last. She had hoped that Hector would be left. Besides Blue and Jamie, he was the Muscle most loyal to Apple.

Hector looks reluctant when she picks him. Before he can lift her off the platform the way he's supposed to, Jemma hops off and lands with an awkward little bounce that the gown disguises. She throws her arms around Hector as if to kiss him.

When her lips are close to his, she says, "I hope you ain't feeling the urge to roll tonight. I got some fun things planned." He's puzzled for a moment, and then he smiles. He knows what she's thinking, or pretty close to it.

"Yeah, I'm down with that," he says.

The final part of the Waking is simple: They get the Mamas drunk. And Lady is ready.

"Bring the booze!" the Priestess says, and two of the younger Muscle bring out ancient bottles of whiskey, aged dark brown.

Lady remembers drinking a clear liquid with Jemma when they were nine until they couldn't even stagger home from the house they scavenged. They lay shoulder to shoulder on carpet so thick it threatened to swallow them in their state. Lay watching the ceiling, plastered with some kind of glinty material, which sparkles with tiny stars.

"Do you ever think, you know, look at the stars and think . . . we part of something so . . . much bigger? Don't you want to—" But Lady couldn't talk anymore because her tongue felt too heavy and thick to lift.

"I just feel small," Jemma said, and passed out.

Tonight, though, at the ceremony, they can drink openly. Only the Mamas can. The Dads don't get any, because their dicks won't work. Lady drinks deep. She holds the bottle up triumphantly, yells, even spills a little on Li, who suddenly kisses her. Maybe he actually does want her, she thinks.

Back there in the chapel, he didn't. He looked at her as if she weren't there, just an empty space where his eyes should be, and she felt cold.

Right before the ceremony, the little Exile approached her, all serious. "Who you gonna pick?" he said.

"It's a secret," she said, giddy.

"Don't pick Li," he said.

"What, jealous?"

"Don't pick Li. He's not safe."

"I know. That's the *point*."

"Don't pick him," Pico said. "I *know* him. He is—"

"You, Exile, gotta get outta here. Come back when you big enough for me." And now, looking at Li, she wonders.

Then they're back on the donkeys, passing the bottles back and forth even as the donkeys sway. The Priestess, Pilar, rides with them, coming back to the village for the first time in weeks. One bottle crashes to the ground, but it's almost empty and no one cares because the mood has changed from ceremony to party, a party that moves through the hills wrapped in a moving cocoon of torchlight, warding off all the death in the world.

By the time they reach the Circle, a giant fire is blazing. It feels different from council nights, as if it's giving off more heat. The bottles keep appearing, from inside bags and under clothes, and it's not just the Mamas drinking anymore. Li takes a long drink of tequila, not caring who sees.

"None for you," Lady says, giggling. "You got work to do."

He just takes another drink. She sees his face slide out of place for a moment, and then it's back like a mask. But another spin around the fire and she's already forgotten it.

She sees Jemma dancing under the stars, even with Apple—even with what's about to happen to Apple. Even Jemma can't help herself when the fire roars and the Mamas dance. *Isn't this life, too?* Lady wonders. *To put down your weapons, to sing, to dance? Is that what keeps you alive when there's so much death?*

Everything is part of her tonight—the fire, the music, Jemma, Li, Apple, Trina, the stars, even the weird little Exile. She dances next to the fire and touches everyone who passes by her. The fire shoots out fingers of warmth; some of them touch her belly. They burn inside until the flames reach every corner. She is ready ready ready.

"Let's go *now*," she says to Li, knowing that she will die if she doesn't kiss someone. If she doesn't roll with him. She pulls him all the way to the Mamas' house, facing the Circle. He follows. She sees Jemma's face on the way out of the Circle, now set hard. *Oh, Jemma*, she thinks. *Tomorrow I'll mourn with you. But tonight I'm gonna live.*

CHAPTER SIXTEEN
THE MAMAS

The drops of whiskey roll down Jemma's chin. She can't have booze, not tonight. But she has to look like she's Waking. That's easier to fake than she would have guessed, because when they reach the Circle it starts to feel real. She finds herself dancing under the stars, feeling the movement in a way she almost never does. The swallow of booze that made it down her throat warms her. She can feel calmness settling upon her shoulders.

One by one, the Mamas and Dads disappear as Jemma watches. Lady pulls Li toward the house, tugging at his shirt. Jemma understands. She wishes her well. She notices Pico making his way silently around the edge of the Circle, moving through the crowd but never seeming to quite touch it.

"You ready to roll?" Jemma says. Hector nods, maybe not as lusty as he should look. She didn't pick him for his acting.

Each of the couples get their own room tonight in a house meant for the Waking. She's made sure she has one with a window facing away from the street. She pulls in Hector, laughing, swishing her gown, and shuts the door.

"Whaddya need me to do?" he says, whispering.

"Nothing," she says. "Just stay here."

"I can help."

"You planning on getting Exiled? Getting a bullet in your head?"

He doesn't answer immediately.

"You can help," she says, "by staying here. I ain't trying to be nice. I need you to stay."

Soft giggles and whimpering sounds filter through the walls. Jemma reaches under the bed and pulls out her Gatherer's pack, which she had Pico sneak in earlier in the day. Hector's face shows he's beginning to understand.

"Make some noise, bang the bed against the wall. Moan if you want," she says brightly. "When they come get you in the morning, say you fell asleep and you don't know where I went."

Jemma opens the window and drops the pack through it. "Got it?"

Hector nods. "You gonna climb out with that dress?"

"I leave it behind, it'll be tough to explain where I went naked," she says.

She puts her hands on the windowsill. "Oh—you can totally tell everyone we rolled. And you was *good*." She hoists herself up, while Hector steadies her foot.

Then a scream tears through the night, not a scream but a cry of rage and pain and the voice of her very best friend.

The gown is complicated, way more complicated than when Lady put it on. Li can't work the zipper. Neither can she, her fingers thick with drink, and they seem to struggle for minutes. Finally she falls back on her bed, and the gown flips up into the air like a bell. "It lifts up," she laughs. "Just lift."

Li is on her, an animal just like she hoped, but then too much like an animal—pawing at her neck, growling in her ear. "Hey," she says.

Both hands slam her shoulders back. "Hey! Stop!" she says. Li slaps her, hard, and grabs a hunk of hair with one hand to pin her to the bed, while the other tears at the gown. She can't move her head.

All the burning is gone, all the flames from the Circle. In its place is the cold of fear. Lady feels a sharp pain under the gown and sees the mask is gone and the only thing on his face is death.

She wrests one arm free. She hits him but he doesn't seem to feel, just punches her in the mouth. She shouts in frustration and anger and fear.

It can't be like this to roll with someone. It won't be. She reaches into her hair, finds the pin that held it up—and drives it into his shoulder.

There are times when it helps to be unseen. Pico's been mostly not seen his whole life, and he uses that tonight.

His pack is on his back. In the time he's been here, he's never unpacked it all the way. Just another place that didn't welcome him. It doesn't bother him, though, because he's found something better. Villages aren't home. People are home.

The Casa de las Casas stands empty and alone. One Muscle usually guards it, but since Hyun and Heather have started their attack on the Muscle, no one's bothered to take the post. He imagines Muscle all over the Holy Wood suddenly asking to be Carpenters or Smiths.

The wood-and-glass case is at the back of the main room, meant to look imposing when the Olders give their speeches. It would be safer if it were built of steel or stone, but then no one would look on it in awe and wonder.

The case is protected more by taboo than a lock. No boy would touch it, under pain of Exile. No girl would, either, out of reverence. The gods would haunt your death and keep you from returning to the Parents. But taboos only work if you believe them. Exile only works when you want to stay.

The breaking glass would bring someone running, so Pico pulls a flat screwdriver from his pack. A few swipes and he's popped the lock's latch. *Is this what keeps the Holy Wood in balance? This thing from the Long Gone?* Pico reaches into the case and touches the wood. He feels it, smooth and ancient and deadly under his fingers. There's a hitch in his movement as he hesitates. Even when you don't believe it, apparently taboos still have power. But his fingers close around the stock, and then he has the One Gun.

Pico fills his pack with bullets. He wraps the gun in the blanket from his pack, but there's no disguising the rifle. It won't fit in the pack. In the streets he keeps to the shadows, with his right hand slung at his side. If he's seen with the gun, he doubts he'd live until the morning.

It's two short blocks to the old pool shed where they're holding Apple. Pico crouches in the deep darkness cast by a hedge next to the road. He watches the Hermanas while he waits for Jemma to arrive. There are four of them here, all awake and moving. There's no fire, so they're not blinded by it. It's going to make it a lot harder for him just to walk in and grab Apple, even with the gun. He wishes that he'd thought to think up a distraction.

A scream splits the night, coming from the house of the Waking. Even from here, it sounds like Lady. There's a long stillness, then shouts. Two of the Hermanas jump to their feet and race toward the tumult. Pico ducks deeper into the shadow of the hedge, but they never glance his way. Jemma must have thought of a distraction herself.

He keeps waiting for Jemma to burst out of the night, breathless, but a minute later, two minutes, she's still not here. He can't afford to waste the moment he's been given. Pico steels himself to step toward the shed. The girls are much bigger than he is, and they seem to have been training as warriors. Then he thinks: *The* gun *makes you stronger.*

The moon breaks through a hole in the trees and lights the grass around the shed. He must look tiny to them when he comes out of the darkness onto the moonlit grass, because they don't react to his steps. "I wanna see my friend Apple," he says.

"Your friend is gonna die in the morning," the left Hermana says. She is almost fourteen, the other maybe twelve. His age, really. What is it that makes the Tweens and younger teens especially want to join the Hermanas? Do they hunger for power, or are they afraid of being left out of everybody else? He suspects it's the latter.

"That's why I wanna see him now." Pico slides the wrap off the One Gun, holds it with the butt close to his waist, and just watches their faces. He can see the exact moments when one Hermana, then the other, recognizes the blue-black barrel of the gun.

"You ain't sposed to have that," the younger Hermana says slowly. As if that will make the bullets hurt less. And their staffs waver.

"I see we all got sticks," Pico says. "Mind putting yours down?"

Gowns aren't meant for running. Jemma finds this out at the living room door when hers traps her feet in poofy layers, sending her crashing hard to the floor. She stares up to see Lady already in the living room, Li towering over her.

"Stay away!" Lady shouts, warding him off with crossed arms. Jemma sees Lady's ripped gown almost torn from her shoulders, the bleeding lip, the white eyes, and she's up again, looking for a weapon. There's nothing, not in the Mamas' house, but she sees a bottle from the ceremony flung in the corner. As she dives toward it, Li backhands Lady in the face and knocks her down.

Jemma has already leapt to her feet and broken the bottle against the wall by the time Li sees her, and his eyes widen at the sight of the jagged edge. "Touch her again, puto," Jemma says.

He backs away, then lunges at her, hitting her hard. Jemma takes a step back, her gown flowing around her. She keeps her feet, slashes upward, and slits his face from mouth to cheek. Then Hector and the other Dads are on them, knocking the bottle away. Jemma struggles with them, but they throw her out the door and onto the hard pavement of the Circle. She jumps up but hears footsteps behind her. Before she can make it back to the house, Hermanas are holding her arms. They march her backward toward the fire.

Now the Dads push out Li, his arms pinned behind his back. He's still tossing them around, but they outnumber him and his movements get smaller. Jemma suddenly remembers what fled her thoughts a minute ago: Pico is at the jail now, by himself. She can't help him. She hopes he's even smarter than he seems.

"What is this?" a voice says behind Jemma. She turns her head to see the Priestess, still clothed in red flames, while in the Circle the fire itself is nothing but coals. Next to the Priestess is Trina, who looks as if she just woke up. There's no Heather, and the Hermanas look uncertainly between the Priestess and the Oldest for cues as to which to follow.

"They cut me," Li says, and Jemma realizes she's never heard him speak. His voice is higher than she thought, like a spoiled Tween.

"You attacked one of the Dads?" the Priestess asks. Her voice is quiet, but Jemma can hear anger rising in it. Jemma is only half listening, though; the other half of her hearing casts for the jail. No shots, no shouts. Yet.

"He raped me." Lady steps out of the Mamas' house, and if you didn't know her like Jemma did, you would have thought all the fear had gone. Jemma can see it in the corner of her eyes, but the rest of her face is as fierce as only Lady's can get.

"What?" Trina says. "You better be sure, Lady." They have the word for it, but they almost never use it. Some of the priestesses think rape isn't even possible. The babies are so important to the survival of the Holy Wood that any way they get them is tolerated, even by force. When you sign up to be a Mama, you have to be willing.

Lady nods, but a little less sure. Sometimes the girl who says she was raped gets into more trouble than the boy. "He hurt me and I told him to stop, and he wouldn't. I stabbed him with my pin and I—I got out of the room and Jemma was there with her knife."

Jemma doesn't say that it was a bottle, not a knife, but it worked on Li anyway.

"They cut me!" Li says.

Trina speaks. "You hurt one of my Mamas, Li. For that, I could cut you myself. Take him away." The Hermanas grab his arms and look tiny next to him.

"No!" the Priestess says. The darkness hides the anger in her face, but it's there. "They ruined the Waking. They gotta fix it for the gods."

"You gotta be shitting me," Trina says. The Hermanas have stopped, paralyzed.

"They both broke it, they both fix it," the Priestess says. "She's a Mama, he's a Dad. They go back in."

"She ain't going back in there," Jemma says.

"Fine. Someone's going in with him."

"No!" Lady says, but for Jemma the Circle has gone cool and clear. In the silence, she notices that no one else is shouting for them. They're alone.

"I would love to go in with Li," Jemma says with a bravado she doesn't feel. "Cuz then I can cut his balls off."

"I'll kill you, bitch!" he says.

"You almost seventeen," she says, so cold. "You better hurry up, then."

"No one's killing anyone," Trina says, not even looking at the Priestess. "We figure this out tomorrow once you've all calmed down."

"They will begin now—"

"It's time for you to go back to your Zervatory, *Pilar*," Trina says, almost spitting out the name. "This is Older biz." And the Dads drop Jemma's arms.

Pilar, looking a young fifteen, steps back nervously and disappears into the night. Only the Oldest could talk to her like that, and only if the Oldest is Trina.

Lady rushes to Jemma and hugs her tight. "Jesucristo, Jemma."

"Trina, he raped her," Jemma says. "You know it. You can't be okay—"

"I know," Trina says. "And I'm sorry."

"Then you gotta fix it."

Trina steps close to them so that only they can hear. Her throat is taut, as if it's holding in words that can't be allowed to escape. "I can't fix it, not now. The other Olders will vote with the Priestess. And Heather's gonna become the Oldest after all this. So . . . whatever you do, it has to happen tonight."

"What?" Lady asks, but Trina just shakes her head.

"Whatever you do. Tonight," Trina says, and Jemma feels as if she's just been thrown a rope.

The crowd disappears quickly once Trina and Pilar do. Hector turns back into the house to grab his stuff, and Jemma nods at him. No need for pretenses. What they need is speed.

"What now?" Lady says.

Jemma looks at Lady. It has to be done. Only Lady's not going to like it, because Jemma now realizes Apple isn't the only one who needs to escape. "Come with me," Jemma says. "We gotta move."

Lady's head can't make sense of the past fifteen minutes: Trina, Jemma, Pilar, Li, pain, and fear. All she can manage is to keep one foot following after the other, following after Jemma. Jemma seems to be leading them deep into the Holy Wood.

They stop at the door of a house. "You okay?" Jemma says. "You need anything?"

"Right now? I like your idea of cutting Li's balls off," Lady says, hard and bitter.

"He needs it," Jemma says, and she pulls Lady toward her. Jemma's not a hugger. Lady wonders how frightened she looks.

"He was the wrong one," Lady says into Jemma's shoulder. Then Lady notices that she's been shaking.

"We need your stuff," Jemma says. Somehow Jemma has picked up her own backpack from the ground without Lady noticing. And now Lady sees she's standing in front of her own front door.

The house is still quiet when they enter. "Why do we need it?" Lady says, but Jemma shakes her head and leads her down the thread-worn carpet of the hall to her own room. Jemma picks up the pack that Lady uses for Gathering and opens it, then stuffs in a blanket.

"Change your clothes," Jemma says.

Something in Jemma's voice is so sure, so strong, that Lady starts stripping off the gown even as she asks questions.

"We going somewhere?" she says.

Jemma nods.

"Tonight?" Lady says. "Why tonight?"

"You heard Trina. What you think happens tomorrow?"

Li's face, leering and bleeding, is all she can see. They wouldn't put the two of them back in the same room. They couldn't. "I didn't do anything *wrong*," she says.

Jemma hasn't stopped. She keeps shoving clothes and tools into the pack. *It's a good thing she knows me so well*, Lady thinks, before wondering why so much is necessary.

"Think of any girl you know that said rape," Jemma said. "Half Holy's Mama, anyone since. How'd that go?"

"You don't think I shoulda said anything." Lady finds herself madder at Jemma at that moment than she's been at anyone since Li lunged at her.

"No. I'm saying that's the Holy Wood. And now we gotta get you out of it."

"I don't want to leave here," Lady says, confused. "This is home."

"Come with me for a few days, and you can come back when it settles down," Jemma says. Lady doesn't nod, but her ability to resist is gone. She just reaches for her pants. She winces when she slides them on.

"We gonna need bikes," Jemma says. "Can you ride—can you ride like this?"

"I think so," Lady says.

Each house has a handful of bikes next to it, and Jemma finds two that have a lot of miles left in them. She squeezes the tires on one and pushes it toward Lady. Jemma takes a patch kit and a small pump from the basket next to the bikes and stows them in her pack. For the first time, Lady notices how thick the pack is.

"I want to be a Mama," Lady says.

"I know."

"Just not like this."

"I know." Jemma touches Lady on the shoulder, lets her hand rest there. "I'm sorry, Lady."

But you didn't do anything, Lady thinks.

They don't head toward the gates by the Circle, which would probably still be guarded tonight. Instead, Jemma winds through the backyards of the houses overlooking the Lake of the Holy Wood until she reaches a small gate that the Parents must have used to walk down to the water. *She's really thought this through*, Lady thinks. *Even with Apple, she's thinking of me first.*

"Your dress," she says to Jemma, who looks down at it absent-mindedly.

"Oh. Right," Jemma says. She pulls the Long Gone gown over her shoulders. She's already wearing her Gathering uniform of shorts and a tank. Lady realizes she never intended to go through the Waking.

They open the gate and wheel their bikes carefully down the slope to the road by the lake. "Ready?" Jemma says, and Lady nods slowly. Maybe a few days away will help her think about this clearly.

Two shadows step out of the woods near the lake. The bigger one she recognizes almost immediately, because no one else is as tall as Apple. She almost shouts to see him alive, she's so happy.

Then she understands that the little shape is the Exile. "He coming with us?" Lady asks. When Jemma nods, Lady realizes she doesn't mind so much.

Until she recognizes the silhouette rising from Pico's shoulder. Few days, or few weeks, all that is a lie. Jemma doesn't intend for them to come back. It's one thing to say that she was attacked. But some things won't be forgiven, and this is one of them. Because the Exile has the One Gun.

"What did you do?" she says, backing toward the slope they just descended. The gate is shut again, but she doesn't think Jemma locked it. She'll tell the Olders she wasn't attacked, she just panicked at being a Mama.

"I—we need you to go with us," Jemma says. The bells start ringing in the village, the bells that mean someone is attacking . . . or someone has escaped with the One Gun. Just like that, the gate above is slammed shut on Lady forever. They'll never believe she wasn't a part of this.

She can't go back.

CHAPTER SEVENTEEN
THE SKYPLANE

Whatever the Hermana did to his collarbone with her staff, it's not going away. Apple attempts to hold on to the handlebars, and every bump and jiggle sends tremors through his shoulder. His left collarbone hurts from the beating. It might be cracked. He shouldn't be on a bike right now, but the clanging of the bells behind him tells him to keep pedaling.

Angelenos try never to travel at night, not without numbers and torches. But the moon is full, and they see the landscape in sharp relief. They pedal past the lake, the moon buried in the water, and Apple thinks he will never see it again.

They glide down the hilly streets, feathering their speed to go through the hairpins safely. The only sound is the whir of the rubber on the crunchy asphalt. They're careful of the dark patches in the road, which hide rough pavement. Pico is good at spotting the cracks. "I'm glad we don't gotta pedal back up," he says. Lady doesn't say anything.

He's alert for any sound that breaks through the rushing wind. Bears and Last Lifers should be in their dens, if the world works the way it's supposed to. Right before the bottom of the hill, a coyote stands on the hood of a Long Gone car. Its head swivels and tracks them as they pass, but it doesn't move or call to its pack.

Lady stops at the bottom of the hill and signals them. She points ahead. The streets are thick with trees, arching and blocking the moon. The way through is a black tunnel, filled with whatever is waiting for them in the night. Even if they dared to light a torch so close to the Holy Wood, the speed of the bikes would blow it out. "You wanna go through that all the way to Downtown?"

"Maybe we can find a house and hole up," Jemma says, uncertainty showing for the first time. She's been hard and clear since they left the village.

"You need to get as much distance as you can," Pico says, pointing to the gun. "Now that we got this thing, we got the whole village looking for us."

"Why ain't they on us?" Jemma says. "If they left when the bells went off, they coulda caught us right off."

"The only reason we ain't fighting off an army is that no one's sure which army should be in charge," Apple says. "Muscle won't follow Hyun no more, and no one wants to follow the Hermanas. But they'll figure it out soon enough."

"Either way, I ain't riding through the dark all night," Lady says. No one can argue against her, and wouldn't if they could. She still looks shocked, angry.

Apple remembers: the 101. They're close to where he and Jemma crossed it last time. The Last Lifers were able to use the height against them. If the Angelenos can get to it, they will have a clear shot to Downtown.

After ten blocks—ten blocks of unidentified noises in the dark—they find another ramp and climb up to the 101. They're on the west side, the empty one, and the road is all theirs except for a few rusting cars. There are no voices or torches on the hill behind them. Maybe they will get enough of a head start, after all.

Apple sees at once why the Parents built the 101. It cuts across the city grid as if it doesn't exist, almost as if it's a stream flowing down from the mountains to Downtown. The 101 looks as if it were grown, not made.

He pushes with his right pedal and they're off, silent except for the soft squeak of Pico's wheel protesting against the night. They ride shoulder to shoulder to shoulder, dark-wheeled silhouettes made half of night. The white pavement of the 101 gleams silver ahead of them all the way to the towers, a river carrying them through the lonely dark to whatever the future holds.

It must be only a few miles to Downtown, but the dark has a way of lengthening the road. The silver of the 101 contrasts with the buildings and trees around them, making Jemma feel as if the world drops off the edge around them. The road isn't as smooth or clear as it seemed. Long Gone cars sprout up in increasing numbers, and in between them cracks emerge that threaten to swallow their tires, if not entire bikes.

They pedal and pedal but the wheels don't turn any faster. Jemma has the gun now; its strap digs into her shoulder, and every stroke and bump knocks the butt into her.

"I'm gonna have a bruise," she says in a whisper, knowing that even though they feel like they're the only people alive tonight, they're not.

"You deserve it!" Lady says. "How could you steal the One Gun?"

Pico says, "We'll need it more than they will. The four of us in the wild?"

"That was your idea, Jemma!" Lady says, and she swerves her bike toward Jemma. She doesn't mean to hit her friend, but the bike aims where you look. Jemma tumbles to the pavement without warning, and the gun flips over her head with a clatter that rings out into the night.

Lady jumps off her bike to help up Jemma—and collapses on top of her. "Goddammit, Jemma! Goddammit!" she sobs. Jemma stays here.

"I'm sorry, Lady."

"You took me from home!" Lady says. "You took me from home."

"I'm sorry. You know I had to. . . ." But she stops. All of it had to be done. None of it fits into the way the world is supposed to work. Finally she says, "There's nothing there for us now."

"There was for me," Lady says, and in that phrase Jemma can feel how Lady's perfect world has crumbled. Then Lady cries. Lady never cries. They don't touch her or talk to her until she finishes.

Jemma doesn't get on her bike right away but looks up the road. When she's still, she imagines she can see farther. She sees a black line across the 101. As the line gets bigger, it takes form. She wasn't sure they existed, but there it is, broken but real: a skyplane, fallen from the air like a stone.

The skyplane must have been moving fast from the north when it landed, a stone thrown rather than dropped. Cutting almost across the 101's northbound side is a ruined line where the skyplane hit first. That lane is ripped completely in half, and the skyplane lies directly in front of her in the southbound lane, half buried in the road. The wings are gone. Jemma recognizes it only by its tall tail and tubular body.

Even buried, the skyplane rises over their heads. The wall is curved and slippery, but Lady dismounts and takes a run at it anyway. For a moment it looks as if she'll reach the roof, but she slides back down. She might make it, given time, but Jemma knows there's no way over it with the packs and the bikes.

"Do we need to go back?" Apple says. He's been deferring to her and Pico on direction. She watches how he favors his shoulder on the bike, too, although "favors" is too small a word. He winces at every bump.

"I hope not," Jemma says. The last ramp is half a mile back, and the streets next to the 101 look impassable. To the north, the skyplane's trench has broken every route, and to the south, a thick jungle of trees has sprung up.

"Through?" Apple says, and as soon as Jemma starts to say it's impossible, she sees that maybe it's not. To their right at the edge of the 101, there's a crack in the skyplane. If it's big enough, or if it goes all the way through . . .

It is big enough, just, if they get off their bikes. Pico goes in first, and Lady pushes her bike and his after him before following. Jemma pushes her bike through the skin of the skyplane, watches it swallowed as if into a giant's sideways mouth.

A last breath of night air and then she's in, too. She has to step down from the roadway into the plane. To her left are the seats where the Parents would have sat. To her right is the front of the skyplane.

She expects it to be dark, but she's not prepared for the sight of the light streaming through the severed head of the skyplane to her right. The fliers must have sat right there. The moonlit city to the south is framed in an almost circle by the jagged walls of the plane. Apple enters the plane behind her. He puts his arm around her, gingerly, and together they watch this sliver of Ell Aye. Whatever madness they've left behind, the world they face together now is stranger by far.

Pico is standing at the edge of the broken floor, looking at the mess of cables and raw metal jutting out. Lady is just behind him, her eyes on the city. Jemma looks down and sees some metal in the trees below.

A groan in the metal startles them, and Jemma takes new notice of where they're standing. "We sticking out past the 101," she says. "Step back."

"Look at all it took to make this fly," Pico says, pointing at the frayed edge of the skyplane.

"Step back," Apple says. And with a sigh, Pico stands up, but not before they feel a jerk. He races past Jemma and stops sheepishly when the plane doesn't move.

Jemma looks toward the back of the plane. The floor of the plane isn't perfectly level with the streets outside. It tilts sharply, so the windows on the far side are almost two feet higher than the side they came in, and the aisle slants to the left.

There's light in the skyplane, from the windows and tears in the skyplane's skin. The moon punches through it in hundreds of fist-size scars in the roof. But none of them look big enough to crawl through. There's no way out. She starts to climb back to the 101, but Lady grabs her arm. "Down there." And Jemma can see, masked by the smaller beams, a wider patch of light that could be anything—maybe even a door.

Finding the light is harder than it looks. The thin aisle pitches them to the left, and they can't push the bicycles along it without bumping into the moldering seats at every row. The seats, and other things. Jemma feels something brush against her right knee, and she realizes it's a hand right as she feels another. The Parents are still in their seats.

"I think they're strapped in, to protect em from the crash," Pico says.

"Didn't do em a lotta good," Lady says, almost cheering up.

Jemma doesn't know how they can still talk. Every bump, every brush of bones, and she feels herself weaken, even with the steady presence of Apple behind her. She breathes in, and all she feels entering her nostrils is the dust of the Parents, rising in puffs when they touch the old seat cushions. Her bicycle tire rolls over something big—a leg? The steady click of her bicycle wheel echoes through the plane, and she wonders who hears it. She sees skeletons everywhere, lit by the moon so the grins are even wider. It's like being back in the Bowl, buried in the bones.

And then Jemma realizes how much of this, the quest for Parents' answers, the nighttime escape, is to get away from what lies there back at the village: more death like this. They can't outrun it. She sits down in the aisle, surrounded by the bones of the Parents who fell from the sky, and gasps for breath.

But they can keep running all the same. She tries to shake off her fear.

"Can we go?" Pico calls from farther down the aisle.

"Shut up, Exile! Jemma's losing it," Lady says, irritated and scared. But before she can say anything more, Pico bounds toward them. He can't get past the bicycles blocking the aisle, so he just steps on top of the seats, hand on the ceiling for support. He jumps off the last one into the row in front of Jemma—and falls through the floor with barely a sound.

"Pico!" Lady screams, and the scream is enough to break the hold the floor had on Jemma. She crawls forward, hands never breaking contact with the carpet, and feels the floor gaping. The crash ripped pieces of the plane away, and one of those holes was waiting to swallow someone as skinny as Pico.

"Pico, you there?" Lady says, and a low groan answers.

"You know his name now?" Jemma says to Lady.

"I'll get him," Apple says.

"With that shoulder? Who's gonna pull *you* up after?" Lady says.

"Hold my legs. I'm gonna look down there," Jemma says.

With Apple on her legs, she threads her torso slowly through the floor, head dropping into the darkness. There's no moonlight, but a gasping light seems to linger on the edges of everything so that as she waits, a boy-shaped shape emerges below her. It's not moving, but it appears to be sitting.

"Pico, can you move?"

"I don't know," the shape says, and its edges blur again, re-forming a foot away. "I guess so, but—ow! Ow!"

"Pico!"

"Not that way." And the voice sounds weaker. "Something's wrong with my leg, my right one."

"Can you stand?"

"Can you reach down and give me your hand?"

She calls to Apple and Lady to let her slide, and now she's buried to her waist. Her hands stretch down to Pico's voice, but she can't find his hands if they're anywhere near. The blood is filling her head, and she feels thick and pulsing.

"If you can see me, Pico, get closer." Jemma hears a rustle, and then a soft *whoosh* and a slap that shocks her when it hits her wrist. Her fingers automatically grab for whatever that was and close on a strap.

"You got it? Pull," Pico says.

She pulls and feels her shoulders strain. Pico is heavier than he looks. She feels herself scraping the side of the hole until her stomach is flat on the floor.

"Get him, Lady," she says, because her arms have lost their strength and she feels pinned to the floor. Lady roughly grabs Pico's hand, and then all of them are jumbled on the floor, panting. There is another shape in the mix that doesn't belong, though, a shining rectangle pinched between Pico's thighs.

"Jesucristo, no wonder you so heavy!" Lady says, voicing what Jemma felt. "Why you pull that out? You're so weird."

"I fell on it, and it felt like a box," he says.

"So?"

"Boxes're usually useful."

And Jemma has to admit that makes a sort of sense. Then she realizes she has seen this before, Pico pulling a silver case from the floor. The blue haze showed it to her. Now he has the case. What else has it showed her that hasn't happened yet? Didn't it show her a charging bear at the Waking? She hopes that one isn't true.

"Can you stand?" Jemma asks, and in reply Pico slowly rises. He takes a ginger step, gasps, then takes another.

"I can't run, but I think I can—yeah, I can walk," Pico says, and he hobbles toward his bicycle, the silver case under his arm.

"Jesucristo, both of you injured now?" Lady says, taking in both boys. "We only been gone two hours!"

The rest of the aisle is clear, and then Jemma is at the door of the skyplane, open to the pavement only a step above.

First she smells the air, rich with jasmine. Then she sees the stars and knows that daylight is not far from them. They need to find cover by morning.

"Can we reach Downtown by morning?" she says, but then sees that the others' attention is elsewhere. Pico is looking at the silver case, and Lady is looking at Pico. His pants are torn, a long slit going from his ankle to his knee.

"It don't open," Pico says.

"You bleeding," Lady says. "You don't feel that?"

Pico shakes his head. Jemma lays down her bike and lifts his torn pant leg.

A patch of skin glistens wet and black in the moonlight. The cut is deep and wide, and not flowing enough to cleanse the wound. "It's gonna feel really bad soon," Jemma says. But she has to get them moving first, especially if the boys are traveling slow.

Pico can mount his bike, but the case is more of a problem than the leg is. He can't figure out how to carry it, and he won't leave it behind.

Finally Apple slips a belt through its handle and throws everything over Pico's shoulder.

"That ain't worth the effort," Lady says.

"I hurt myself to get it," Pico says.

"You hurt yourself cuz you didn't watch where you going," Lady says.

"I'm still hurt," he says.

Jemma looks down the 101. The Downtown are ahead of them, the Holy Wood and Last Lifers behind. The sky is starting to glow behind the shapes of the Towers. If there's enough light for her to see the Towers, there'll soon be enough light for their enemies to see them.

CHAPTER EIGHTEEN

THE SILVER FLOWER

They crawl the last miles into Downtown—that's how it feels. Pico can only pedal with his left leg, and Lady can hear a lopsided rhythm every time he pushes with his left and moves the right leg around without putting pressure on it: grunt, tire squeak, wheel clicks, grunt, tire squeak, wheel clicks, grunt.

Apple doesn't make a sound, but when Lady catches his unguarded face she can see him wince.

They have to get into Downtown before dawn—but Lady has no idea where they're supposed to go when they get there.

"The Library Tower," Jemma says when Lady asks.

"What? And what's a library?"

"The biggest tower in Downtown," Pico says.

"Oh, you mean the biggest thing in the sky? Say that first."

The Downtown tribe doesn't live Downtown, but they guard all the roads into it to keep their sacred place empty. This place means something to them that it doesn't to the rest of the Angelenos, but even she can understand the pull it holds on the horizon. She's visited the Downtown twice in their village, built into a giant stadio from Long Gone. And even though she knows their faces, even though they are sisters and allies, Lady knows this: If they find the people of the Holy Wood entering Downtown, it will mean death.

She almost thinks they can make it there in the dark, but when she can see where the 101 enters Downtown, the sun bursts between the towers.

"They can see us," she says to the others, but realizes that if anyone has been watching, they already could. They'd just need enough light—

Enough light to aim.

Beneath them, beneath the 101, is the other great road that marks the boundary of Downtown. The cars on it look on fire in the morning sun, and then they're gone as the bikes cross into the sacred city.

The walls and buildings around them take a whole new shape, and she sees what the Muscle would see—too many places to attack, not enough places to hide. They're on a wide concrete plain sparsely populated with cars. Ahead is a steep canyon with giant buildings looming. They're bristling with arrows in Lady's mind. If the Downtown were guarding the 101, wouldn't this be where they are?

Apple sees it when she does. He would have seen it sooner if he weren't dulled by pain. "Stay as low as you can, everybody," he says. "Stay low and by the cars."

The first arrow doesn't make a noise until it hits the car to her right. It would have torn through her neck, but it clatters off the window. "Hide!" Jemma says ahead of her, and all of them are off their bikes and pushing them behind cars. Lady collapses against the side of the car and hears two more arrows, one of them clanging off the metal. It takes four more breaths before she can look up to see that Apple is next to her, and Jemma and Pico are safe behind another car ahead of them.

Not for long, though. The next car is fifty yards away, so they can't move from car to car without being seen. If they stay, the Downtown can walk right up to them and slit their throats.

Fortunately, they brought their own Muscle.

Apple nocks an arrow and waits for a movement. He pulls the string back—

And screams. The string snaps back without the arrow, which drops harmlessly to the ground, and Apple holds his collarbone in agony. He collapses against the side of the car just before two arrows, tracking his screams, sail overhead.

Lady can see the building that launched the arrows. It's nearly windowless except for a glass block of a tower at the top, capped with a giant corkscrew of metal. She watches it for movement, and then she sees a slender shaft flying from the roof below the corkscrew.

She's not strong enough to reach the archer with that bow. The Downtown have practice and gravity on their side.

But then Lady almost laughs out loud: *They have bows. We have the gun.*

She calls to Jemma in a whisper that just carries between cars, and Jemma nods. Lady watches Jemma unsling the gun from her back.

An arrow glances off the glass in front of her. Lady doesn't think the gun will have the same problem. And now they have a target. She gestures to Jemma, who follows her finger to the roof and sees the archer's head.

Jemma lays the gun on the car, keeping her body hidden as much as possible. She squeezes the trigger.

The stone next to the archer shatters. She fires again and it hits the stone below. If noise alone could kill the archers, they'd be fine.

"You're the worst shot I've ever seen!" Lady yells at Jemma.

"I don't know *how* to shoot!" Jemma shouts back.

"Let me try!"

Jemma shakes her head at first, but then slides the gun toward Lady along the road. Lady's never held it as a weapon before, but she's seen the Oldest use it and thinks she understands it. She pushes the brass shells into the chamber, flicks the safety switch, and crawls toward the flattened rear of the car.

The gun feels at home in Lady's hand, and she can see in its sights the head of the archer, too stupid to duck even when his targets carry a gun. She breathes, stilling her chest until nothing can move the gun, and squeezes it so gently that she doesn't realize she's fired until she hears the crack—and then a shriek.

She didn't hit her target in the head, but she hit him. He won't fire again.

"Ride!" she yells, but Lady sees Pico and Jemma already pedaling hard from the corner of her eye. She makes sure Apple has made it onto his bike and then she rides, too, the gun across her shoulders and her bike in motion before another Downtown archer can step to the ledge. Lady and Apple catch up in a few seconds, because although Pico seems to have forgotten his injured leg, he still can't pedal as fast as she can.

A short ramp opens to their right and they peel off toward it. Jemma chances a look over her shoulder and shakes her head, grim. "About five of em. On foot, thank gods," she says.

They pedal through brush so thick that the buildings above seem to glow green, filtered as they are by the leaves. And then it opens up in front of them, more a giant silver flower than a building. Lady has never seen it from the Zervatory, has never seen anything like it ever: a steel structure not made of walls, but of sinuous, curving petals like a rose that opens up to welcome them. As they ride cautiously toward it, she sees it's covered with thin panels of metal. Some of them have been peeled back as if a giant were opening an orange, and green is bursting out of every crack, but it doesn't take away from the grandeur. She feels as if she's stumbled into the garden of the gods.

A thin stairway beckons them up into the blossom, and Lady feels compelled to follow it. She hesitates, thinking of Pico and the blood caking on his leg.

"We can make a stand here," Apple says, looking at it with a Muscle's eye. It's overgrown, it's easily blockaded, and it can give them as much protection as anything else around. And Pico shouldn't be riding on that leg.

Pico makes it up the steps with his arm over Jemma's right shoulder, and his bike in her left arm. Apple can put a bike on his good arm if someone else lifts it for him. Lady carries the other two bikes, and they climb slowly up the stairs.

Metal gates, covered with a mesh of wires, block the stairs almost at the top. One of them is open, and they shut it behind them. The lock doesn't work, long rusted in place, but a sturdy branch locks it for them.

If Lady thought she was in the garden of the gods before, this is a garden for very small gods. It's filled with trees and flowers crowding out a path of winding flagstones. They push into the garden and find another rose, a fountain made out of shattered blue china. Lady knows it's a fountain because water is miraculously still bubbling up. The water and the rose are edged with slime, but when Lady sips it, it still tastes pure.

"I never seen a fountain still working," Lady says, awed. "This's gotta be a sign from the gods."

"The gods can wait. Right now, I want to clean this leg," Pico says, a trace of his old self pushing through the pain.

So Lady opens her pack to her store of medsen. The Gatherers cut themselves sometimes on their foraging trips, and they can't count on making it back to the camp for supplies. She has ripped cloths and stuff for pain. Jemma dips her canteen into the fountain and pours its contents over Pico's leg, over and over until the wound seems clean and open, and Pico winces. The pack has nothing for fections. The Parents taught them that fections are things you can't see but can still kill you. A lot of Children die from fections.

"I wish we had booze," Jemma says.

"To drink," Lady says, so quick and deadpan that even Pico laughs.

When they have bound his wound and tried to immobilize Apple's shoulder with a sling, they collapse on springy tufts of grass growing up along the pathway.

"What is this place?" Lady says, and she thinks of how rarely she's ever asked that question.

"I saw the words 'hall' and 'concert' on our way up," Pico says, and Lady almost chokes.

"Oh yeah, he can read," Jemma says.

"That explains a lot, you freak," Lady says. "That news to you, too, Apple?"

"I knew," Apple says. *Of course.*

"I think this place is for music," Pico says.

Lady's thoughts are climbing up the silver petals, in a direction they're not used to going. They sing in the fields of the Holy Wood, but to build this?

The travelers are beat after traveling all night, so Jemma and Lady draw straws to stand watch, and Lady loses. Pico and Apple they let rest.

Next to the stairs is a narrow passageway that twists through the metal to a low wall, where Lady can crouch and just see the street where they came from. With the trees it's only a narrow band, but she'll spot anyone who comes their way.

The search party, when it arrives, is not as motivated as expected. They glance toward the steps, and Lady reaches for the One Gun, but it's almost as if they don't want to see the hiding place. And she thinks she's right: They don't want to see her. The stairs are easily defended, and if she's really there with the gun, which she is, she can kill all five of them before they reach the top. They're Angelenos. They don't want to kill Holy Wood any more than they want to die.

The Downtown party moves east, toward the morning sun, and from the way the sounds trail off, she thinks they turn north to the 101. She holds her post while the others sleep. After all they've been through, they need some peace.

Doesn't she need that, too? Lady's alone with her thoughts for the first time since Li attacked her, and now she wishes they would go away. She's not used to thinking about her feelings, and they stretch her mind like an unused muscle.

She thinks about a village of girls pretending that rape isn't a word, about Jemma saving her from it and then ripping her away. She shakes her head, refuses to give Li a permanent place in her mind.

She hasn't slept since yesterday morning, and she isn't sure she can make it through the watch. So she explores the garden. The moment she moves along the silvery curtain of the hall, Lady is awake. The walls above her flutter in shining waves, holding down and reflecting the blue of the sky.

Glass doors, broken by time, split the wall. She walks through without having to touch the handles, into a silence she hasn't known—the interior is as hushed as a grove of trees, and every sound seems to disappear into the fir beams jutting from the wall. Then she notices more: bear droppings, tiny animal skeletons, and, farther in, human skeletons.

What if a bear still lives there? She hopes it doesn't come home while they're here. But something about the still of the hall draws her in, deep into a giant room filled with seats that remind her of their church in the Zervatory. Light filters down from a tear in the roof. Otherwise, she wouldn't be able to see a thing.

"So this is where you sang." The words hang in the air for a moment longer than they should, and the feel of them pushes a song to the surface, one that she hasn't thought of since she was in Daycare.

Her throat is tight, choking on tears that won't come out. But where the tears won't, the notes will, and they rise through the light like motes of dust.

I could be a farmer
A tailor, a doctor
A fighter, a lover
None of it matters
All of me in this world is you.
You will not know me
No one will tell me
The steps that you take
The hearts that collapse
All of me in this world is you.
So stay with me, child
Drive back the wild
The world has no life
Beyond the one in your eyes
All of me in this world is you.

The room still rings when she finishes. Now she understands why they built it, to make music soar like nowhere else in the world. The words still swim through her head.

She won't cry. She won't be a victim. But she still wants that fat little baby. She wants the swell in her stomach. She wants to touch and be touched. *Screw you, Li, for turning a roll into something to fear.*

Searching for a familiar sensation, she combs through the curls of her hair with her fingers as she has every day of her life since she was a toddler. No one else in the Holy Wood has those curls. But this time they brush across something hard, sharp.

The hairpin. The one she stabbed Li with, which probably saved her life. She'd left it in her hair in the scramble down the hill from the Holy Wood. This one is as long as her hand is wide, with a flat shimmering back that looks like abalone shell. She picked it because it looked like something the Children could never make.

But now she only sees the point, a tiny dagger still crusted with Li's blood. She doesn't wipe off the blood. She wants to remember that she drew it. Lady has always worn her hair loose and tangled, but now she pulls it up in one hand like she did for the Waking and slides the pin in place. Not because she wants to look like one of the old priestesses, but because she always wants that pin within reach. For the next time.

The sun has crossed into the western side of the sky, and sharp beams glance toward them from the silver rose, before she wakes them. "It's afternoon," she says.

Jemma stirs and says to Pico, "If you want to find your books, we gotta get there in the light."

"We looking for books?" Lady asks.

"Looking for the answers. Pico thinks they'll be in the library." And Lady realizes Jemma hasn't told her everything. Anything, really.

"Something caused the End," Pico says. "If the Parents knew what, it could be in their library. That building."

"So . . . we trying to stop the End?" Lady says, the look on her face not even close to belief.

"To understand it. Maybe to stop it," Pico says.

"Then why didn't you tell me about it first?" That's the question that's been hurting ever since she saw Pico and Apple by the lake. Not that

Jemma was trying to drag her away. That Jemma was never going to tell her she was leaving.

"You wouldn't a wanted to go. But you'd a gone anyway," Jemma says.

Lady takes in a deep breath, shaking it all away. She looks around at this strange place. She knows that when she closes her eyes tonight, she will see the silver petals twisting over one another and wish that she could lie below them until the light is gone. How could all this have been at the feet of the Holy Wood and none of them known it? *Because we stayed where we're sposed to*, she thinks.

"Where's the tower from here, anyway?"

Jemma points behind Lady, and, rising over the south wall, she can see its tip. She hadn't noticed the whole time they were in the garden. But then, Jemma is the one who looks at the sky, and because of her everything has gone wrong.

CHAPTER NINETEEN
THE LIBRARY

The Library Tower is only blocks away, but, it turns out, this isn't the library. The real library is a building across the street, capped by a blue pyramid set with a golden sun. Lady laughs at Pico getting it wrong.

The door to the library sits inside a darkened archway. It's heavy steel, propped open by rust and debris. Game trails crisscross the deep dust on the floor, as if they were still in the hills. Unlike the other Parents' buildings, which smell of dust and death, this one smells like life—messy and earthy and green. When they enter the light coming from their left, they can see why: The library opens into a giant atrium flooded with sunlight and carpeted in plants.

At the top of the room is a great glass ceiling, mostly gone, which let the light and the rain and the seeds in until now; a forest is growing where there was once only stone. Jade pillars thicker than pines run from floor to ceiling, covered with creeping fig until just a little of their stone peeks out from under the vine. Steps drop down and down toward the back of the atrium, each one tangled deeper into the library woods. Groundwater has broken into the building, and a thin waterfall drops over the lip of the lower floors.

"Nature wants this building back," Apple says.

Pico sees the nature, but more than that he sees the intentions buried under the vines: the grand pillars, the airy ceiling, the sweeping stairs. This place was meant to be a temple, a church, as much as the Zervatory. Beyond the greenery Pico smells the dust of books, can almost sense the memories of the Long Gone, the big thinks buried here. This is Pico's temple.

"Books!" Pico says, and points to low-ceilinged rooms branching off from each level of the atrium. Compared to the expanse of the atrium, they look like caves. "There's so many!"

They rest their bicycles carefully against a green pillar and make their way down the steps to the first level. Pico lays down the silver case, which has banged his butt since they left the metal building. Jemma still carries the gun and her pack. There's a sign for the level, but Pico has to puzzle it out. "Bus eye ness?"

"I thought you could read," Lady says.

"Not good enough," he says, his face screwed up. "Not the right words. I don't understand any of this."

Pico pushes deeper into the dark of the shelves, and a loud shrieking drives him back. He can't place the sound until he sees the mask: a grown raccoon. It bursts out of its den in a bottom shelf and screeches at them, teeth bared.

"Stupid raccoon," Lady says, and throws a book at it.

The next level has more for Pico. The light filters into the cave, but less than the level above. "Science," he says.

"What's that?" Jemma asks.

"How stuff works. How all of the Parents' stuff works," Pico says. He grabs a book with streetlights on the cover, glowing. He's never seen them lit before.

"Do you realize? Do you realize what's in these books?" he says, close to shouting. Everything is connecting in his head—cars, Lectrics, guns. "This is all the Parents' stuff, in this building. Just *one* of these books is more than *all* the stuff we know. Than all the Children know. But with all of em . . . you could—you could make everything run again."

The others watch him as he flips through the pages, maybe awed, until Apple says: "If you had enough time." Apple understands what time means.

"If I had enough time." Pico is quieter now. The pages blur together, and a few shapes jump out. He looks up, and the excitement is gone. "I don't understand any of this. Like, maybe a few words. It's gonna take a long time."

"Get reading, book boy," Lady says.

"I think I'm starting to hate you," he says, and retreats into the shelves.

What did he expect? That he could unlock the Parents' mysteries in the first five minutes, that they would be laid out for him to discover like Chris Mass?

Because when he disappears into the stacks, the sheer weight of the books threatens to overwhelm him—they soar over his head, fill every part of his vision. The dust floating off them threatens to choke him. But as he passes through, he catches pieces of words, pictures of machines, and starts to understand what he's looking at. The books subside into orderly piles.

Pico thumbs through a book on Teevee. From the words he does understand, from the pictures, it looks as if it's just another Lectric. Magical, yes, this stuff that made the world run, but not a god. His mind should be reeling from that, but he found the gods hard to swallow in the first place. If they had so much power, they shouldn't have let the world End.

"Pico! You got something?"

Pico looks at Apple and realizes he's nowhere near to an answer. "What do you guys got?" he says.

"Since we can't read," Lady says, "not a whole lot."

"Look for pictures of people dying, maybe?" Pico says.

"I kind of wish I could read," Jemma says. She's running her hand along a plastic map of Ell Aye.

"Start with the things you know, and see what words're next to em," Pico says. "It's a start."

Jemma points at the map, which is bigger than just the Holy Wood or even Downtown. It has bumps the shapes of the Holy Wood Hills and Malibu, but the ocean seems to go along its edge for hundreds of miles. Jemma points at a thick red line. "Is that the 101?" she says.

"Think so. Keep going," Pico says. As he goes back into the stacks, he sees her tracing the line south.

Still he finds nothing, and the enormity of trying to understand what happened to the Parents settles on his shoulders. There are too many words here.

At the lowest, darkest level, Pico has almost given up. He can barely read the spines in the dark. When he finds something that looks promising, he has to take it out to the atrium to see the pages. And none of it is right. "Everything here is old," he says.

"Well, yeah—" Jemma starts, but Lady cuts her off.

"Cuz everyone is dead," Lady says.

"No," Pico says, "it was all written a long time before the Parents died. Books must have taken a long time. So if everyone died fast, they couldn't write about it."

"What do you mean?"

"I mean," Pico says, "the answers ain't here."

What do they do now? They're the first people maybe since the Parents to enter the library, or at least the first to understand it. Apple had started to believe they would find answers there, if they searched hard enough. They have the books and they have the Exile, and no one's had anyone like him in generations.

Still, there's nothing out here for them. Could he convince Jemma and Lady to go back to the Holy Wood, give up, become Mamas, try to live their last years the way they're meant to be lived? He's about to say that, but he stops himself. They can't go back, after all they've done. But it's more than that. Apple doesn't want them to go back. He decided to live for Jemma, and now, selfishly, he wants to know what that's like. He's ashamed to think that way, but there is Jemma. That's what he wants.

"Maybe—" But he doesn't know how to finish the sentence. They've failed. The last of the light to make its way to the depths is fading, and they've lost the day. They need to find shelter before dark, tend to their wounds. Tend to the things that matter.

They move toward the door of the atrium when Lady pauses, holds her hands up. "You hear that?"

They drop even quieter than they were before and strain to catch any noise. There's nothing, but then, wait—was that a snuffle? Like someone clearing her nose? Apple is completely still but doesn't hear anything. They hold for almost a minute until a shared glance gets them walking quietly toward the door. None of them even seem to be breathing, they're walking so quietly.

Pico said to look for dying people, and all of them see the pictures at once on a large folded square of paper, yellow and crumbling: bodies lying on a street, unburied and unburned.

Pico is already reading the words. " 'San Diego Falls While Disease Spreads,' " he whispers, puzzled. "What's San Diego?"

"I think it's a place," Jemma says.

"How do you know that?" Apple says, a little in wonder.

"I saw those letters on the map."

"Can you show it to me?" Pico says.

Apple claps his hands over both their mouths. He hasn't forgotten why they were whispering. It's so quiet that Apple can hear the pulse in his ear. Then something else, the pad of footsteps. They're soft, but they carry weight. He can almost feel a tremor through the metal of the shelf under his hand.

Whatever it is stops, and this time Apple can hear it sniff, take a few steps, and sniff again. It's between them and the door. And it's hunting them.

They're still frozen in place when he spies the first flash of brown fur between the shelves, the grizzled tips catching the dying light from the atrium. The creature moves into the row next to them, and even before he sees its hump Apple can tell it's a bear, one of the big brown ones. You can scare the black bears off sometimes. Not the brown ones.

The shelf next to them is filled with thick books, which must be the only reason the bear hasn't seen them, although surely their scent must be all around it. Apple fingers his machete but knows it's too short to help on a bear that big. He can't draw his bow with his collarbone separated or broken.

He looks to his right at the others and nods at them while placing his hands flat against the shelf, flexing. He pantomimes and they place their hands against the shelf, too.

Apple holds up his hand, three fingers showing. The fingers flex, ready to count down.

The heavy head of the bear comes into sight. It starts to turn toward him—

Three, two. One.

They push the shelf, and there's a roar of recognition from the bear, and the shelf rocks but doesn't move, and they're attacking the shelf with their shoulders, slamming into it again and again. Apple is using his good shoulder, but still the pain jags through his collarbone. A paw swipes through the bottom shelf, just missing Jemma's legs, and then the shelf topples, hitting the bear in a cloud of ancient books and pinning it between the floor and the next shelf.

"Get the paper!" Pico says, but when Apple lifts it, it crumbles in his hand and falls away, the black letters floating to the floor. He feels its loss like a punch in the stomach, but he's running with all of them toward the door and away from the roaring pile of books.

Pico slows at a desk near the entrance of the atrium to scoop the papers into his arm. "You crazy?" Lady says. "Get on!" She can see Pico can't climb all those steps. She hoists Pico onto her back, his hands holding tight over her pack, and starts taking the stairs two at a time.

There are hundreds of steps. They didn't notice them on the way down, but now they stretch endlessly to the top, each flight jogging to the left before going up. Halfway up Lady has slowed down so much she's barely walking, and Pico is slipping. "Trade," Jemma says, and slips off the rifle.

Pico climbs awkwardly onto her back, holding tight around her neck. "Why didn't you use the gun, Jemma?" Lady says.

Apple's thoughts sharpen, as they always do during a fight. Lady now has the gun, but she's shot it only once. What else do they have? His bow, as long as he doesn't need to draw it. His machete, if he's way too close. "Get ready to shoot, Lady," Apple says. It's good she has the gun. Lady's the highest up the stairs and will have the most time to react.

On the second-to-last landing, the bear's roar seems to split the atrium in half. He looks down and sees that lightning brown bulk, bolting up the stairs. It'll be on them in seconds.

Lady aims, pulls the trigger. Apple hears the shot but can't see where it lands, just a louder roar. Lady scrambles to the top of the stairs and fires again while they climb. Apple grabs Jemma with his good arm and tows her and Pico up the steps. Jemma's legs waver, she pitches forward, but Apple keeps pulling. They tumble over the lip of the stairs.

The bikes on the landing are no help, not with Pico's leg. "Next level!" Apple shouts, but his voice gets lost in another shot. Lady is standing her ground, and the bear seems to have slowed, wary of this stinging bang.

The next steps lead to a short hallway and then a huge rotunda, bigger than the one at the Zervatory. They hear nothing for a moment, thinking that maybe the bullets really hit. It's long enough for Apple to steal a glance at the ceiling, a bold yellow sun set in a blue sky, but then the bear stalks into the rotunda, as if it knows it's trapped them. As it probably has.

They back up just as slowly, and Apple feels a breeze at his neck. A doorway or something, behind him. One more step and he can see the door itself, a heavy steel grating that should shut out the bear, if it will move.

He speaks evenly. "Jemma, get ready to shut the—"

Lady lifts the gun, and the bear closes the gap in a breath. Lady fires, but the bear's paw darts and knocks the gun to the floor with a clatter. The bear jerks at the boom of the gun, momentarily rocked back on its heels, then lurches forward.

Apple grips his bow at the end with one hand and swings it like a whip. It whistles through the air and cracks the bear across the snout. It won't hurt the bear but might startle it into thinking it's been hurt. Apple remembers Jemma and the lion, and he's making himself as tall as he can, screaming at the bear with everything he has.

It rises, tall, so tall, taller than any of the Children. Apple sees the others pushing on the doors and the bear bats the bow away but the bear is two steps and a bite away from his Jemma and he remembers the machete and how it's only good up close but he can get close. He rips the machete free from its sheath and steps into the bear, under its chin, finds himself swallowed up and suffocated in the fur. *How soft is death?* he wonders. Claws tear at him, at his back and arms and everywhere, and death isn't soft anymore. He drives his blade upward toward the throat.

He misses it. He knows it. It sank somewhere in the fatty shoulder. But the bear howls, falls away, and in that pause Apple stumbles backward and Jemma and Lady slam the doors. They slide a metal bolt in place moments before the bear slams into the door. It shudders, holds, they stumble backward, and Jemma falls on the floor.

"Ow ow ow," Pico says, muffled beneath her. Jemma rolls off and he's lying on the floor under her pack. Apple can't feel his back. The bear is biting and swiping at the holes in the grating, but it's outside the door. And they're inside.

CHAPTER TWENTY
THE BOOK AND THE BEAR

It takes checking every door in their new room, barricading two of the doors, and ignoring the bear pacing outside the grating before they can take stock of where they are. Ignoring is not quite possible, when they can hear every grunt and growl of the bear, and it stops to clang the bars every few minutes.

As soon as they're safe, Jemma examines Apple. He has deep cuts crisscrossing his back and shoulder in rows of four. They have only their drinking water and Gatherers' field medsen. He needs the Little Doctors, and she tells him so.

"You seen their hands?" he says. "If the bear don't got fections, those kids defintly do."

She realizes they haven't been alone since they rescued him. Her hands brush across his skin, and she wants to brush it more, but everyone can see them. It's not even close to private enough.

"You could have Ended," she says. He shrugs, as if to say: *Soon enough.*

This part of the library feels older—the materials and the curves are richer, and the ceiling rests on sturdy wooden beams. And unlike the other sections, it seems to have been made for small children—the posters on the wall are brighter, the books have pictures on them.

"Kids could read?" Jemma says.

"You could read, Jemma," Pico says.

Jemma picks up a book, opens it. Inside the letters are bunched so close that they seem to be leaning on one another for support.

"Not like that," Pico says, and moves to a nearby shelf. The books there are thinner, with colors that peek through the dust and age. He thumbs through them until he finds a book thinner than his pinkie. On its cover are some animals and familiar shapes of letters. "Look, a bear!" Lady says brightly.

"It's a code," Pico says. "You just gotta figure out what letters go with what sounds. But it's mostly sounds and words you already know. The Parents called em the ABCs."

First page is a fruit. "Apple," Jemma blurts out.

"That looks nothing like me," Apple says. Jemma had almost forgotten it was a fruit. Apples only grow in the hills where it gets cold enough. Traders from the San Fernandos bring them to the Holy Wood once every few years. She still remembers the crispness, the delight at that first explosion of juice.

"So you know the A makes that sound, or at least one of its sounds," Pico says.

"And 'bear'?" Jemma says, involuntarily checking to make sure their bear is okay. It seems to have bored of them, and right as she looks to the door, it collapses to the ground in a *humph*, its huge back pressed up against the grating.

"The letter is B, sounds like the word 'bee,'" Pico says.

"Like the bug?" Lady says. "Oh, that's another B."

They flip through the pages—car, donkey, mouse. When the book is done, Jemma draws the book into her lap and folds her hands over it, not wanting to let it go. This rectangle, full of a child's paintings—it's the key to the world the Parents abandoned.

Pico hobbles closer to the grating. "The bear's bleeding," he says. The edges of its fur are tinged with blood, dark red blotting out the brown.

"Maybe it'll die," Lady says.

"I hope not," Jemma says before realizing that's how she feels. "How long do these things live, Pico?"

"Forty years, I read."

"So this . . . is the oldest thing in the Holy Wood." She's awed by it.

It was old enough that it could have lived when her Mama did, when her Mama's Mama lived. She touches her fingers to her lips, and says, "Salud, viejo. Live a long life."

"It ain't supposed to be here, you know," Pico says.

"In a library? Yeah," Lady says.

"No, at *all*. I read that kind of bear, a grizzly, got wiped out around here. Whatever happened to the Parents, the animals got a chance to come back."

Jemma inches toward the bear's fur, spilling through the cracks. It's lush and rank all at once, and her hand slips toward it. Then she's petting it with two fingers, as if any more of her hand would make it notice. It twitches its ear as if flicking away a fly, grumbles, and settles closer to the floor. What has it seen? What does it remember? More than they ever will.

"We need both your hands," Apple says, pulling her away from the beast with his tone as much as the hand on her waist.

"If it don't get bored enough to leave, we better hope it dies," Lady says. "We gotta get home, and it's blocking us."

"It's blocking the gun, too," Jemma says.

"Yeah, we're gonna need that, too, if we wanna go home," Lady says. No one responds to that.

They debate whether or not to start a fire, and with what. "We surrounded by kindling," Lady says, arms open to the books filling the room.

"You want to burn em?" Pico can't hide his horror.

"Get over it, Exile! You the only person in the world who can read!" Lady says.

He relents when they pick only the books that have more than one copy, and even he smiles when a fire is flickering—on the tile, far away from the bookshelves—and gives him enough light to read.

Jemma hands out rations—fruit and dried meat. But Lady doesn't really eat. Jemma notices that her jaw muscles stay tense even after she's done chewing, as if they're wrestling with unfamiliar, violent sounds. "When we going home?" she says.

"Home?" Apple says.

"Yeah, Apple, home," Lady says.

Jemma doesn't speak at first. She thought Lady would never want to go back. Not after what happened. Maybe even she misunderstood how deep Lady's love for the Holy Wood went.

"Jemma, you said just a couple of days," Lady says.

Jemma stands up and walks to the heavy book she saw before, one she decided not to burn, because it's full of maps. It starts with an A. "I was thinking . . . I was thinking we could go to the map of the words."

"San Diego?" Pico says.

"Yeah, that place. Maybe whatever killed the Parents started there."

"If it started there," Pico says, "then maybe we can tell what caused it."

"The place on the paper? Is that even real?" Lady says.

"I saw it, Lady." And Jemma's fingers race through the A book, not sure where she'll find it, but knowing it has to be there. And then she finds the same map, flatter and brighter and smaller, but with San Diego and Holy Wood both marked. She can't explain it to Lady, not even to Apple, but somehow the haze sparked when she saw those words. It wants her to go to San Diego.

"How far is that, Jemma? Do you know? Days? Weeks? And you know that the first thing after Ell Aye is the Wilds?" The Wilds are the lands south of Ell Aye. No one has lived there for a hundred years—just dogs and pigs and the occasional Gatherer. "You know how to get through that?"

"I don't," Jemma says, small. Then she speaks a little louder. "But I want to. I want to look for a cure."

"Cure? There's no cure. It's not a disease. It's life."

"Answers, then," Apple says.

Lady wheels to him, then back to Jemma. "I see why you want it, Apple. I even see the Exile, cuz he's got nobody. But Jemma and me—"

She grabs the A book from Jemma and stabs at the map with her finger, nails punching through the ancient streets. "San Diego ain't real," she says. "Our home is real, and it's not days from here, it's hours."

Home. Even if Jemma could return the gun, even if they would take her back, even if they would spare Apple, was there a home anymore in the Holy Wood? She looks at Lady, sees the curly-haired little girl she snuggled with on a mattress for warmth, who punched her for a mango. Lady looks back into her eyes and knows: Home is no more real for her than San Diego.

"You ain't never going back," Lady says.

"We can't."

"*I* can," Lady says, determined. As if she's not talking about going home anymore. As if she's trying to get back the life that was stolen from her.

Lady packs. The briefest of hugs, a couple of tears, and Lady is belly down on the windowsill, sliding backward into the night. Jemma watches her land safely and turns away from the window before the real crying begins. Apple holds her tight, but her ribs ache from sobs that she doesn't bother to hide.

"Why would she go back?" Pico says. "It ain't safe for her there."

"Lady loved the Holy Wood, and she lost it," Apple says. "She wants to be a Mama. She wants it all to be safe and normal."

"She didn't lose it. Li took it from her," Jemma says. "Li—and the Priestess and the Olders. There ain't no more normal."

"She seems like the kind who's always gonna be okay," Pico says, awkwardly patting Jemma's shoulder.

"Shut up, Exile," Jemma says, and the echo of Lady makes the sobs come harder.

When she curls inside Apple's body on the slick tile, it's all comfort, no desire. He's the only thing keeping her from melting into the floor in exhaustion.

"Maybe I was wrong," he says into her ear. "Maybe I wanted to live so much that . . . maybe I was wrong to take you out of the Holy Wood."

No. It might have started as a way to keep him alive, but she's the one who grabbed on to the mystery of the End, who even now can't face the prospect of early death. She needs him to want to hang on to life as badly as she does. "No," she says. "I took you out of there. Don't ever forget it."

Sleep seems far away, and she waits hour by hour, wondering if Lady has made it to the 101. Finally she drops into sleep as if she were falling into a well. She hears a scratching at the edge of her mind, as if the haze is trying to break in and tell her something, but she's too tired to see it.

Her eyes fly open, and she fights for breath as if it's the first one in minutes. Apple sits cross-legged across from her, smiling toward that window, the window where the scrabbling must have really started. Through that window pops Lady's bushy hair and her out-of-breath face.

Jemma jumps up and pulls Lady from the sill roughly, clutching her to her chest. "Mija!" she says.

"Jesucristo, girl, I've been gone half a night," Lady says, pushing her away. "I made it to the skyplane and just realized—it's dark out there, and there's a rapist in the Holy Wood that you saved me from, and the only thing I really loved in that whole place was you. So . . . you all suck."

They hug again, this time Lady not fighting her.

"You came back," Pico says, his smile the widest Jemma has seen it. He reaches toward them.

"You hug me, Exile, and I'll kick you in the nuts," Lady says.

He hugs her anyway and she doesn't kick him. Jemma nestles into Apple's arms, holds Lady's hands, and they all sleep puddled around the book fire, even after they learn that bears snore.

CHAPTER TWENTY-ONE
THE WILD

The bear is gone when they wake, the only sign that it was there a clean patch on the floor where its fur mopped up the dust. Blood, too, but just a few drops. Lady's relieved it's gone, scared it lurks around the corner, but Jemma looks sad to see it go.

They argue about the route out of Ell Aye in the library. The shortest way to San Diego, it seems, is the road marked with a 5. But that takes them through the Wilds, a place of warehouses, homes, and train tracks that had turned to jungle when the Parents disappeared. There are no sure sources of food there, and traders from the Downtown peoples said it was ruled by packs of wild dogs and pigs that would rip your throat.

But Lady points out a line of blue on the map, heading almost straight south to the sea as if it were drawn into being, not born from the earth. That was the Ell Aye River, which the Holy Wood shares at its source with the San Fernando. The water is clean, filled with frogs and birds. They can follow it and then turn to the east before they reach Palo territory.

The first stop when they leave, after scouting the library for signs of the bear, is a broken storefront just south of the library. Behind the window is a long wooden bar, some bottles still intact.

Pico's steps this morning are uneven and forced. When Lady peeled back the bandage, she had to freeze her face so that Pico didn't see what she saw: swollen flesh, red streaking out from the edges and past his knee. The wound was living and angry. They should have searched harder for medsen. Apple's aren't as bad, yet, but red lines the edges of the cuts.

The library could have waited.

Pico hoists himself onto the bar, exhaling sharply at the effort. Jemma twists open a dusty bottle of vodka, and Lady places her skinning knife on the counter. Jemma splashes it with alcohol, running her fingers wet with vodka along the knife's edge. It smells burning and clean. She pours it on Pico's leg, inches from each edge of the wound.

"You want to do this or me?" Lady says. They'll need to slice open the fections with crisscross cuts, release whatever poison bubbles inside him. They haven't told him that.

"You can," Jemma says, moving to Pico's head.

"Um, thanks," Lady says.

"Do what?" Pico asks, his voice still calm.

"Save your leg," Lady says. "You'll thank me later." And then, low: "A lot later."

He screams less than she would have thought, but they wait the day in the bar to let him rest.

They reach the river the next day after a breathless rush through the streets, an eye out for Downtown scouts and on Pico's seeping bandage. The river looks different. In the Holy Wood it's filled with trees and brush that give cover to the animals. Here it's a mossy cement ditch, with only bursts of grass breaking the banks. Even the water looks smaller. Lady starts to doubt her course, then spots a fishy, silvery glint. There is life, even here.

When the Parents encased the river in concrete, they built in flattened edges, half as wide as a street. It would have been a tight fit for a car, but it's perfect for bicycles. They don't waste time looking at the river, just turn right and head toward the sun. It's already past noon.

Their bicycles pass silently beneath a bridge that soars overhead, sliding from a bluff down toward the city. Lady wonders what it would have been like to ride toward those towers when they were full of life, not decay and fear.

The map says this goes all the way to the sea where the ships float still, bigger than a village. Pico had told her about a ghost ship that moved past the Malibus, so slow and so big it took a week to clear Point Dume. On the deck they could see skeletons of the Parents on reclining chairs, as if they were just resting and taking in the sights of the orphans below.

There's no sign of the sea here. Just concrete.

"Where the people at?" Pico says. "There should be people fishing it."

"No one lives here," Jemma says. "It's too hard and empty."

Pico gestures at the river walls, surrounded by Long Gone warehouses, but no houses. "Rivers mean life. But it's almost as if the Parents turned their backs on this part."

"Maybe Ell Aye was dying even before the End," Apple says.

This path won't be as easy as a road, as much as it looks like one. Debris blocks the path in ropy drifts that stretch as far as they can see. Every time they bump over them, Lady hears Pico or Apple groan. Rains or quakes, take your pick, have pushed parts of the path into the river, forcing them to skirt the holes. Once the entire path crumbles away.

Apple points out the remnants of once-living moss on the bank, only a few feet below them. "Rains was high this year. Lotta flooding."

"That's why the Parents walled em off, I guess," Jemma says.

Apple settles into a rhythm. The collarbone can't be healing, but he seems to ignore it. But the gasps of Pico's pedaling grow into constant noise as they ride down the path. By late afternoon, each stifled cry seems to cut into her until she doesn't feel sorry as much as annoyed. She wants to punch Pico. Jemma looks as if she feels the same way—so it must really be bad.

A colony of freshwater mussels gives them an excuse to halt. Lady has seen these along the water upstream where they fished. "Let's grab some of these things for supper," Lady says.

"It's not suppertime," Pico says.

"You think you could make it till supper?" Lady says, curling her lip.

"I could try," Pico says.

"And then you'd be useless tomorrow," Apple says. "Besides, there's food here."

By the time Jemma has a bag full of shellfish, Lady has a fire going where the path intersects with an industrial street that touches the river. Pico lies flat on his back, sweating even though he's found shade.

They roast the mussels until they pop and eat them until they feel as if they're popping themselves. Even Pico perks up.

Apple stands watch while they rest. The girls lie down next to Pico, one on each side. The late-spring afternoon is growing cold, and his body is somehow warm.

"We got some things to talk about," Pico says.

"About how you can't walk?" Lady says. Someone had to say it first.

"About how I'm gonna die," Pico says.

Not even a flutter passes her eyelids, and she sees Jemma go equally still. "That's not true, Pico," Jemma says.

"I got a red line running up my leg, and every step I take is moving it that much closer to my heart," Pico says. "We in the Wilds without medsen. What else is gonna happen?"

"The gods," Lady says.

Pico just smiles at Lady. "So . . . I'm gonna die."

"What do you want us to do?" Jemma asks.

"Someone braver than me would tell you to leave me behind to die," Pico says. "But I kinda like the idea of living. So . . . I guess we just focus on the not-walking part."

An old bed frame has washed to shore, rusted nearly through. A family of coots drifts by, chasing the fin of a carp. Both Jemma and Lady see it at the same time.

"Let's float," Lady says.

Boats are in low supply for a river, Jemma thinks. Lady finds rotting planks within sight of their camp, but they're so soaked with water they barely break the surface. With people on them, they'll scrape the bottom.

The three leave Pico at camp, armed with the One Gun and his books. They spread into the low warehouses, fighting through a thicket of collapsing garage doors. There are skeletons here, not many, but so far from Children that no one ever moved them. The bodies sprawl on the floor in overalls emptied like a water skin.

"Look!" she hears Apple shout from outside the building. He's in a passage between the warehouse and an outbuilding, next to a stack of blue barrels. They're plastic, filled with water that reeks of chemicals, and completely intact. It's as if the Parents filled them yesterday.

The barrels are meant to be lifted by grown Parents with machines, not Children. By the time the kids have pushed them over and unscrewed their lids, they shake and sweat. Even Apple looks worn. No, Apple *especially* looks worn. But the liquid smells evil, and they roll their first two barrels away without a rest. Apple stays behind to dump out more.

Pico is hammering the silver case with a rock when they get back to camp. Jemma forgot it while they rode, because Pico's groan drowned out its light thuds against the bike. But Pico hadn't.

"I need your hatchet," he says to Jemma.

"Why?"

"Cuz . . . it's sharper than a rock?"

"Don't ding my hatchet," she says, slipping it from her waist.

"Okay," he says, and swings. The hatchet glances off and hits the rock. Sparks fly.

"Pico!" she says, and then she turns away.

"He better be dying," she says to Lady.

"It'd be faster if we shoot him," Lady says.

After they bring back the second set of barrels, Pico has stopped chopping at the case. His skin is gray, covered with a sheen, and his head hangs down. How can he push so hard when he needs to hold every bit of energy he can muster? Jemma feels something tug at her chest. She pushes the barrel into place and pulls the hatchet out of Pico's hands. "Here," she says. She swings once at the case, and it sinks between the case and the clasp, and she's there in the Bowl watching the hatchet fall into the furrow between Andy's surprised eyes. "Here," she repeats, her voice suddenly gruff, "here."

"Thanks," Pico says, and he holds her eyes as if he were carrying something fragile.

"I'm gonna go build a boat," Jemma says, and turns away.

They break apart the crates in the warehouse into large squares. There are hammers and nails and enough rotting rope that they can weave everything into an unwieldy but floating mass.

They finish the raft in the final breaths of light. The raft is made of twelve of the barrels in all, in six rows of two, with planks as a deck, forming a rectangle about six feet wide and ten feet long. It's blocky and awkward but should handle the shallow river. With the lazy current in front of them, it doesn't need to be seaworthy.

Pico has pored over the contents of the silver case for the past two hours, and when Jemma turns away from the raft she sees him holding up a sheaf of papers in the firelight. Jemma takes the last of the mussels, throwing some to Lady and Apple. "Papers, that's it?" Lady says, cracking open the cold mussels. "I expected treasure. Holy weed, maybe."

"Papers," Pico says, not bothering to look up. "But . . . papers."

"What do they say?" Apple asks.

"I don't know," Pico says, and Jemma can't tell if it's exhaustion or defeat creeping into his voice. "The writing—it's weird."

He holds up the yellowed paper for Jemma to see. Instead of the blocky letters like the Holy Wood sign, the lines curve and fold over one another. She can barely tell where the words end. Nothing looks like a letter.

"Can you read it?"

"No," Pico says. "But this letter is an A, and this is an M. Unless they used different letters that I haven't seen, I should be able to figure out what the other letters are. If I have enough time."

Jemma flops down between the fire and Apple. He hasn't said much since they built the raft, but she reminds herself: *He just got attacked by a bear.* She leans into his left shoulder and he flinches. *And he broke his collarbone.*

"Sorry," she says. "I'm good at finding the spots that hurt."

"It all hurts," Apple says. He starts to kiss her, but something doesn't make her want to kiss. "What?" he says when she pulls back.

Just Pico dying. "Nah," she says.

"I ain't going anywhere," he says.

"It's just that Pico . . . It just sucks that—" Tears come, surprising her, and she shakes them loose. "No point being sad."

"It's okay," he says. "I think being sad made the Parents the Parents."

"They lived forever," she says. "How could they be sad?"

"All that living meant they was always seeing someone die," Apple says. "There's no living without losing. Being sad just means you loved."

"In that case," she says, leaning into him and kissing him, "I'm gonna be real real sad when you go." The thought hits her with a panic. She will.

Desperation and fear and longing pile into one and she's kissing him and he's driving back against her, tracing her shoulder blades with his good arm. She recognizes the thirsty feeling of never wanting to let go.

There are people next to them, next to the fire, and she doesn't care. *They can't see us. We're invisible because we made a place all our own.*

Her mouth leaves his for a moment and traces a line along his jaw: sharpness of bone, the last remnants of baby fat. As if she can feel him becoming a man under her lips. Her tongue reaches his ear and he gasps inward. It's then she remembers that she needs to breathe, that she's holding her chest still as if it would keep the bubble they're in from breaking.

Apple is breathing enough for both. She feels his lungs, labored and ragged, under her chest. He lets go for a minute, panting.

"Sorry," he says, "I gotta—" And then she sees the sweat on his skin, his eyes strange in the firelight.

"Apple," she says, but before he can say anything, she hears the buzz. It's almost inaudible now that she's gotten better at seeing the visions, but she likes the warning. The haze swirls out of the night and four-legged shapes appear in the middle of the blue. Even with the crude outlines, she can see them licking their chops.

She leaps to her feet and pulls her hatchet from her belt. She nods at Apple, who gets to his feet less certainly and picks up his machete.

"What is it?" he says.

She motions out at the night where the haze tells her they would be. They don't come for a long time. But at the skritching of claws on pavement, she knows she was right.

Dogs.

So when the dog slams out of the blackness farther from the river, a blur of blacker black and fangs, she isn't surprised, but she's still not ready for it because it's heavier than she is, and it smashes her into the ground inches from the fire. She feels the heat of the flames next to her ear even as she flails against the dog. It has tan marks around its eye. She strikes again and again with the hatchet and nothing lands, and then Apple's machete cuts into its neck and the dog crumples.

Jemma throws off the dog, grabs a stick, and lights it in the fire. Apple holds his machete grimly. With a hatchet in one hand and the torch in the other, she looks into the darkness on the opposite side.

The fire won't scare the dogs like it would a coyote. Nothing does. The dogs are larger than the coyotes, stronger, and they hunt the parts of the city where the humans are rare. Sometimes they even break into the Holy Wood and attack the little kids. She's seen pictures of them in Parents' houses and know they lived with the families. It's as if the Parents' friends had come back to haunt them.

The rest of the pack emerges from the darkness, all colors and sizes. They look almost casual, as if attack is the furthest thing from their minds, but Jemma knows it will start any second. When they attack, they pile on Apple first, maybe because he doesn't have the torch, maybe because his left arm hangs useless. He hacks his way out from under two of them, and she brings down another with the hatchet.

"Get behind us," she says, yelling to Pico and Lady.

"Like this?" Lady says at her ear as if she's telling a joke, and then the gun is firing, once, twice, and the dogs are falling and running.

"You gotta remember we got this thing," Lady says, running her fingers along the gun.

There are five dogs on the ground, none of them moving. Lady nudges the big black form by the fire with her toe. "Kinda wish we'd been attacked by pigs. Taste better."

Apple hasn't moved from his spot near the fire. He stands, machete at his side, and slowly looks up. He looks as if the fight has drained everything from his face.

"Apple?" she says.

Then he collapses, falling hard on his side on the pavement. It's the bad side, and he doesn't even whimper. Jemma scrambles toward him. He feels flushed and feverish, like—like Pico. She checks his back for wounds. They seem to be healing as they should. But he reaches to his right hip, and she tugs at his waist. There's a scratch from the bear that she didn't see, only an inch long but deep into the skin. In the firelight it looks as if it's bubbling.

"I didn't even feel it till now," Apple says, and then he's gone.

CHAPTER TWENTY-TWO
THE RAFT

The letters come to Pico during the night, looping around him in lazy spirals. Sometimes a C will come into view, sometimes an M, but the rest spool out in liquid threads, never taking shape.

He tries to talk to them, to ask why they won't come clear, and all he feels is a fevered shake in his jaw. He wrestles free of the ropy words, but they settle on him, tight and familiar as an old coat. One winds around his leg, and he wonders why it's pulling at his calf, why it's carving a line through his skin. Another settles on his shoulder—

They put it on a skyplane. They guarded it with a locked case. It holds secrets that strange letters can't keep silent. Look for the letters you know first.

The letters uncoil and climb his leg, straight for his heart. Learn the letters and you stop the climb. The C wraps around his neck, squeezes. Pico tears it off. Opens his eyes, then opens the case.

"There is no 'back,'" Apple says. He's so tired he can barely argue anymore.

They've spent most of the morning trying to figure out how to fight the boys' fections. Apple knows there's no hope. Pico knows there's no hope. But Jemma and Lady, both, think there's a way to go back.

"The Angelenos got medsen," Lady says. "I know they got Zithmax.

I Gathered it myself." Zithmax was a medsen the Parents used to have. It was the only thing that could beat a fection like that.

"The Holy Wood?" Pico says. "I steal the One Gun, and they gonna give me Zithmax?"

"Fine," Lady says.

"The San Fernando and the Downtown," Jemma says. "They're even closer than the Holy Wood. They can help."

"They won't," Apple says.

"Maybe they give us the medsen," Lady says. But they all know that's not true. No one will give them anything. They don't have anything to trade other than the One Gun, which would get them killed by the other Angelenos. That's the difference between being with people and being on your own. You get sick, you get injured, and there's no help.

"I been through this before. Been an Exile," Pico says. "Only thing that saved me was you."

"Plus, the Last Lifers are out there," Apple says.

"You killed em," Jemma says.

"We killed some," Apple says. "That Last Lifer came from the San Fernandos. They could be coming from all over Ell Aye—and going to the Palos. We go backward, we're likely to cross their path."

"We could find the Zithmax ourselves," Lady says reluctantly. "We Gatherers."

"I wanna keep going to San Diego," Pico says. "I'm finally starting to understand stuff."

Jemma looks at Apple, silently trying to convince him to go back. This time, though, he can't give her what she wants. This way, there's a tiny piece of hope, fragile as a spiderweb, but hope. "It's only forward for me," he says.

The river would be more beautiful, Lady thinks, if it weren't for the kids dying on the boat.

They are on the raft at first light, looking for a break in the Wilds.

Before they can find the Zithmax—*it starts with a* Z, Lady thinks—they have to find a spot where there are stores and houses. It's called the Wilds because it's been abandoned since long before their Mamas' Mamas' Mama, because so much of it—the warehouses and the parking lots—are unlivable. It's known for the beasts that live there, not the people. But there will be houses. There should be houses.

Mist floats up from the surface of the water in a slender band. The tendrils start a foot from the water and end two feet higher, so their bodies cut through the cloud while their heads float above it. Above the fog, the world is cold.

But Pico—Pico is lying down in the midst of the mist, shivering more than he should be from the moisture, and when Lady feels his body it seems as if he's carrying the fire with them. Apple doesn't shiver, just lies quietly on the deck, his eyes tracking the waterline.

"San Diego," Pico says, under the fog.

"What?" Lady says. She leans under the fog blanket and it shreds at that moment, as if a giant is tearing a dandelion puff with gentle breaths. There were tendrils of white, and now there's only mossy river glistening under the sun.

"The papers say San Diego," Pico says.

"You figured out their words?"

"I'm starting to," he says. "Some of the letters look like ours."

He settles back into his study. Lady takes another look at their craft. Two of the bikes are lashed to the raft and to each other to make a triangle, with the other bikes forming a back wall. If it gets hot or rainy, they can throw a blanket over the frames to make a tiny shelter for whoever needs it most.

The river is so choked with brush on either side that branches graze the sides of the drums with a scratchy hiss. They guide the raft into a groove carved into the bottom of the concrete. In the center the river is deeper, and their short poles just touch the bottom. By summer, she thinks, the groove will be an emerald line surrounded by blinding white banks.

The water is so still that she can feel Pico's shakes through the deck of the boat. But the pages keep turning. He's there with his stupid case, muttering and tapping the paper, his head still racing even as the poison climbs.

Lady has only begun to believe that this journey could matter. If Pico dies, none of this matters. She watches for an opening in the bank that looks promising, balancing on the edge of hope.

Maybe she can find Zithmax, even in the middle of the Wilds. No way the Exile gets to out-stubborn her.

They find the one place where green breaks up the warehouse walls along the eastern shore, and Lady steps out lightly onto the bank, bicycle over her shoulder. Lady leaves the gun with Apple, since Jemma can't seem to shoot it straight.

Jemma pushes the raft into the water and floats slowly away with her sick cargo. Since she can move so much faster on bike, Lady will meet them a few miles downstream when she's done looking for the Zithmax.

They're in the wrong kind of place for medsen, Lady can tell almost immediately. There are houses in front of her to the east, but not the big ones. The bigger the house, the more the Parents needed medsen.

Lady smashes away the weak wood in the front door of the third house, the first to look good. She scans the tiny front room and kitchen quickly. Other than a vine tearing through a duct in the floor, it looks untouched—but it's not.

When she enters the bathroom, she pushes aside strips of wallpaper that carpet the floor like autumn leaves. The medsen cabinet is empty, just a moldering box of bandaids covered with pictures of a puppet frog. Lady sees a word written in the dust of the window behind her, so clear the window hasn't had a chance to film over the writing. She never could have read it before Pico showed her the ABC book.

"Hi," it says. Smiley face.

Gatherers already knew how to read, she realizes, even though she didn't call it that. The Parents had medsens for reasons she can't imagine. They had to understand the shapes of the letters on the medsen to know which would heal.

That's why she almost checks over her shoulder when she sees the words. It could have been written by some kind of Gatherer. It could have been written today.

There are soon at least six homes that no longer have a working front door, thanks to Lady and her anger at Li, her fear for Pico and Apple. But mostly she's racing the unseen Gatherers who have found everything before she did.

The other Gatherers seem not to care for food as much, so she gleans cans from the kitchens. She gleans tidbits about the mystery Gatherers, too. Strange bicycle tracks in soft dirt, heavy and rolling three wide. Two sets of footprints on a dusty floor. Every house put back to bed like a nanny with her Daycare brats.

The latches are newly oiled and locked. They want to keep the houses for themselves. These aren't Angelenos. Lady stops, feeling cold. She doesn't know *who* lives in the Wilds.

She's always been the last person to worry. The Holy Wood swaddled her perfectly and kept her from harm. But now, cut free from her people, she seems to worry all the time: About Apple, who seems to have shrunken in size in days. About Jemma, who carries weight on her that she can't release. Mostly, she's surprised to find, about the Exile. Because he holds their fates, yeah. Also because he's turned out to be a decent sort of runty know-it-all.

She finds them under an overpass downriver, breaking night. Jemma's face is tight and red, as if she's been thinking about crying.

"Any better?" Lady says.

Jemma shakes her head. "Anyone get better?"

Lady collapses in a pile on the ground with a grunt. She peels off her pack, reaches in, and tosses Jemma a can. "Peaches."

"No bulges," Jemma says, twisting the can in her hand.

"A whole cubberd full of em. Carried what I can."

Jemma doesn't say anything while she opens the can but speaks after the wheel cuts through the last thread of metal holding the lid with a *tink*. "You didn't go for peaches."

Lady lies back. Stars jut out of the clear night sky, wrapped by clouds on the north and south. She can't look Jemma in the eye. She can't even look at the piles of blankets by the fire. She keeps eye contact with the stars instead and tells Jemma that the good stuff is gone.

"We can look tomorrow," Jemma says, quiet.

"Yeah." Lady is just as quiet.

Jemma carries a can to Apple. Lady scootches toward Pico on her butt and peels back the blanket. His hair is doused with sweat. His eyes, when they open, look as if they're staring out from under the surface of the river.

The peaches don't look like peaches anymore, and Lady wouldn't know them if she hadn't seen the picture. She fishes out a browning mushy lump with her fingers and holds them over Pico's mouth. "Food for you, Exile," she says. The words are harsh, but her tone isn't. His mouth is open, and Lady lets a few drops of peach juice fall between his teeth. She can imagine the way the drops feel, sliding cool over a cracked throat, the way they'd make you want to swallow even when you didn't think you could.

Pico does swallow; she can see his throat move. "Good," he says, and opens for more. Lady gives him the whole lump. He chews, and the chewing seems to wake him up. He doesn't stop looking like he's dying, but he stops looking like he's dead.

"No medsen today," Lady says.

Pico shrugs. "That's too bad. Cuz I figured out my papers."

"Really?" Lady says.

The End came so fast, the Parents so unaware, that no one had time to write it in a book, Pico says. But that didn't mean no one was writing about it. Whoever was on the skyplane must have been a Doctor or an Older or something like that, trying to figure out what caused the End.

When she knew a little, she got on the skyplane to tell someone else. The plane fell out of the sky, and the secrets fell with her.

The first people who died lived in the mountains outside of San Diego. The End spread from there, and in weeks almost every Parent in San Diego was dead. Other places had it, too, spread by skyplanes and cars, but San Diego was first.

There are lots of words Pico doesn't know, like "government" and "scientist," and Lady knows even fewer when Pico reads them aloud. But one sentence catches them all. "'The disease attacks the brain,'" Pico says.

"What's the brain?" Lady says.

"I think it's in your head." They're all silent then, and Lady guesses they're thinking about the Malibu boy, Leong. He hurt his head, and he didn't die.

"But how?" Lady says. "What does it do?"

"I don't know. The people who wrote the papers didn't know."

"Is there more?"

"Yeah, but a lot of it's numbers. I don't know how to read numbers like that."

"Sounds like we really do need to go to San Diego," Lady says. For the first time, she's looking forward, not back to the Holy Wood.

"Everyone's dead there, though," Jemma says.

"Everyone's dead everywhere," Lady says.

Lady's eyes are the first open in the morning, and she counts the generations of bird's nests on the overpass in the rising light. They've camped under the junction of two great roads, and ramps soar high above them, curving to connect the highway. The curves are so perfect, the pillars are so high, that her breath catches a bit. *What is wrong with me?* she thinks. *I'm looking at Parents' stuff like Jemma now.*

Pico is next to her, but she can't make herself look toward him in case he's not moving.

When she does, he's not, and she shudders until she places her palm over his mouth. Warm breath washes over her hand and then stops. Startled, her eyes jump to his face—to see his eyes staring at her.

"Stop it, you freak," Pico says. "I'm still here."

"Good," she says, and gets up to find breakfast.

Talking about the End wakes Apple up from the sleep that seemed to be swallowing him. "What about the book?" Apple says. "The one the Half Holy gave us?"

Pico carries it in his pack, but he rarely opens it. He's focused on the silver case.

"There's not much in it," Pico says. "Mostly pictures." But he fishes the book out of his pack.

Apple follows the motion and Jemma follows him. Jemma seems tied to him by an invisible string for the past two days while Lady looks for medsen. The push and pull seem to tear at her so much that tendon lines emerge in her cheek, in her neck. They're so tight he can almost read her thoughts along the lines.

"Go," he tells her. "Let Lady watch us."

"I can't leave," she says.

"You can't stay here no more." He wonders if she can see something that will happen if she leaves.

Apple asked her about it last night. "How'd you know bout the dogs?" he said.

"I—I didn't."

"I didn't hear em. You was up and ready for em before they ever got close."

"I guess I saw em."

He knows that isn't possible, not the way they were both too close to the fire, the way their eyes were on each other. "Not with your eyes, though."

Jemma doesn't answer, but by the droop of her shoulders, he can tell he's right. "How do you see em?" he says. And she tells him about the Bowl, how she called for help from the gods and the haze showed her what to do. How she sees more and more visions in the haze and how they mostly seem to show her what is to come. He pulls her tight.

"You two," he says gesturing at Pico's blanket, "you two are a wonder. The way he understands the world. The way you . . . see it."

Jemma shrugs.

"You gotta get him safe, Jemma," he says. "You two need each other."

"I'm doing what I can."

"Do everything," he says.

Right now he sees a thirst in Jemma's face to do, to run, to fight, and he helps her act on it. "Look for some medsen," he says. "Go." And she leaves on the bike. Shortly after, Lady pushes them into the river for their long float to nowhere.

Apple feels the rough boards of the raft through his pants. That's almost worse than the wound. His hip throbs where the bear gouged him, but he's beyond pain. Everything hurts, everything aches, so he can tamp it down as long as he can focus on the puzzle.

They have the Half Holy's book between them. Pico is right. There are only a few words in the book, usually small ones below the pictures. Pico reads them out loud, but none of them make sense. *We're too far gone from the Parents*, Apple thinks.

Then Pico says, " 'The plague has puzzled sci—scientists, who say in its speed of death and contag'—I can't say that word—'that it acts unlike any other known disease.' "

"Diseases the same as fections? So are plagues?"

Pico nods.

A disease that surprised even the Parents, that was new and frightening to even the science people.

"Maybe it was made by the gods to punish the Parents," Apple says.

Pico raises his eyebrows. Apple knows what he thinks about the gods. "Maybe it was made by someone," he says.

"Like with magic?" Apple says. The Priestess says they used to have that kind of power, before the End.

"Or like cooking in a pot," Pico says.

A splash, somewhere across the river. The clean sound of a heron ripping through the water for prey, not the flop of a fish. Apple feels every movement and sound in his skin, twice as big as he would have felt it before.

"You two are loco," Lady says.

"Help us, then," Pico says. "End ain't gonna fix itself."

Lady jumps in, throwing out ideas about fections and invisibles. They float down the river with the sound of their own words drowning out the ripples.

Then the truce Apple's had with the body ends, and a lightning bolt shoots out from the point on his hip where the bear pierced his skin. He is dying, he is dying, and for a moment he almost wishes for the End. At least then he would feel the Betterment, his body knitting itself together one last time before it stopped.

"The Betterment," he says out loud, and only when the others look at him does he realize it matters. "What kind of fection fixes you first?"

"Hush," Lady says. "I hear someone."

Apple hears it at the same time and wills himself to stand. He can't. Still the voices continue: Jemma shouting, and someone shouting back.

CHAPTER TWENTY-THREE
THE LECTRICS

Jemma hacks through a park so thick that she immediately starts looking for higher ground. She wraps her arm around a tree to climb it—and then she sees something higher.

It's a bare metal tower, held together by rusted girders, nothing else. It stretches above the trees so high that she can't see the top through the leaves.

The tower beams crisscross like a basket weave. It's no trick to inch up one angled beam and jump to the next beam cutting the other direction. At each turn the sides push closer together, until finally she can almost touch both sides at once. She hooks one arm over a girder and takes in the Wilds. She's still in them, she can tell—everywhere to the south and west is a dirty gray, and two freeways rise up out of the gloom.

She should have recognized the tower. It's one of the Lectric towers, strung with wires flowing south in a line of towers. Somehow the wires ran everything in the Parents' world. Pico says it isn't magic, but how else to explain what it used to do? Or why the magic doesn't work anymore?

The wires are mostly still intact, except for hers: Some giant hand sliced one of them, and it tumbles into the greening below. It's inches from her fingers.

They don't work; they haven't worked for tens or hundreds or thousands of years or however long the Parents have been gone. Yet something draws her to the wire. When she touches it she feels a shock, a hum, and then a flurry of blue hazy images. They're the same kind of images the haze has been showing her, but when she touches the wire there are more. And they're sharper. Complete.

Jemma removes her hand, and they disappear. She follows the Lectric wire from pole to pole until they disappear on the horizon. The visions, the blue haze, somehow they're attracted to this wire. When she touches it, they must flow toward her like water through a straw. When she touches it, the visions are clearer, more numerous, than any she's seen before.

She imagines the haze, focused and strengthened by miles and miles of wire. It's like the antenna above the Holy Wood sign, designed to draw the signal of the god Teevee and share it with others. The more Lectrics, the sharper the haze comes into focus. This time it stays as long as she looks at it, and it slowly morphs into shapes: a boy with a faintly clinking bike hung with pots and fruit, a girl on a horse, a small boy in a pipe, cannibal after cannibal—

She gasps when her fingers burn and then again when something says *Hello.*

She touches the wire again, and the voice is gone, and so are the shapes. Are those shapes waiting for her along the Lectrics?

Someone is showing her the future, some god or angel. But can she believe it?

Jemma shakes her head, and the movement feels so violent it almost knocks her off her perch. She clutches the metal tighter and turns to the east. The houses meld together in a sloppy jumble of roof and tree, and it's tough for her to pick anything out of the mess. But to the northeast, she sees a familiar white van, two of them, lined up outside of a low building. Those look like ambylances. Which makes that a hospital. Maybe with medsen.

Jemma starts to climb down the girders, when an impulse makes her grab the wire again. Could she see the hospital from here? She can't see it with her eyes, but if she holds the wire and focuses, the Lectrics show her. In the haze she sees cars that look blown backward by a desert wind, a pile of bones crisscrossed haphazardly in the hospital. But the hospital is bare. No medsen here. Its empty shelves stand bleak in the haze.

She shimmies down the tower. Maybe the haze was wrong. Maybe there's another hospital after this one, or houses where the Zithmax still rests.

"Wait," the voice says. It's the one that said "hello," and just the fact that it's still talking makes her slump against the tower.

"I don't got time," she says.

"Wait," it says.

None of this makes sense, but Jemma doesn't make sense to herself anymore. Why could she never accept life in the Holy Wood? Partly bravery, partly fear, partly love, partly because it couldn't have been the life they deserved. But it was life. It was short and brutal, and she can't stop the friends she loves from leaving it.

I shoulda rolled with Apple, she thinks. *I shoulda rolled when we could.* In that moment everything she ever wanted is wrapped up in his touch. Maybe the Holy Wood doesn't know everything about living, but they know that: The touch is life.

You need to save him, Jemma. Not just to save him but to make it worth it. A little voice, small because it feels so disloyal, says: But if Pico could stop the End, would that make it worth it, too?

Did she want to live with Apple, or just want to live?

Then the voice cuts through the haze with the telltale buzz: "Looking for the Ice Cream Man?"

"Who's the Ice Cream Man?" she says, out loud. And she remembers the name from something before, maybe something Apple said.

The voice says, "You better run if you're going to catch him."

For a startling moment she catches hold of a hazy image, of a boy on a jangling bike. And she can see that he's about to cross the river, ahead of Lady, ahead of her. This isn't a future. This is now.

CHAPTER TWENTY-FOUR
THE ICE CREAM MAN

Pedaling after the Ice Cream Man is hard. The streets feel broken by a giant hammer, the pavement cratered. Cars rest deserted in the streets. Straight lines are impossible, and Jemma zigzags so tight that her right hip glances off a car. Never once does she slow down, just trusts her tires to hold the corners.

There are only two more blocks until the river—she can tell from the Lectric towers still flanking the water like onlookers. She slows down, not sure what she'll see at the river. Is she afraid that the Ice Cream Man will be there? Or that he won't?

When Jemma breaks through to the riverbank, she sees two things: Upstream, to her right, the low rectangle of the raft. Downstream? A boy on a jangling bike.

She rides downstream.

Closer she rides, and sees more details. The bike has three wheels, with a huge box slung between the wheels in the front. Tattered umbrella flying above, and so many things hanging from the box it's stopped being square.

Closer still, and she makes out the outlines of things. Two frying pans. A hose. A hammer.

She's so close now, she can see the boy's smiling profile, his pants cut off into shorts. He looks like he's thirteen. "Kid!" she says. "Ice Cream Man!" He turns, and she sees only half a mouth of teeth.

Then there's a rustle in the bushes, a stick in her spokes, and the world tumbling with her as she flies through the air. Then there's the pavement.

A smaller boy, maybe ten, emerges from the brush, bow and arrow in his hands, pink hair on his head, look of pure murder on his face. The haze couldn't have shown her that? She picks up her bike and backs away quickly, but there's nowhere to go.

"Ain't no touchin the Ice Cream Man!" The arrow is nocked, the string is drawn.

Jemma steps back even farther, the bike wheeling back with her. "That's—that's the Ice Cream Man?"

"You an idiot?" he says. "You the one yelling his name."

"Oh," Jemma says. "Guess I was."

The bow drops a little. She can see his arms shake.

"Hold still, idjit. I'm a crack good shot," Pink Hair says. She moves anyway.

He lets the arrow fly and has another one on the string before she can charge him. Jemma thinks it's flown wide but looks to her right in time to see her bike's front tire hissing air from a finger-size hole.

"You shot . . . my bike?"

Jemma has forgotten the Ice Cream Man, but now he's tinkling toward her in his box-on-a-bike. The box is covered in faded pictures of candy foods that once must have been violent pinks and reds and blues. But the pictures are hidden by a tapestry of hooks and hanging things: shovels and fishnets and shoes and pepper strings.

"Crack good shot, Alfie," the Ice Cream Man says. "You aims for the wheel?"

"Yeah," Alfie mutters, and from his tone Jemma wonders if he was actually aiming at her. Did he not want to kill her, or was he just not up for the job? Neither one of those thoughts brings any relief, with the next arrow even closer to her chest.

"You the Ice Cream Man, right?" Jemma says, throwing her hopes at the one who hasn't tried to kill her yet. "I saw you—I think I'm sposed to ask your help."

"You saws me? You saws the Ice Cream Man?" The eyes over the box sharpen.

"Just"—the truth is starting to feel deadly—"just from up the river. So I came running."

"Just comes runnin. And guesst my name."

"Just . . . came running."

"First time sounds like you believes it," the Ice Cream Man says. "Take the bag, Alfie. And her hatchet."

He opens his mouth and a crack and a clang drown him out. It doesn't hit Alfie, but she sees the Ice Cream Man ducking behind his box and a pot flying through the air.

"Pinky! Drop the bow!" Lady says, holding the rifle to her shoulder.

"No," he says. Brave or stupid. Probably stupid.

"I got a gun."

"I gots a bow. On yer friend." Or not so stupid.

"Box boy!" Lady says. "You in charge?"

"Yeah, I am," the Ice Cream Man says, head poking around the box.

"You wanna get killed, or not killed?"

"Not kills, I guess."

"Tell Pinky to take the arrow off his string, I put down my gun. We got a trade for you if you good."

The Ice Cream Man sighs, waves at Alfie. "It good, Alfie. Just keep em close." Alfie lowers his weapons. He looks mad, but Jemma thinks she sees some relief.

"Why's your head pink?" Lady says to Alfie.

"Oh, this," Alfie says, and touches his head. He slips off a wig, and underneath the wig is hair that's dark like theirs but not. It gently waves and, like the Ice Cream Man's, is streaked with blond.

"Matches my bike," he says, and wheels one out of the bushes, pink with white tires and tassels streaming from the handlebars.

"So . . . who're you, box boy?" Lady says.

"The Ice Cream Man. The trader of stuff, the finder of things, the drawer of the map." And then she remembers the traders Apple said he met at the Downtowns, the ones who had left Ell Aye and traveled the world.

The Ice Cream Man isn't the only Ice Cream Man, he says. His tribe is full of them, and boys and girls alike call themselves the Ice Cream Man because of their carts full of trade goods. They scavenge the Wilds for treasures. The kid, Alfie, acts as a scout.

"You took all the medsen," Jemma says, making sense of everything she's seen.

"The what?"

"Medsen."

"Yeah. The meds." The Ice Cream Man nods and grins. "You gets a lotta trades for that. Pigs. Loads of salt. Once I gots a baby."

Jemma freezes. "To eat?"

"No, jest a baby. To grows." He sees their look and stops.

"Why?"

"We dying," Alfie says.

"Not yours to tells, Alfie."

Alfie shrugs. "We needs babies or we don't get bigger. No more Ice Cream Men. So sometimes people gives us babies."

"Okay, Ice Cream Man," Jemma says, and steps up to the cart. "You got some medsen in there or not?"

"Yeah, I got some," the Ice Cream Man says, and the half-toothed grin sets harder.

"We looking for some Zithmax."

"Just fer you and your friend here?" The Ice Cream Man eyes them. "You don't look so sick."

"We know someone," Jemma says. If the Ice Cream Man knows that the boys are dying, they lose any leverage they might have had.

"I bets your friend's pretty sick, or he'd be standing there."

Jemma sees the situation slipping. "Look, you got some?"

"Yeah, I do," the Ice Cream Man says. "I just wanna knows how bad you wants it offa me."

"I could give you my ax," Jemma says, feeling its loss from her waist even as she says it.

"Like that?" He points at three of them dangling from his cart.

"Hey, them's your friends down there?" Alfie calls from the riverbank. He's wandered over without either one of them seeing it, and must be standing over the ramp. "Two of thems? That bunch of mostly deads under the blankets?"

They don't answer.

"The price just wents up," Alfie says.

"Okay, they're dying," Jemma says. "You gonna let someone die?"

"People dies all the time," the Ice Cream Man says.

"Not these ones," Jemma says.

"Tell me again what you gots," the Ice Cream Man says. The rifle is on Lady's shoulder without Jemma seeing it lifted, but Jemma's already jumping at Alfie, knocking the bow out of his hand. She picks it up and turns. The barrel of the One Gun is aimed at the Ice Cream Man's chest.

"This is what I got," Lady says.

Fear is there on his face, but not like Jemma expected—just a dusting across the brows. "If you trades, you knows the Ice Cream Man always carries an egg. Not for eats." He holds up a metal egg, battered gray-green. It looks heavy, wrong, even from where Jemma is. There's a ring at the end, and his finger is through it.

"What's that?"

"Gift from the Parents," he says. "You shoots, it falls off the pin into this box. And all your meds, all of the stuff you tries to steals from me, just . . . blows up. You know 'blows up'?"

"I can figure it out," Jemma says drily.

"But, good news," says the Ice Cream Man. "I think you gots something for trades." He looks straight down the barrel of the gun.

The trade takes forever, with Jemma trying to make Lady and the Ice Cream Man put down their weapons at the same time. When they finally do, Lady takes out all the bullets. "You ain't getting these till we leave," she says.

The Ice Cream Man digs through his box for several minutes, bringing out things that even Jemma hasn't seen as a Gatherer: a set of socket wrenches, perfectly preserved bicycle tubes. Finally he pulls out a decaying plastic bag wrapped several times around a small flat object. He peels off the bag and fishes out two packets covered on one side by a metal paper, on the other with bubble shapes. Jemma knows the packages from Gathering, but it's been months since she's seen one.

"This alls I got," he says.

"That's enough," she says.

"Enough for one," he says. It takes Jemma extra heartbeats to figure out what he means, and then her heart seems to seize in her chest. The space between heartbeats is filled with a brutal silence.

"What'd you say?" Lady says.

"Enough for one," the Ice Cream Man says. "Zithmax don't works so good no more. Takes more."

"But you told us you had—you told us—" Jemma fumbles over the words. To search for days, to get this message from the gods, and now this? Half a cure?

"I got Zithmax," the Ice Cream Man says. "You got Zithmax. Just figgered you'd rather have one dead friend than two."

"Puto!" Lady lunges for the gun on the top of the bicycle box and grabs it away. She digs for the bullets in her pockets and has one in the chamber before anyone else can react. The Ice Cream Man doesn't budge.

"Shoots," he says. "I gots what I gots. Now you gots to deals."

Jemma hasn't moved since he placed the packets in her hand, feels as if she can't ever move. She pictures the two blankets down by the river. One of those blankets might never leave.

"You want the trade or not?" the Ice Cream Man says.

"Course we want it," Jemma says, and saying so gives her power to move again.

She walks away from the Ice Cream Man toward the river but stops at the top of the slant of the bank. Lady walks with her, stops with her. Jemma can't look at the raft, or the boys next to it. She only sees the fading green of the water running away to the sea and feels the risk of running along with it.

Lady wraps up her arm, nestles into her shoulder. The feel of Lady's tangled hair against her skin gives Jemma something to grasp, and she comes back to that spot against her will. She doesn't want to be here, deciding this. She wants to be anywhere, everywhere. Not here.

"Could you pick for me?" Jemma says. Somehow if Lady chose, she could live with it.

"No," Lady says. "No, mija. It's not for me."

"Give me reasons, then." She knows she knows them, but she needs to hear them. They've escaped her somehow.

"Pico's sicker. It might not work," Lady says. Jemma nods. "Apple might get better. But then what?"

The reasons fly at Jemma now, too fast to grab them all. *Pico is smart. Apple is strong. Apple has always been there. That's not Pico's fault. Apple will keep us safe. Pico offers a chance. Apple's just for me. Pico is for everyone.*

Apple's my love. Pico's the answer. None of those are things any Child should expect to have. And still she can't walk down to the water.

"I don't know the answer," Jemma says.

"Cuz all the answers're wrong," Lady says.

That's when she decides. "We never get to be happy," she says. "We never get to want what we want."

Lady's face is still, her whole body is still, as if she's holding it in place so that no emotions will escape.

"No one gets to be happy," Jemma says. "But I will."

The raft is beached on a bench of concrete at the bottom, and next to it on the bench are the two blankets. She crouches in between them and reaches down.

Pico looks dead already. Would if he weren't still sweating. She checks his neck and feels a pulse, irregular but there.

"He's still with us," Apple says, stirring next to her. She's so grateful that he's still there that she falls on him, sobbing without sound. She wraps her arms around him, but he can't wrap back. He doesn't ask her what's wrong because, really, what isn't?

When she speaks, she speaks into his neck while he holds her. "I see things," she says.

"Like you saw the dogs," Apple says.

"Like that. Like lots of things." Still he doesn't look surprised. "Like this." She holds up the Zithmax packet, clutched in her hand this whole time, too much of a treasure to ever let out of her sight.

A look of wonder crosses over his face. He pulls her tighter. He would never admit that he's scared to die, that he's greedy to live, but it's there.

"The gods showed me how to trade for it, and when they showed me I thought it was cuz they wanted us to be together, to somehow beat the End. Why else would they show me?" She shakes the packet. "Only this, Apple, only this is not enough medsen for both those things."

"Ah," he says.

"So I . . ." Her voice trails off. She can't say it. But she sits up and starts to open the first bubble on the first packet. She has to give the first bubbles from each packet at once.

"Tell me," he says. "When you saw things, did you see us, together . . . after now?"

"I dunno what you mean."

"We riding the river together, we exploring together? Or is it only you?"

"Why you wanna know?"

"I don't," he says. "I want you to know. Whether this world is supposed to have me in it."

"Just cuz I didn't see it—"

"But you didn't."

He's the boy who waited his whole life for her, until she discovered she had been looking for him. They found each other now. She owes him the rest of that life.

"You gotta do it," Apple says. "You know it. You gotta be smart. Pico, he might be able to fix things. That stops if you pick me."

"I don't—"

"I ain't in your pictures. All this future you see don't got me in it. Pico, though—Pico gives you the future."

"I wanna be with you," she says, the sobs starting deep in her gut. This time they have an effect on him.

"Don't make me do this," Apple says. "Don't make me beg you not to save me. Cuz I want to stay."

"I'm not letting you go," she says. "I'm too selfish for anything else."

"I know that," he says, his face threatening to give way. "I know you, Jemma. But maybe you oughta really be selfish. Hold out for more than a few months with me."

He's right. The selfish act, for her, is to bet on her own life.

"That's just a trick," she says, sniffling.

"You got a chance to do something that no one has done since the End," Apple says. "For you, for Lady, for the whole Holy Wood. That part's not selfish."

"Maybe," she says.

"You know," he says.

Apple looks up at her from under the blanket, and with that look, that Child's look in an almost-grown body, she remembers: *My first memory is of Apple.* He must have been watching her in the Daycare, stepping in for a nanny. He handed her a bow and a practice arrow sharpened to a wooden point. Then, as now, she didn't really know how to use it.

She took the arrow in her hand and stabbed him in the thigh. He didn't flinch.

He doesn't now, even when he sees the motion of her hand, the look in her eyes, but something must fail for him at that moment because he seems to collapse, asleep, and is breathing deep and regular in just seconds. As if he can't stop it if he can't see it.

CHAPTER TWENTY-FIVE
THE MAP

Jemma is standing up when Lady reaches the raft, shaking, holding out her hand. "Give Pico this," Jemma says, with the Zithmax in her fingers.

"You sure, mija?"

"You gotta give it to him. I can't."

"Jemma—"

"Give it to him before I take it back." The packet slams into her fingers, Jemma's in such a hurry to get rid of it. Jemma disappears into the night along the riverbank.

Lady wonders if she did right, by making Jemma make this decision on her own. But she would have always chosen this exact thing.

Pico's head seems to blend in with the blankets. Lady touches him on the temples. "Wake up, Peek," she says, and thinks she's never called him that before. They haven't known each other long enough for a nickname that wasn't mean. "Wake up. We got some medsen for you."

A slow blink from the blankets. She puts her hand under his neck, feels it swallow compulsively.

The mouth is too dry and the pills stick to his tongue. When Lady pushes them down, Pico gags. Finally Lady crushes the pills into a swallow of water and pours it down Pico's throat. He gasps at the wetness. This time, though, the medsen stays down.

"Gods," the Ice Cream Man says, sliding down the slope and seeing Pico's face. "I shoulda tooks your ax, too."

The Ice Cream Man is back to a happy gap-toothed kid once he has the gun. He and Alfie don't seem in a hurry to go anywhere. Since Jemma has disappeared, Lady decides to let them stay.

They're good dinner guests, though, because the ice cream cart contains such wonders: strange spiny fruits, delicate dried meat, candy from the Parents still sweet in its wrappers.

And the stories.

The Ice Cream Men live deep in the Wilds, but they constantly move as they pick the buildings around them clean. They call their group the Fleet. They keep chickens and goats but trade for fresh food. Right now, they live in a hotel with two hundred rooms.

"Got so many beds, where your babies? You boys ain't up for a good roll?" Lady says, and then she's thinking about rolling. And then she touches the hairpin instinctively, and she doesn't want to think about rolling anymore.

The Ice Cream Man only smiles. "Takes two kids in a bed to makes some noise. When I gots there, all the ladies gone."

They return to the Fleet every week or two. Longer than that, and the Fleet could disappear. They used to have Ice Cream Men wandering around looking for the Fleet, so they started to leave maps for one another.

"Maps? You got maps?" Lady says. She never thought of maps as important before because she had everything mapped in her mind in the little world at her front door. This world, though, is too big to keep only in your mind.

They do, but the old ones are so fragile that they only pull them out when they're desperate. The Ice Cream Man marvels at Pico's plastic map, as clear as the day it was made, and then shows her his map.

"This is the best thing I'm gonna makes in my life," he says, leading her to his cart and lifting the lid. On it is a map written in neat pen strokes on the white bottom of the lid. She sees Downtown at the top, the mountains, the Palos peninsula, the lands below. It's the entire world of the Ice Cream Men.

"Pico and Jemma need to see this," Lady says.

At the bottom of the map, somewhere between Ell Aye and San Diego, along the ocean, are harsh bold lines, drawn again and again with pen to keep anyone from crossing. "What's that?" Lady says.

"Them's the Dead Lands," the Ice Cream Man says. "The Parents, they runed it fore the End. You gets sick you go in."

The map is a story of people, too. A group of warriors riding on horses like the Long Gone days, but the Ice Cream Man doesn't bother to explain. Lady's eyes are drawn to the low rise of the Palos, rough figures drawn with sharp blades and pale skin. "Them's the Biters," the Ice Cream Man says.

"The what?" Lady says.

"The Biters. You know, the ones . . . who eat people?"

"Oh, you mean the Palos," Lady says.

"That don't makes no sense," Alfie says. "They *eats* people."

"Wait. You trade with em?" Lady says.

The Ice Cream Man shrugs. "We trades so they leaves us alone. And cuz they useful."

"But they eat people," she says. "You just said so."

"Only sometimes."

Lady feels cold, feels rage. They see the face of evil, and they just offer it a frying pan. She wants to cut them. Then she thinks: *If we could get the Palos to leave us alone, wouldn't we?*

The Ice Cream Man describes everything without judgment. Nothing is good or bad. They're either useful or not useful. Dogs, useful. The people of the south, useful. Biters, useful.

But the Biters are growing.

"They're not just in the Palos?" Lady says.

"They never was," he says. They live in pockets between here and the dark black lines. The Newports are Biters, really good with boats. And people seem to be flocking to the Biters, even the ones that aren't white.

"They gots a new leader," the Ice Cream Man says. "They calls him

Little Man—I guess cuz he growns like the Parents. And he brings them all together. The Newports and Palos never used to talk. Now they do. And they works with the Last Lifers."

"You seeing Last Lifers with the Biters?" Lady says. She remembers what Pico and Apple said about them.

"Yeah," the Ice Cream Man says. "Moves south, maybe one Biter likes he's herding them."

"That seem weird to you?" Lady says.

"Any times the Last Lifers don't acts crazy, that's weird," the Ice Cream Man says.

"Them Last Lifers have guns?"

"They got guns, the Biters gots guns. They always gots lots of guns," Alfie says.

"You selling guns to the Palos?" Lady says.

"We ain't stupid. We sells to them, everyone gets mad," Alfie says.

"But they gots them," the Ice Cream Man says. "More and more."

"Jesucristo," Lady says. Think what happens when the Palos get ahold of a whole bunch of guns, when the Last Lifers are following them south? "You useful to em? That many guns, you gonna find out," Lady says. And the Ice Cream Man doesn't answer.

Jemma's voice comes from beyond the fire. Lady doesn't know how long she's been there, but she suspects for a long while. "What's ice cream?"

The Ice Cream Man smiles. "You seens ice?"

The hunting parties have seen it before in the mountains, but Lady's only seen it once, after a winter storm that froze all the oranges where they hung on the branch. They blackened and rotted, and for months the Holy Wood had to take their chances with the cans they found in the houses. One kid died from starvation, one from the contents of the bulging can she was unwise enough to try to eat.

But that winter, Lady found ice. A puddle lay before her on the street, hard and cold and almost like a mirror. She poked it with a stick and the mirror crackled around the tip. When she put the puddle in her mouth, it melted and her tongue went numb from the cold. She craved that sensation all day, but the ice was gone as soon as the clouds peeled away.

"I seen ice," Lady says.

"Thinks on ice, and thinks on honey and strawberries and milk. That's what the stories says it taste like," the Ice Cream Man says. "The stories says the Old Guys use to brings it to the Ice Cream Men."

"Who are they?" Jemma says. If she's asking that now, then she must really want to know.

"They Parents who still alive. They comes to the kids and helps and teaches."

"For real?"

"For reals," Alfie says. "But they gones now. Just tales now."

"What else you know about the Old Guys?" Jemma says.

"They real old. They smart. But they gone." *Pico needs to know about them*, Lady thinks. The Ice Cream Man still wants to talk about ice cream, and somehow so does she, about the sweet and milk and cold and the everything gone from the world.

"The Parents hads magic to keep it cold on the hot hot days. They mades it and carried it in these carts, and it's never gonna get mades until the Parents comes again."

"Until the Parents comes again," Alfie says wonderingly.

"Then it's lost forever," Jemma says.

CHAPTER TWENTY-SIX
THE BETTERMENT

By the time the sun climbs high enough to break over the bank, Jemma's sure she can see it, as if there are two buckets attached to a yoke. Every drop of life that goes into Pico seems to siphon from Apple. Pico's breath eases, Apple's struggles; Pico cools and Apple burns. How long before one bucket is completely empty?

As much as she wants Pico to be full and living, she can't help but hate him for emptying Apple. But Pico opens his eyes and sees her. He doesn't speak or move, and she's not sure he could, but his eyes are warm and liquid and, she thinks, grateful.

They agree to stay where they are near the river. The Ice Cream Man scouts out a Long Gone old gasplace a block from the water and helps them move the boys by draping them across the box of his ice cream cart. A huge awning shields the glass front, where three of the four panes somehow still hold. A palm tree splits the platform where the gas pumps rest, and one of the pumps has tipped over. Another palm grows up from the floor through a hole in the roof. They set up camp between the empty shelves.

As they haul Pico's stuff into the gasplace, the pack falls to the floor and the Half Holy's book drops out of it. Jemma doesn't think to hide it, because who else but Pico would know what it means?

"Where you gets that book?" the Ice Cream Man says. Jemma sees that it's opened to the gruesome pictures of the End.

"In the Holy Wood," Lady says. "Why?"

"Ice Cream Men finds em all over the Wilds. In big shiny places like the bookhouses, bookskins you gots to touch." *Libraries*, Jemma thinks. "Insides are End pics, always pics, on newy paper. They don't fits."

"Someone left it?" she says.

"They just waits on you to touch. People try to trades to me, but what I gonna do with books?"

And Jemma nods. What, before now, would they have done with books?

Then the two are gone, although she can hear the tinkling for minutes after the cart disappears.

"How am I still alive?" Pico says, sitting up. "Am I getting better?"

"We got you medsen," Jemma says.

"You Gathered?"

"We traded," she says. For everything.

Pico's not sure he'll ever move again. It isn't the sharpness of the pain, although it still burns fierce in his leg. It's the way the pain seems to be everywhere at once, even in the parts of his body that shouldn't hurt, as if the rest of his body were just feeling sorry for the leg.

The case rests under his hand, hard and cold and smooth. Did the girl bring it to him?

Jemma. Jemma is the girl, the sad one. There's a curly-haired girl here somewhere.

The boy next to him, wrapped up in blankets and sweating—that was him a day or a week ago. "Is the boy dying?" he says.

"His name's Apple," Jemma says.

Apple. And then he remembers it all. If Pico's awake, Apple should be, too. They were sick together. He motions to Apple, as if he could communicate all that with his fingers.

"There was only medsen for one of you," Jemma says.

Then he understands why Jemma is sad, why maybe she will never be not sad again. He's sad, too. Apple was the first one to trust a useless

Exile. He saved them from the bear. He believed they could find the answers to the End.

In the confusion, in the grief, Pico pulls back to the silver box. At first he can only rest with the case, dozing between breaths. He dreams it's being carried away, and he pulls it under his arm like a doll. No one will take it away now.

The mystery of the case breathes life into his mind. Those tendrils of wonder creep into his head, unlocking doors that had been shutting down, and consciousness throws those doors wide. He doesn't know when it happens, but his eyes are fixed on the case, watching his thumb as it flicks at the latch.

"You want some help with that?" Lady says. He's not sure when she came back.

"No," he says, still weak. "By the time I'm strong enough to open it, I'll be strong enough to look at it."

"You sure?"

"I'm not sure I'm even here right now."

She lies down by him, and he's grateful for the warmth against his side. He hasn't felt warm for days. "Still cold," he says.

"You feel hot. Wonder when your fever's gonna break?"

His fingers don't seem to be any better at the latch, as if they just can't get the feel for the metal. But he doesn't want to wait longer. "I was wrong," he says.

"What?"

"I want you to open it."

She opens the case and drops the ancient paper into his grateful hands. He's too tired to thank her, but he knows she knows he means it.

Pico can't focus on the words yet—all those scrawls require too much concentration—but having the smooth roughness under his fingers brings the words he's already seen back.

It attacks the brain. If the brain changes when you become a Parent, what if it doesn't change? Is that how Leong survived the End by getting hit in the head? Do the Touched die first because their brains are more like a Parent's?

The papers fall into the case again, his cheek against the floor.

It's noon and the sun through Long Gone streaked glass finally soaks through his skin. "Time for Zithmax," Lady says, her eyes studying his face, looking for breaks in his illness. She looks relieved.

"How you think Apple is?" Pico says.

"Bout the same."

That's what it looks like to Pico. If anything, Apple seems a little stronger.

Lady tilts a litro and helps him drink. "You turning into quite the Mama," he says, and is just alert enough to know he's used the wrong words. There's a flash of something across her eyes and forehead, and then it's gone.

"It's just that you a giant baby," she says. She leaves. Jemma left minutes ago, and it's just him and Apple.

Apple hasn't moved all day. By the way Jemma acts around him, she doesn't expect him to move again. He's sorry for it, but he's never been so glad to breathe in his life. This is why the End matters. Because not Ending just feels too good.

He flips through the papers, maybe too fast, because they blur dizzily together. He looks up to see Apple, tired and sickly but definitely alive, sitting up and trying to make sense of the room. He shouldn't be sitting. He should be dying.

"Hey, Piquito," Apple says. "You figure the case out, or what?"

The girls are closer than he thinks. One shout from Pico and they come running.

Apple is tired. He's been swimming in rivers of brea, fighting the current and the pull of the earth. It wants him under. The Last Lifer in the tarpit is there, small, smaller than Pico. She clings on to his shoulder like a snail, inching up toward his neck as he sinks into the brea.

"I got you," he says.

"You don't got nothin," she says.

The fight leaves him, and the moment he stops kicking is the moment he realizes he doesn't have to. The brea is thicker than water. It bears his weight and the Last Lifer's. He revels in the way it cushions his limbs. *You don't have to swim*, he thinks. *You wait for the current to carry you to shore.*

Then the brea is rift by fire, by streams of light. Whatever held it together separates as if he's tugging on a cobweb. It's not black and dank. It's honey, it's gold. He's Apple, and he will live.

Apple is awake.

He opens his eyes and speaks without quite knowing what he says, sees Pico staring back at him. Then Pico is shouting and Jemma and Lady are staring at him, too. No one expected him to wake. It makes him wonder if he's already dead.

Lady tackles him in a hug that almost knocks him back to his blankets. Her chin tucks in behind his neck, her curls covering most of his face. She feels real. He must still be here. "Jesucristo, Apple," she says.

"Was I gone a long time?" he says.

"Long gone," she says.

Lady steps back and for the first time since he woke he really sees Jemma. She's rooted to the tiles just inside the door. Her arms are rigid, her hatchet halfway up as if she forgot she was lifting it. Her face is rigid, too, like a cast she's made of herself. Nothing moves on the outside, but the inside Jemma threatens to burst.

Her eyes flare. She is sharp and terrible and beautiful—as the version of Jemma in his head has always been. And he's so glad he could wake up to her again.

"You came back," she says, and then she collapses into his arms, soft again. *Without my help* is the part she doesn't say.

"Is it possible to get better without Zithmax?" Jemma says that night after they light the fire. It scorches the tile floor. The smoke winds its way up to the hole torn by the palm tree.

"Clearly," Lady says. Apple already looks as if he's taken most of the Zithmax bubbles.

"Apple's a lot stronger than most kids. Maybe strong enough to fight fections on his own," Pico says.

"True," Jemma says.

"Could be," Apple says, but he wonders.

"I got some new stuff to talk about from the case," Pico says.

"Maybe not tonight, Pico. Tonight I wanna hang with Jemma," he says. With his girl? There isn't a word for them in the Holy Wood. There's nothing to describe what it is when you have each other.

Jemma's face floods with light and something else. She helps him outside, but he can walk pretty well already without her help. His leg feels better.

They sit on the hood of a car, a car built for speed like a falcon but now grounded. Ivy grows through the tires. The gasplace windows are lit up from the fire like a lantern. Any fighter in a mile could see the glow, a sign saying to come attack. "We need to move the fire back, make it smaller," he says, needing her to think more like a Muscle now.

Jemma nods. "That ain't why you wanted to come out here."

"Nah? Why then?"

"Cuz I didn't pick you. When you knew I was gonna pick you. You talked me out of it, and I let you."

"What you want, Jemma?" he says. Not offering her condemnation or especially forgiveness, because that she could never forgive. Just letting her say what she couldn't say the night she let him die.

"I wanted you," she says. "Even when I picked Pico."

"I wanted you, too," he says.

He remembers the feeling in the Stacks that he was floating away like a kite and the tug of Jemma pulling him back to the ground. She's the reason he's still here at all.

But now he feels planted, and when they kiss, this time, it's as if he's towing her in by a rope wrapped around his hand while her feet fly up in the air in a giant wind. She's the one who needs mooring.

"I wanna roll with you," she says.

"I wanna roll with you. I always have." But still—

If they don't roll together tonight, she will regret it. If they do, she will regret it even more, because she will never separate the rolling from everything else about to follow. Because, he believes, it soon will follow.

"Maybe tomorrow, when I feel better," he says.

"Not agreeing to anything like that," she says. "Gonna take advantage of your miracle cure." He understands. He's waited for tomorrow too often for this. No one in the Holy Wood waits. Nothing in him wants to wait.

"Tomorrow," he says.

She looks stung, but just a little. She kisses him so close, clings to him so hard, that he almost changes his mind.

"I been thinking about your visions," he says.

She sits back, puzzled. This isn't what she expected, but there are things he needs to say, words he needs to leave as a gift.

"They don't mean nothing," she says. "You know now they don't."

"They mean something. Mean the gods picked the right person to talk to."

"Why would they pick me?" she says. "I ain't that strong. I ain't that good."

"You strong and good enough," Apple says. "But maybe it's how you imagine the world to be. You see what it was before. You believe it can be more. No one believes like that. Maybe the gods come to you cuz you needed it. Cuz you opened up a crack to let em in."

Jemma's ribs move under his hand. He's aware that she's speaking in response but feels it as a vibration under his fingertips and not a voice in his ears. He smiles at her and his face seems to split. His body lurches—no, his insides lurch, falling through him toward his feet.

He's shivering when a second ago there was no cold. "Can you get me a blanket?" he says. Jemma slips into the gasplace, and the moment she closes the door, Apple staggers away, each step rooted in the ground while his shoulders wobble through the air. Like no earthly thing he's felt. This has to be it.

Wild images flash before him, outlined in golden haze. The gasplace right now, a cannibal shivering in a pipe, a boy on a strange kind of bike, a man from the Long Gone, with a beard and wrinkles. None of it from right now except the gasplace. He wills himself to find something real, and then Jemma's eyes are there. Squinting, brown, skeptical. Smiling.

Hold them in the center, he thinks. *Hold them.* They float above him, and he pulls them to his chest. Then he floats with them. The feeling changes.

The haze around the gas pumps floats like sparks from a hundred fires, falling on him with no heat and no terror. The sparks are gold. They look like something he's seen before. They cling to the hairs of his arms.

When he breathes, his lungs double. His heart stops pounding, stops pulsating in the night. The feeling—as if he's lit a fire in his chest, but it's warm and good and threatens to eat up all the evil in the world. The feeling that he's stronger than he ever has been. As if he can't be broken.

Tingling, too small to see, moves through his chest. He inhales and something sharp enters his nose, a scent come to life. His vision is sharper. He can see the sparks flowing through the sky. They stretch out into the night, until the sky is a web of glowing gold haze.

Then he knows where he's seen the sparks and the images before, or at least who has seen them. He has to get back to Jemma.

The gods didn't mean for us to feel this much. He never wants to stop feeling it.

When Jemma emerges from the gasplace, Apple is standing well clear from the car, slowly spinning under the stars. He shouldn't be able to move. He was all but dead this morning. For the first time, she's afraid of the healing.

"Apple, you okay?"

"Never better," he says, as if he's struggling over his own tongue. She draws closer and he points to his waistband above his left hip. He motions to her to pull it down.

She does. There, below the arc of his hip bone, is the ugly mess of the bear wound. But it seems to have disappeared in the firelight. She looks closer, and it's there, but getting smaller and smaller before her eyes. She looks at his shoulder where the lump of his broken collarbone jutted out yesterday. He's better. He's not supposed to be better.

When she looks up, she sees a mix of fear and awe in Apple's eyes. Hers would only show fear. She's never seen this happen before, but she knows how it works.

"The Betterment," she says. The moment before the End when your body becomes right, when it starts to fix itself. That's what brought Apple back from the dead.

"Jemma," he says, trying to hold her in the center of his vision. Every word seems to take everything. "The End. It's like your haze. But I see gold instead of blue."

"What?"

"The haze is like . . ." His voice trails off, distracted by whatever else is struggling in his head.

"Apple, I don't care about the haze, I—"

"Jemma," Apple says again, but something is wrong with his voice; it's tight and raw, then something's wrong with his face. Blood is trickling down his nose, down his ears. She can't mark all the changes in his body because soon she knows it will be much, much worse. He collapses.

His eyes are confused, but he can still speak. "I didn't—I thought I knew how—"

"Apple, don't," she says, sobbing and squeezing his hand. He gives her a strange smile. A holy smile. His eyes are kind and nothing. She knows what will happen, what always happens, but still she has to act it out. She will run into the gasplace, screaming, and Lady will pull out her bag, and they will try to stop the bleeding. They will chant and moan and finally close his eyes and light the body fire.

She knows all this, and maybe she just can't find the will because it's her Apple and he's fading. So when Jemma steps into the gasplace after kissing his lips again, she says it so quietly that at first the other two can't hear: "It's Apple. He's at the End."

CHAPTER TWENTY-SEVEN

THE FLAMES AND THE FLOOD

Pico lights a torch and drops it into the pile of smashed furniture under Apple's body. All his scars are gone, even the ones Apple carried from the lion. His body is straight and smooth and new as the flames ignite around him. Pico thinks: *Before the End kills you, it tries to fix you first.*

Why does the End try to heal you? And why don't you stay healed?

He's not sure why his head is still trying to solve the puzzle even when he's mourning the first person who truly grasped what he was. But that's how he's always dealt with harshness: by setting his brain to work. The body fire climbs. Emotion, so rare for him, creeps into his face. *Your friend fell to the End, just like everyone. This is the perfect time to ask questions about it.*

Jemma, next to him, is still and stone. She has cried for Apple, most of the night, but now that's done. Something about the grit in her jawline makes him think it will be a long time before she cries again.

It was Jemma's idea to set the gasplace on fire, with Apple in it—the biggest body fire they've ever seen.

"That smoke is gonna draw anyone in ten miles," Lady said.

"Then the gods gonna see it, too," Jemma said.

"It's gonna be really big," Pico said, almost apologizing.

"Can you think of anyone who should have bigger?" Jemma said, and smashed another chair. They piled the furniture and pallets up to their waists in the middle of the floor, doused it all with the sludgy remains of a gas barrel.

The smoke is sooty and thick. It billows up toward the clouds and rubs them out, till all Pico can see is black. If the tires next to the gasplace catch, they'll see it from the Holy Wood. It's a sign that says: Someone's alive in the Wilds.

Pico keeps his eyes on the blanketed bundle in the center until it's swathed in orange, until he's sure it's really on fire. The heat pulses against his face. It stings. It makes him feel clean. The flames burst higher, pooling against the ceiling as if someone poured them there. Pico turns away from the body fire.

"Someone gonna come soon," he says.

"Then we better get the hell outta here," Jemma says, turning without looking back as if it cost her nothing. He knows that's not true. He wonders if hiding it will end up costing her more.

The raft is already loaded at the river. Pico's not ready to ride yet. He has no choice but to float his way to San Diego, at least for another day.

The raft is too big without Apple sprawled next to him. But when he opens the case, the world seems to close around him like a cocoon. The puzzle insulates him from the absence of Apple, from the fatigue in his arms, from the pain and stiffness in his leg. Thinking always feels safer than being.

The bicycle tent will just let him sit cross-legged if he hunches. He hunches anyway to see the papers. He spreads them carefully across his lap and onto the deck as the mossy water slips away noiselessly beyond the rear bicycle's diamond frame.

"I thought the storms was over," Jemma says.

"Yeah," Lady says. They both move toward the end of the boat, talking over his head.

"Not up there," Jemma says. Pico lifts his head up to where her finger must be pointing. Angry clouds surround the mountains in the north, pushing them back into the ground. He can see the rain from here: long, gray streaks slanting into the slopes and the hills just below them. With the sun spraying down on the thunderclouds from the south, it's an odd, beautiful sight.

The handwritten letters step off the page for him now. Pico reads them almost as easily as he can read printed ones, but still—still, they make no sense. He knows what they are, but he doesn't know what they *mean*. He imagines these Parents spending whole lifetimes, two or three Picos, to get to the point where they could write words like these.

But yet—not everyone could understand the inside of the head, could they? He's seen enough in his books to know that not everyone studied these things. Science, they called it. Not everyone is a scientist. So Pico tries to find the parts where they explain things to not-scientists.

Those live on the edges, he finds, crammed into the white space on the edge of the paper in another hand and another pen. "Ask those bastards up in the mountains," one furious scrawl says. Next to the letters "TLLP" is "The Long Life Project." That one makes Pico squint, perplexed. One note gets repeated, over and over, underlined in red. "Why doesn't it act like a virus?"

He leafs through the pages absently but carefully. They're already starting to tear under his hands. Only being in the case has preserved them this long.

Pico speaks to the girls without turning his head, still watching the clouds. "They couldn't see it. How can it kill you if you can't see it?"

"You couldn't see the fection," Lady says, her voice floating over his left shoulder.

"No, but it came from something in that skyplane. It touched my cut. This comes from nowhere."

"You can't see whatever makes you an idiot," Lady says.

"Don't ever be nice to me," Pico says.

"She's only nice when you're knocked out," Jemma says.

The green rivulets off the back of the boat, the gray rain in the distance, the distant sound of seabirds—all make the papers feel heavy in his hand, his head heavy on his neck. "I'm going back to sleep," he says. "Steer this thing without me?"

"It only goes in a straight line," Lady says.

Pico curls up under the bikes, the papers barely making it back into the open case before he dozes off. And then he's deep deep in sleep, rocked on the water like the oldest memories of himself in Nursery. He looks up and sees someone who isn't his Mama, just some Middle on her shift.

The Middle in his dream rocks harder and harder, angry that her shift is lasting through the night. The Children hate the night, fear it more than almost anything. She rocks and rocks and rocks until he fears for his little body. Her face contorts with fear, yelling in his ear now: "Wake up, Exile! Wake up, Peek! You gotta wake up!"

Pico finds himself again on the boat, and when the girls finally shake him awake he's lying on his right cheek, facing upstream. The green is gone, though. In its place is a furious wall of gray.

"Flood!" he screams, and arms yank him through the tent into the middle of the boat. Jemma is staring down at him, terrified.

"You gotta move," she says. "We can't carry you!"

His legs are out of practice and they seem to be asleep. They flop woodenly on the deck. He tries to pull them under his hips but can't. "Help me up," he says, and sees the front of the flash flood almost on them. The rain may have fallen in the mountains, but the concrete river has pushed it here without slowing it down.

She grabs both of his hands and yanks him up, and he's standing unsteadily. But the boat is pitching now as the first rough water reaches them, and he can't stand up without Jemma's help.

Lady jumps from the boat and lands safely on the sloped bank. The flat bench has already disappeared, ahead of the gray wall. She reaches her hands out for him. "Jump, Pico!"

"You crazy?" he says.

"You gotta jump, Peek," Jemma says, her voice calm in his ear. "I'll help you. But we gotta get off."

"The case!" He sees it gleam from under the bicycle frames.

"No time! Jump!" Jemma says. And as he pushes against her to go back to the case, she throws him off the boat.

This would have worked better if I'd jumped. He flies toward Lady. She reaches out her hand. He reaches out his. Then he splashes into the water just as the flood hits.

The waves wash over him, push him down, and he struggles to the surface. The water is choked with mud and logs and everything the river has picked up on the way from the mountains. It roars around him in violent waves. Even when his head is above the water he can't see the shore. The sound is even more disorienting. It fills his ears until all he can think of is the river.

Pico is a good swimmer, all the Malibus are, but this would have been too much for him even if he were healthy. He flaps helplessly in the water, then decides to save his energy for thinking.

The walls of the river have gotten steeper, almost vertical. Even if he could reach the shore, even if he had strength in his limbs, he couldn't climb out. But the river ahead of him is clear, and he can float. He lies on his back and points his toes downstream so if he hits something, it won't be with his head. He watches for a way out.

The flash flood still rages around him, and he tries to calculate how long it can last. The concrete won't slow it down, not without trees and grass on the bank. But it can't keep on going to the ocean . . . can it?

The river sweeps under a bridge, and Pico thinks it must be slowing. He starts to watch for places where he can leave the water, and paddles closer to the edge with little flutters. The banks slope more gently again, and soon he'll be able to get out and inch himself up the concrete to safety.

Unless there's a giant trailer in the river blocking his way. Which there is.

The trailer is the kind that used to be pulled by a truck. It's been there a long time, wrapped around the pillar of a bridge, creased at the fold like paper but not broken. Logs and machines and everything the river has carried are trapped under its wheels. Pico knows that if he hits that jam, the water will wash over him and he will die at the trailer before the flood does.

Pico lunges toward the shore with everything he has, his body forgetting his pain and fatigue in the desperation just to live. His fingers cup together, tear through the water. Submerged reeds pull at his legs, and he scissors free. He reaches the bank but can't hold on to anything. The current tumbles him along the bank and the rough concrete digs into his shoulder, his chin, his elbow, his chin. He falls back in again.

A dark circle looms out of the cement, something with an edge that Pico can hold. It's a drainage pipe built into the side of the river at the water's edge. It comes at him almost too fast to grasp, but he does, with four fingers of his left hand, then his right. The metal digs into his knuckles, and he almost lets go. He stops to breathe and rest, then hoists himself painfully out of the current, the water sucking at his legs and threatening to pull him back into the river. At last he's flat on his belly in the pipe, gasping like a fish. His hands are at his sides and he's too tired to move them. Too tired to move at all.

After, he's not sure how long he was there. Minutes, certainly, though they feel like hours. When he's strong enough, Pico rolls over onto his back and sits up. He curls in the mouth of the pipe, his head and feet climbing up the sides. The pipe, like the others that puncture the river all along its length, is four feet high. At one time it must have been meant to drain water from the streets near the water, to funnel the water down to the sea.

Off his right side, the river still boils past right below the pipe. In a regular storm, this pipe would be pumping out water from the streets above, but since this storm was only in the mountains, the pipe is still dry. It will keep him safe until the storm passes, but there's no getting out. Unless—unless the pipe tunnels under the riverbank to a street beyond the river. It had to start somewhere, right?

Pico peers into the darkness, where the walls of the pipe disappear. If only he had a torch. Or his pack.

Or the case. For a moment grief swallows him as the river failed to do—he feels it as a real sensation, wet and cold. So many secrets, so many clues, and they've sunk to the bottom of the river.

A skritchety sound in the depths draws his eyes to the dark of the pipe again. A rat escaping from the flood, maybe, or a dog. He's not scared of rats, but a dog would be trouble.

The thing grows nearer, echoing off the metal until he's not sure which sounds are footsteps and which are just their echoes.

A human face emerges from the tunnel, white against the blackness. It's a boy, smaller than he is, younger. "There's no way out that way," the boy says. He looks more frightened than Pico.

He's short enough that he can almost walk in the pipe without bending. His clothes are as wet as Pico's. When he steps into the light, Pico starts. The eyes the light is shining upon are blue. He's heard the stories, and he knows where the blue comes from. He's looking at a cannibal.

CHAPTER TWENTY-EIGHT
THE CANNIBAL

They look like drowned puppies, puppies that just happen to be trying to kill one another. From outside the drainage pipe, they sounded like cats. Lady heard them while she ran down the riverbank and wasn't surprised to find that it's not cats but a tangle of boys rolling out of the pipe toward the river, throwing feeble punches at one another, and that one of the boys is Pico, trying to bite the ear off a cannibal.

She's not surprised because she believed, even when Pico floated away. Jemma looked grim and started to cross the river along a pipe, looking for their bikes. "You ain't gonna look for them?" Lady said.

"He's gone," Jemma said. "That was a waste." Lady could tell she felt the loss of both Pico and Apple in that flood.

"Not gone until I find his body," Lady said, and ran down the riverbank, following the blue of the barrels of the raft. If she can still see those, she's near his body. She caught up to the barrels at a huge jam in the river. That's where she found this pipe.

Lady dives into the pipe, grabs the little cannibal around the neck, and pins him against the side of the pipe. He struggles and spits until she pulls her knife. Pico scoots backward, deeper into the pipe.

"You trying to eat my friend?" she says, jabbing the blade at him. He goes limp, and she begins to think the legends of the Palos warriors are just talk to keep everyone in line. He's small, even for a kid. Eyes brilliant blue, unnerving blue. Hair, the pale yellow only the Palos have, shaved on the left side and long on the right. They're supposed to have tattoos for kills, but his wrists are empty.

"No no no," he says, his teeth chattering. She notices that his skin is blue. Caught in the flood, too, no doubt.

"Really?"

"I—I think he was trying to eat *me*," he says, and she has to look at the cannibal's face to see if he's trying to be funny. "He attacked me."

"I doubt that," Lady says. "He's been mostly dead all week."

"It's true, I was," Pico says from within the pipe.

Pico is shivering, and so is the Palo. She wants to question the cannibal, but it can happen just as easily near a fire.

Gatherers are good with knots. By the time Lady is done with the little Palo, he's lashed to a light pole while she builds a fire. She guesses that he doesn't mind being tied, as long as he knows he'll get warm. So she makes sure she builds it just far enough from him that he'll take a long time to dry.

On the other side of the fire, she lays out the contents of her pack to dry. No dry blankets or clothes, so Pico's going to have to stay near the fire. When she's done, she squats in front of Pico. "How you feeling, Exile?" she says. The name has lost all its sting, and Pico smiles at the mention.

"Weak," he says, and he's not exaggerating.

Lady speaks softly so that the Palo can't hear, and Pico does the same. "You so weak, why'd you jump a Biter?" She likes that name better than Palo.

"Got no choice," Pico says. "He came out of the pipe and he couldn't know how weak I was."

"You ain't that strong anyway," Lady says.

"And I ain't that strong anyway," Pico says. "But what if there was more Palos around?"

Lady freezes. What if there *are* more Palos around? What was the chance of a little Biter wandering around the Wild by himself? Jemma would have thought of that, would have put the camp in a spot that's easier to defend. Hell, maybe even put them in a house nearby.

Where was Jemma, anyway?

Apple's bowstring is wet, but it'll still shoot. Lady picks up the bow and an arrow and holds both in her left hand. She crosses over to the cannibal, facing the darkness so that nothing takes her by surprise. She avoids looking into the fire. Can't lose her night vision now.

"Where your friends, Biter?" she asks. They're facing the same direction, so they look almost like two buddies sharing a sidelong secret.

"I don't have any friends," he says.

She pokes him with her arrow. "I said, where your friends?"

The Biter shakes his head. "I—I ran away."

"Why you do that?"

"It's hard to be one of the Chosen."

"Who are the Chosen?"

"You call yourselves the Chosen? Someone feels good about themselves," Pico says from the fire.

"Why is it so hard to be a cannibal, Cannibal?" And Jemma steps out of the darkness, a bicycle under each hand and Pico's pack over her shoulder. She's soaking wet, too. There's no weapon in her hand, but Lady knows her well enough to know that the Biter should be scared.

"That's not what we call ourselves—"

"No one cares what you call yourself," Lady says. "You the ones who butcher people. Why you so scared?"

Jemma crosses into the firelight and drops the bikes. "Why'd you run away?" Jemma says.

The boy breaks down. "I can't be like them! They kill, and they—and they—"

"We know," Lady says.

"But you can't just stop being one," the boy says, and Lady can see tears falling in the firelight. "You got to run. I had to run."

"You a long way from home," Jemma says. "Why you so far away?"

"Raiding trip," the Biter says.

"Who was you raiding?"

"The Kingdom," the boy says without hesitation.

"They're powerful, right? You got a big army?"

"No, a raiding party. The Kingdom's got people along the harbor—and the water is ours. It's the Chosen's, I mean. I ran when I got to the river. I saw this smoke along the river—"

"Smoke, huh?" Lady says, sneaking a look at Jemma's face. No reaction.

"So I headed north. Until the flood."

"How many raiders?" Lady asks. If it's too small, this kid's absence is more likely to be noticed. She can tell Jemma is thinking the same thing.

"Twenty-five. Well, twenty-four without me."

"Someone gonna miss you?"

"Nah," the cannibal says. "No one wanted me to come in the first place. They won't come looking for me."

"You got a name, Palo?" Jemma says.

"Tommy," the kid says, and he seems grateful to be spoken to like a human. Jesucristo, he's so small, like the kids she used to watch in Daycare.

"Well, Tommy," Jemma says, in a voice so low Lady can barely hear her even right next to her, "sorry you got stuck here with us."

Jemma turns away from the Biter, and they both cross the campsite to Pico. Jemma takes her hatchet off her belt. It somehow looks small in her hands. Jemma turns to the Palo. "Really sorry." And lifts the hatchet.

Lady grabs at her arm. "What you doing?" she says.

"Killing the kid."

"What? No you ain't. Pico?" She looks at Pico, who shrugs as if he's being asked about farming. Couldn't care. Lady pushes Jemma away from the Biter.

"He's so small. Who's he gonna hurt?" She turns to Pico. "What the hell, Pico? Peek?"

Pico winces at her words, then his gaze hardens. "Do you know what I could do at his age?" Pico asks.

"Probably not kill another person," Lady says.

"That's what *they* do," Pico says.

"How do you know?"

"I had one friend," Pico says, "one friend in the Malibus, a kid named Roberto. Smart like me, but better at hiding it. Then the Palos came up in one of their boats with the white sails while he was fishing, killed everyone. They took him away, dead or alive, I don't know.

"So yeah, Lady," he says, "if I'd been strong enough, I woulda killed him at the pipe."

Lady looks back at the light pole and the tiny cannibal. He doesn't even look like he's trying to hear, just slumping at his ropes.

Pico can kill because he hates, because he's not always good at wearing someone else's skin. Jemma can kill because something died with Apple, and she knows she's expected to be ruthless. But the girl who saved the little Exile is still there. She's still there, but Lady has to wake her up.

"You ain't being smart," Lady says. "You being scared."

"I'm being careful," Jemma says.

"We don't kill people cuz we careful!" she says. "We kill people when it's the only way." She wants to add. *We work so hard to make life. We shouldn't be killing anyone.*

"We could leave him tied there and let the animals get him," Pico says uncertainly.

"That's just being a dick," Lady says. "Kill him ourselves or let him live."

Jemma says, "His friends could follow us, Lady! We—"

"You pendejas so smart, *so smart*, but sometimes you too stupid to know the way the world works. If the Biters are coming, they're on the way already, and they're not coming to rescue him. It don't matter if he's with us or not. What's he gonna do, drop some bread crumbs? You going deep into enemy lands. You don't know nothing about em. You got a Palo right here, who wants to leave, who wants to talk . . . and you want to kill him before he can."

"That would be stupid," Pico says. Thank the gods the kid has no pride. But Jemma . . .

Jemma shrugs, and Lady knows that look, one she's earned more than once. *You win. I don't agree. Now what?*

"I gotta check one thing," Lady says. "Two."

The tiny Palo watches her cross the circle. She's not sure what he heard, but it doesn't matter. She squats in front of him, locks on those creepy blue eyes. How is she gonna look at those things every day?

"You ever kill anyone, Biter?" she says.

"No," he says, and he looks like he's not lying.

"You ever eat anyone?"

He starts to shake his head, and she interrupts him.

"No? Not . . . just a little bite?"

Tommy flushes, and with his pale skin she can see it even in the firelight. "I—I didn't want to."

"How'd it taste?" She has to know, if this one has a soul, so she asks questions she doesn't want to know the answer to.

Unblinking blue, tired of hiding. "Like the world was ending."

CHAPTER TWENTY-NINE
THE PRISONER

When Jemma wakes in the dark, only one thought fills her head: *I drove Apple out. I let him go.* The night is still cold. So is she.

The Biter is tied to a kitchen chair outside her door, in the house she forced them to march to in the middle of the night. She hopes his arms are turning black from the rope. She wanted to kill him last night; she still does. Not because he did anything, not because she thought she would gain from it.

The death alone is what mattered. If she could take life from him so easily, maybe she has some control over it, after all.

The sky turns gray, then rose.

The bedroom starts to take shape around her: a musty landscape of statues. Someone carved ducks out of logs. They found the rambling, barely red house a few blocks from the river, on a gently curving street. They're tucked behind a high brick wall, tucked behind the trees, tucked away from sight. The house is dressed with split shingles, and as the paint has peeled away, the walls have turned back to forest.

Apple pushes into her mind in the still, and she pushes him back out with an elbow and a knife twist. She can't afford him there. The miracle of his return from death and then his true true unavoidable death—how could she have been fooled? She's angry at him, but not just for his death. It's that, with Apple, she let herself hope that life without death was even possible.

Pico came to her last night, when he heard a sound that might have been sobbing. But it wasn't sobs—just Jemma's anger. "I miss him, too," Pico said, rubbing her shoulder with the touch of someone who knows that touch is important but can't quite imagine why.

"You don't know nothing," she said, and turned away. No one gets to feel sorry for her.

Jemma thinks of Trina, who Jemma hated but who was so good at being Oldest. Trina, who hated Jemma but saved her, who must have lost her job as the Oldest when they stole the One Gun. Trina, who would never feel sorry for herself.

Trina would drop dead before she felt sorry for herself.

Neither will Jemma.

Pico disappears into the library almost as soon as they find it. The Parents in this house loved to read. Tommy sees him go, and asks Jemma, "Can he read?"

"He likes the smell of paper," Jemma says. She's determined not to answer any of his questions.

If the Biter is a spy, Jemma thinks, he might be the worst spy ever. He tells them everything, even when he doesn't ask.

"Where was you going?" Jemma says.

"North," Tommy says. He wiggles the wrist that seems to have been sprained in the flood. It's tied to the chair arms.

"North to where?"

"To the Towers. I could see them from our hill, and I thought I could escape there." He could see Downtown from his hill, just like she could see the Palos from hers.

"The Downtown people would kill you if you went."

"They live there?"

"No, they guard it." She wonders if she should have told him that. He doesn't ask that many questions but seems to get the answers anyway.

As they surround him in the kitchen, they find out more about the

Palos. Their numbers are smaller than they thought, no more than the Holy Wood. If the Angelenos combined, Jemma thinks, they could defeat them.

They dwindle every generation: They aren't capturing enough children and have almost stopped having babies. The other people they capture aren't allowed to breed.

"Why not?" she says.

"They're the wrong color," Tommy says, not apologizing. "The Chosen can't change the color of their skins."

"Why you all pink?" Lady says.

"*White,*" he says. "We was always white."

"Why you care about white?" Lady says. "Everyone in Ell Aye is all pieces of other colors. The old colors don't matter no more."

"We care," Tommy says. "I mean, my people used to when I was one of them."

"And now you're inbred and crazy cuz you only roll with the other whiteys," Lady says.

Tommy shrugs. "You ain't wrong."

"That why you steal other people's kids? That why you eat people?" Jemma says.

"The world was always ours," Tommy says. "We're just taking it back."

"The Little Man—" And Jemma remembers the name from the Priestess, maybe the Ice Cream Men, and she knows it matters.

"Who's the Little Man?" she says.

Tommy shakes his head. "Uh-uh."

"C'mon, Biter," Lady says, pushing him.

"The Head. The leader of the Cluster. You wanna stay away from him. He's dumb, but he's mean mean mean. He brought the Palos Verdes and the Newport tribes of the Chosen together. The Newport head said he wouldn't fight with the Palos Verdes peoples. So Little Man sailed to Newport to talk about it and cut off their leader's head."

"There's more than one of you?" Jemma says, a flare of fear rising.

"The two great centers of the Chosen world, Palos Verdes and

Newport. Newport is far down the coast, past the Kingdom," Tommy says. "Where there was riches and where there was boats, that's where we grew."

"How can you tell them apart?" Lady says.

"By their lances," Tommy says. "The Newports dip theirs in fire so that the shafts are black. The Palos dip theirs in blood. So Little Man is bringing together both the smoke and the blood. It won't last, though—too much hate between them."

Jemma hears something strange in the way he talks about Little Man. It's half admiration, half fear. Were they rivals somehow? This boy couldn't rival anyone.

"Little Man is bringing guns to the Last Lifers," Jemma says, remembering what Apple told her, what Pilar had said in the Waking under the influence of the haze. Pico walks into the kitchen with an orange.

Tommy falters. "That can't be true," he says.

"It is," Pico says.

"Why would we work with the Last Lifers?" Tommy says.

"Exactly. Why?" Pico says. "But we know you did."

Tommy shakes his head, and Pico keeps talking. "I heard it from a Last Lifer myself."

"I feel like we heard it from everyone," Jemma says, thinking of what the Last Lifers told Lady.

"The Last Lifers are beneath the Chosen."

"Perfect for you to put in front of an arrow in a war," Pico says. "I don't think you'd turn down a thousand new warriors."

"I just don't—I don't know anything about it."

Pico leans on Tommy's wrist, the one that's sprained. It's all the cannibal can do to keep from screaming. "The most talkative cannibal in the world, and now you don't got nothing to say?"

Jemma's never seen Pico like this, but she didn't know how much he hated the Palos until last night. "Pico!" she says, and pulls him off.

"I'm just trying to help," the Biter says, breathing hard. He looks at Pico with pure hate, and then, miraculously, the hate disappears.

"Cannibals're super helpful," Pico says. "Hey, Cannibal, what happened to my friend Roberto?"

A flicker passes through Tommy's eyes. "I don't know a Roberto."

"What, you take away their names?"

"No, the Lowers get to keep their names."

"Lowers. That your name for the people you steal? Your slaves?"

Tommy nods, and Pico says, "Well, at least they get to keep their names."

"There's no Roberto."

"But you stole him from the beach in front of the Malibus. I saw you."

"Some boats don't make it back," Tommy says. "A couple of years ago, the Lowers revolted against the captain of the Chosen. They killed all the Chosen but accidentally set the boat on fire. It came into the harbor, burning down to the water. Maybe your friend was on that boat."

Pico doesn't blink at the news.

"I'm sorry if that upset you," Tommy says.

"I don't get upset," Pico says. "I fix things. So if my friend got killed by the Palos, I . . . I will fix that."

This time, the Biter is the one who doesn't blink.

"I'm going back to the library," Pico says.

The library is no match for the big Library, just four walls and one room. But for Pico, who knows any book could unlock the past, it's a jumble of wonders. He sent himself in there to decode what he remembers from the case and finds himself distracted by the rows and rows of book spines. Each book inspires Pico to leap from one to the other, from cars to medicine to animals to poetry to planes. He doesn't understand everything. He feels like a Toddler. But his world gets bigger when he enters the room.

Pico floats a raft down a wide wide river, just as he did in real life, he swings from a vine with a boy in a white wolf suit, he creeps through a closet door to a lamp post in the woods. A heart beats under a floorboard. With every beat he feels his own blood pumping.

He feels giddy in here, soaking in this world that didn't exist until he turned those pages. He thinks Parents must have been in love with learning. He thinks they must have never stopped reading. If you could read, why would you do anything else?

The Long Life Project is harder to find. These Parents didn't read scientists. They have the books Pico is drawn to, but they mostly seemed to like soft books with shirtless men and almost-shirtless women. These books with their decaying pages come off the shelf in musty blows that hit him between the eyes with a headache. A few reads of those, and he wonders whether the Parents knew even less about sex than the Children do. Why would they roll with someone if they couldn't make a baby?

Finally he finds a stack of thin books, made of thin paper, with a thin red frame around the edge and "TIME" on the cover. There are thirty or forty of them, identical in everything but the picture on the cover. Pico handles them gingerly, remembering the paper that fell apart at the library. He thumbs through seventeen of them until he sees a picture: a man, very, very old even by the Parents' standards, and a boy just older than the Children. Their faces are merged together as if they're the same person at opposite ends of life. But it's the words that pull him in. "The End of Death," the words say.

The End of Death. If that's not what the Parents were seeking, then what was? A Long Life?

There's nothing about the Long Life Project, but everything about why it could have come to be. The Parents were as frightened of death as the Children are, maybe more—they lived generations longer than their descendants but spent most of those years trying to fight death, with creams, with clothes, with doctors' knives.

Death came anyway; they just looked younger than they were supposed to when it did. Until scientists started to believe they could find the cure by getting the body to fix itself. The body fought diseases by itself, and infections, but maybe it could do it better. If Apple was right, that the End started out as a fix, then it could have started here.

The last person the book mentions is a doctor, with a last name Pico can't read. "Someday the brain will be able to tell the body how to fix itself," the doctor says. The brain, that thing that's in our heads, where the End starts.

The doctor worked in San Diego. Also where the End started.

It's time to leave.

Lady has never done indoors well, and as their stay in the house stretches into its third day, the stillness and the stiflingness get to her. Enough to make her talk to a Palo. "What did you do there?" Lady says to Tommy, who hasn't complained about his chair.

"When I wasn't eating people?" Tommy says. Cannibal humor.

"Yeah. When you was taking a break from all that."

"Fixed stuff," he says.

"Like what?"

"I studied the Grown-Ups and what they built. Some of the machines are too big. But bikes, guns, pumps—

"Guns."

Tommy stammers. "A people who like to fight, they like to have guns."

"We never seen Palos with guns." Except for the ones who were bringing the guns to the Last Lifers, if Apple was right.

"Not until me," Tommy says. "Now that I'm not there to fix them, maybe you won't."

He's more important to the Biters than they thought, she thinks. Would they send someone to find him?

"Can I ask you a question?" Tommy says.

"Maybe," she says.

"Why'd you leave home?"

"Why do you care?" she says.

"I know Angelenos. They—there are a lot of them in the Lowers. And they miss their hills."

Jesucristo, I miss my hills, she thinks. The hills and the Lake of the

Holy Wood and the Tweens swaggering around the Circle not knowing they don't own it yet. And the babies in the Daycare. *When will I see the babies again? I could travel through the Wilds forever and never see another baby. Jesucristo, I miss everything.*

To him she says, "Sometimes they do."

CHAPTER THIRTY

THE FACE IN THE BOX

San Diego is southeast, but they will travel east and a little north first. That's because Tommy warns them of danger on the map. Jemma feels herself warming to him. He seems to want to avoid danger as much as they do.

"You go south, you're gonna hit the Chosen," he says.

"*Cannibals*," Pico says. Tommy ignores him.

"Pretty much anyplace east of here, you're in the Kingdom. Maybe even here."

"You scared of em?" Pico says.

"Course I am. I'm dead if they see me," Tommy says. "But don't think they're gonna treat you much better."

They stop at the river first to fill up their litros before the day's travel. Jemma slides down the slanted concrete bank and squats next to the water's edge, filling all their bottles while Lady guards the prisoner up top. The new sun sneaks over her left shoulder, starting to light up the opposite edge of the river.

Jemma fills up her first two bottles and turns toward the others. She stops. All three kids—Lady, Pico, and the Biter—are frozen still, their arms pointing toward the opposite shore.

Last Lifers on the far bank. A raiding party of five or six, she thinks, but that can't be right—it would be unlikely to find the Last Lifers so far into the Wilds without villages nearby to raid. As she watches, she realizes how wrong she is.

Last Lifer after Last Lifer makes their way down the bank single file. Not five or six. A hundred or more, lit with the half gold of morning. They're all armed, some with guns, most with lances or machetes, and in between are splashes of blond that mean the Palos. None of them look toward the morning sun, toward Jemma. It takes them minutes to pass.

When she finally dares to climb back up the bank, she's shaking. Apple had told her this was happening. Even Pilar's vision did. But now she's seen it.

"They *are* at war," she says.

"Yeah, but with who?" Pico says. And they move slowly away from the southbound army.

Pico is riding in a wagon. Tommy fixed it up, a rusting pile of red under a tarp in the garage. Lady pushed for her to untie him—"No one else is gonna be able to fix a ride for Pico," she said. Jemma resisted, but Lady was right.

The wagon trails Jemma's bike by a thin orange rope. She's the only one strong enough to pull Pico, as light as he is. Her legs burn early. Pico nests in the middle of a pile of books, although he doesn't look at them while Tommy is there. He's facing backward, supposedly to watch their rear, but she knows he doesn't want to let the Palo out of his sight.

Tommy walks while the rest of them ride, tied by a rope on his waist to Lady's bike. Because of the drag on Jemma, he can keep up even with his short legs.

After lunch Jemma starts looking for places to rest—Pico looks tired from baking in the sun, and she's straining to pull the wagon. They move at less than walking speed. *Pico better heal soon*, she thinks. *I can't haul him to San Diego.*

A wall of green looms in front of them—a Long Gone park overgrown into a wilderness, nestled against a crumbling highway.

It's the kind of park where they used to hit balls with metal sticks, where trees crowd grassy greens, where mansions cluster close like gossiping Tweens. It's the place now where animals live thick and dense. Even in the Holy Wood, they could count on these parks for game when everything else failed.

To their right is a thicket of white carts, almost like cars but smaller and with open sides. Jemma has seen them in the parks before, always next to the sticks. Half of them are toppled and falling apart. One of them is driven by a skeleton dressed in a rotting sweater.

"One last game of sticks before the End . . . ," Lady says.

"These carts are all over the Palos," Tommy says.

"You fix em up?" Jemma says, thinking about how Lady told him he repaired the guns.

"Nah, they're useless," Tommy says.

"I don't know bout that," Pico says. "Nothin's completely dead."

"These are."

There's a stiffening in Pico's shoulders, and Jemma sees the challenge in his face. He nods toward the carts, and Jemma tows him closer so that he can look. "Leave me here," Pico says.

"We ain't leaving you here, Peek," Lady says.

"Check out the park and come back for me," Pico says, already trying to lift up the hood of the closest cart.

Tommy tugs on the end of his rope, and Lady jerks him back. "Not you, Cannibal," she says. "Unless you wanna give Pico another chance to kill you."

They leave their bikes with Pico, along with a hatchet and a stick that will let him pole around the carts in his wagon. They move into a long meadow surrounded by sycamores. Scars of game paths cross the meadow, as if this were under heavy use. Lady takes the cannibal's rope while Lady pulls out Apple's bow.

"This don't look like deer country," Lady says, and when Jemma looks closer, she sees she's right. Deer eat nuts and leaves and buds and flowers, but they don't usually touch grass. This grass looks as if it were mowed, and the parts that aren't are trampled flat. Droppings as big as plates cover the grass.

Lady nudges her, then points up the meadow to the creature walking right through the middle of it.

It's bigger than any deer, almost as big as the bear, with longer legs. Black and white, with heavy horns and heavy boobs that swing between its hindquarters. She's never seen it before, but she recognizes it from the brightly colored picture in the ABC book.

"C is for cow," Jemma says, before realizing the Palo is there.

"You can read?" he says, but she ignores it. Lady lifts her bow.

The cow turns sideways and it's almost like shooting a car, it's such a big target. Even Jemma could hit it. But something is strange about it. "That's someone's cow, Lady," she says.

"What?"

"Someone wrote on its butt." Behind the black-and-white cow, she sees more cows walking toward them: red, brown, all black. As if someone were herding them.

"They ain't here," Lady says. Her arrow flies right into the cow's heart, but cows are bigger than deer and maybe even horses, and it doesn't fall. It bellows in panic. It staggers and bleats and still it doesn't fall, until Lady puts a second arrow in its heart and a third in its neck.

"What did you do?" the Palo says, at the end of his rope. He's breathing hard. Anyone in a mile could have heard the cow.

They creep through the meadow toward the cow, as if they expect it to spring back to life. When they reach its flank, somehow still twitching in the sun, they see the letter burned into the hide.

Tommy pokes at the letter with his feet. "K is for Kingdom," he says.

Jemma thinks, just for a flash: *He knows his ABCs, too.*

"I'm eating it either way," Lady says. Jemma nods, because they really could use the meat.

They tie the cannibal's rope to a tree next to them. Jemma slits the cow's throat in the thick neck—so much more powerful than a deer, she thinks—and drains the blood while Lady carves a line from tail to chest. Even though they weren't Hunters in their village, they helped butcher the animals that the Hunters brought home.

"They got extra stomachs!" Jemma says as they pull out the guts. "Jesucristo, what is this thing?"

Their arms are deep in the cow when they hear the sound of hooves. They've heard horses before in the Wild, so they're not alarmed, just curious.

Then a horse bursts into the meadow, twenty yards away—and there's a girl on her. *Children don't ride horses*, Jemma thinks. The horse pulls up in front of them, stamping its feet, but all Jemma really sees is the rider. Her skin is about the same color as the Angelenos', and her hair flows backward in long, thin braids tied so close to her head that her scalp shows between rows. She carries rope in a coil at her waist. Just as Jemma knew she would.

"I seen her before," Jemma says.

"You seen her? How?" Lady says.

"In a sorta dream."

The rider speaks, her voice formal, as if the Parents were still talking. "Trespassers, you have killed a cow in the forest of the King," she says, "and the penalty is death. You'd better run."

Six other riders, in black wide-brimmed hats, emerge from the brush. "I didn't see this part," Jemma says.

They run.

Tommy runs until a rope jerks him short, a rope anchored by heavy balls at the ends so they can be thrown by the riders. A rider scoops him up and Jemma sees his blond hair flopping over the back of a saddle.

Jemma with her long legs and Lady with her stubborn speed make it farther. They bound toward the trees, and more hooves pound closer.

Jemma feels something wrap around her neck, cutting off her breath with coarse, ropy squeezes. Something punches her in her chest. Then something whips around her legs, tying her together and pitching her forward on arms she has suddenly forgotten how to use.

Lady runs past her but turns back when she sees Jemma fall. Jemma curses her friend's loyalty right now. "Go! Get help!" she shouts, before remembering that the only help is Pico, lame Pico. Then a rope spins through the air, three arms of rope with heavy balls at each end. It catches Lady around the ankles, and she hits the ground so hard Jemma worries that her neck will break.

The two of them are trussed on the ground, just feet apart. Hooves approach, and Jemma can just see them from the corner of her eye: brown, with just a brush of white across the toe.

Jemma wants to bite her tongue, to appear brave. But being brave doesn't keep you alive. She opens her mouth and screams and screams.

The rider dismounts, steps between them. Jemma sees the rider's face, not unkind, staring at her. "Honey, you have to shut up," the rider says. "We have work to do."

Jemma just keeps screaming.

"Okay," the rider says, shrugging her shoulders. And hits Jemma in the head with the butt of a whip.

By the time Pico hears the cow and the screams and hobbles toward the meadow, he's too late. He sees the riders, and his friends and his enemy slung over the horses' backs like blankets.

The only weapons he has are the hatchet and his stick. All he has is Lady's bike. Even with those, he's too small and still too sick to do any damage. The riders head out of the park, and his mind is already out there with them.

You can't save em like this. If you charge in, you all gonna die.

The girl finds herself in blackness, flying as much as falling. With no walls, no landmarks, she can't tell if she's even moving. There's no fear, because there's no bottom.

Her left hand scrapes against the wall and there's a trail of blue sparks. Not sparks. Stars. The blue flares and fills the blackness with light, and then it's gone again.

She reaches out with both hands, and her fingers brush the sides, trailing fire. She slows. The sparks grow brighter. It's the haze, but different somehow. Where the haze was in her world before, trying to assume the shapes she would recognize, she seems to be in its world. The sparks start flowing past her, as if she could ride it like a river.

She's inside the haze. Is she trapped inside a Lectric?

No, she's in a nothing, with no true walls or sides. It's a place in between. She becomes aware of outlines in the haze, alerting her to presences. People. They're people. She can see their shapes. They're near her but they don't know she's there.

Except for one, a boy. He looks familiar. He's watching her. The Palo? He shouldn't be inside the haze, but he is. He doesn't try to talk, he just watches. She shivers, and the motion sends tremors through the haze.

The glows is brighter in front of her, and she pushes toward it. There's a box floating in the air, a little smaller than a Teevee screen. It looks almost like a picture frame, but inside of it, there's a man.

A man.

Not a kid, not a ghost, a real man. What the Ice Cream Men called the Old Guys. He can't be real. But he's more sharply defined than anything else she's ever seen in the haze. She pokes her head through the frame.

He's seated at a table and looks up, startled. "That computer doesn't work," he says.

"What?" another voice says.

"That computer hasn't worked in ten years," he says to someone off to his side. "Something's wrong." She can't quite focus on his face, but he has hair on it. His face looks wrinkled, but somehow still youthful, as if someone had overlaid a child's face over one of the Long Gone Parents.

"A compo what?"

"It's still talking to me," the Old Guy says.

"I ain't an it," she says.

"You're not a glitch, are you?" he says.

"No, I'm—" She remembers that she has a question for him. "Do you know the End?"

Some sort of realization passes over his face, even as it goes in and out of focus. She's losing her hold on the room. "Where are you?" he says.

"I—I need to go back. This is in-between."

"This is real," he says. "Who are you?"

"I'm—I'm Jemma," she says. And the knowing is enough to drag her back into the day.

CHAPTER THIRTY-ONE
THE RIDERS

Lady can't think of a less comfortable way to travel. Her arms are tied behind her, her ankles are tied together, and all of her is tied to the back of a horse that, as far she knows, learned how to walk from an earthquake.

The riders aren't there for them. They're there for the cows. Lady has to hang on while they roust the cows out of pockets of green.

"What you doing?" Lady asks the rider, who's only a long muscled leg in Lady's eyes. She doesn't answer at first, but even riders must get tired of not talking.

"We're pulling the cows out," the rider says, after minutes of silence. Lady heard someone call her Tashia. "They've been grazing for the past few months in the Wilds. These went wider than usual. Springtime is when we bring them home."

"Where's home?"

"Oh, honey, you do not want to find out where home is," Tashia says. "Because that's where someone is going to have to kill you."

By the time the riders are done, there are maybe thirty cows. One drags the dead cow on a triangle-shaped litter behind her horse. The cows blink at Lady with a calm curiosity, as if she's just another creature from the wood.

The roundup—that's what Tashia calls it—is bigger than just those cows. As they ride out of the park, they're joined by individual riders and groups of five, six cows at a time. They come from alleyways, from front lawns where they graze on close-cropped Parents' grass, from parking lots where the vegetation has run wild. All of them have the K.

The cows swell in numbers, from the dozens in the park to twice that. They drive down the main street, under the red and blue of a gasplace awning, black hides brushing against the pumps. Past cars, past Parents in cars, past orderly rows of palms, past libraries and hospitals and abandoned stores. Even hanging from Tashia's horse, Lady can see new herds pushing in from the dead ends and the parking lots.

Some of the animals have horns, and when their horns toss near Lady she jerks her head back. The hooves clatter on the pavement, the cattle moan, and it all builds in volume until Lady can no longer hear Tashia's halfhearted responses to her questions. It's the most noise she's ever heard outside of a thunderstorm.

These streets were never intended for cows, Lady thinks, with the tiniest of thrills, pushed down by her pain. *This mess of smelly, noisy life whirling down the pavement was only intended for machines. The Parents never planned this, and yet we are here, in the middle of cows, slung on the back of a horse.*

If only I could get off the horse.

Jemma is still unconscious, a little blood on her temple. Their heads jostle close together, and Lady can see that she's still breathing. The cannibal is awake and seems to not notice the fact that he's strapped to the back of a horse. He chats up his rider, asking him about the herd and the roundup and their weapons, the ropes that tangled their feet.

"Bolas," the rider says. "For the cows."

That word means "balls" in the Holy Wood, and Lady can see why. Each rope is actually three ropes tied together, heavy stone balls at each end. The riders fling them at runaway cows, the balls whirling through the air until they wrap the legs and the cows trip and fall the way Lady did. But how did the riders discover those?

"We only killed a cow," Lady says to Tashia, after a while longer.

"You killed one of *our* cows," Tashia says.

"So?"

"So, honey, you'd have been better off killing one of our kids."

There's nothing in her voice to give Lady any hope. But the moment Lady felt that rope bite into her arms, she stopped hoping anyway. Still, she has to keep talking, and there's so much to know that it's easier than she thought.

"What's a king?" Lady says. "Is that like a Kingdom?"

"You never heard of a king?"

In the ABC book Pico and Jemma showed her, a king starts with K. But she doesn't know what they do.

"He's in charge of the Round Table and the Knights."

"So—furniture in the night?"

"No, Knights. Warriors. They meet at the Round Table."

Lady's confusion must come through in her silence, because Tashia laughs. "Poor kid. You'll meet them soon enough."

Lady feels some tension in the way Tashia talks about the Table, and she pokes at the weak spot. "The Knights better than the riders?"

"No, those idiots aren't better than us. We're the cowboys. Cowboys make this Kingdom. The Knights just take—" But Tashia stops herself, looks over her shoulder warily. Lady can't tell if she's eyeing her or the other riders.

"Can a cowboy be a . . . a Knight?"

"You have to win a fight with another Knight in order to become a Knight. But . . . why would you want to?" The question is for herself, not for Lady.

Ahead Lady sees something she never thought she would see here: a mountain, covered with snow. It's smaller than she imagined, but undeniably a mountain, pushing up from the ground like the beak of a giant. Snow has dusted the mountains in the distance, but never so close. She's drawn to it with a sort of hunger that feels like home.

"What the hell is that?" she says.

"End of the line, honey," Tashia says. "Home."

The road opens up to their right into a giant plaza, and the cows wheel toward it, making temporary lines in the herd like spokes. The cowboys ride along the left flank to move the slower cows onward.

At first Lady thinks she's in an old mall, the trading place of the Parents. But this is different. A concrete track mounted on columns passes overhead. The thing on it is like the baby of a train and a skyplane, sleek with metal sides that drop down on each side of the single rail. It's maybe twenty feet long, the first car in a train that's mostly missing. It's a relic of the Parents, some imagined tomorrow the Children will never see. And it's towed by four cows.

The cows tug against wooden yokes tied to thick ropes that angle up to the front of the train. Where there must have been glass, the windows are covered with wooden slats, and cabbages show through. The drivers sit at the front of the little train in a sort of nest. That window is completely gone, and the drivers' nest juts out like a lower jaw. With its faded red paint and the ribs where the windows are missing, the whole thing looks like a boiled and cracked crawdad.

Tommy's eyes widen. Tashia doesn't wait for their questions. "The Mono," Tashia says. "It sat there my whole life, but Grease got it moving. It carries food and stuff between the Kingdom and our sleeping place."

To their right is a huge hotel. When their beds wore out, Parents would buy new ones in these buildings, hundreds of people at a time, and stay there until their beds were fixed again. The Children of the Kingdom have taken it over; there are clothes and bedding drying out the windows and the shouts of Toddlers from the courtyard below. An entire village or three could fit in it. It looks as if they do.

Another sweep to the left, toward the mountain. They're facing a wall maybe ten feet high, stretching to the right and left as far as she can see. The original wall was a spiked fence, but now it's backed with paving stones and concrete chunks. The gate is another kind of train, with rubber tires, covered with heavy metal plates in a sloppy patchwork. The closer she looks, though, she can tell that the patchwork works—there isn't more than a finger's gap between the plates. She sees bullet holes and spear scratches in the steel.

"Bring the cows in," Tashia says to three of her riders. "Tell them we're six short, one of them killed by these fools. We'll go look for the rest tomorrow when our herd gets counted." And the riders take the cows through the gates behind them, into a parking lot ripped up and replaced by pasture. A broken scaffold of steel—some kind of train track that went in a loop?—rises above the pastures, where she can see hundreds of cows.

Tashia and the rest of her riders stop at the gate. Rifle barrels poke through slits in the gate. On three of the poles on the fence behind are heads with white skin and blond hair shaved on one side. She spares a look at Tommy to see if he reacts to it—and he doesn't—but mostly she thinks about herself and Jemma. A person who will put a head on a pole probably doesn't care what color it is.

The barrels swivel to point at them. If she thought she lost hope when she felt the ropes tighten, she knows she's really losing it now. She instinctively jerks her hand to touch the pin in her hair, but they're tied.

"Cowboys at the gate!" Tashia calls, never turning her head to look at the guns. She carries herself with a surety that Lady can't imagine. "Cowboys at the gate, with prisoners for the King."

"Name yourself, cowboy," a voice booms from behind the gate.

"It's Tashia, jackass. Are we going to do this every time I come to the gate? Because if we are, I can make sure you're not getting any more meat."

"So hard to get good help," Lady says.

"Sorry, Tashia." The voice is smaller this time. "Who are your prisoners?"

"Two cow thieves. And a Biter."

"Good. I'll take them to the King."

"No, *I'll* take them to the King," Tashia says. "There's no way you're getting credit for this."

"Okay." There's silence behind the gate, and no movement.

"You want your dinner?" Tashia asks. "Open the damn gate!"

There is the sound of latches being thrown, the creaking of wheels, and the gate slides slowly to the right. When the opening is five feet wide,

Tashia rides through and the other riders follow her. Lady can't quite make them all out, but the rider pulling the cow is right behind her, followed by Jemma's rider and Tommy's. Jemma's eyes are open. That's one less thing to worry about.

As they trot past the gate, Lady sees how the gate works. Four sturdy kids push the train from a waist-high bar attached to the train at each end. Gunners sit inside the train itself, protected from incoming fire by the narrow slit and thick iron plating bolted to the fence. Who taught them how to make these things?

In front of them is a stately building of red brick. People and gun barrels are silhouetted on the roof line. She takes a closer look at the gunners on the gate, the sentries on the buildings. These people are at war against the Biters. The only question is, have they always been, or is this new?

The riders duck to the right under a small overpass—it, too, ready to be closed off with a gate if someone breaches the first wall—and then they're in a plaza in front of a small city street. The top floors of the buildings get shorter as they go, as if someone wanted the street to seem longer. She hears babies crying above one of them.

At the end of the street is . . . a castle.

Pico showed her a picture of a castle when he was trying to explain the Kingdom, but even he didn't know what it was. It was just a Long Gone story, old even in the Parents' time. The building has heavy stones, a tall spiked roof. It doesn't belong in Ell Aye.

Tashia laughs when she sees her expression. "What, you think we had a Kingdom and no castle?"

The plaza and the street have been torn up, the ground turned into soil. Horses and cows graze nearby. At the center of the plaza is a patch of peas, protected by an ornate steel fence, and in the center of that is a statue of a man holding the hand of a child-size mouse. She's seen that mouse before, in the houses where she's Gathered, but she doesn't know what it means.

Except for the hooves and the strange buildings, the compound feels a lot like an Angeleno camp. Little ones race past on tricycles. Middles tend the crops. Tweens sneak away to kiss behind a sign. Everyone stops what they're doing to stare at Tashia and her strange cargo. Lady feels a pang of homesickness. So good to see so much life.

"You don't get a lot of visitors, huh?" Lady says.

"We usually shoot them before they get to the front gate."

They clatter to the front of the castle, across a bridge flanked by two ponds. The ponds are full of fish. Girls—not boys—are dipping in with nets to catch them. Two heavy doors, studded metal, block their way.

"Cowboys at the gate!" Tashia says again. "Prisoners for the King!"

Lady hears a shout back, but the doors don't open. They wait for what seems like an hour. Tashia shifts from side to side next to her.

Then hands are on her, loosening her legs but not her arms. They untie her from the saddle and yank her to the ground. She's standing almost without noticing it, and feels needles racing into her legs.

Lady is stamping the life into her legs when she sees Jemma slide down the side of the horse as if she were poured, all limp and liquid. She hits the ground hard.

Lady bolts toward Jemma before she has a chance to think it through—what would she do without hands, anyway?—and is stopped by a gun butt to her shoulder. She drops to the ground, two feet from Jemma. Jemma stirs, lifts her head, and Lady starts to lift her own.

It's Tashia who crouches between them. "You have to be more careful," she says. "People are gonna think you're trying to escape."

Tashia pulls them both up. Jemma wobbles, but this time she's able to stand. She looks around her uncertainly but catches Lady's eye. *How'd we get here?* her eyes ask.

"The Kingdom," Lady says, quiet.

"You're about to meet the Round Table," Tashia says. "Time to stand up real straight."

Suddenly the front doors bang open, pushed by a clot of kids carrying swords. They look similar to the Holy Wood Muscle, maybe a little taller and broader. They wear their hair short, shaved along both sides.

A tower of a kid leads the way, six feet tall with a scar from left eye to scalp. Lady thinks he's the leader, but he's only the tip of the spear. The rest of the boys walk close together, guarding something in the middle, but she can't see what. Or who.

When they reach the captives, the spear formation opens and a boy steps forward. He's smaller than the boys in front, but his knuckles are split with the scars of many fights. His cheekbones are sharp, his eyes are sharp, and everything seems to flash when he speaks.

"Tashia," he says, his voice higher than Lady expected, but with a scratch in it, "who are these trespassers? Why are they bothering the King?"

"They killed a cow in the King's forest," Tashia says. Lady notices how carefully Tashia is keeping her tone free of accusation, even as the words accuse. She also sees a flash of anger that seems to be directed at the King.

"We didn't know it was your cow," Lady says. "We didn't know it *was* a cow."

The tall kid puts his sword to her chest, faster than someone that big should move. His voice is deeper than she's ever heard. Maybe he's about to End. "You don't talk to the King. Not until he talks to you first."

"I want to hear this," the King says. He's angry already, she can tell, but curious.

"You gotta name?" Lady says. "Or we just call you King?"

The King's boys—the Round Table, she guesses—glower at that, but if anything the King's face relaxes. "I see the High Tongue has escaped your people," he says. "But in our nation, the King forgets his name. He is only the King."

"Is it Sam?" Lady says. "Just feeling lucky."

The King nods to the tall one. "Othello, if you would?"

"Where are you from, and why are you here?" Othello draws a sword.

"Easy, Gigante," Lady says. "No pointy things. I'm Lady, from the Holy Wood, from the Angelenos."

"We don't know the Angelenos," the King says.

"From the hills below the mountains, from the land beyond the Towers," Jemma says. "I'm Jemma."

"I've seen the Towers," the King says.

"Why are you here?" Othello says.

"We just wanderers from the Holy Wood, looking for a way south," Lady says.

"Wanderers. You didn't think I'd notice that you brought a Biter with you like a pet?"

"See, they use 'Biter,' too," Lady says in an undertone to Jemma. Lady looks back at Tommy, quiet and pathetic next to Tashia. He's as threatening as a mushroom. "The Biter is a prisoner."

"You're at war with the cannibals?" the King says.

"We heard they was building in the south, so sent a raiding party to look for them," Jemma says, mirroring his formal speech. "We captured this one. We saw more of them, lots more, heading south with an army of Last Lifers. We heard that the Kingdom was the Palos'—the Biters'—greatest enemy, so we wanted to bring this prisoner to you and warn you, with the hopes that we could join forces to fight the Biters together."

"We have nothing to fear from the Last Lifers," the King says.

"Unless they're getting guns from the Biters," Lady says.

"You were coming to warn us," the King says, "and yet you were found on the eastern fringes of our territory, killing our cows like thieves."

"We didn't know where you were—and we didn't know you had cows," Jemma says.

"You knew we hated the cannibals, yet you didn't know about the herd?"

"No, I—"

"Let's assume you're telling the truth. You sent an armed party of warriors into the Kingdom. You say it was to find the Biters. I say that a party of warriors from the lands of the north is a threat to my entire Kingdom."

"That ain't true," Lady says. "We didn't know—"

"It doesn't *matter*," the King says. "Here's what I know: You killed a cow. You harbored a Biter. Either of those things mean I can kill you. I've had a pretty long day. So . . ."

The King turns to Othello, with his sword. "If you would, Othello."

He turns and walks back toward the castle, stopping at the door to watch. Othello leads them to a Long Gone slatted bench. Blood stains the concrete below the bench. Without ceremony, he forces all three of them neck-first to the bench. Lady wonders for a moment if he could cut all three heads off with a single stroke.

"Sir," Tashia says, "we could learn from them for the war. They have to know things. It's a shame to waste them without asking."

"Kill them," the King says, and walks back toward the castle. The Round Table stays, watching Othello.

That's when Lady hears the noise.

She's never imagined anything like it. The Children's world is almost completely silent, except for birds and laughter. This tears that world open. Bigger than thunder, bigger than waves, bigger than gunfire. A steady roar that gets louder and louder, as if it's tracking them. She holds her ears. She thinks if it gets any louder, she might go insane.

None of the Round Table notices it, though. Tashia just looks annoyed.

But most important, the King stops at the doors and turns around. "Hold up, Othello," he says. "Let's see what Grease wants."

CHAPTER THIRTY-TWO
THE BOY AND THE MOCYCLE

Pico has nothing left in his legs, not even to pedal Lady's bicycle. All he can do is listen to the cows fade into the distance. So he thinks about where they could have gone.

He finds the trail of the herd easily enough. He smells it first. Then, big piles of poop in the middle of the street, tracks in the dirt, dust still lingering in the air where the cows have kicked it up.

They can't be going that far away. The Kingdom must not be able to keep the cows in their village because they would eat all the grass. So they let them loose in the surrounding streets and parks, maybe under the watchful eyes of a few riders.

The riders would have wanted to keep the cows closer to home. If they were too far away, they couldn't watch the cows. Even with their horses, they would have to travel too far to get to them.

The map. Tommy guided them around the northern border of the Kingdom in a sort of circle. Their village has to be somewhere in that circle. *I should have asked Tommy where it was*, he thinks. *I shouldn't have let my anger get in the way of my curiosity.*

Pico sits down in the dirt next to the street and digs out his map. He finds the center of the circle quickly enough, but their base can't be there. Too many streets, too many buildings. Cows need a lot of grass and a lot of room. He needs to find the emptiest spot on the map. That's where they'd put the cows.

A minute or two of studying, and he finds a possibility—the

biggest hole on the map, marked by the word "Kingdom." Could it be that easy?

If he's right, the base where the riders came from is about ten miles away. Time for him to catch them, even going as slow as he is. Time to think of something to save them before they get killed.

If only I could move my legs. He lays down in the dirt, with his head in the shade. And then he's asleep, without meaning to fall asleep.

He's at the lake where he fished with Jemma and sees the biggest koi he's ever seen, pale gold with lazy whiskers. It looks up at him with liquid eyes and flicks toward the surface. As it does, it opens its mouth, wider and wider and closer and closer until it's the biggest fish he's seen, the biggest anything. It closes its mouth, and when it opens it again a sound comes out. It's louder than anything, than the cows, than the monsoons, than the wildfires. It splits open his head.

It splits open his head, and when it does Pico opens his eyes and there's a boy riding up the street toward him. He's on a bicycle—but *not* a bicycle. A mocycle. Its wheels are fatter, it's thicker and heavier. Smoke belches from two long pipes. There's an engine shaking the frame and it's shouting out thunder.

Pico sits up while the boy stops his cycle. The boy is tall and gawky, with short hair shaved on the sides. "That's an internal combustion engine," Pico says.

The mocyclist looks surprised, but it's hard to tell because his eyes are hidden behind two windows of glass attached to his face. The frames are something that the Parents would have worn so they could see better, but the glass looks rough, as if the rider had shaped it himself.

"It might be," the mocyclist says.

"It is," Pico says. "How'd you get it going?"

"It might be," the mocyclist says. "How did you know what it was?"

"I can show you," Pico says. "If you can take me to your camp."

"I don't let anyone ride my bike," the mocyclist says.

"I can show you a lot more than that, even," Pico says. The truth.

The only hope the three of them have now is telling the truth. "Like why you gonna—wait, how old're you?"

"Fifteen."

"Like why you gonna die in two years."

"If you can show me that, I can give you a ride," the mocyclist says.

There's no fighting their way out, Jemma can tell from the moment she wakes up. This is a tribe built by war. And so the only way out is by talking to a group of kids who don't feel like talking. That's why they're kneeling at the bench.

Jemma has failed. She's sorry that she led her friend to this bench. But she stops being afraid. When you live that close to death your whole life, it's almost an old friend. She thinks about Apple. She thinks about her Mama, the tall one. She thinks maybe she would like it better with them.

The sword is about to drop when the sound splits open the sky.

Pico could probably explain it—especially since he's on the back of the thunder bike as it roars into camp. A goggly-eyed tall kid is on the front, and Pico has his arms wrapped around him. Wrapped is not the right word, though. His arms are so tight the other kid probably can't breathe.

The goggly kid skids in front of the castle, the way the little ones did in Daycare when they were showing off on their bikes.

"Grease," the King says. "You picking up prisoners now?"

"Yeah," Grease says, "but one thing, sir. I'd humbly request you don't kill him."

"Hmm," the King says.

"Or my friends," Pico says.

"Or his friends."

"Grease!" Othello says, and Jemma gets a long history of exactly this kind of conversation by the way he grinds his teeth at Grease. "You can't keep stopping the King's executions."

"If you kill them first, then I can't hear what they have to say. Listen, *then* kill."

The King interrupts, not by clearing his throat or speaking but by looking at Grease until he stops talking on his own. "So . . . what is it, Grease?"

"The kid knows how to read," Grease says.

"Good," the King says. "Keep him, and kill his friends."

"No," Grease says, unfazed. "They know more than that."

That's what they should have told, Jemma thinks, not her rushed lie. The truth about why they were roaming the Wilds, why they'd left the Holy Wood. No stories.

"Yeah?" the King says.

"Tell him, prisoner," Grease says.

Pico climbs off the bike, and Jemma sees that he's jittery. But Pico knows when to be dramatic.

"Sir, we been learning stuff, and we know how it works. How the End—how the End starts. We know a kid who ain't Ended."

Everything about the King changes then, from anger and boredom and bemusement to alertness, as if he's watching over the wall for an attack. He looks around the crowd, and Jemma follows his eyes—to Jemma, to Lady. To the tall girl rider, to the Round Table, to Tommy. To the little Biter who knows they can read and knows how the End came. The King says, "Let's take this inside." And the rider and the goggly kid and all of them follow the King.

They push through the double doors of the castle, whatever that is, and Jemma blinks. She's expecting something on the other side—a fort, maybe, or a building like the Zervatory. But it's just a passageway with a room or two on each side, and then more sidewalk. It's fake, she thinks. As far as she can tell, the castle has never guarded a thing. Why would they have built it, if not for war?

On the other side she sees girls. There was that rider outside, Lady's rider, but none of the Muscle were girls. Inside, there are dozens: cooking, cleaning, holding babies to their boobs. One of them catches Jemma's eye, short hair and baby on her chest, and glares. Jemma's glad to see girls, then wonders: *Why aren't they outside?*

A few more steps and they're standing in the middle of giant teacups, faded purples and pinks. The Kingdom uses them for tables, but she sees pictures of kids in them. *What is this place?*

At the base of the little mountain, a pair of sturdy cows is tied to a wheel set horizontally in the ground. She thinks of the water pump for the Great Field in the Holy Wood, drawn by donkeys, and realizes almost immediately that is sort of the same thing. The wheel turns other wheels, smaller and smaller, until they turn a chain in a train track.

In those tracks are little train cars. They point up the hill. They look more skyplane than train, created for speed: low, three seats stacked one behind the other, painted white with what must have been a red stripe.

"They used to be run by Lectrics. Or fire juice. I don't know," Grease says. "So I set them up with the only thing we still got: hooves."

They climb into the cars, and a cow driver clicks his tongue at the cows. The wheel slowly turns, and the train cars begin to climb straight up the mountain. Gears clank below them, and the cars jerk toward the top. She's sure the track will give way at every click of the gears, and they'll plummet back to the ground.

"We're on a mountain," Lady whispers, and Grease hears her.

"It's called the Horn," Grease says.

"Why?"

Grease shrugs. "Maybe it's shaped like one? I don't know—it's always been called that."

The cavern opens up for a moment to their left. Was that . . . some kind of snowy monster? It looks like a human but isn't. Still they climb.

"These things go down?" Pico says.

"Oh yeah. The rollertrain? Down is what they do best."

The cars reach the top and roll left around a gentle curve on the section of track closest to the peak. A gate swings across the track and holds them in place; the cars seem to have no brakes. They get out onto the tracks. The track is no higher than the Lectric tower Jemma climbed, but it feels taller. Jemma can see south and west. Is San Diego that way?

Pico hasn't talked much since he got off the bike, and his face has a reverent quality. As if he's finally seeing the things he knew must be true but had never seen.

"It's just—full of wonders, isn't it? And you brought it back to life?" Pico says to Grease, who seems to flush.

"There's nothing like the Kingdom, in this life or our last one," Tashia says.

"What is it, though?" Pico says.

"It's more fun if you figure it out yourself," Tashia says.

"More fun for us, anyway," Grease says.

"If we live," Jemma says.

CHAPTER THIRTY-THREE

THE BEGINNING

The snow is fake. It's paint on rock. Lady wanted it to be real. The moment she saw that snow, she thought of the ice and the ice cream and everything the Parents had taken away forever, and thought that it might be coming back. But when she climbs out of the rollertrain at the top of the track, she can feel the painted snow under the fingers.

Othello nods toward the tunnel where the track goes into the Horn again. There's a door built into the wall of the tunnel, meant to look like rock. Lady can barely see the seam. They climb a short, winding flight of stairs into a cavern of a room. She sees the girders of the Horn, a web of wood and steel that supports a concrete skin. Holes are punched throughout the walls, and boys with telescopes are watching through them.

A large round table—*Ah*, she thinks, *now I get it*—fills the center of the room, and above it, a ball hoop. She's seen them attached to houses and schools, but not in a place like this. Why would you build a hoop in a mountain?

A better question: Why would you build a mountain?

A wooden staircase climbs even farther up, and they climb it now. The last section is a ladder. They climb up it and push outside through a door onto a platform only six feet by six feet wide, jutting out from the very tip of the Horn, exposed to the air. There wasn't a railing around the platform originally, but someone has built a sturdy one of steel. On it rests the longest rifle Lady has ever seen, with a telescope.

Lady drifts closer to the edge, and a moment of vertigo makes her flail. She brushes the gun's tripod, and—

A hand slaps her cheek so hard that she reels backward into the hatch and just catches herself on the rail. "Stay away from the gun," Othello says.

"I wasn't touching your gun, puto," Lady says.

"I don't know what that word means," he says.

"I bet you can figure it out. *Puto.*"

Othello lunges at her, but the King is there. He doesn't touch Othello; he doesn't have to. He just holds his hand in front of Othello, who backs down as if he's been struck.

Lady watches the King and his Round Table. The King lives in his own skin, Othello is stretching his, but the others seem to quiver and burst with energy, ready to explode at any moment. In the Holy Wood, boys like these would have been Exiled long ago, too full of rage to be safe in the tribe even as a Muscle. But these have been pulled into the King's inner circle.

She's aware that she's watching a completely different kind of tribe, and it's one that makes her guard her every motion. This tribe is run by boys.

"This your village?" Jemma says, pointing outward.

"No, not my village," the King says. "My Kingdom."

"That don't mean nothing to us," Lady says, because she really doesn't know what it means and because she wants to take the wind out of the King and his gasbags.

"There's nothing like it in this life or our last one," he says, echoing Tashia's words. "Imagine your village, and then think of something so big and powerful that it could fit a dozen of them," the King says.

Your head, she almost says, but remembers they only recently almost died here.

She can see all of the Kingdom from there. All the world, it feels like. She tries to take it in but can't. Her head can't put it into the right buckets. The Kingdom is divided up like spokes in a wheel, centering on the castle. Each section of the Kingdom seems to have a different life. The quiet street they walked through, the castle, and the Horn. To her left is a place seemingly made of skyplanes, white towers, and smooth metal. To her right is desert and painted rock, followed by a small lake. Next to that is a jungle.

On the perimeter of the Kingdom is a thick berm, an earthen bank maybe fifteen to twenty feet high. It's so regular that she thinks it must have been built by the Parents, but on top of that is a patchwork of fences and walls—steel plates salvaged from streets and sheds, sharpened wooden poles, barbed wire—that must have been built by the Children over generations. Huge buildings make up the rest of the defense, their blank walls making it impossible for invaders to climb or get through. They have to feel so safe here.

The buildings all remain, but the rest of the Kingdom has been suited to the Children's needs. The streets are turned to the green of vegetables and fruits. A couple dozen cows are penned next to the soaring white towers. Kids fish in the lakes. A little girl milks a cow tied to a rocket, and a boy is carrying a heavy bucket of milk toward the castle.

"You've seen what we have," the King says, motioning back down the ladder. "Now let's see what you have."

"What's with the cows?" Pico says. They're standing before the Round Table back inside the Horn, where the King and his Knights sit in rolling chairs. Jemma is still stupefied by the sight of the Kingdom and isn't sure where Pico found a voice to speak.

The King doesn't change his expression, just swivels his chair and settles in. "The story of the cows," he says, "is for people who are going to live."

"Tell us *that* story, then," Pico says.

"Tell me your story first, and we'll see," the King says.

"My name is Pico, and I'm from the Malibu tribe of the Angelenos," Pico says. "I never met my Mama, and my Dad was the Dad of half the village."

"Start later in your story," the King says, amused. "A lot later."

Pico tells them the story of Leong, hit in the head and still living.

"How?" Grease says. "How would that stop us from dying?"

"I think . . ." Pico looks around the room, gauging how much truth he has to tell to leave the room alive.

"Pico." Jemma puts a hand on his arm and nods. "Tell him everything." They don't live if he holds anything back.

"Send the Palo away, though," Pico says. Even though he uses the wrong name, the King nods, and a Knight leads Tommy back out of the room.

When the room is clear of the Biter, Pico says, "I think the End hits the brain."

"Brain?" Grease says.

"The thing in your head that does the thinks. The End hits your brain when you get old. But Leong will always be eight in his head."

"How do you know this?" the King says.

"He read it," Grease says.

"Something the Parents left behind, some papers. They thought the End attacked the brain. And—" Then Pico pauses.

"And they got killed before they could fix it," Jemma says.

Lady continues the story, and she seems to believe what she's saying. "And we, the three of us, we wanna figure out what they couldn't figure out. We wanna know why we End. And we wanna know how to—how not to End."

The King doesn't say anything, just watches her until she stops, then starts.

"Why do you keep calling it the End?" the King says.

"It's two kind of Ends," Pico says. "It's when the Parents all died. And it's the end of our lives."

"We don't call it the End," he says. "We call it the Beginning."

"That's . . . really weird," Lady says.

The King swivels back and forth in his chair, his toes pushing lightly off the floor to set the chair in motion. "It depends on how you view the changes. What do your stories tell you about yourselves before the Beginning—before all of this?"

"Not much," Lady says, remembering the wall in the Casa de las Casas.

"We remember all our stories," the King says. "We were many peoples before we became the Kingdom, just like you—pinks, browns, Mexcans, Veets, island people. But we all were, even before the Beginning—we were warriors. We were kids, and we were warriors. We were a gang."

"A what?" Lady says.

"Lots of gangs, I guess. A group of kids," the King says. "We were the ones shut out, the ones they made poor. We were beaten and jailed and murdered for walking down the wrong street. So we fought back, we killed, we took. We stuck together because the Grown-Ups were gone or against us; we fought because the whole word stunk and we had nothing to lose. Like—"

"Like the Last Lifers," Jemma says. That's what it must have been to be in a gang. To be freed of consequence. To let go of the world. Sometimes, like right now, she can see the appeal.

The King just nods and keeps talking. "We fought the laws, we fought each other, we fought the Grown-Ups who still tried to control us. Until they all died. The world went bad, and we were the only ones who knew how to live in it," he says. "The gangs were mostly kids already, we were organized, and the young ones just stepped up and took over."

"Took over the gangs?" Jemma says.

"Took over the world. We started with the police places because that's where the guns were. Then things were fine enough, but we were exactly the way we were before, only no one to fight but other kids."

"Just like now," Jemma says.

"No, not like now," the King says. He points to the inside of the Horn. "This didn't come from a gang. No—one day one of us realized we'd been fighting the world, and now we owned the world. We were fighting the Grown-Ups, but *we* were the Grown-Ups now. Time to become the Grown-Ups."

"The Philosopher King," Grease says.

"Fill a what?" Lady says. "Pico, what's that?"

"I have no idea," Pico says. That must hurt.

"It's a thinker," Grease says. "Not just about eating or staying alive, but how we live. The Philosopher read a lot when the Kingdom used to be able to read. He thought we should be more. When he took over, we changed how we lived."

"He loved a story, about a king and a knight and a Round Table," the King says. "We found this place, and it was already a legendary Kingdom. It even had our castle. We took it over and made it our home. The Philosopher King said you could be strong and save the world. So he started the Round Table. All us colors used to fight each other, but we took the best warriors of each gang and made them into the Round Table."

Jemma thinks about this—about erasing the fights between peoples, and about creating a new one. How the Mamas of the Holy Wood must have done the same thing, but with a different Story.

"He start the cowboys, too?" Jemma says.

The King nods. "Ell Aye was city, but the Philosopher King's peoples were from the land. They had been farmers, far away. When they came to Ell Aye, they brought the land with them, and some of it survived the city. Some of the gangs learned to ride horses, they were taught about goats and cows."

"Cows ain't from Ell Aye," Pico says.

"The Philosopher found them at a place that taught kids about farming," the King says. "There were only a few of them, maybe twenty, and they were starving. You can go to the telescopes if you want to look how many of them there are now."

She doesn't have to. There are dozens of cows inside the walls of the Kingdom, hundreds more in the lot outside the gate. Enough to feed the Holy Wood for a year. Enough to feed the Angelenos for a year. They had built something here.

That was the King's point.

"So now you know why we don't need your help," the King says.

"The little one can become part of us because Grease says he knows things we can use, and anything Grease doesn't know is worth letting you live."

Pico doesn't let his relief show if he feels it at all; he just watches Jemma and Lady until they know what their fate is.

"The Biter will die when we've learned what he has to tell us. But you girls—" The King shakes his head. "I have no use for more girls."

It takes Jemma a full second to understand what the King means. And she sees Tashia's outrage before it closes up again.

"But I'll give you a chance. At the feast of the new moon in three weeks, in twenty-two days, you can enter the Kingdom the way all our people do—by hand combat inside the Night Mountain. If you win, you become a part of the Kingdom. If you lose—well, then you die as our enemies."

"But we can help you beat the End!" Jemma says.

"There's that word again," the King says. "Look around you, Holy Wood. None of this would have been possible without the Beginning. We went from gangs to the greatest people in the world. We became who we were supposed to be. So . . . why would we want the Beginning to end?"

CHAPTER THIRTY-FOUR
THE FAKE PLACE

No one will talk to them after the King's sentence; no one will even tell them more about what the King's sentence means. Jemma looks for the rider Tashia, but she has disappeared. So instead they wander around the Kingdom, trying to make sense of the place. The people of the Kingdom look curiously at them but then seem to float away as they draw closer.

The first place they look for is the Night Mountain. It's the arena where all the fights are held. It doesn't look like a building. It doesn't even look much like a mountain. More like a temple, maybe—a round white shape like a bowl turned upside down, with a dozen great ribs climbing straight to the summit to a dozen spires.

They creep in through a long tunnel, and Jemma understands why they call it Night Mountain. There are no windows. What they can see from the light of the outside is a sand floor over concrete. There are steel girders everywhere, as if the side of a skyscraper were blasted off and the skeleton still remained.

Running through them is the same kind of rollertrain that they rode into the Horn—but this one doubles back and forth on itself, stacks on layer after layer, until the entire building is filled with track. She sees a rocketplane-looking car that must have tumbled off the track years ago, still smashed on its side against the floor, as if someone were holding it down until it said mercy. Loose steel bars hang off the scaffolds and lie on the ground. So many places to hide, so many potential weapons.

"They fight here? In the dark?" Pico says. "That's . . ."

Impossible. It will be impossible, unless they can train here and memorize the terrain.

"You can't be here," a voice says behind them. It's one of the Round Table, but they never heard his name. "This is for fighters only."

"We wasn't fighters until your King made us fighters," Lady says. "You was there."

"You're only a fighter when you become one of the Kingdom."

"How we sposed to join the Kingdom if we can't win the fight cuz we couldn't fight at the place where we're sposed to have the fight?" Lady says. But they leave.

"Tomorrowland," Pico reads from a sign on the plaza outside. They silently note the strangeness around the Night Mountain: sleek lines, the Mono, rocketplanes, a pile of rusting mini cars, one of which Jemma has seen towed behind a horse. "This feels wrong," he says. "These kinds of things didn't really exist in the Parents' world. It's like they wanted to show what their future was gonna be. But they never got it." Instead, they got this—their Mono being pulled by cows.

The Angelenos push westward, past the castle. Painted red rock spires push up out of the ground, like a desert set in the middle of a city. The Children have colonized the caves going through the rock, and laundry hangs between the rock towers. Jemma remembers Apple's stories—of red deserts and trains that go in loopdy-loops. Was this that place? He had talked as if everything was possible, and she hadn't believed him. But here, it was.

"They really like trains," Lady says. "And none of the trains go nowhere."

They move toward the patch of jungle that they saw from the platform, drawn like any Ell Aye kid to green land, because it means water and life. They soon find themselves in the middle of it. The trees there seem wrong, too—too green, too straight. Their leaves are dusty, but underneath there's still a luster that Jemma can't believe.

"These trees . . . ," Pico says. He's hobbling but seems to be getting better. He stares at the jungle for a moment, then plucks a leaf. It resists, but he yanks it free, sniffs it—and then bites it.

"Plastic?" he says. "They grew plastic?"

"It's all fake, dummy," Lady says.

"That . . . makes no sense," Pico says.

But it's true. Someone built this whole world, to look like other worlds outside the Kingdom. Once Jemma knows that, she looks at the scene with a fresh eye. Bright flashes of birds, frozen on branches. The heads of huge lizard creatures, sticking out of what was once a Long Gone river and resting on iron struts. Buildings of every style. "This place looked Long Gone even before the End," Jemma says.

One of the buildings next to the jungle is cracked open like a shell by time or earthquake. Jemma strains to see through the gloom and—there's someone in there. A man, bearded, wearing a strange hat and carrying a sword. Jemma freezes the others.

Then Jemma realizes: He's a man. Despite everything else she's seen, she doesn't believe those still exist. Something about this one, about how still he is, makes her step closer.

"Careful," Lady says, but Jemma shrugs and looks. The beard is faded, chewed by mice. The clothes are falling off. The sword is plastic, and so is the man.

Pico runs his fingers across the plastic skin, finding a rip in the neck. He tears at it, to expose gears underneath. "Look at this," he says. "They made people out of machines."

"What?"

"They made machines that looked like people, anyway. I don't know why."

"Servants, maybe?" Lady says.

"Maybe," Pico says. "They needed cars to drive em places. Maybe they needed machines to do everything else."

The more Jemma looks, the more she can see the gears, the plastic, the concrete underlying this place. She just can't see the why.

Lady is the one who figures it out. "It's all for kids. It's a Fake Place," she says.

"Why do you say that?" Pico says.

"Those teacups that people rode is what made me think it. It's the way they made the baby rooms in the Parents' houses. Lots of colors, lots of toys. Only these're bigger."

"A lot bigger," Jemma says. She shakes her head, trying to make sense of it. "They built this whole place to play?" The Children played, of course, but even their play was serious business, a way of learning to hunt and fight and Gather. If you didn't play right, you wouldn't live.

She marvels at the imagination and the skill that made fake castles and rocks and machine men, and thinks, *What a waste of skill.*

And then: *If life would let me, I'd be glad to waste it, too.*

The wonder of the Kingdom wears off soon for Lady, who says, "We still gonna die here."

"Not necessarily," Pico says.

"Just cuz you ain't gonna die don't mean you gotta get all snotty about it," Lady says.

"No, we just gotta figure out how to make ourselves so useful they don't want to kill us," Pico says. "And if that doesn't work, you guys gotta learn how to win."

"Oh, that's all," Lady says.

"What? We got three weeks to do it."

"Okay," Lady says. Pico doesn't complain about things, he fixes them, and he's right about fixing this. "You work on that Grease kid. He makes everything go here. Get him on your side. But us—we gotta make other friends so we can be useful, too."

Jemma has been thoughtful since they left the center of the Horn, but she slowly locks on to their conversation. "The cowboy. She liked you. Maybe she could tell you what we're gonna be fighting. And more about the Night Mountain."

"I got her, Pico's got Grease," Lady says. "What about you?"

"I can talk to the King," Jemma says, "if they let me. Also, I think I gotta find that Biter."

"Why him?"

"He's been building guns to fight em; he should know em. Maybe we can learn something before they kill em."

They circle back toward the stables, where they've been told to sleep, past a lake with a rotting wooden ship sunk in the middle. Its masts must have been chopped down for wood. Lady isn't sure why they didn't just burn the rest.

The cowboy Tashia could be at the stables. If she is, Lady could talk to her. But the image of Tashia on a horse brings a memory floating back to her from their capture. "Jemma? What did you mean in the park?"

"What?" Jemma says, blank. Maybe she really doesn't remember, since she got hit on the head.

"You . . . saw the cowboy. Whaddya mean, you saw her?"

She can see two ideas at war on Jemma's face—fear of saying whatever gets said next, and relief at being able to say it. It takes a long time for her to make up her mind. "I . . . see things. Before they happen."

"Like what?"

Jemma flushes. "The Ice Cream Man. The dogs that attacked us. Pico's case. Lots of things." And she describes the haze, how she's just starting to understand how it tells her things, how it connects her with others. How sometimes it misses things, but mostly lets her see what will come.

For a moment Lady's in awe. Her friend speaks to the gods. And then—it's just one more thing Jemma hasn't told her. "Puta! When was you—"

Jemma puts a hand on her shoulder. "I ain't known that long. At first I didn't know what I was seeing, and then Apple helped me figure I was seeing true." Her face brightens. "When I was knocked out, I saw the ones the Ice Cream Men called the Old Guys. The ones who was supposed to survive the End." And she tells them what she saw.

"Like, real old people just . . . alive?" Pico says, skeptical.

"If I saw the cowboy and she was real, if I saw the dogs and they was real, couldn't the Old Guys be real, too?"

"They might," Lady says. "But we gotta get outta here to know."

"You shoulda told us," Pico says. "We coulda used that."

"I was afraid people would think I was a witch."

"We ain't *people*. We your friends," Lady says.

"And you ain't the only one been called a bruja," Pico says. "They kicked me out of the Malibu for it. We woulda understood."

"We all gonna die here anyway," Lady says. "Seems like a real good time to have our own witch."

Jemma finds the Biter in a yellow metal boat in an empty pond, with kids of the Kingdom jeering at him. Other boats surround him. This is their prison. In the boats on each side of Tommy are two other Biters captured in some other skirmish. These two are true warriors, with marks on their wrists for the people they've killed. *The Kingdom isn't letting Tommy in with them so that he can't learn anything from them*, she thinks.

All he would learn from them is how soon he can die. The metal boxes bake them during the day, freeze them at night. They seem to have sweated their muscles away.

The Kingdom kids drift away from her as they did before, as if they're not quite sure if she's a ghost. There's a metal hatch at the top that seals Tommy in, but she can talk to him through a broken round window. He's huddled at the corner to escape the sun but scoots forward when he sees her.

"They let you go?" Tommy says.

"No. We gotta fight our way into the Kingdom."

"Figures," Tommy says. "That's all they care about."

"You're alive," she says. "That's a surprise."

"Until the King finds what he wants to know." He knows that's the only reason he and the other Biters aren't impaled on the gates.

"I could tell him you fix guns. He might think that's good to know."

"And?"

"You gotta help me figure out how to beat them."

"Easy. Be stronger."

"Whatever." She turns to leave, if he's not going to get serious.

"No," he says. "They only care about strength. You gotta be stronger, or find some way to use it."

"That the best you got?"

"I just got here, too."

"Stay cool, Biter," she says, and turns away.

Tommy calls after her. "You're looking for the End," he says, so low the other Biters couldn't hear him even if they were well enough to listen.

Jemma doesn't answer but looks back.

"If you are, I'd like to help you," he says, even quieter.

She shakes her head, slowly, never breaking contact with his eyes.

"Who else here cares?" he says. His words go with her when she goes. Even if Tommy's serious, if he knows something about the End, he can't be trusted. He's a cannibal. His help is poisoned.

Pico won't like her talking to the Biter. But she thinks of Trina, who cared about the Holy Wood even when people hated her. Who risked her position, as long as they were safe. Trina would take help where she could find it. So will she. Jemma will find a way to use the cannibal, even if he can't be trusted.

She won't let her friends die in this Kingdom.

The cowboy Tashia is unsaddling a horse. The saddle is made of old carpet and tire rubber. Tashia nods when Lady walks up to the fence.

"It hard to ride em?" Lady says.

"At first. You feel like you're sitting on a mountain."

"We hunt em, in our village. No one knows how to ride."

Tashia's face darkens. "They're the center of the Kingdom. Without them, we'd lose the cows, we'd lose the battles. You can't hurt them here."

"Wouldn't want to," Lady says. She holds out her hand, knuckles curled under, and the horse's lips feel around them as if to make sure she's not food.

"She don't normally let people get that close," Tashia says.

"Why you let me, then?"

"I wanted to see if she'd bite off your hand."

Lady almost laughs but turns serious. "Who gets to live here?" she says. "Inside the Kingdom, I mean, not in the hotel?"

"Everyone does, in wartime."

"But all the time?"

"The King's people. Those who are important, I guess. The Cowboys, the Knights, their favorite girls . . ." But she wrinkles her lips at that. A little disgust showing?

"What's the deal with the Night Mountain?"

Tashia pauses, as if deciding something. "Probably the last thing you're gonna see alive. They used to have the rollertrains inside. They used to use the Lectrics to light it up, but now it's just black in there. No windows."

"I saw it. It ain't so bad."

"It is. You don't know the Night Mountain, but the Knights do. They know every inch. They're going to put one Knight in there for each of you. Maybe he ambushes you. Maybe you climb up the rollertracks and he throws you off the edge."

"Why you telling me this?" Lady says.

"I don't expect you to live."

"It's sposed to be by hand, ain't it?"

"Swords aren't the only way to get yourselves killed, honey," Tashia says. "There's lots of old junk in there from the rollertrain—steel bars, Lectric cables, bricks. They'll use them as weapons."

Lady looks at Tashia more closely and sees signs of wear—a two-inch scar above her cheekbone, a crooked left ear, a swollen ring finger, purple bruises on her skin. She remembers what Tashia said about fighting her way into the Round Table, and starts to form an idea.

Without saying anything more, Lady picks up a brush from the fence and steps closer to Tashia's horse. The muscles jump under the brush, as if they're welcoming the bristles.

"Stay away from her back leg. She might kick if she can't see you," Tashia says, and continues to put away her gear.

Lady understands how big the horse really is, how powerful its legs and teeth are.

"This thing's so much stronger than you," she says. "How you control it?"

"She doesn't know she's stronger," Tashia says.

"How you get the mocycle working?" Pico says. He's found Grease in a huge workshop at the back of the Kingdom. The building is littered with the parts of mocycles and cars and lawn-mowing things.

"It's called a mocycle?" Grease says.

"Yeah," Pico says. "But how you get it to work if you can't read?"

"I see machines, I can kind of see how they work in my mind. This one started with the fire juice in the tank."

The goggly kid talks as if it's painful for him to speak to another person, but sometimes the words bust out as if escaping from a pen.

"Gas," Pico says.

"Gas? Like the fart?"

"Different. Cars and stuff used gas."

"Gas. I figured out it must use . . . fire juice . . . to run. And if it used fire juice, then it needed some kind of fire, and some kind of spark to light the fire." Grease climbs on the mocycle and starts it with a kick to a pedal. It sputters once, three times, then purrs. He raises his voice to talk over it. "I found an old book that had pictures. I cleaned everything out and put it back together. It was all about getting the fuel and the fire together."

"That makes sense, I guess."

"It took me two years," Grease says.

"What about cars?" The Parents had so many of them.

"Cars are hard," Grease says. "Bikes are simpler. I can kick them awake."

Pico revs the handle like Grease showed him, and the purr climbs to a roar.

"The King wants me to fix a whole bunch of them."

"Cool."

But Grease's face doesn't say cool. "He wants to use them with the guns."

"Oh," Pico says, and he sees the Knights racing toward the Biters on two-wheeled hurricanes, rifles bolted onto the handlebars. The horses are advantage enough. But these would be so fast, so loud, so hard to shoot at, that they would grind down anyone in their path.

"You fix the guns, too?" Pico says.

"Guns are easy," Grease says. "Make sure the powder's dry, the bolts are greased. But . . ."

"But what they do is hard."

"There's so much death already," Grease says. "What's to like about something that just brings more death?" That's how Pico learns that Grease doesn't agree with the King on everything, even though the King values him more than anyone else in the Kingdom.

"Why you guys fight so much?" Pico says.

"We know we're going to die, but the most important thing is to die strong."

"The most important thing is not to die," Pico says, and Grease only nods.

CHAPTER THIRTY-FIVE
THE KINGDOM

Pico teaches Grease his letters when no one watches, although reading won't get Grease Exiled like it would in the Holy Wood. Grease's eyes wrinkle with joy behind the thick glasses the first time he makes out one of the words on the Kingdom's walls: "Snacks."

In turn Grease shows him how to take apart the mocycles and clean out the rust and spiderwebs, how to find extra parts from the pile of scrap he's collected. Pico's hands have always been a disappointment to him, a little too shaky and weak for machines, but they steady under Grease's training. Pico learns how Grease got his name when his own arms are blackened to his elbows at the end of the day, but the pieces of the machines start to click together in his mind and in real life.

"It supposed to sound like that?" Pico says, looking at the motor that's smoking and knocking as if someone were inside with a hammer trying to get out, but really he doesn't care because it's the first engine he's ever fixed, and it's actually running.

"It's the gas. It's old," Grease says. "The stuff in cars won't burn, usually. Only good stuff I found was at the place where they keep the skyplanes, about as fresh as the Grown-Ups made it. I gotta get some more."

"How you get the stuff back?"

"I can carry a little, or talk someone into throwing it on a cart."

"You need something with four wheels to carry stuff." *Or more people,* Pico thinks. "Like a car."

"But if we had a car . . . then we'd have a car."

"What if it was only *like* a car?" Pico says. Then they'd have a way to San Diego.

The cannibal's white-pink skin is red-pink after a few days in the boat. He's not getting enough water, Jemma sees, and she sneaks some to him on the third day.

The Biter on the right is almost dead, and the one on the left watches her with dead eyes. He looks like Andy before he joined the Last Lifers, she thinks, but the kid is completely gone from this Biter. She doesn't know if he gave up life or if the Kingdom took it from him, but this is what it looks like when you stop living.

"They ain't treating you so good?" she says.

"As well as they treat anyone who eats them," Tommy says, and she laughs. The little burst of humor makes her think she can ask her question.

"So . . . what do you know about the End?" she says.

He smiles, as if he knew what she would say. "You're not the only one who has seen someone live after the End," he says. "We had one of the Chosen, trampled in battle by the King's horses. He's still alive and almost nineteen."

"That's how—" Jemma makes herself stop.

"It's his head," Tommy says. "The brain."

"I didn't know you heard Pico call it that," Jemma says.

Whatever Tommy was about to say comes out empty, and he closes his mouth with a snap. "I must have," he says a moment later. "What does Pico think?" he says.

She doesn't want to give too much away. But she wants his help, and he seems to have figured a lot of it out on his own. "He thinks—he thinks the End works on Parents cuz their brains changed somehow when they grew up. That's why the Touched go first, the kids who're smarter, more mature."

"That makes sense."

They speak carefully. They don't trust each other, and each seems to think the other knows more than they say. But they need each other, she thinks.

"You're going to need to get us out of here soon," he says.

"Us?"

"You need to leave. I need to not be dead."

"I ain't agreed to that," she says. "Also, they're too strong."

"There's your answer," Tommy says. "They're too strong to care about being smart."

"That's not an answer," Jemma says.

She leaves his prison, unraveling the problem like an old yarn doll. The Kingdom is as strong as Tommy says, with a code that doesn't break. And strong as warriors, because they don't Exile the ones who start to rage. She's seen them at one another's throats already, teenage boys, like a sack full of rats. That's . . .

Othello is leaning in the shade of the Horn, watching her and the prison.

"You got a thing for the little Biter, don't you?" he says, pushing out from the wall. "Want to make a little pink baby? You're going to have to wait for his dick to grow."

She wills herself to be hard and tall, to bury her fear the way she did with Lady and Li the night they left the Holy Wood. But that was for her friend, not for herself.

"Don't you got a horse to roll with?" she says.

Othello grabs her throat. "I could kill you for that," he says.

"If you could, you would," she says.

His arms are so strong, his fingers so tight she feels them inside her throat. But she is strong, too, the strongest girl in the Holy Wood, and she squeezes a point in his wrist until he lets go, and she never lets go of his eyes. "You ain't never lived with girls in charge."

"Doesn't matter," he says. "You're in the Kingdom now." He raises his hands, smiles light and easy, and glides away.

Helping Grease means Pico gets to leave the Kingdom, holding on to the mocycle under the roar of the internal combustion engine. He learns to love the wind on his skin, the buzz of the motor.

The first place Pico asks Grease to take him is the park where the riders attacked them. He shows Grease the rows of carts, and Grease understands.

"It's a golf cart," Pico says, when they've explored the garage where the Parents fixed the carts and he's read the signs. "That's what the sticks are. Golf sticks." Inside a panel on the rear of the cart, Pico can see a motor that's much smaller than a car's, with fewer tubes and wires and none of those black boxes that Grease can never crack. "You think you could figure this out?"

"Most of it. We got a lot of parts here. For the rest of it, I have this"—he tosses a thick book toward Pico—"and you."

"'Golf Cart Maintenance and Repair,'" Pico reads, for a moment only thinking of the fact that he can read "Maintenance" but still doesn't know what it is.

"Where I get stuck, you read our way through."

"We only got seventeen days before the fight," Pico says, as if both of them know what it's for. Somehow, in five days, Pico has won Grease over, and he's not sure why. But he's glad.

"So easy," Grease says. Grease and Pico look at the cart, not at each other. They see what it can become. If they can fix it. But he knows they can.

"You realize," Pico says, "this is gonna die with us."

"What?"

"Your machines. My books. What we know about the End."

"The King loves my machines. So will the next King."

"Yeah, but there ain't gonna be a you to fix em," Pico says. "No one's smart nuff, no one lives nuff. And cuz we're smart, that means we're Touched, and we gonna End even faster."

"Yeah," Grease says. His face is somber.

"One or two people gonna remember what we did but ain't gonna be able to teach the next. The next time someone smart nuff to figure this stuff out on his own comes along, the machines are gonna be rusted to pieces. Life ain't long nuff for all that when everyone's just trying to live."

"In that case," Grease says, "this really is the End. You know what the Preachers call it? They go way back to the old book, the oldest book."

"The Bible," Pico says.

"How did you know?"

"I read, remember?" Pico says. "But I gotta tell you, it ain't a very good book. I never got past the snake."

"Well, they call it the apokalips."

"What does that mean?"

"The end of the world."

"Wonder if the Bible saw this," Pico says.

Tashia has Lady and Jemma running errands for her horses. Fresh vegetables from the kitchen, new leather from the tanners, ointment for hooves.

Lady is retrieving a bundle of grass brought in on the Mono from the fields beyond the wall. The Kingdom dries them out and stores them in the stables so it's always easy to feed the animals.

Grease told Lady that the Mono uses rubber wheels so it glides above them quietly. The only sounds that give it away are the moos of the cows pulling it and the shouts of its drivers.

The Mono will never work as the Parents would have intended, not without Lectrics, because of the wall surrounding the Kingdom. The Mono track carves a long loop throughout the Kingdom. When it leaves the Kingdom, it crosses over the wall far above the ground through a hole in the fence, and the cows have to stop at the wall. The momentum carries the Mono mostly over the wall, and then the girls on top fish up the tow ropes and throw them over to the drivers waiting on the other side. Those drivers take the Mono to the hotel and the gardens and return in a loop to the same spot at the wall, loaded up with goods for the animals and people of the Kingdom.

As the girl from the Mono swings her the bundle of grass, her attention catches. Lady looks behind her to see what she's watching. In front of the Night Mountain, she sees a boy and girl, maybe thirteen, holding hands on a bench. No, not holding hands—they hover an inch apart as if magnets keep them from touching.

Lady remembers that feeling, but it seems to have buried itself since she left the Holy Wood. There are boys here, strong and tall, and she still feels twinges of longing when she passes them. But since Li, she's not as in love with muscles. She knows what they can do.

The boys are strange to her, too. They don't flirt or show off like the Holy Wood boys. They don't talk to you and they don't touch your shoulder if they do. Here in the Kingdom, they just stare at her when she walks by. She knows that look, and it feels like Li.

Tashia says it's because they don't talk about rolling here. Some kind of Preacher thing. They have to roll to keep the Kingdom alive. The strongest kids have a duty to make the strongest babies, but they're not supposed to like it.

Lady doesn't understand. Rolling is the most important thing. Rolling is life. How can it be swept aside, as if it's shameful . . . as if it's something to be feared?

These two at the bus stop aren't rolling together, not yet. But these two have marked each other with their eyes, a trail of invisible fingerprints climbing across the shoulder blade to the side of the neck to the lips. There's something more than rolling going on behind their eyes.

Like the way Apple used to look at Jemma.

Yes, like that.

Lady smiles at the way they fit each other—willowy, gentle, maybe too fragile for this world. Maybe that's why they break their gazes only to check over their shoulders, why they shrink into the corners of the bench.

That's when she sees Othello striding toward the girl as if she's something he dropped and just remembered to pick back up. Othello grabs the girl, shakes her just once like a nanny with a runaway child, and pulls her away from the bench. From the looks of the people nearby, that's what's supposed to happen. The girl slips her hand from his giant fist, though, and yells at him. Now all the girls near the plaza are watching.

The boy is sitting so small on the bench he's almost invisible. When Othello turns his back, the boy launches himself from the seat and tackles Othello in the leg. For a second Othello might go down.

He doesn't. He sways, roars, peels the boy off his side. He flings him into the bench with one hand, and Lady swears she can hear the wood crack. Lady's hand searches her hair for the pin, desperate to stab. But her arm freezes there.

The girl hasn't given up all fight yet, and she collapses to the ground like a Toddler as Othello pulls her away from the bench. Othello drags her along without looking back at her trying to dig her fingernails into the cracked pavement.

The plaza in front of the Night Mountain is empty except for a streak of blood from the girl's thumb.

But the girls at the edge of it make the air vibrate with fury. Lady watches them, their arms slicing through the air as they talk.

She's been watching so long that she doesn't notice that the girl who helped her load the bundle of grass is standing at her shoulder.

"Was she . . . his girl?" Lady asks.

The girl's voice is having a tough time making it out of her throat. "When you're a Knight, everyone's your girl. Whether you want it or not. Because they're strong."

"That ain't right," Lady says, already losing her bearings.

"Whether you want it or not," the girl says. "Can you imagine that?"

Lady doesn't answer.

Yes, she imagines it. The hard part is to not.

CHAPTER THIRTY-SIX

THE GIRLS IN THE RING

Tommy doesn't say anything, but every day Jemma wonders if he's the next Biter to die. The others' heads are on the wall. His skin is blistered from the sun and cut from when they torture him. She has learned to stay away from the castle when the screams come.

Somehow he survives, even with the little water and food Jemma can sneak past the guards. Tough little pendejo.

She's curious about something. "Why you Biters even bother trying to attack the Kingdom?" she says. "That wall ain't goin nowhere."

"There's an answer to every wall," he says. "This one's too big. They can't man it properly. I bet you I could find three places where someone could get through."

"Yeah? Where would you climb?"

"Where the Mono comes through, for one," he says.

Something about the Biter's face just then makes her recall a vision she must have had through the haze. He was in it, but the details swim away before she can see what he was doing. She's worked on seeing the haze every day and can sometimes call it up at will. The images are sharper, the buzz has faded, as if it finally understands how to speak to her clearly. But Jemma doesn't always know what is real. The haze seems to show her the paths most likely to happen, not the ones that will surely come true.

"I'm glad you decided not to kill me," he says, and his voice softens. "In the Palos, the big ones stole my food, beat me up from the time I was three. I never had anyone who cared. Never had anyone to protect me. I think you might be her."

Right then, he changes. Not an enemy. Not a threat. Just a kid.

"You think you could teach me to ride?" Lady asks Tashia without turning away from the horse she's feeding. If she could ride, they'd have a chance to leave these walls. Tashia doesn't come up to the horse, though, stops just short of entering the corral.

When Lady turns around, she sees that today is not a good day to ask Tashia anything.

The cowboy's face is tight, but not crying. Lady almost doesn't speak, unsure if she wants to release the tears. "Something wrong?"

Tashia lifts up the front hoof and inspects it, running her fingers around the edge. "You hear about Othello and the girl?"

"Yeah," she says. "Tashia . . . Tashia, I know how you feel."

She doesn't see Tashia's face. Doesn't see Tashia move. Just feels Tashia's arm on her neck, slamming her into the fence. The bars dig into her shoulders. She pushes off them and Tashia is staring at her down an outstretched fist, one eyebrow arching above the knuckle.

Then the fist shows up in Lady's gut. The air rushes out of her lungs, and Lady struggles to pull it back before it escapes to the clouds. She doesn't feel she's being attacked by Tashia but by floating fists landing so fast on both sides of her body that she can't trace the swings. Lady collapses against the fence and draws Tashia in, closer, closer, until a punch lingers long enough on her torso that she can grab the forearm, until she can hold it tight, until she sees Tashia's eyes widen at the grip that doesn't let go.

Until her own right hand connects with Tashia's jaw two, three times and rocks Tashia's head backward and Tashia is sitting in the dirt, still not sure how she got there.

Lady braces herself for Tashia's rush, but Tashia shakes her head twice, slowly, and only her eyes smile. "Damn, honey," she says with her mouth. *That's a hell of a punch*, the rest of her says.

"I ain't saying sorry," Tashia says.

"Me neither."

Tashia scoots across the dirt to the fence and leans back against it. Lady slides down the fence, inches from the horse's nose. It hasn't budged. It doesn't care what they do to each other as long as it's got its food.

"She's my sister," Tashia says. "Not *our* sister like we all are, but my true sister, from my Ma. My Ma was so young when she had me, maybe fourteen, that I remembered her before she passed. 'That's Jackie,' she said. 'She's yours now.' And she has been since."

"Never had a sister," Lady says. "Just Jemma."

"I taught her to walk. I showed her how to throw the bolas, how to ride, how to find the only mushrooms that won't kill you. And now Othello—I'm gonna kill that—"

"Puto, is what we say," Lady says.

"What does that mean?"

"Means someone like Othello."

"Ha!" Tashia sags just a bit.

"Can't the King do something?"

Tashia snorts. "The King? X isn't going to do anything."

"X?" *Like the letter,* she almost says, but it's just a sound to Tashia.

"He hasn't been the King forever, honey. Before he was the King he was a kid named X. X was a beautiful boy, strong. Strong and sweet. And he was mine."

"Oh," Lady says. She thinks back to every time she's seen them together, and can't see anything but a simmering hatred, and realizes that she's only seeing the underbelly of their love.

"He was my boy, since we were old enough to know that boys and girls were different. Then the old King, the Cleaver, took me, and he wasn't beautiful or sweet."

Lady sees Li lunging for her, her fingers fluttering toward the hairpin.

"X challenged the King to fight at the next feast in the Night Mountain and barely walked away alive. And then he challenged him at the next one and the next. Each time he got a little closer, and he got stronger, and one night he caught the King in the kidney and X stomped him until he didn't get up again."

"He became King for you," Lady says, a little bit awed.

"No, honey, not quite for me," Tashia says. "He came up to me and said, 'I took you back.'"

She watches Tashia's face, the way the old pain plays across it like a distant storm, moving away but still splitting the sky. "I said no," Tashia says, "you didn't take me. No one gets to take me ever again."

That's why there's a kinship between them, across tribe and captor and captive. Two girls who wouldn't be taken.

"So you gotta fight them?" Lady says.

"I'm gonna fight Othello. But I ain't strong enough yet," Tashia says. "The boys won't train with me anymore, and the girls are too small."

"We'll fight you. Me and Jemma. Teach us how to fight, and we'll fight you."

"Please."

"We only got sixteen days before they throw us in the Night Mountain. We need it."

"You're just going to be a punching bag."

"Yeah, maybe," Lady says, "but now you know I can take a punch."

Tashia nods and then motions toward the dirt of the corral. "Whenever you're ready."

"Just—just a minute." Her fingers are searching for the hairpin again, but they're lost in all these curls. In the things that are supposed to make her a girl. She had so much pride in them, the only girl in the Holy Wood with curls. Now they're in the way. She sees a large pair of shears on the wall, used for cutting leather and rope.

She fishes out the pin and lays it down, and Tashia seems to understand. The shears are heavy, but she can slice through the curls well enough if she gets a thin hank of them.

Nothing for the boys to hold on to, when they come for her. Nothing to distract her, to fall over her eyes when she's swinging her fist.

The curls are all gone now, in a fluffy black-brown pile in the dirt. For a moment, she feels as if she killed something and she's looking at its body. Her hair is just long enough to slide in the hairpin, to slide it back out again when she needs it.

Lady steps toward Tashia, holding her fists up to guard her face.

They sleep in the stables, in an empty stall. Jemma is alone there as evening starts to fall. Even though there are no blankets, Jemma has found she can burrow into the straw to stay warm. Pico is off with Grease, as he's supposed to be.

Somehow, being surrounded by the warm smell of horses, the sweet smell of hay, the rich smell of leather, makes it okay that they're prisoners here. That they're going to die.

Then the more she thinks of it, it's not okay at all. What has she done?

She tried to find a new life with Apple, and he died. She tried to find an answer to the End, and they're trapped here with more questions. She wanted to be free of the Holy Wood, and now she's fighting someone else's fight. She starts to cry, warm in the straw.

Lady bursts into the stables, bringing a current of energy with her. "Tashia's going to fight with us!" she says. "She says she'll train with us if we—"

Lady falters when she sees Jemma looking at her hair. Lady looks like a boy. Not like the boys of the Holy Wood, who wear their hair long and shaggy. Not like the boys of the Kingdom, who shave the sides of their heads. But like the boys of the Parents' time.

"If we . . . ," Lady says, and loses her thought. Her ribs pulse in and out, as if she's trying to hold her heart in place. "When Li attacked me, he held me down with . . ."

Jemma stands up. She meant to hug Lady, and instead she touches her hair. Jemma tugs at the roots of what used to be curls. Her fingers slip through. There's not enough to grab. Her hand rests on the hairpin, tucked into the longest part, above the right ear. The ornamented head is beautiful but the point emerging from the other side is deadly. That's beautiful, too.

"It's perfect," Jemma says, taking Lady's head in both hands and pulling it close to her chest. Lady's head rests just under her chin. This time they both sob. They've both broken pieces of themselves they didn't think could be broken.

While he waits for Grease to find the right wrench, Pico draws out the book the Half Holy had given him. Although the case floated away, Jemma saved his pack. The book is warped and moldy from the water, but he can read it.

"What's that?" Grease says. Pico tells him how he got it, and Grease looks increasingly agitated.

"What's wrong?" Pico says.

"Nothing. Maybe something. But I got two of them."

Grease disappears and comes back with two books like his. The first is about the movies, which is some kind of Teevee. A way of seeing new worlds. In the first few pages he recognizes pictures from the Holy Motel. Those priests and priestesses—they were people from the movies.

The last few pages of the book are a different type. Whiter, newer, rougher. Just like his. His fingers quiver when he turns the pages, and he finds himself clenching his teeth. It's another book about the End.

The same pictures are there: stacked bodies, panic in the streets. The same bold letters, too. San Diego. New disease. Symptoms that seem like a cure, not a sickness.

The words are someone trying to make sense of something sweeping the earth almost faster than she can write them down. The fear is there in every line. For all that, there's only one line with new details. "'The Wind Plague, as it is now called, is believed to have originated at Camp Pendleton, the Marine base near San Diego,'" he reads out loud.

The Wind Plague. Because it traveled on the wind? Because it killed as quickly as the wind moves? And Camp Pendleton and Marines. "What are Marines?" he says.

Grease points to a picture, six bodies laid in a row, rifles at their sides: soldiers.

"I found these in book places, as if somebody left them for me. I didn't understand them, but they looked important."

Pico's mind jumps from the clue to the fact that the clue is there in the first place. The Ice Cream Men found some; so did the Half Holy. And they're picked up by people who understand they're important. If the books aren't from before the End, which everything tells him they're not, then someone is leaving them to find.

Someone who can read and write. Someone who can work with paper. Someone who knows about the End. Why, though? They pick books that are thick and glossy, that stand out. They add pages—not enough to tell everything about the End, just enough for you to know they're about the End.

"Who did this?" Pico says.

"The Old Guys, obviously," Grease says, and Pico looks up. The Old Guys are a legend of the Ice Cream Men. Not something someone like Grease would believe.

"Those are just stories," Pico says.

"They're one of our oldest stories," Grease says, "but where the other stories fade away, they stay clear . . . because they're still there."

"What does that mean?"

"The Beginning came and took all the Parents with it. We scavenged from the houses and the buildings, and every day we had to roam farther from the Kingdom into the lands of the dead. We found the cows and horses but didn't know what to do with them.

"A year or two later, the Old Guys walked into the Kingdom. They were all colors, boys and girls. Men and women, they called them. They taught the Philosopher King how to tame the horses, how to tend the cows, how to plant the crops that would feed the most people."

"Jesucristo. And now they're gone."

"No," he says. "The stories say the Children got into a fight against the Old Guys, so they retreated to the south. What if they left the books behind as a trail?"

The books are meant for someone who could read, a chance so slim it's almost not worth taking. They're meant for someone willing to explore Ell Aye when most Children never leave their village. But if the right Child read it, if that Child cared about what they read . . . then that Child might follow the clues home.

"Okay, there's something you gotta see," Grease says.

Jemma had promised Tommy she would talk to the King about his ability to fix guns, but she hasn't been able to get close to the King. He always passes by surrounded by his Knights, and every time she approaches him, five or six swords leave their scabbards.

Until the day she sees the King, alone, looking for a skewer of meat between meals. None of the other girls are around, and he doesn't seem to know where they keep the food. She shows him the place where the kitchen girls, now that they know she is working with Tashia, will sneak her food.

"Thanks . . . prisoner," he says after she hands him the skewer. For once the King looks unsure, as if he doesn't know how to act without his Knights. He probably doesn't. "Have we . . . have we treated you nobly?"

"I don't know what that means, but I'm a prisoner, so . . ." She's aware that he could have her killed, but she doesn't think that killing is his first choice. So she speaks as freely as she dares. The more she speaks, the less she's afraid.

The King actually looks embarrassed. "It can't be helped."

"We don't gotta be prisoners. We don't gotta fight. We could just help you. We're the best Gatherers in the Holy Wood. We can fight, we can think. Even the Biter"—the King's attention flares, darkly—"even the Biter could help. He's their Grease and Pico put together. He got their guns running; he knows things about the world."

"He never told us these things."

"Because he knows you'll kill him no matter what. Promise us safety, and he'll help you. We all will."

"No, I, it's just—" And for once she can see behind the King to the fifteen-year-old who's still in there. X, Tashia called him. And then he looks even younger. "They won't let me." She can see who the "they" is by the way he says it.

"You're the King."

"It's hard to be king, you know."

"Is it?"

"I didn't want to be." She knows he didn't, that he fought just to get Tashia back. He ended up with a Kingdom—but without a girl. "I can fight a war. But all of this . . ."

"All you got is soldiers in your Round Table," Jemma says. "You need smart people like Grease, like Tashia."

"They have to be strong," the King says.

"Look at this place," Jemma says, pointing at the Fake Place. "Think they built this with strong? They built it with smart."

The King starts to speak, shakes his head, speaks again. "They would never let me do that," the King says.

"We gotta fix the End," she says, knowing she may never get a chance to say these things again. "You call it the Beginning, but the rest of us're just hanging on. Every year, there's less babies, less food. Ain't you seen it? Even in the Kingdom, things are falling apart." She grips his arm. He doesn't show alarm.

"Because I say things to you in front of my Knights doesn't mean it's all that I believe," the King says quietly, urgently. "For every person in that room who is my ally, there are two who see themselves as King. I could be King for two years or another day. They have to see me as strong."

"Yeah, well, there's seeming to be strong," Jemma says, "and there's actually being strong." Jemma sees one of his Knights coming, and she drops the King's arm. "Hope you know the difference," she says.

CHAPTER THIRTY-SEVEN
THE MACHINES

"This is what I wanted to show you, Peek," Grease says. He's adopted Pico's nickname even faster than the girls. It sounds different on Grease's tongue, as if it means something new.

They have finished loading the fuel into a wagon at the skyplane place, and the wagon drivers have returned to the Kingdom. What he shows Pico is a room in the skyplane tower full of dust and maps and books. Grease has seen it on other trips but couldn't read then.

They find maps for the mountains north and west of San Diego. The maps are so big and detailed that the mountains turn from green blobs to vast ranges with every canyon and creek marked. He doesn't need to look long for the place, though—it spans several mountains. Camp Pendleton.

"What're them?" Pico points at a wall of shelves filled with black binders, each three inches thick and labeled with four numbers on the spine.

"Loooog," Grease says. "It says 'Log.' I couldn't read it until I met you. It's like a record, I think, you know, everyone writing down everything that happened."

"It is."

"I think they're in some kind of order." Grease runs his finger along a set of numbers: 2024. "What does that mean?"

"I think it's the year," Pico says. "The Parents had so many of em they had to number em."

"I never thought to keep track of any years but my own," Grease says.

"2025—that's the highest number," Pico says.

"And that's where it ends," Grease says. "Look."

The first books in the line look ordered by a straightedge. The last books are thrown as if no one cared where they fell.

"I think they stopped caring about the books. Because of the apokalips."

They start reading the books. It isn't the last page or even the last book when something jumps out at Pico. Two weeks before the last entry, someone wasn't allowed to land at all. It's the name that catches him. "Camp Pendleton. 'Helicopter from Camp Pendleton carrying Marines,'" Pico reads slowly. "What's a helicopter?"

"Some kind of skyplane. They used to spy us on when we were just gangs."

"Something's wrong with the soldiers. They wrote down the way they talked to the helicopter." He reads the rest directly to Grease.

"These men are sick. They need help."

"We know they're sick. That's why we can't give you permission to land."

"I got two men bleeding through their nose and their ears."

"Can't allow it, sir."

"We are United States Marines. I'm ordering you to let us land."

"Sir, we have orders not to let you land. From the United States government."

Pico can imagine the frantic shouts to whoever in the helicopter could still make decisions. None of that shows on the paper, but he can hear the panic. He's seen the End enough to know it.

"We are landing. We are heavily armed. If anyone tries to stop the landing, we will shoot without warning."

"Sir, you are not authorized to—"

"Aww, shit. That was the pilot. He's bleeding now." Another pause, Pico imagines. Resignation after the panic. *"It's the goddamn machines."*

"Sir? Machines in the chopper?"

"No, they're in us. The Wind Plague. The machines are inside of us."

"Sir? I'm—I'm sorry, sir."

"Just hope the crash kills me first."

The book is suddenly heavy in his hand, and Pico puts it down.

"So . . . two weeks before people stopped writing, this happened," Grease says.

Pico doesn't answer. He's reading the last lines over and over. He looks up. "It's machines," Pico says.

"Yeah, they were in a machine."

"No, don't you see?" He grabs Grease's wrists, holds on, and the words rush out. "Don't you see! It's machines. Machines on the wind. Machines you can breathe. Is that possible?"

"I didn't think so until now," Grease says, seeming to notice more the hands on his wrist than his own words. "But they made machines fly. They could do whatever they wanted."

"If it was a fection, then there's no hope. But if it's machines . . . maybe you can fix em."

"Fix machines you can't see?" Grease says, shaking away a cloud. "How are we going to fix this when the Parents couldn't?"

"Dunno," Pico says, "but maybe we see things the Parents couldn't."

"Guess we'll find out at the camp," Grease says.

Pico looks at him. Grease seems to be having a tough time breathing. "You—you'd go with us?"

Grease seems grateful for the question. "All I got here are guns that need oiling, guns to go on a mocycle, and guns to go on a fence." Just death. Outside, there's the tiniest chance at life.

"If the End is like any other sickness," Tommy says, "why's it still here?"

"What?" Jemma says. She's on the ground leaning against the yellow boat. A "sub," Tommy calls it.

"Like the flu," he says. "It comes in, kills a bunch of kids, then it's gone. But the End—the End, it just kinda hangs out waiting for people to get old? That's weird."

It *is* weird. She likes the way Tommy looks at things. A little like Pico, but a lot less annoying.

"Maybe it's made different," she says. She passes some salted meat back through the window.

"Like how?"

"Like, whoever made it wanted—" And then she remembers that it's Pico's discovery. Pico's and Apple's. And she clamps her mouth shut.

"Who? Who made it?" She can tell that Tommy can tell she meant to say more, even with her back to him.

"The gods, I mean. Who else? Maybe they made it different."

"Yeah, the gods." He's quiet for a few moments. "That's smart. But you're so strong, I bet no one ever appreciates you for being smart," he says, and touches her on the shoulder through the broken window.

Something in that touch makes her turn, and when she does, there's something in that face. As if the smile is about to slide off, as if the eyes would rather be somewhere else.

She's seen that face somewhere.

"I don't think the Kingdom knew what they caught when they got you," he says.

That's the face. From Heather, the Older. The day she came to Jemma, already on her way to being the strongest girl, and asked her to become an Hermana. "You deserve more than what they give you, after all you do for the Holy Wood . . ." Jemma listened, flattered, until she realized that the smile was not for her. That the voice would promise her the Holy Wood and never mean to give the Holy Wood to anyone but Heather.

His face, his voice, would promise her everything.

She gets up slowly. "Better get back," she says.

He calls her back. His voice sounds a bit more urgent, a bit more strained. Then she realizes: She's never heard him strained. *A prisoner should feel the strain.*

"I meant to tell you," he says. "Something I heard about the End."

"Yeah?"

"When people are about to End, sometimes they see things." And when he says that, she remembers the dream she had when she was hit by Tashia's whip. How it seemed more real, how she felt like she was inside the haze itself. And the other person inside that haze was Tommy.

"Like what?" she says carefully.

"Like the stuff that makes the End happen. Like—like they're connected to each other." He wasn't a dream. He was really there in the haze with her.

Tommy watches her face, and for long seconds she can't control the feelings underneath or the memories coming back. Apple said something to her, and she's tried to forget everything about that night.

The End. It's like the haze.

If Tommy said it to see if she knows something, now he knows she does. She has to tell her friends what she remembered.

"I think I heard something like that," she says. Saying otherwise will just make him wonder.

"Do you think they can see things that are gonna happen, too? Like a dream?" His voice is light, his eyes are clear, but something in them tells her: *He saw me in the vision. When I imagined him, I wasn't actually imagining him. He was in the haze somehow, watching me. And he knows I was there.*

He's just making sure.

CHAPTER THIRTY-EIGHT
THE GOLF CART OF THE APOKALIPS

Pico has them meet in the shed where he and Grease work, and he can see that Lady and Jemma are as agitated as he and Grease are.

"We gotta get out of here," he says.

"I know," Jemma says. She tells him about her talk with Tommy, her story of Apple's End.

"Wait, you told the cannibal how the End works?" Pico says.

"Well—not completely."

"Oh, puta," Lady says, shaking her head. Pico's still not used to the sight of her without her curls. But he's starting to like it.

"I thought I could trick him into helping us."

"Ha!" Lady says. "Not that pendejo. He's slippery."

"You wanted to save him," Jemma says.

"Yeah," Lady says, "but I wasn't the one who gave our biggest secrets away." And that's the end of it. Maybe back in the Holy Wood, they would have fought about this. But they've both been through too much to care about anything that doesn't help them survive.

"He sees the haze, too," Jemma says.

"Shit," Lady says.

"I think others do, too," Jemma says. "Pilar had a vision at the Waking, I know that. And the way Apple talked about Pablo, I think Pablo had them. I think the haze convinced him to start the rebellion."

"So the haze isn't good," Lady says.

"It ain't good or bad," Pico says, beginning to understand. "It just wants someone to talk to. It picks someone who will listen and then shows them what they need to survive."

Jemma starts to tell them about her dreams. "We know about them," Grease says.

"You don't know *how* they happen," Jemma says. She explains how the buzz in the ears tells her she's seeing things, how the haze sculpts the visions to life. Then she tells them how the wires sharpened her visions, made them bigger. Pico imagines the wires, humming with living dust. He sees Grease take apart the words in his head, inspecting them, putting them back in place.

"Maybe they're Lectrics," Grease says. And then Pico tells the girls what they learned about the End.

"I used to think it was the gods talking to me," Jemma says. "That it was magic."

"We used to think Lectrics was magic—till Pico ruined that," Lady says. Pico nods. So does Grease.

"I told Apple about the haze, what it felt like, what it looked like," Jemma says. "After the Betterment . . . before the End . . . he told me that—that the haze and the End was the same kind of thing. Except he saw it in gold, not blue."

Pico and Grease react strangely. They smile. "How's that?" Lady says.

Grease answers first. "We think the End might be made of machines. Lots of tiny machines. And if it's made from the same stuff as the haze, that means Lectrics and means maybe we're right."

"You saying that the haze and the End are caused by the same kind of thing?"

"Not just the same kind of thing," Pico says. "Exact same thing. Whatever caused the End is the same thing that's helping you."

She understands how that could be important but doesn't know why. The pieces won't fit together in her mind. "What does that mean?"

"It means, Jemma, you can see into the End."

No one speaks for long seconds.

"You think the answers really at this Camp place?" Lady says.

"If there's any answers left."

"Then we gotta get there soon," she says. And that's the moment Pico knows she's made herself a part of this. She's no longer stuck in the Holy Wood.

"So . . . just gotta wait for the fight in Night Mountain, then?" Jemma says.

"We can't let you go in there," Grease says. "Because of the unfortunate fact that we still need you alive."

"We leave the night before the feast," Pico says.

Grease says, "They'll be roasting cows and preparing for the feast, and maybe they won't notice us as easily when we leave. Maybe."

"What about the fight, then?" Jemma says.

"Keep fighting and learning to ride," Pico says. "That still gives you five days more to train—in case things don't work."

"We don't got a way out," Lady says. "They'd catch us on their horses."

"We thought of that," Pico says. He opens the rotting tarp they've set up in the corner of the shed like a curtain. They pulled the frame in by horse like a wagon and brought the rest of the cart in piece by piece, from seven different carts. No one noticed when Grease brought it in, just thought they were his usual piles of motor junk. It's going to be harder to smuggle out.

The cart is no longer white. Pico came up with the idea to paint it gray and green, like old soldiers' cars, so that it would be harder to see and shoot. They found cans of paint still intact at the skyplane place but had to dig through a layer of plasticy paint to get to the color. Grease covered the open doors with steel plates from an old road repair, and spikes from a gate line the front bumper. Baskets in the back will hold gas cans, hooks hold everything else, and a stand will mount a gun if they can get one.

"What the hell is that?" Lady says, not sure what it is but seeming to like what she sees. She walks her hand around the edge, then climbs in as if they're leaving right now. When the cart first ran, it moved at walking pace, until Grease found a switch that kept the cart from speeding. Once they removed it, the cart traveled faster than a bike—more important, faster than a horse over long distances, with more people.

"This is your way out," Grease says.

Pico runs his hands along the steel plate, pleased. He's still awed by what he and Grease could do. Has the world seen anything like this in a hundred years?

"The golf cart of the apokalips," Pico says.

Tashia has been training with them for days. Even though they're leaving before the Night Mountain, both Lady and Jemma keep fighting. It helps them to avoid thinking of the things they don't want to think about. Except for today—today, it jars the memories.

They never talk about why Tashia is helping them, because it's grown from just training. There's a subtle shift of allegiances—from a Kingdom of boys to a friendship of girls, from ruler to subjects. Tashia wants what they want: to be free, to live long, to pick her own boy. They haven't tested that bond, but Jemma thinks it would go a long way.

Today Jemma fights while Lady watches. Lady has proven herself a fierce fighter, with knuckles as sharp as her tongue. She doesn't back down, even after she's been hit. Jemma and Tashia are better matched—both strong, with arms that reach past Lady's defenses.

But Tashia is faster than Jemma.

That was Jemma's weakness, she knew even from her training with Apple. She can rattle jaws with her punch—but she has to catch the jaw first.

Tashia moves like a waterfall. Fury and force flow without effort, her blows touching almost the second they leave the shoulder. She lands three punches for every one of Jemma's.

Jemma circles around Tashia, noting the way that Tashia's right hand dips for half a second when her left strikes. Tashia's right eye is open and vulnerable. Jemma winds up and swings hard. Tashia ducks, so close that

Jemma can't correct and falls into the dirt. Tashia kicks at her with those sharp boots of hers while she's down but stops just short.

"Just broke your ribs, honey," she says.

"Too fast," Jemma pants.

"Othello's faster," Tashia says. "Just trying to keep you alive, honey."

Just keeping you alive, Jemma. That's what Apple said when he used to spar with her. No, not spar. He hit harder than Tashia does. And Jemma never beat him, either.

Suddenly Apple is here, just like he was then. Every time a fist breaks through her defenses and crashes into her face, Jemma thinks of Apple. She hasn't wanted to think of Apple, but the pain won't let her shut him out. The fight echoes with fights, with taunts, that she's had with him before.

A fist to the cheekbone. "Where's your guard?" Apple would say.

A punch to the gut. "Why you giving me such a big target for such a skinny girl?" Apple would say.

A blow that falls short. "Don't swing for my face. Swing through the back of my head," Apple would say.

Apple. You should be here. I left for you.

A tear falls down Jemma's cheek, and Tashia must think it's from the pain. "Suck it up, honey! It's gonna hurt a lot worse!" she says.

"Shut up," Jemma says, teeth gritted. Talking to Apple. Trying to get him out of her mind. She's pushed him away so far. She can push more if she needs to.

"It comes from your hips, not your arms," Tashia says, "like this." And Jemma sees the flex of Tashia's hip the second before she feels the pain in her ear. She sees Apple's hip as it presses close to hers. *What did we think we would find out here, Apple?*

Jemma swings, connects, but Tashia doesn't look as if she's been hit.

The last night with Apple, feeling things that the Children stopped finding words for a long time ago. Holding everything in the world, right there. *What did we think we could find?*

That's not quite right, she knows. She didn't leave for Apple. She left to live.

Can you still do that, chica?

Get out, she thinks, and her mind goes clear. All she can see is Tashia and the haze, which outlines her like a cloak.

The haze is supposed to show her what she needs to survive. *Well, haze,* she thinks, *I need a way to be faster.*

The haze blurs, Tashia's outline getting less crisp. Jemma's not sure exactly how the haze has changed at first but starts to make sense of it. It's like a shadow of Tashia, trailing her—no, it's like a shadow in reverse. Every time Tashia moves, the haze goes first. When Tashia swings, it swings first. As if it wants Jemma to know where to hit. Because that's what Jemma needs to survive.

She watches the haze, and it's half a second in front of Tashia. A full second. It knows where Tashia's going to go, Jemma thinks. Or it's really good at guessing.

Tashia taps her again and again, those rapid punches that would have been impossible to dodge. But now Jemma lets them land so she can study the haze and start to use it.

Tashia hits with her left again, and the haze says she will go high, will open herself up for the flash of a second. Jemma ducks to the right, her body tightening up like a corkscrew, like a Long Gone clock, tighter and tighter until the only way out is through Tashia's face in that moment, like threading a needle. Jemma pushes through her thigh, her hip, her shoulder, and her fist, and Tashia goes down, surprised to see the dust so soon, feels the blood rising on her cheek.

"How'd you see that hole?" Tashia says when she gets her breath.

Jemma doesn't answer, just thinks of the way the haze showed her the future of her fight, and how powerful it made her feel. It almost makes her wish for a chance to fight in the Night Mountain.

There are people coming out of every building. More than Lady's ever seen in the Kingdom. Before the feast, wagons go in and out of the Kingdom all day. Whole cows, to be roasted behind the Castle; vegetables from the parking lots to the south. The Mono goes back and forth without stopping. The usually placid cows towing it are showing signs of exhaustion and annoyance.

Grease's plan to get them out is pretty simple: They're going to walk out through the midst of all those people getting ready for the feast. A motor on the cart would attract attention. Put a horse in front of it, though, and no one will notice.

They load the back of the cart with crates and cover the crates with fenders and auto parts. Outside it looks as if Grease and Pico are hauling out trash to one of the dumps just outside the Kingdom. But Lady and Jemma can ride inside the crates until they're out of sight of the castle. By the time the Round Table realizes Grease is gone, they'll be miles down the road, untraceable because of the rubber tires.

It's almost dark when they meet Grease and Pico in Grease's shed. A horse is tied up outside, a sturdy dappled female that can pull the weight of the cart on her own. She'll find her way back to the Kingdom walls once they're free.

Jemma climbs in first and lies on her side, and Lady nestles in front of her like a spoon. "Don't fart," Jemma says, and Lady laughs.

"You gonna have to be quieter when we go," Pico says. And they're off.

The cart is taller and skinnier than a normal wagon, so Grease has to walk the horse slowly. Lady hears noise all around her as they move through the crowds. She can tell, even through the crate, a change in the energy of the Kingdom. The Children are excited about the feast—and more than that, she realizes, the fight. *We ain't gonna be here to give you a show,* she thinks.

The cart stops in front of the gate where the guard is watching traffic in and out. Grease says something in greeting, and the guard grunts back. The cart lurches forward again, and they travel twelve steps. Lady counts the hoofbeats. She hears the swearing of the closest kid as he pushes on the strut that rolls the gate open. Another kid joins in.

"It's a feast," one of the kids says. "They should just leave the gate open all day."

That's when the bells ring. Lady has never seen or heard them, but they seem to surround the cart. They go on for almost a minute, dozens of handbells, until she can feel them in her chest.

"Jesucristo," she says so low that only Jemma can hear. If they're caught, they'll never make it to the Night Mountain. They'll be put to death on the spot.

The bells stop. Before Lady had been aware of the irregular sounds of a crowd, of kids padding back and forth. Now all the feet seem as if they're running in the same direction, the sound rushing toward them and washing over them like a wave.

"Hold up, Grease!" one of kids at the gate says. He keeps speaking to Grease, but Lady can't make out the words through the walls.

There's a thump against the side of the crate, as if someone is testing to see if it's hollow. Lady tries not to breathe. All she can think of is how everything—her clothes scraping, her heart beating—makes too much noise.

But the thump isn't followed by a second.

"Biters!" she hears, from a place high above them, somewhere on the wall. "Biters in sight!"

The cart suddenly starts and swerves, and Lady and Jemma tumble together, Lady pressed flat against the wall. They straighten out, and Lady can tell they're rolling over the leftover stones in the Main Street. Shouts are everywhere. Then they're in the shed, and Lady hears the door slide shut.

The crates open and they're back, too soon, in the garage. Pico looks frightened, for once, and Grease looks serious.

"We under attack?" Lady says.

"The bells are for sightings. If there's an attack, they bang the drums. They spotted a bunch of Biters in the streets beyond the Kingdom," Grease says. "In a second I have to go to make sure the defenses are set."

"That ain't good," Lady says, but thinks, *What are a few Biters to this place?*

"We don't know if they're spies or the front of a raiding party. It doesn't matter. When those bells go off, everyone comes in. The cows, the kids in the hotel, everyone."

"I saw this in the haze. They don't catch us at the gate," Jemma says, confused.

"No, they don't catch us. But they shut the gates. Nobody comes in. Nobody goes out. Not until at least after the feast."

Ah. Lady understands.

"I'm sorry," Grease says. "You're going to have to fight in the Night Mountain."

CHAPTER THIRTY-NINE

THE NIGHT MOUNTAIN

"Ain't they going to go get the Biters?" Jemma says. She keeps thinking of those Biters out there, watching, just out of reach. She saw them herself from atop the wall.

Tashia shrugs. They are walking toward the feast. "We get a lot of Biters knocking on our door. We can't go chasing all of them."

They turn the corner and the Night Mountain rises in front of them. Jemma's shoulders spasm briefly, uncontrollably, the way they do at night when you're just starting to fall asleep.

"I'm sorry," Tashia says under her breath.

"Why you doing this? Helping us?" Lady says.

"I'm not helping you," Tashia says.

"Yeah you are," Lady says.

Tashia pauses. "The Kingdom is the greatest thing in this life and our last one," Tashia says, that phrase edged with exhaustion. "It's great. But it ain't good." That momentary lapse into Angeleno speech makes Jemma smile.

"We're going to have to change a lot of things here if we're ever going to be good," Tashia says, "starting with how we treat the people who walk through our front door. And that means putting more girls in charge."

"Like you?" Jemma says.

"Well, no one's quite like me," Tashia says, smiling.

They haven't been back inside the Night Mountain since the first day.

When they walk in tonight, Jemma realizes how much she missed the first time, and how much more terrifying it is even than she remembers. There's steel twisting everywhere.

The feast of the new moon is set in a vast room that they didn't see the first time in the dark. It's at the base of the Night Mountain, where they used to launch the rollertrains. The trains are all gone, and a wooden floor has been constructed over the tracks where they ran. The wall between the launch room and the rollertracks has been torn down so that everyone feasting can see inside the mountain.

"Space men," Pico says, pointing up at the ceiling. Two men in space suits hang upside down from what looks like a rocketplane engine.

Jemma and Lady get as close to the floor of the Night Mountain as they can, trying to memorize everything about it. Jemma realizes for the first time how much debris is in the Night Mountain—metal bars, bricks and rocks, pieces of the rollertrain. Weapons there if you can find them fast enough, Tashia had said.

She doesn't get much of a look, though—the fighters aren't sitting there. Grease nods to two ramps leading out of the launch room, climbing toward the ceiling of the Night Mountain. They take the ramp on the right and enter a tube that would once have carried the rollertrain up. The tube opens up to the sky, and she sees Othello and other Knights trudging up the tube on the left. She hadn't seen them enter. Othello smiles, deathly in the dim light.

The King's platform is built at the very top of the ramp, where the rollertrain tracks would have fallen toward the floor. That way the Round Table can see every fight that happens inside the Night Mountain. The friends sit as far away from the King as they can, with younger fighters in between them and the Knights.

Servants carry huge platters of cow up clanging steps from the floor of the Night Mountain. Despite her terror, her mouth waters when they place a seared steak in front of her.

Lady has already dug in. "Jesucristo, I can't believe you get to eat cow every day," she says, her mouth full. They'd never had it before the Kingdom, and it's already their favorite food.

"You can get sick of anything," Grease says, eating squash instead.

"Don't get too full," Jemma says, thinking of the fight ahead.

"If I gotta die," Lady says, "it's gonna be with a stomach full of meat."

The inside of the Night Mountain blazes bright, as if someone had turned on the moon. Grease and Tashia had tried to explain it to them, but they still aren't prepared for it.

Jemma looks along the balcony and sees three metal canisters, each over a fire. There's a glass lens on the front, like Grease's goggles, and a mirror behind them to focus the light. The light operator drops a thick metal shade over the lens to block the light, lifts it to shine it again. "I built them for the Wall," Grease had told them, almost angrily. "I guess this is a better use."

The King speaks briefly, and the fights begin. The first is a pair of younger kids, twelve-year-olds, trying to win their way fully into the Kingdom. But they're not fighting Knights, and as far as Jemma can see, no one is trying to kill them. She points that out.

"They didn't kill a cow," Tashia says.

The fights at the feast are the way that everything is decided in the Kingdom. The girl who wins will go on to become a cowboy, something important. The girl who loses will go to the kitchens or the fields.

The two girls circle each other, feinting and ducking, in the light. Suddenly the lights go out in the ring, and there's darkness below. The shades have dropped over the canisters, by some whispered signal between the operators. The only light comes from the candles and firelight in the platform and the feast room. Jemma tries to make out the fighters, tries to see them in the haze, desperate to understand a way to help her and Lady win. But the haze stubbornly stays dark.

When the lights come up again, one girl is straddling the other in the sand, pounding away with her fists. There's blood on the sand. The crowd cheers.

"It's the hardest kind of fight," Tashia had said when she was training them. "The Night Mountain tests strength, agility, all your senses."

There are three more fights before theirs. The last one is a boy challenging to become one of the Round Table. But the Knight who accepts the challenge is John, a huge friend of Othello's. John throws the boy off the rollertracks to cheers.

The King stands. The words he uses seem familiar to everyone at the feast. "There is nothing like the Kingdom, in this life or our last one," he says, and the crowd echoes it. "We came out of the darkness. We turned the danger and the chaos of the End into the Beginning. We tamed the darkness and made it light.

"Each new member of the Kingdom goes through the same journey. They enter the darkness. They face the dangers in the Night Mountain. Tonight, outsiders ask to become part of the Kingdom; they ask to join their strength with ours. That is not something given freely. They have to win it. If they emerge whole from the Night Mountain, we embrace them as our own. If they lack the strength to do so—" He shouts the last line, leaning on every word. "If they lack the strength to do so . . . they were never meant to be one of us!"

Jemma's limbs feel numb, as if they might not move when asked. But somehow she does stand when he calls their names, when the crowd rocks the room with mostly boos, when they are herded down the towering steps onto the floor of the Night Mountain, when they wait for the King to announce their opponents. Sometimes the opponents are picked, Tashia told them. Usually they're volunteers.

The two Knights climb lightly down the steps. They always knew Othello would be one of them. He fights every chance he can get, and he hates the Angelenos. The other one is a Knight named Sipu. He's not as tall, not as broad as Othello, but moves with a sinewy grace.

"Stick together," Lady says, and grasps her arm around the wrist.

Othello looks at Jemma with a slow, confident smile. He lifts his finger to his throat and slices across it.

The lights go out.

There is nothing around them but darkness. Lady takes a half step forward and stops, vertigo washing over her for a moment. She can't balance because she can't tell which way is up.

The crowd is way too loud for this. She listens for footsteps in the arena, but all she gets is the static of shouts. *All of my senses are gone,* she thinks.

"Can you see anything?" she says to Jemma. Not with her eyes, of course. But with the haze. If Jemma can use the haze to see the outlines of the fighters, they just might win.

"It's still dark," Jemma says. Lady hears the scratch of sand and then a fist clubs her in the side of the head. She wriggles away, losing her grip on Jemma's hand. These boys can't see any better than Lady can—but her voice gave them a target.

The lights blast on, and the crowd roars. She blinks once, twice, and sees Sipu charging her. She ducks, and he just misses, stumbling to the ground.

She spots a steel bar underneath a section of rollertrain track, which swoops close to the floor but doesn't quite touch it. She memorizes the location—twenty steps, maybe fifteen at a run—and sprints across the sand.

The dark comes back, although she's not surprised by it this time. She finishes her steps, hoping her direction held, and slides into the sand feetfirst, hoping to hit the bar with them. She doesn't. She scrambles for it in the sand.

The rollertrain track clangs above her head, sparking. She can see Sipu's face for a flash. He found some kind of club, but the track above her blocked his swing. She huddles beneath the truck, realizing it's the only safety she has. Her feet churn up the sand, trying to find the bar. Had she run the wrong direction?

The club strikes her across the side. Sipu found her. In a panic, she reaches up and finds the tube of the rollertrain track and flips herself up on its top. She inches herself up the track, hoping to distance herself from the ground. She tries not to scream, not to pant. She can't give herself away.

The lights go on again, and her heart sinks. She's only climbed a few feet above the floor, within Sipu's reach. The crowd laughs at the sight of her clinging helpless on the bar, like a rat in a storm. This time the light gives Sipu plenty of time to reach her, and his club smashes into her wrist before she drops onto the sand and runs away.

Lady looks around for Jemma and doesn't see her.

The crowd goes quiet with the light change this time, as if they sense that Sipu is closing in. She's cradling her arm, weaponless, waiting for him to finish her off.

Only not weaponless. They didn't take her hairpin. Maybe they didn't know about it, or maybe they think it won't matter. Maybe it won't. But she pulls it out of her hair. She tests her wrist. Sore, stunned, but not broken. She waits in the dark and thinks.

Sipu knows this place. But he doesn't know her.

She spotted a dense thicket of girders in the center of the Night Mountain that holds the King's platform. That's where she can draw him in. This time when the lights go up, she walks deliberately, almost slowly toward them. The slow speed seems to help, because it doesn't trigger his peripheral vision. Sipu doesn't spot her until she's nearly to the thicket, and she pauses for the lights to dim before she goes in.

There's a closet-shaped hole in the thicket. She doesn't go into that, but ducks under a bar into a tighter space next to it. She picks up a handful of sand and waits until the arena is quiet. She drops the sand, hoping it will make noise, and it does. Sipu barrels toward her, into the closet-shaped hole, and slams into the bars. Her hand darts out, trying to grab anything.

She finds his hand. And drives the hairpin into it with all her force.

Sipu swears and drops the club, which is what she really wanted. She picks it up from the sand, slithers to the opening of the closet hole, and swings with all her force at whatever's in there, again and again.

Something crunches. His screams tell her he's still alive—but that he's not going anywhere.

The arena is silent at that, as the crowd waits to find out what happened. In the quiet she hears Jemma's voice from maybe thirty feet away.

"I see you, Othello," Jemma says.

The haze doesn't come to Jemma right away, and she has to fend off a flurry of Othello in the dark before she wiggles away. *I don't know how to turn it on*, she thinks. *I can't use it if I can't turn it on.*

She tries to remember the way she held her mind still to see the images before, but all it can manage is *He'll kill me*. Her mind won't clear in the panic.

The light blasts her eyes, and she blinks. Othello is right in front of her. He punches her so hard her head snaps back, and he hauls her back by her collar so he can hit her again and again. It doesn't matter when the lights turn off again, because he has her.

With that thought comes acceptance, and then comes clarity. Images start to float in. She can see the outline of Othello, the dots making up his face in the haze, the snarl in his lips up close. She can even trace the shape of the track, the girders, the old lights, the room filling up with straight blue lines in the haze. *Of course*, she thinks. *These were all Lectrics.* It's a huge antenna to focus the haze. She can see even better than when she was fighting Tashia.

She smiles.

Othello isn't using the terrain of the Night Mountain, he's that confident in his strength. So he stands toe to toe with Jemma and hits her with everything he has.

Only she's not there.

The haze shows her where he'll go, a second before he does, just like with Tashia. She ducks and clips him in his neck. He swings again and again, and again and again she's not there.

The light flickers on, then off again, as if the kids running it couldn't decide whether they needed it. The moment it goes off, she hammers straight at the spot in his throat where the haze says will be unprotected.

Only it's not. When she misses, Othello knees her in the gut.

Because it's not like Tashia. Othello is faster than Tashia is, more unpredictable, and the haze can just barely catch up. Sometimes it's wrong about his motions, as if it guesses them incorrectly. Half the times she tries to connect with him, he's not there. And half the times she tries to dodge him, he connects.

Her face is bloody, she can tell. Her ribs ache. Every blow means that much less of a chance for her to walk out alive. She starts to hide from him, to scramble across the tracks and the girders using their blue silhouettes. He follows, not as gracefully, but somehow he can sense her.

Jemma climbs up a set of girders, a tower on the opposite side of the Night Mountain from the feast room. She steps out onto the track they support. Othello is several feet below, and the light still hasn't come on. "I see you," she says, and she crouches to jump. She's going to fall on him and break his neck.

But Othello tracks her voice and jumps up toward her, barely touching the girders as he climbs up. His arm wraps around her ankle, and he yanks her down against the track. Her head bangs against the rails, and the haze stutters for a moment as she struggles to concentrate on it. She shakes her head clear of pain and she can see the outlines of the Night Mountain in the haze again. This time the haze comes back even stronger, the rollertrain tracks clear and sharp.

Othello pulls himself up, still pinning her down. She wriggles out and scrambles upward to the next loop of track, trying to evade his flailing hands. In the next flash of light, he grabs her with both arms and squeezes. He leans on her, smashing her back against the track.

Her ribs start to give. She gulps and he squeezes harder, forcing all the air out of her lungs. The lights turn off again, and this time she can't tell because she sees light dancing inside her head from lack of air.

The haze stays by her, though. It seems to fill her lungs even when the air doesn't; it flows into her limbs from the track in her hands. It strengthens her. She reaches out to it, to the rollertrain tracks holding the haze like a giant pulsing web, and forces herself into the haze.

The lights burst on. Not Grease's torches, but the real lights, the Lectric ones that used to guide the rollertrain. All the lights that are intact, that the haze can still touch, turn on. She sees a blazing night sky, a swirl of meteor red, an exploding sun. She hears bursts of sirens, whistles and wails, sounds unheard by Children in a hundred years. And then the floodlights overhead, like Grease's searchlights but a thousand times brighter.

Othello's face is frozen above hers, not just because he's blinded but because he never thought he would see or hear this. No one did. Jemma folds her legs to her body and kicks out as hard as she can.

Into Othello's chest. His body flies backward, downward, and it hits a girder and then the track and then the floor. It lies still in the sand.

The lights overhead stay on, the noise stays on, because Jemma doesn't know how to turn it off. She climbs down slowly to see if he's alive.

He is, although is leg is broken badly, and he seems to be unconscious. He won't threaten them now.

"You do that?" Lady says, next to her. The lights and the sounds from the rollertrain dim, as if the haze knew its job was finished. For the first time, Jemma realizes that there's no noise from the crowd. Then a single shout, followed by another. She looks up and sees angry, frightened faces peering over the edge of the platform. The King's is the last of them.

"Witch," they say.

CHAPTER FORTY
THE ROLLERTRAIN

"I only have one question," the King says, in his room in the Horn where they've dragged her after the fight, along with Lady and Pico. He's calm. No, not calm—contained, as if any second all his anger and fear will come bursting out.

She knows more or less what the question is but waits for him to ask it. "Are you a devil?" he says. Saying it out loud unleashes all the anger in the room, and the Knights begin shouting. The one holding her shoves her face down on the Round Table. She feels a knife at her throat.

"No!" The King's voice cuts the air like a whip. "She's one of us now. And if we punish her, it'll be as one of us."

She stands back up, quiet. She won't bend. "I dunno what it was," she says. "It ain't ever happened before."

"Are you a devil? A witch?"

"Do I talk to demons or something? No."

"But that power—it comes from some kind of god."

"No, King, it doesn't." The King jumps when Grease speaks, as if he and Jemma had been the only two people in the room. "Something talks to her, but it isn't a god. It's some kind of machine, some kind of Lectrics. It was part of the End."

Harsh, frightened whispers at that. The King may say that the End is actually the Beginning, but his Knights live in fear of it.

"We came here cuz we wanted to know about the End." Jemma shrugs. "Turns out the End wants to know about me."

Pico and Grease explain enough about the haze, about their theories about the End, that the King seems truly interested.

"She's not a witch," Grease says. "But she matters. We hurt her, we lose our only chance of figuring out the End."

"I don't care about—"

"I do," Grease says. She never thought him capable of saying those two words in front of his king. "We all do. We don't have enough time to be great. Every year, we get smaller. We lose more people, we lose what we know."

The King seems to relax. He's thinking now, not bristling. Grease saying what he did could give the King cover to say what he really thinks, not what the Knights think he should say. "Maybe you're right," the King says. "A power like Jemma's, as terrifying as it is . . . it would make all the difference in the war against the Biters."

I'm not a weapon, Jemma thinks. *I'm not a weapon.*

A guard bursts into the room. He's winded from the run up the stairs, but he doesn't pause for breath. "The little Biter," he says, "the little one that was locked up. He's escaped."

Dammit, she thinks.

The King pushes her. "You were friends," he says. "All of this was a way to distract us so he could get away."

She thinks about the things Tommy said. The way she started to trust him, even though she knew that she shouldn't. The things she must have told him about the Kingdom, about the Angelenos, without even realizing it. The things she certainly told him about the End. She can't even shake her head at the King, because he's right. She helped Tommy escape when she thought she was using him to escape.

Before she can say anything to explain or defend, the alarm drums start clanging.

They're attacking the southeast wall. Grease knows because he built the drums with a different tone for each part of the wall. So he immediately goes to the scopes on the southeast edge of the Horn. The things he sees:

The Biters, battle ready and screaming, lit by the pots of burning tar for their arrows. 150 of them. The fire gleams off the single shaved side of their heads; the smoke from the tar drifts between them and makes it look like there are twice as many of them. Beyond them, he sees something else, darker skin. Have they brought the Lowers, too?

One in three of the Biters carries a bow; the rest bristle with swords and long rusty spears ripped from iron fences. It's not rust, he knows; it's blood. Only—some of the lances aren't covered in blood. Some of them are smoky black, the black of the Newport tribe of the Biters.

He turns away from the scope, reeling. They've joined forces, the Newports and the Palos. The main thing that has saved the Kingdom from the Biters in the past was that the Newports and Palos hate each other almost as much as they hate the Kingdom. They've never attacked together. But here they are at the fences, the blood and the smoke.

"The Biters, sir," he says. "The Newports and Palos are both attacking."

The King doesn't notice; the King hasn't moved. Neither has the Round Table. They should be riding out on the enemy's flank, but all their attention is focused on Jemma and Lady. "Who sent you here?" the King says. It sounds almost like a cat's growl, it's coming so low and deep within the King's throat.

"You captured us," Jemma says.

"You killed a cow so we would capture you and you could take over."

Lady steps in front of Jemma, as if to shield her. "We killed an animal that we never heard of to get captured by a place we never heard of?" She shakes her head.

"You're working with the Biter. You talked to him every day, and he's escaped."

"We just wanted to know what he knew," Jemma says. And then her face brightens. "He said there was a place they could climb in. The Mono track."

Grease has warned the King about the track before, about the way it pierces the wall, but the King just shakes his head now. "That track's twenty feet off the ground."

"It's not that far with a rope," Grease says.

"Whatever magic you're working, the Biter is helping you make it," the King says.

"Give my girl some credit," Lady says.

"I can see them in the haze," Jemma says, and Grease can't tell if she's telling the truth or not. "But it's shown me a way to stop them."

"Neither of those things are true," the King says. "You're working with the Biter." But Grease steps to a different telescope, pointing at the Mono track outside the wall. He can't tell if they're climbing it or not, but he sees Biters below it. Jemma's right.

There's more, though. Whatever caused the Biters to hold off attacking, they've started now. The sky lights up with burning arrows falling like stars into the Kingdom. The gunner on top of the Horn starts firing, deep guttural shots. Below him, on the wall, other defenders fire as well.

"The enemy is at the wall." Grease says it slow and loud enough for everyone. "They're firing at us. They're at the Mono track. We need to close up the hole."

"The wall will hold until we're done here."

"Sir, the enemy is at the wall."

"We could help you," Jemma says. "We can stop them."

"The wall will hold." There's something unsure, a dangerous amount of unsure, in the King's eyes. "It'll hold until I've taken care of these girls."

Grease punches the King in the face.

"Forget about the girls! Be a king!" Grease says. The words break through, but it's the fact that the King has been hit by the one person in the Kingdom who doesn't fight, who hasn't hit anyone since he was seven, that snaps him around.

The King looks as if he wants to add Grease's head to the ones on the gate, but the reason comes slowly back. He turns to his Knights, who have their swords half drawn. "Give me the room."

They file out, and the King stares at the Round Table without meeting their eyes. He sighs. "All these signs of strength . . . for what?" When he looks up, it's to Jemma. "What was it you said? There's appearing to be strong, and there's actually being strong."

She doesn't say anything, as if it will break whatever spell he's under. He says, "Are you sure of her, Grease?"

"I know what she can do," Grease says, and his gaze opens to Pico and Lady, too. "More importantly, I know that they're strong and they're good. Just . . . listen to them."

"You have a plan?" the King says. "Tell me fast."

Jemma tells him, and it's a good one.

"You okay if that happens to the Mono?" the King says.

"It's just stuff," Grease says. Then Grease tells him about the golf cart of the apokalips, and the King raises an eyebrow but nods.

Grease remembers how smart the boy X was, before he became the King. How kind he was. Grease remembers when people used to make fun of him, as a Tween, playing with the machines, when he first got his name. Only X gazed in wonder at the little motor puttering away inside the yard mower, the smoke rising in the air. Only X saw the power. "You got to make more of those," X had said.

A little of that X comes back into the King's face. "I think you're both right. I want your help. So . . . this is me actually being strong." And he points to a different door than the Knights used. "You'll want to take the fast way down."

Rollertrains are meant to go down. Lady keeps telling herself that.

They tiptoe along the tubular rail as it ducks through outcroppings and grottos until they get to the rollertrain car. The wooden gate on the track is the only thing that holds the rollertrain in place, and Grease opens it while they climb in. She gets in the first car with Jemma straddling the seat right behind her.

When it moves, it lurches once, as if to warn them. But then it travels smoothly, gently, around the bend. "This ain't so bad," Lady calls to Grease, who jogs along and then hops into the back seat behind her.

"That's what everyone says at this part," Grease says. The next moment the rollertrain glides through a jeweled grotto—and the bottom drops out. Lady screams, involuntarily, and realizes she's not sure if she's scared or not.

It feels like nothing else she's ever experienced—like flying down a zigzag path on a bicycle, if the bicycle were crossed with a goat and bucked and jerked at every step. Beams zoom over her head, rocks fly past her hands, sharp turns threaten to tumble her out of her seat.

She hates it. She loves it. She's never been in anything built just to thrill—and this thrills.

The track careens around the Horn, falling closer to the ground.

"One other thing," Grease shouts above the noise. "They made this without brakes!" They'll reach the bottom soon. Were there other cars at the bottom? She can't remember. The train swoops down the last curve away from the Horn, and she sees a flash of the night sky above and the ground below and a long line of train cars ahead.

Then there's a bang and a jerk and she doesn't feel pain but finds herself slamming into the lip of the rollertrain car in front of her seat.

Her breath is gone, but when she sits up she pumps her arm in the air. "Wooh!" she says.

She can't wait to do it again. She knows she never will.

"Is that how this thing stops?" Jemma says, stretching her neck as if it's hurt.

"We never got the seat belts to work," Grease says, shrugging.

The stairs to the Mono station are at the base of the Horn. Jemma and Lady roll plastic barrels toward it, delivered by Grease from his shed after they came down the rollertrain. They carry swords and a pistol that Grease had stored in the back of the cart.

The Mono stands empty, torches still lit around the drivers' nest, the two pairs of tow lines dangling slack below the track. They'll need more rope. Jemma sees several coils of it on the outside of the pen and starts to pay it out and cut it to length. Lady takes one end of the ropes and runs it up to the front of the Mono, where the driver normally sits.

There's a pen of cows a few paces away from the station. Some of those cows are used to pull the Mono. The others are used for milk and food. They'll need all of them now.

Lady drops rope after rope from the track. Six. Seven. Eight. Ten ropes in all. Now they need to find enough cows for them.

At first it's simple. She ties the ropes around the necks of the cows that usually tow the Mono, and they don't budge. But the fourth cow snorts and jerks its head, and Lady accidentally smacks it on the nose. It bawls and shies away, and then all the cows are jostling her. She isn't worried about tying the loops anymore, she's worried about being crushed.

Lady slides down one of the ropes to the side of the pen, but she can't calm the cows, either. They've sent Pico and Grease to load the cart with food and weapons. They won't be getting any more help.

"Your visions show you this?" Lady says, a little panic in her voice.

"Wasn't *quite* a vision," Jemma says, and throws a loop over the cow closest to her. "Just a good idea."

"You see the Biters climbing the track, at least?" Lady says.

"Mostly," Jemma says. Lady flips her off.

A cow knocks Lady down, and Jemma dives between the cows to pull her out. A hoof strikes her, and she's not sure how she'll get up again.

A whistle splits the air, and the cows somehow separate. In front of them, on her horse, is Tashia. Her cowboys line up next to her. She shakes her head. "I thought I told you two to leave the cows alone."

Jemma points at the slot where the Mono passes through the fence and says, "We plugging the gap." She tells Tashia their plan, and Tashia nods and motions to her cowboys. Within moments, all ten ropes are tied to cows.

This is the moment when they know if it will work. Four cows can pull a full Mono at walking speed. Ten cows and empty Mono? It should move the Mono as fast as they need, enough to shove the train halfway across the wall.

The cowboys pull down a section of the fence, so the cows have only one way to go. Jemma and Lady carry the barrels up the stairs and to the front of the Mono. They open the spouts and stuff short lengths of frayed rope in the mouths.

"See ya on the other side," Lady says, and the cowboys wheel to the edges of the herd. Tashia smacks the last cow with her folded bolas. Another cracks a whip, and they all shout and slap at the cows' flanks.

Jemma and Lady plant their feet inside the Mono, waiting for it to lurch into motion. Lady holds up the pistol and fires it. The cows start to run.

The Mono train they're on is two hundred yards from the wall, crossing it almost square, just below the track of the return loop. Jemma can see the gap they'll need to pass through and plug with the Mono. And the four Biters who emerge from the gap, walking along the narrow Mono track.

"They're in!" Jemma shouts, pointing at them so that Tashia can see. Then Lady fires a pistol at them.

It's a tough shot from a moving Mono at that distance, and Lady misses widely. She kneels down on the floor of the Mono, rests her barrel against the lip of the drivers' nest. The pistol flares and a Biter drops from the track—no sound, no flailing, just a cold drop to the hard ground.

There are archers on the wall who see the cannibals, but they're too far away, without a clear shot. *This is too much wall,* Jemma thinks. A bullet clangs into the metal support above their heads, and Jemma and Lady get as low in the Mono car as they can. The Biters have at least one gun.

One of the cowboys has a bow, and she brings a Biter down. Another Biter just seems to trip and fall. The bolas.

The Mono wall is coming up close, a stretch of steel plate and razor wire on top of a fifteen-foot earthen bank. They're not going fast enough. The train curves toward the wall, and the cows are barely trotting.

Worse, two of them are pulling to the side. They need to go at full gallop so that half the train gets thrown across like a slingshot, using the full mass of the train to block the gap. Anything less and the Biters could just slip through.

"Faster!" Jemma says. Tashia clicks to her horse and it cuts toward the herd, squeezing them together. Tashia grabs a cow's line and gallops faster, practically dragging the cow along. The other cowboys do the same, and the Mono almost doubles its speed. Twenty animals, aiming them for the wall. The wall comes quickly now.

Without having to say a thing, Jemma and Lady grab a torch and hold it to the ropes in the barrels. They're soaked with skyplane gas. Lady's lights right away, but Jemma's refuses to catch. The wall is at sixty yards now, at fifty, and thirty, and still it doesn't light.

Three more Biters climb onto the track, just on the other side of the wall. The Biter who had the gun is still there and fires again. Jemma's too busy to duck. What if the barrel doesn't light? And how long will they have when they do?

The flame on Lady's barrel spurts up, as if it's tapping into the gas below. Then Jemma's catches, finally. She makes sure her sword is ready. Lady has another loop of rope in her hands and gives one end to Jemma.

Twenty yards. Jemma nods, and they both lean out the window and slash at the lines that hold the cows. The speed still carries them toward the gap.

The Mono breaks through the gap, flaming now. They see below dozens of Biters waiting to climb the track, dozens more on their way. The Mono hits the first Biter, and he's inside the drivers' nest for a moment, biting and scrambling. Lady swings at him with the pistol, and he falls off—but so does the pistol. Another Biter jumps away from the flames, and the third just bounces away from the front of the Mono like a pebble on pavement.

Lady holds one end of their rope, Jemma the other, and each stand on the edge of their side of the Mono.

The cowboys reach the bank, and the horses climb up it before they peel away to the right and left. Some of the cows stop, confused, when there's no place left to run, and the other cows pile into them. The Mono slows with the cows cut away.

The girls jump. The Mono comes to a rest with its nose fifteen feet through the gap, exactly where they wanted. As the girls fall down on both sides of the track on the outer side of the wall, the Mono catches flame. That way, no one can climb through the Mono to the track beyond.

No one will get through the gap now. Including them.

The Biters who watched them fall from the sky slowly turn toward them, lances up.

CHAPTER FORTY-ONE
THE BITERS AT THE WALL

Lady laughs at the Biters' expressions when they appear. Those stupid faces. The Biters might have expected boiling oil, or rocks, or a hail of arrows. They didn't expect two girls dropping out of the sky with flame at their back.

The girls stay close to the Mono tower and move with their backs together, their swords in front. Lady feels the heft of her sword and wonders how it will swing. Heavier than a machete, shorter than an ax, sharp on both edges.

"Do we slice or poke?" Lady says.

"Anything you can manage," Jemma says, and the Biters attack. The Mono flares overhead.

Slicing or poking is more than Lady can manage. All she can do is block the thrusts of the spears, frantically batting them aside and letting the weight of the sword do most of the work. Luckily, most of the Biters aren't by the track, so she has time to get the feel. She disarms a girl with a sharp downward blow and swings a sword at the Biter's neck. She accidentally hits with the flat of the sword instead of the blade and the girl goes down, unconscious.

I hope I didn't break her neck, she thinks. *Actually, who cares.*

Jemma wields the sword like it belongs in her hand—after the training she used to get from Apple, maybe it does. Lady meets Jemma's eyes for a moment and then they flare and Jemma lunges past Lady. Lady spins in time to see a Biter's sword at her neck, and then it's on the ground in a pool of blood—with the arm.

"You cut off his arm!" she says.

"There're a lot more of those," Jemma says, and Lady can tell she's not being clever.

Lady's never seen the Palos in action. Everything about them is designed to frighten—the screams that sound like they're strangling themselves, the oiled skin, the necklaces of human teeth. Now she knows why the Kingdom never let down their guard until now, and what it might cost them.

The army blurs together for a moment, and when it separates again she sees people who are not Palos in the midst.

In the blond hair, black. In the blue eyes, brown. But brown eyes rimmed with charcoal, like the faces that haunted the Holy Wood.

The Mono explodes above them, and they hold up their arms to shield themselves from the heat and debris. They step back from the track.

"Do you see em?" she says to Jemma. "Do you see em? Apple was right."

Last Lifers.

Their two worst enemies, in the same army. Jemma knew it could happen, but it's something else to see them shoulder to shoulder.

Jemma can't think about that now, because the Biters hit them hard in the glow of the Mono, as if they've been waiting for someone to give them permission to attack. Her blade barely blocks the spears again and again until one of them slices through and her left shoulder burns. She still holds the sword with two hands, but she has to lead harder with the right.

Then—then the Biters in front of her make way for something worse. Something lumbers through the night, pushing its own soldiers out of the way like reeds. She catches glimpses of it through the flashes of steel, hears its bellows. Then its bare chest is behind the soldiers attacking her and he's a Biter, but he's also a giant.

The giant towers over the others, his chest stretches outward in a muscled V. He smashes a club made of a piano leg into another Biter as if he didn't know the Biter was there.

It's his face, though: There's hair on it. Not the wispy things on the boys' lips, but so much it covers everything but the nose and the eyes and the teeth set in a snarl.

"Little Man!" she shouts.

Little Man. Is he the Biter who Tommy said lived to nineteen? Is that the size the Parents always got when they lived so long?

Little Man roars, not like an animal but like a kid who lost a toy, and swings the piano club. She ducks, and the club glances off her calf. If it were direct, something would have broken. She can't beat him. When he lifts the club again she darts under his arms, running to her right along the fence toward the main battle. She cuts between a squad of Last Lifers and the fence, and Little Man is too big to squeeze between and follow.

She's free of him, on the other side of the Last Lifers. But the Last Lifers are still there. And Lady isn't.

The golf cart is ready. After they took the skyplane gas barrels to the Mono station, they loaded it up with food and fuel and weapons. Pico thinks, *Are we really going into a battle?*

The engine comes to life in a putter, not a roar like the mocycle. The Kingdom would hear it on a quiet day, but not tonight, when the Children are shouting and there's a soul-deadening scream coming from the southeast wall. The night will swallow it up.

Pico drives so that Grease will be able to shoot. The crowds get thicker as they near the wall, and they pass buckets and bullets and arrows traveling hand to hand to the defenders. The gate is in front of them.

Grease hesitates, and for the first time Pico sees how much of his heart is still here. It's the first time Grease sees it, too. "Peek," Grease begins, and it's the sound of him changing his mind, of him abandoning the quest. His throat catches, but the next sounds are of guns going off one right after another.

"They got lots of guns," Pico says, knowing it from his reading. "We gotta go."

"I know," Grease says. The fighting is happening a hundred yards from the main gate, so there will be time for the cart to slip out and to close the gate up again. The guards, three girls and a boy, step in front of the cart. "What's this thing?"

"Weapons, for the battle," Grease says. "King's orders."

Everyone's so used to Grease that if he rolled a giant teacup through the door, the guards probably wouldn't have noticed. Even so, they don't open the gate. "You can't go out with the Angeleno kid," one says.

"It's the King's orders."

They open the gate.

"Stop." A blocky shadow, all arms and head, steps away from the wall. "No one leaves." It's one of the Knights, John. Othello's friend. Grease flinches. They could have talked their way past anyone, but John lacks imagination.

"You heard the guns out there," Grease says. "It's the King's orders."

"The King isn't down here. Maybe recovering from that punch of yours," John says, and there's something ugly in his face. Has he turned against the King? "Only the Knights leave."

"You gonna tell the King he doesn't get his weapon?"

John says, "The King isn't—" And then he stops. Two of the girl guards have their swords at his neck, and one covers the boy guard. That girl is Tashia's little sister, Pico realizes. Dozens of girls surround the cart, carrying swords and clubs and bricks.

"Why?" he starts to say, and looks behind him. Tashia and her cowboys are mounted on horses behind them.

"I'm going to be so tired of saving all your asses tonight," she says.

At first Lady finds herself separated from Jemma when Little Man comes for Jemma, then she finds herself in a thicket of Biter spears. One grazes her neck. She runs a Biter through the stomach. The Biter drops on the ground, clutching her stomach, and suddenly they all fall away in a curtain.

Not because of her.

A Last Lifer, almost as big as Little Man, blocks her path. He waves off the Biters, who retreat. Some kind of commander, then.

She sees something in the way he stands, even though his face is dark with the Terminal's fires at his back. She says a quick prayer that she's wrong, but when he turns his cheekbone the fire catches a fresh scar that runs from his cheek to the edge of his mouth in a disaster of a smile, a scar given to him by a jagged bottle. That scar—she almost wishes he didn't have it, because it's what she sees when she closes her eyes at night.

Li.

He carries two machetes. His eyes are lined with charcoal like all the other Last Lifers, but she can see past the black lining to a deeper blackness. He wants her dead.

"Figures," she says, working her fear into a sneer. "You always was a Last Lifer. Finally found people almost as dead as you."

"You never shut up. Just like that night." He swings the left machete lazily, and even so it comes so close to her ear that she feels a puff of air. He's fast, too.

"I was just bummed that your little Li wasn't as big as the rest of you." Make him angry, she thinks. *But he's always angry.* Lady jabs at him, and he retaliates with both machetes. She manages to block them, but one slides along her blade and cuts her thumb. He presses on her with a flurry of machete blades, each hand windmilling toward her. A machete strikes her sword dead-on, and sparks fill the space between them.

He's so strong. The wildness of his attacks shows her something, though. As big as he is, he's never had to learn how to fight—not the way the Biters or the Kingdom have. He slices as hard as he can and trusts his speed and strength to do the work. Worse—for him—he follows each blow with a look that says, *See what I can do. I bet he flexes in front of a mirror,* she thinks.

"Why you here?" she says. She wants him to talk to slow him down—but she really does need to know, in case they survive this. He's part of the story of how the Last Lifers joined the Biters, and she has to know it.

"The Holy Wood kicked me out cuz of you. All afraid of how strong I was," Li says, pausing between blows, circling her.

"No. It's cuz you only half human," Lady says.

"The Last Lifers made me their leader. I *made* em make me their leader. I killed anyone in the first Last Lifer den who wouldn't do what I said, and then we killed other groups who didn't do what I said, until dozens of Last Lifers followed me. Then Little Man gave us guns and promised us long lives."

A way to keep growing without the End. Can Little Man really give them that? "You believe that?"

"I don't believe nothin. But the Biters is on our side now."

"You just their favorite dog," Lady says. The sneer is real now. "I hope I'm there when they eat you."

Li lunges at her, tackles her down to the dirt, and then she's staring at his shoulder the way she did that night, afraid now as then that she'll never crawl out from under his body. She feels him rubbing against her, hands tearing her clothes. Not again. She'd rather die.

Only of course she wouldn't. Dying would give the puto what he wants. And he's dropped a machete and she still has her hairpin.

Better. She has a sword.

Lady wrests her right hand from under his body, grabs the sword, and hacks at him blindly. From his scream she knows she cut something on the back of his leg, hopefully deep. He rolls off her and she scrambles away.

When they both regain their feet, she can see the blood pouring down his calf. If she'd landed her blow an inch higher, he'd be hamstrung. While she's circling him, Lady scans the crowd for Jemma. But Jemma is surrounded by Biters, visible only by the rise and fall of her sword.

So is Lady, still. Even if she beats Li somehow, the Biters will kill her. Not this puto, though. He won't be the one.

Li jumps at her again, machete flashing wild. She parries the blows, barely, and each one feels as if it will drive her into the earth. Her muscles threaten to give out, but she holds on until his arms drop, triumphant. *Ha!* his face says.

Until she stabs him in the chest.

The blade doesn't hit his heart. She can tell, because he can still scream with the blade stuck below his collarbone. Lady pulls it out and sees the blood running down that chest and the pain tearing through that ugly grin. More screaming, high and petulant. She thinks: *I will never get sick of that sound.*

Under the scream, Lady almost misses the hoofbeats.

CHAPTER FORTY-TWO
THE THUNDER GUN

Lady is jerked through the air, away from Li, by a hand in her armpit. Then she's struggling to climb on a horse behind Tashia, settling into the saddle behind her.

"Puta! I had him!" Lady says, pounding Tashia's back in anger.

"Yeah? Who had all the Biters right behind him?" Tashia says.

"I was gonna kill him," Lady says.

"Wait. Li?" Tashia says. She has heard about Li from their talks, and she understands.

"He got away now. Somewhere away from the wall." Lady's shaking almost too hard to hold on to the horse.

Bolas whistle through the air. The Biters nearest them go down. More cowboys burst through the attackers, their horses herding the army like runaway cattle. Most of the cowboys are girls, who don't usually fight for the Kingdom, but these have machetes and swing them with glee.

The cowboys scatter the invaders for a moment, and Lady thinks they might hold. But the Biters are seasoned, fearless, and they jab at the horses with their spears. The horse next to Lady collapses, a spear in its side, and its rider disappears into a furious pile of Biters. Screams, shouts, and then Lady has to look away.

Hooves, more of them, and this time from the right. The Knights are coming, the King is coming, and Lady thinks: *We will win this.* Because, she realizes, no one fights like the Knights of the Kingdom.

They ride in formation, sweeping aside or trampling every Last Lifer and Biter in their way.

The Knights carry lances made by Grease from skyplane struts, featherweight lances that will never break. They wear vests, helmets, and shields, the kind that used to protect police from bullets, and nothing the Biters have can penetrate them. An arrow shatters on the King's clear shield.

Almost as if on cue, the last of the Biters loses nerve, and they run away from the fence. The Knights bunch together and gallop after them, closing the distance between them in seconds.

That's when thunder and flame rip open the night.

"Don't know what you think you gonna do with those," Pico says as Grease unlatches the guns from the side of the cart.

"Guns are easy to shoot," Grease says. "That's what makes them scary." Grease holds on to the side of the cart behind Pico and watches Pico as he drives. Grease thought he was happy in the Kingdom. Somehow, though, being outside the wall with Pico makes him happier than when he discovered how to make the engines go. Is it freedom? For the first time, freedom to be what he wants?

They drive toward the clamor. The cart has no lights, so they travel only by the light coming from the Kingdom, passing through splashes of yellow-white and back into darkness. As they reach the southeast corner of the Kingdom wall, the battle hits them with a blast of sound.

That's probably why the Biters who are clustered at the edge never see them coming until the golf cart of the apokalips is upon them. Two of the Biters are dead before the others can even see where the gun is. Pico swerves right and drives in a circle around the edge of the battle, while Grease fires from his spot at the door on the inside of the circle. Another one goes down.

Only one Biter has a gun, and she probably can't get a lock on the cart. Between the new moon and the gray-green paint, it slips through the night; the battle covers up the sound. She can only fire back at the muzzle flashes. Grease shoots the Biter next to her and then her. There's only one left, and that one can't shoot them.

The shots coming out of the night are too much for the Biters, and they start to edge away from the wall and into the darkness, where Grease keeps picking them off.

There is one knot of Biters left, rallying around a giant. *Little Man*, Pico thinks. And he seems to be fighting Jemma.

The thunder gun is unlike any gun Lady's ever seen, black with gills like a fish. A big Palo—who would've seemed bigger if she hadn't seen Little Man or Li—is firing it with one hand.

Each trigger pull unleashes a stream of fire and a rat-a-tat that she's never heard in this world. Worse, every burst cuts down horses and boys and girls, and there's nothing to do but—

"Get out," she says in Tashia's ear.

"Not while that thing's there," Tashia says, and spurs her horse toward the gun.

The gunner looks bored, as if he only cares about death when it's harder. While most Biters let their hair flop down over their eyes, he pulls his into a topknot.

"We never gonna get close enough," Lady says.

"Honey, close is for Knights," Tashia says. Lady sees the bola in her hands.

Lady ducks behind Tashia's back so Tashia has room to throw, feels the muscles ripple under Tashia's skin as she twirls the rope. They release. Tashia's arm points at the gunner for a second, and then the ropes shimmy through the air.

The bola wraps around the Biter, locks the arm to his chest. The gun falls to the ground. Tashia is still galloping at full speed toward the gunner. "I'll get it!" Lady says, and launches herself off the left side of the horse. She didn't mean to do it, but when her feet land on the Biter's shoulder with a crunch, it feels good anyway.

The cannibal slows her down, but she's moving too fast when she hits the ground for her feet to catch up with her, and she tumbles to a stop. She manages somehow not to roll on the sword on her hand.

Lady overshoots the gun by about ten feet. As she lunges toward it the Biter shakes off the bola and dives at the gun, too. He hits the ground and reaches. His fingers close on the stock.

Lady slices them off with her sword.

The Biter rolls away, screaming and cradling his hand. Lady calmly picks up the gun and points it at him. She should hold one of these more often.

"Not so big without this, are you, puto?" she says.

Jemma feels the Biters drop away, as if they've lost focus. The Last Lifers are running away from the battle. *When were the Last Lifers ever afraid?* she wonders.

There's a roar along the fence. Little Man, again. She had hoped the knights had killed him, but he's found new prey. She sees the giant, a foot and a half taller than everyone else, swinging his piano club high in the air.

Below him is a Knight, fighting without a lance and losing. The Knight blocks the club with his sword, but the blow seems to drive him into the ground. The next attack from Little Man knocks his riot helmet off, and the Knight spins toward Jemma. It's the King.

No one could stand long against Little Man, she thinks, but the King seems to prove her wrong. He dodges the next blow. Little Man twirls after the miss, a flurry of limbs and piano club threatening to fall under its own mass. Little Man is slower, and the King is under his outstretched arms and slicing toward his shoulder. Blood spurts out from the joint. For the first time Little Man yells in pain, not just in anger.

Jemma watches Little Man, watches the way the other Biters act around him. They give him room, lots of room. Clearly they know his strength, and they don't want to be accidentally crushed. But when he's hurt, no one comes to his aid. Shouldn't they, if he's their leader?

Maybe he's turned them all away from him, from the purges Tommy said he made. Maybe they secretly hope he dies. Or maybe that's the way all Biters treat their fellow soldiers.

The King slashes against Little Man's legs, and the look of shock on Little Man's face reminds her so much of a baby. Tommy said he wasn't smart, that he was propped up by their council. But she sees no signs of intelligence in his eyes, no signs at all. How did he talk the Biters into joining them if this is who he is? What wasn't Tommy telling her about Little Man?

The tide turns against the King. One moment he is hacking against the piano club, carving off chips of wood as Little Man blocks the blows. Then Little Man rages, and the club rises again and again, and the King shrinks before him—just one more speck to be beaten into the ground.

She charges in with her sword, and the King doesn't register surprise as much as resigned gladness. Together they battle Little Man, slashing at him whenever they get an opening. Little Man falls back.

But he's still too strong, and they're weakening from the strain of the battle. Jemma's left arm is numb. It's only moving because she wills it to move.

The end comes too fast to track. Her sword is gone, somewhere behind her, and her hands are stinging. Little Man knocks the King down. He knocks the King's sword out of his hand. The King could cower, but he doesn't, so she stands up straight, too.

Little Man looms over them. She can see the scowl on his face turn to a smile—and then the golf cart of the apokalips runs over him.

The cart flies in from her right, hitting Little Man with the hardened spiked-steel grille, sending him flying through the air, and then, when he lands, running him over. *Thump. Thump.*

The cart stops and backs up. There's a beeping sound in reverse. *Beep. Beep. Thump.*

Little Man's body is pinned under the wheels. The driver's door opens, and Pico steps out over Little Man's legs. He looks a little puzzled and a lot pleased. "The golf cart of the apokalips!" he says.

"Is he dead?" Jemma says.

The King steps behind the cart with his dagger drawn, and returns a moment later, cleaning the dagger. "If he wasn't, he is," the King says. He looks around at the three of them.

"You killed Little Man," Pico says.

"I think you did," he says.

They all hear the same thing: silence. The Last Lifers are completely gone, and Biters are running after them. The fall of Little Man, the loss of their gun, the failure of the Last Lifers to hold the line with the Biters—all that must have caused the Biters to lose their nerve.

"Did we . . . ?" the King says. Jemma nods.

"This was a pretty good first day in the Kingdom," she says.

"You might have saved the Kingdom. I owe you . . . I owe you everything."

Tashia trots up, with Lady behind her on the saddle. A look passes between Tashia and the King. Longing, anger, sadness. "Tashia," he says, opening a door.

"King," Tashia says, shutting it. Jemma sees the beginning of a war that will go on long after they leave. Because they are leaving.

"Oh," Jemma says, "we ain't going back inside the Kingdom. I ain't gonna be your weapon. We gonna find out about the End, and when we do, we'll come back to you and tell you what we know."

"I'm going with them," Grease says. "I have to know."

To her surprise, the King doesn't answer right away, and when he does, it's not with anger. "You did save my life," he says. "And Grease has earned the right to do anything he wants."

"We can make it look like an escape," Jemma says. There's hope for this King yet.

"That would help," the King says.

CHAPTER FORTY-THREE
THE DEAD LANDS

Grease tells Lady this isn't fast. His mocycle was faster. So were the cars and trains and skyplanes. But for Lady, whose only experience with speed was that minute on the rollertrain, the golf cart moves as if it has wings.

It took them days to get to the Kingdom. Now the cart flies down the 5 road, at least when the road is clear. When there are abandoned cars, the cart is skinny enough to sneak by. And so it is that in just an hour, they leave the living lands.

It happens gradually, in that first mile. But then Lady sees that everything has become black and brown and rust—rotten tree trunks, leaves just clinging, pine needles red as if they're lit on fire.

What made the ground so sick that it still kills? Lady resists the urge to hold her breath. The land is quiet, too. Even in the middle of the city, birds chirp, squirrels chase one another across the Lectrics. Not here.

She remembers the talk with the Ice Cream Men. Jemma was in grief, Pico unconscious. But she remembers the black line scrawled on the map. "These are the Dead Lands," she says.

Don't drink the water, the Ice Cream Man had said. *Don't eat anything but what you carry.* As Lady looks on the waste of the Dead Lands, she wonders why anyone would ever. This whole place is a warning.

They should be quiet, too; that's what the Dead Lands are telling them. Something in Lady doesn't want to listen to the land, though. She speaks loudly, she sings, she laughs. *We are the happiest people in the Dead Lands*, she thinks.

Still, the death wears on them. Funny to live in an entire dead world, where the Parents' bodies still litter the street, and have death mean anything at all. Life still goes on in the rest of the world, though. In this place, you have no hope. The Ice Cream Man was right—before it made you sick, it would make you crazy.

The singing starts to feel forced. They leave the houses, into what must have been a wide plain shouldering up to steep hills.

"Hey! Boobies!" Pico says. It's so unlike a Pico thing to say, and his voice is so bright, that it takes her a moment to realize he's pointing at them.

These are definitely boobs: a huge pair of buildings, half spheres each maybe a hundred feet tall and two hundred feet wide . . . with a structure shaped like nipples on the tops. She's not sure why the Parents built anything in that shape, but she can tell from the lack of windows that they weren't made for living in.

Lady looks at the boys. Grease is barely reacting, and Pico is wearing a goofy smile. "You're a boy, after all, Exile," Lady says.

"I'm sprised as you," he says.

The Boobs are right up against the ocean. "The ocean," she says, trying to keep the wonder out of her voice. It fills the horizon.

"You never seen the ocean?" Pico says.

"We only seen it from the hills."

"Me neither," Grease says.

"Could we go to it?" Lady says. She and Jemma used to talk about going to the ocean when they were young Gatherers, when the ocean was just a shimmering crescent at the end of Ell Aye. Lady feels a pull in her stomach that's almost what she used to feel around boys.

"Nope. Still Dead Lands," Pico says.

Lady looks closer at the Boobs and sees a crack down one of them, as if someone hit it with a giant hatchet.

"What is this place?" Jemma asks.

Grease points at huge Lectric towers running to the Boobs. "This thing made Lectrics, a lot of them. These must have been really strong," he says.

"So . . ."

"So maybe whatever was so strong on the inside broke out when the Parents died. Like, no one knew how to control something so strong."

They've drawn closer to the Boobs, and Pico has them pause so he can read the sign. "Nu-clear Power Fa-cility," he says. "I think you're right. It made enough Lectrics to feed cities. And then it all went bad."

Lady looks at the two of them: Grease with his understanding of machines, Pico with his understanding of words. If anyone could bring the world back, they could. With Jemma to help them ask the right questions.

The land beyond the Boobs is barren. The plants have gone, and there's no concrete or houses to hold down the dust. It piles up against fences and stumps, threatening to overwhelm them. It's as if no one has ever lived there. She's never known land where no Parents lived.

A wind hits them from the ocean on their right, and she imagines it filled with the poison that killed the Dead Lands, ready to sting her eyes and fill her lungs. She doesn't have to imagine it for long, though; soon so much dust chokes the air that without the cloth she pulls over her face, she'd be choking.

Off the 5 she sees a lump. Multiple lumps, in a field of rocks. "Stop the cart," she says, and climbs out. They walk toward the lump. Half buried in the dust, she sees that her mind wasn't lying about the shape. Bodies of Children, recently dead.

Pico squats, looks at them closely. "They don't smell that much, so I'm guessing a day or two."

"That wasn't done by a human," Lady says.

"That's the Dead Lands," Grease says. On their skin Lady sees big blisters and scabs, as if someone attempted to rub off their faces. What were they escaping? What were they hoping for in the gray of the Dead Lands?

The wind rises, the dust along with it, and what's left of the daylight is swallowed up. Lady looks south and sees a brown cloud roaring toward them, as tall as one of the towers of Downtown. "Get to the cart!" she shouts, and runs toward it.

The cart is only a hundred feet away, but the cloud hits them with thirty feet to go. Lady stumbles, panicked, because the cart suddenly disappears. The dust is everywhere, stinging her eyes, filling her nostrils. She spreads her hands wide, blind.

Lady doesn't stop moving, afraid that if she stops she'll forget which way was forward. She leans into the momentum, trusting her body to follow the line it had been taking.

A rock snares her foot. She catches herself, takes one, two steps more, and something bangs her left hand. The front plate of the golf cart. If she'd been even one foot farther past its nose, she'd have wandered off into the storm.

"Here!" she screams into the wind. "The cart's here!" Pico and Grease were to her left, Jemma right behind her, but they could be in any direction now.

She holds on to the cart and stretches out her fingers, hoping to catch anyone who comes by. No one does. No touch, no sound, but then—the cart rocks as if someone is climbing into it. Again even harder, feeling like two made it on this time.

"We're on, Lady!" Pico says.

"We held hands," Grease says. Lady should have thought of that, having them all hold hands so they could find the cart faster and lose each other less easily. But they made it.

"Let's try to block the sand," Lady says. They pull blankets over the sides of the cart to keep out as much dust as possible, and inside the blankets it feels like a fragile cave.

And in that cave Lady realizes: *Jemma's not here.* She's out in the poison.

Jemma is only five feet behind Lady when Lady disappeared in the dust, so she keeps running as Lady did. She expects to smash into the cart, but it doesn't come.

She's taken at least thirty steps. The cart would have taken only fifteen. She missed it. She's lost. She gulps in the storm and dust fills her lungs. And then she reminds herself that she can see.

At first she can't remember how to call up the haze, rattled as she is by the dust. Flecks of blue appear but get swept away with the wind. Then she breathes twice through the bandana, getting some almost clean air through the cloth, and she feels the haze connecting to her.

She still can't see anything—because she's pointed the wrong way. "Here!" Lady says, and Jemma spins toward her. The haze lights up. Outlining the frame is a coat of blue haze, glowing softly through the dust. So are her three friends, already in the cart.

Jemma steps forward confidently, now that the cart is in sight. She forgets that the haze can see people and metal pretty well, but it doesn't pick up everything. She lays her foot down, too hard, on a rock the haze didn't show her. It rolls under her and she pitches forward, twisting through the air.

A pain shoots through the back of her head where it strikes the ground. It feels like another rock. The haze blinks out. So does she.

The light wakes Jemma, so bright it's split in two. Her head is half buried in dust, and she lifts it slightly. Her vision blurs, which is the only way to explain what she sees next. Behind the split suns, she sees a figure, a tall one. It has large green eyes that mean it's something new, because when it lifts them up there are regular people eyes on a face that isn't regular at all. The skin is pink, lined with lines that don't belong on skin. The hair is . . . gray? That can't be. No one is gray.

The face leans over her, its green bug eyes and regular human eyes both looking at her. It would be concern, maybe, if it were human. And then the very human eyes, blue and crinkly around the corners, widen.

"You," it says.

Hers might widen, too, if she could keep them open. Because now she understands. "You're . . . old?" Then the face is gone.

CHAPTER FORTY-FOUR
THE OLD GUYS

She's not completely unconscious in the next hours, but she wishes she were. She feels bouncing roads, lights that make her puke, soft bandages, firm hands, Pico's touch, not all in that order. She's going somewhere, but when she tries to understand *where*, she starts to lose her *who* again, so she stops.

She is Jemma, and apparently she is alive. She's alive enough to feel thankful for that, until she passes out again.

When she wakes up Grease has made the golf cart bigger, louder, bouncier. "We're safe, Jemma," Lady says, whispering in her ear over and over. "You won't believe it."

"Try me," Jemma says, and is gone.

Lights, more lights. Does this world ever run out of lights? Running along the ceiling in long yellow strips. She feels as if she's flying along a road to the sun.

Then there is white and softness and a relief she hasn't felt since before Apple, and more strange gray faces and her friends, all of them. Then sleep.

How long she sleeps she doesn't know, but she goes under longer each time. When she opens her eyes Pico is there, then Grease, then the gray face, then Lady. Almost always it's Lady. Even when she's not there, Jemma dreams she's there.

None of the dreams have the haze.

"Where are we, Lady?" she says. Maybe it's a dream.

"Exactly where we wanted," Lady says.

The last waking comes after long black hours, and when it comes, she's truly awake. The kind of room she sees in the old hospitals, but this one seems to still work. A machine pumps with sucking sounds, and numbers flicker across a screen. The lights are overhead. Everywhere, Lectrics.

We're somewhere where the End didn't happen.

Lady stirs in the corner. She's been there the whole time.

"You really awake?" Lady says. "Cuz mija, I'm sick of your lazy ass."

"I . . . I guess?"

Lady presses a button. When it doesn't work fast enough, she yells, "Hey! Dummies! Get in here!"

Pico and Grease skid into the room, their faces unsure. When they see Jemma, they light up. Pico tackles her with a hug. "Didn't know you was a hugger, Peek," she says, coughing.

"I didn't know you was going to live," he says. "So . . ."

Grease hangs back. "Hey, Grease," she says, and hugs him, too.

"There's a lot to tell you," Lady says.

"You—you just won't believe it," Grease says.

"So many answers," Pico says, most excited of all.

"I only want one for now. Two. Where we at? And how'd we get here?"

"The Old Guys," Pico says. "And James brought us."

"None of that makes any sense," Jemma says.

"It'd be easier if I show you," says a gravelly voice behind her. Standing in the doorway, for who knows how long, is the gray hair she saw that night in front of the lights. It's shaggy, parted to the side, but what really interests her is the face below. Because it can't exist.

"You—you're alive. You can't be," she says, shocked. It's the face of a Parent. But more than that—his was the face she saw in the well during her dream.

"This is James," Lady says. "He found us in the storm."

"We met," Jemma says.

"You called me," James says. "It's a genuine pleasure to meet you in real life." He talks funny, she thinks. The words, the tone, they're all a little wrong, dug up from whatever hole he's been hiding in.

"So . . . you really was in my dream?" Jemma says.

"It wasn't a dream. I was sitting next to a computer that hadn't worked in ten years, and it turned on and there you were, talking to us through the screen."

As James steps closer, she wonders if she's right about his age. He's covered with spots that she's never seen on a person before, deep brown stains larger than freckles. There are a few of the lines she knows are called wrinkles.

But the face—it reminds her of a Tween, somehow, a smoothness under the spots. She's seen pictures of the Parents, of the really old ones, and they're gnarled like logs. There's something of the child in him.

"Where we at?"

"Let's show you."

"Can she move?" Lady says.

"She's been able to move for days. It's her brain that wasn't ready," James says. "Have you had multiple concussions lately, Jemma?"

"I don't know what that—"

"Have you been hit in the head?"

She holds up three fingers.

"I wish we had a CAT scanner," he says. "It's probably nothing, though." There's something in those words that makes her look twice, some kind of edge, but his face doesn't give anything away.

He helps her up, and her legs feel steady, but he motions to her to sit. "This is a wheelchair," James says.

"We have *wheels*," Jemma says, all acid on the tongue.

"I'm sorry," James says, in a distracted voice that seems part of him. "I never know what anyone knows anymore."

They roll down a long concrete hallway, and she can tell that they're underground—moisture on the walls, mustiness in the air. Lectrics dot the walls every ten feet, but some of them are fading.

"How'd you find us?" she says, realizing her third question.

"I saw you coming from our lookout on the top of the mountain. We don't get a lot of visitors, as you might expect, so any moving motor vehicle is particularly interesting. I saw the storm coming, and thought I could guide you in."

"He's got Lectrics to see in the dark," Grease says. "They look like bug eyes."

"Sometimes I just need a reason to get off the mountain," James says.

"Last time," Jemma says, growing impatient. "Where we at?"

They reach heavy double doors, metal painted with paint that doesn't flake. "A place designed to outlast the end of the world," James says, pulling a lever. "In a way, I guess it did." The doors rumble open and the outside pours in.

It's her first daylight in days, and her eyes stream. The outlines of the place start to emerge, though. Four concrete buildings like the one she just left form a square. They're half buried in the earth, so the square seems to sit at the bottom of a shallow bowl. The bowl is covered with short and even grass, almost like carpet, as if it's cut by some kind of machine. Deep dirt trails slice through the grass. The people who live here rarely walk anywhere else but here.

Lady wheels her forward to some trees in the middle of the courtyard. Beyond them, in a gap between two buildings, she can see the shimmer of the ocean.

They sit in chairs under the trees. For the first time she realizes they're not alone in the courtyard. Other gray-hairs are there, too, tending to the gardens. Legends walking the earth—but, by the appearance of things, hugging the edge of the courtyard as if something dangerous lies in the middle. James notices Jemma watching them.

"You'll have to excuse them. They get frightened around Children," James says. To him, Children means something different, something optional. For them, though, Children are all that is left. "The last few years haven't been kind to them."

"The last few years ain't been kind to the Children, either," Pico says drily.

"No. No, they haven't."

"Are you a Parent?" Jemma says.

"No, I'm not a Parent. I'm just old enough to be one."

"*I'm* old enough to be one," Jemma says. "That ain't what I meant."

"I know, I know. It's been so long since I've been around the Children that I'm not used to the way the words have changed. Fifty more years and we won't be speaking the same language."

Fifty years? She can't comprehend it. But she asks, "You used to come around us?"

"We used to. We tried to help them. But most of the kids we talked to didn't want answers, they didn't want help. They wanted someone to blame," James says. "They started to attack us when we came to them, so most of us just gave up. The last thing we did was leave the books all over the Southland."

"I knew it," Pico says.

"We figured the kids who could handle the answers could piece together enough clues to find their way to us. Like you. But no one came. That was fifty years ago."

"You keep saying years that don't exist," Jemma says. "No one's that old."

"How old do you think is old, Jemma?"

"Twenty, twenty-five?"

"I'm a hundred and sixty-two years old," he says.

She blinks. "But the End—"

"I was old before the End, and I'm still here."

"When did the End happen, then?"

"A hundred and four years ago," he says gently. "One person could live that long before the End, if they got lucky. But you—you've probably had nine or ten generations during that time."

"That's why we lost everything," Pico says.

Jemma looks at Pico, and Grease, and Lady, all the hopeful faces who've traveled so far for just this moment, just these answers, and thinks: *Maybe it was worth it.* "Can you tell us?" she says. "Can you show us how?"

"How . . ."

". . . to live. The only thing that matters."

"We can tell you about the End."

"How you know so much?" Pico says.

"Well," James says, "we caused it."

Jemma searches that ageless old face, for regret and sorrow and everything else that must be there. And it is. She should have so much anger, but this is bigger than anger.

"But what is the End?" she says. "What causes it? Where does it come from?"

"You're breathing it," he says.

She's stunned. "Then how am I not dead?"

"The things that do it, they're always there. We call it the Wind. It's floating in the air, doing nothing—until you grow up and your brain does, too. Your brain constantly changes until your twenties, but sometime around sixteen or seventeen, the Wind starts to recognize you as an adult. It's like it's watching for the brain to assume the right shape. Then what used to sit there quietly suddenly attacks you."

"It's just waiting for us to get old?"

"Not just old," James says. "Better at seeing the world, at accepting it. That's why some of the smarter, the wiser Children die younger." The Touched. Like Apple. Like Pico and Grease and Tommy . . . and maybe her. "That's the real irony. The second you become like an adult, you die."

"It's machines, just like we thought," Grease says. "Machines you can't see or touch."

"Nanobots," James says. "Machines smaller than the smallest speck of sand. They're simple and weak by themselves, but if you have billions of them floating around you, they can do almost anything."

"Why would you make something like that?" Jemma says.

"The first nanotech was used in clinical trials for cancer. It got adept at sniffing out the cancer, removing it."

The children stare at him, blank.

"It could cure cancer," James says."It could cure the worst disease of our time. More than that, though—we discovered nanotech could communicate to the brain and help the body repair itself, over and over again. The Wind was supposed to fix grown-ups, to make them live forever. Only grown-ups, because kids were still changing. But the nanotech didn't fix people. It shut them down."

"Not you, though."

"No, not us. We had other . . . procedures done, in the first part of the Long Life Project. Before the End came, before the Wind. It can't touch us, partly because it no longer recognizes us as exactly human."

"We don't understand that either," Pico says to Jemma, "and we been here for days."

"You will," James says. "But it would have been hard even for the, as you say, Parents to have understood in my time."

"If you know this, if you started it," Lady says, "why can't you fix it?"

"We've tried, and we've failed, many, many times. There's not enough left of the old world. Not enough technology, not enough people. Before I met you, I would have said it's no longer possible. Now I would say—I don't know what's possible anymore. Whether we fix it or not is entirely up to you."

"What?"

"The haze, Jemma," James says. "You can use it to see, can't you? You can use it to talk to others."

She nods.

"The haze and the Wind are the same thing," he says.

Like Apple said. He never claimed to be smart, to be especially kind. He just saw everything. She misses him so much.

"The Wind is simply endless networked nodes that communicate to each other, powered by a supercomputer," James says, and shakes his head at their blank faces again. He starts over. "Imagine all of these things floating through the air, floating inside you. Their only job is to take fuel from the sun, to create more nanobots—and to talk. They listen to the body, they watch the world for signs of trouble, and they report it."

Jemma's head can barely keep up with James, but she is starting to understand him because she knows the haze. She can visualize these nanobots hovering in the air, wanting to show her things. Wanting to be heard.

"This all matters, Jemma," James says. "We've always known it was theoretically possible. If the nanotech can talk to other simple circuits, then it could talk to computers, it could talk to other machines, it could talk to you."

He leans toward her. "Theoretically. But it's always been theory until now. The Wind connected you to us, through a computer that stopped working years ago. It wants something from you. It's not only causing the End, it's giving you visions. It's speaking to you. And in the hundred and four years since the End happened, this is the first time I've known it to speak."

The old man won't say more, and offers to walk them to the kitchens. The boys leap at that, at a whole world of food that disappeared with the Parents. Jemma starts to follow but is caught again by the sight of the ocean. Lady stands at her side.

"We'll go there soon. To the ocean," Lady says softly, and squeezes her shoulder.

"I don't think I can handle any more new stuff this week," Jemma says, and hugs Lady tight. They don't lose sight of the ocean.

So much lost. Apple, Zee, the Holy Wood. Their innocence. But the four of them, they're still here. "Let's go in," Lady says, then beams like a Kinder. "You gotta try the ice cream."

EPILOGUE

The captain cradles his arm, the one with the missing hand, as if he's lost a baby. Lose one hand in battle and he can't stop showing it to the whole town.

Tommy's stopped paying attention to him. He hates the way his mouth moves. "It was a rescue mission. A big one. So I took it serious."

"So . . . serious," Tommy says. "So serious you brought a machine gun? You brought the Last Lifers? To rescue one person?"

"Those were our secret weapons," the captain says, a stubborn stupid look on his face—*Stubbid*, Tommy says to himself. Captain Stubbid.

"Yes. Secret." Tommy smiles kindly. "Any idea why we didn't paint a sign on the Kingdom that said, 'Our gun is bigger than yours'?" *Besides the fact that none of you can read.*

"Ahh." And to Stubbid's credit, the seriousness of what he's done hits him now. What little color that was in his face is now gone.

"Are your troops ready?"

Stubbid nods. "Rested from their march. Ready to go when we get the word."

Tommy motions with his hand for Stubbid to stand. "Thanks for rescuing me, Captain," he says. "But be careful out there, okay? You lose another hand, and the Little Man may not have a use for you."

The captain gets paler still, gets out the door before Tommy can say another word. The Little Man causes fear, even here in Newport.

He didn't mean to get captured. He couldn't see that. But he was headed south from the Flat Lands of Ell Aye after recruiting Last Lifers and saw Jemma, saw the haze thick around her, and knew he had to get closer. So he left his armed guards and searched for her. They stayed as close as they could, the Chosen warriors, but none of them counted on the flood. He couldn't see that, either. Turns out the haze wasn't good at seeing a lot of things that were kind of important.

But it had worked, hadn't it? Found out about the Holy Wood, a mystery in the hills of Ell Aye. And got inside the Kingdom when none of the Chosen warriors had ever gotten out alive.

He could have left sooner—the Kingdom's cages hadn't been meant for someone who knew anything about machines. A thick pin in his sleeve let him wander around the Kingdom at night, marking their defenses and their machines. The mocycles that Grease had made? He has to have one. What could the Chosen army do with those?

Then, when he was ready, he signaled the army, and they attacked in the places he'd known were weak. Only Jemma had actually listened to what he'd told her and was ready. He almost wishes he hadn't talked so much to her, but he could never resist winding people up.

Tommy slips into the streets of the Newport harbor, smelling the familiar smells of fish guts, trash, and smoke. What a dump. All along the harbor, the Newports built tin shacks slopped on top of one another so no one has to walk to the main street of Balboa. Two of them washed away to sea in a storm last month.

There are no fortifications like in the Kingdom, but also no worries of attack. The Kingdom will never leave its home, like a turtle in its shell. Until someone bigger scoops the whole thing up and throws it in the pot.

Tommy hates it here in Newport, can't wait to get back to the Hill, where the breeze never seems to stop blowing and he can see what feels like the whole world from the tower.

This, though, stopping in front of a wharf—this is why he's here. Boat after boat, sails of white, decks of white, ready to run with blood. From here they can raid the coast, look for new homes and new kinds of Lowers to take captive. Tommy read a story once, of a blond race of warriors called the Vikings, who raped and pillaged their way through a mystical land. If ever there were Old Ones to belong to, it was them.

We will be Vikings.

Everywhere along the streets are the soldiers who will fill the boats, lounging on the docks, playing dice. Last Lifers roam the streets, still capturing dirty looks from people not used to seeing brown skin wandering without the Lowers' brand. That's fine. They have their purposes.

Li steps in line behind him. This one has been useful. Tommy hates to admit it, but he wouldn't be that far without the giant Last Lifer. The Last Lifers were too fragmented, unfocused, for his promises to work on more than a dozen. Jemma's boyfriend and Pico killed those.

Tommy almost gave in then, already ready to tell the Cluster that he had changed his mind and have the Last Lifers slaughtered, when Li marched up the street with a hundred Last Lifers. "Heard you got guns," Li said. Tommy had looked around at the Last Lifers and realized: Li is the only thing they fear besides the End. Another look at Li's eyes of blackened souls, and Tommy knows why.

In the Ferry Square, three Kingdom warriors hang from a scaffold spread-eagled. The bodies are rotting now—the ceremonies have already claimed the best parts for eating. Tommy ate a tongue.

They still need more guns. He is going to have to get them from the Ice Cream Men, who won't want to trade them. But he'll get them anyway. The weapons will change the face of the upcoming war.

The soldiers grow thicker together, and Tommy sees the first of his giants. The giant nods, scowls.

No one wanted to trust him, to trust an eight-year-old, when he told them he could stop the End. When he was desperate to be accepted here, to show he deserved to survive, the haze came to him. It showed him how to cut a nerve in the brain that keeps the Giants from maturing, so that the End skips them over. Now the first of the Giants is nineteen, and growing still. Tommy promised the Last Lifers that they could become Giants, that this isn't the last of life, after all.

Guns? Last Lifers? These Giants are the real secret weapons.

There's a twinge of jealousy, though. His way might stop the End, but it's not one he would take. The people the Giants used to be are gone. They fall backward into childhood. Jemma and Pico and Grease, though, they're looking for the real end of the End. They know more about it than he does. No matter how much he questioned them, how much he tricked them, they never gave that up.

Other people have been able to use the haze before Jemma. One of his gifts is to see it on them like a blanket, and Jemma is swaddled in it. He's always had those people killed so he doesn't have to share the haze.

The three have disappeared from him in the haze, mostly, after the escape. Once he's met others, he can pull them up at will, watch them as easily as checking his own reflection. Jemma stays dark.

In a wide spot on the waterfront, the Chosen line up, in rank: Palo, Newport, Lowers, Last Lifers. The only place, the only time in history where they've all come together. And he brought them there. They'll roll forward from this town, roll through the Terminal as if it weren't even there. They'll roll up the Ell Aye river and into Malibu. Everything they see will be theirs, and once he discovers the source of the End, it will be theirs forever.

The warriors look at him expectantly as he climbs onto a pile of crates above them. They smell of fish and blood. One of his lieutenants steps to his side.

"They're ready for you, Little Man," the lieutenant says.

He doesn't speak right away. They can wait for the Little Man. He half closes his eyes, and casts once again for Jemma. This time he sees her, just for a moment. She's laughing. Next to her are Lady and Grease and Pico—and a man. Even through the haze, he can see that the man is older than anything else on this earth. A man who doesn't belong in this world.

"Oh, this won't do," Little Man whispers, and steps to the waiting crowd.

THANK YOU FOR READING THIS **FEIWEL AND FRIENDS** BOOK.
THE FRIENDS WHO MADE

MAYFLY

POSSIBLE ARE:

JEAN FEIWEL
PUBLISHER

LIZ SZABLA
ASSOCIATE PUBLISHER

RICH DEAS
SENIOR CREATIVE DIRECTOR

HOLLY WEST
EDITOR

ANNA ROBERTO
EDITOR

CHRISTINE BARCELLONA
EDITOR

KAT BRZOZOWSKI
EDITOR

KIM WAYMER
SENIOR PRODUCTION MANAGER

ALEXEI ESIKOFF
SENIOR MANAGING EDITOR

ANNA POON
ASSISTANT EDITOR

EMILY SETTLE
ASSISTANT EDITOR

SOPHIE ERB
JUNIOR DESIGNER

OUR BOOKS ARE FRIENDS FOR LIFE.